PENGUIN

MASSACRE AT JAL

Stanley Wolpert received his Ph the University of Pennsylvania. He first visited India in 1948, on the day after Mahatma Gandhi was assassinated, and his impressions of the time led him to write his bestselling novel *Nine Hours to Rama*. He has written several non-fiction books and monographs on India including *A New History of India* and *Tilak and Gokhale*, which won the American Historical Association's Watamull Prize for the best work on Indian history. Stanley Wolpert teachers history at U.C.L.A., and lives in Los Angeles.

STANLEY WOLPERT

MASSACRE AT JALLIANWALA BAGH

PENGUIN BOOKS

Penguin Books (India) Ltd, 72-B, Himalaya House, 23 Kasturba Gandhi Marg, New Delhi-110 001, India
Penguin Books Ltd, Harmondsworth, Middlesex, England
Viking Penguin Inc, 40 West 23rd Street, New York, N.Y. 10010, U.S.A.
Penguin Books Australia Ltd, Ringwood, Victoria, Australia
Penguin Books Canada Ltd, 2801 John Street, Markham, Ontario, Canada L3R 1B4
Penguin Books (N.Z.) Ltd, 182-190 Wairau Road, Auckland 10, New Zealand

First published as *An Error of Judgment* by Little, Brown & Co. 1970
Published in Penguin Books 1988
Copyright © Stanley Wolpert 1970, 1988

for Dorothy —
from your old friend

Lahore

November 19, 1919

1

WILLIAM felt himself shudder as the General entered the hearing room. More than a quarter century on the bench had, he thought, inured him to brutality, yet last night after rereading the General's written statement he had scarcely been able to sleep, and now the inner rumbling continued as the red-faced figure in khaki approached, eyes narrowed, cold as the barrel of the pistol slung over his bulging hip. Was there no rule about witnesses bearing firearms? Surely even in Lahore there must be such a regulation? Only this wasn't a trial, of course, merely a Committee of Inquiry, to investigate — how had the Viceroy's letter to him put it? — the "recent disturbances" in the Punjab. Yes, there have been disturbances here, William thought.

The General slapped the leather of one boot against his other, and stiffly, unsmilingly saluted.

"Were you, in April, in command of the Forty-fifth Brigade?" William asked softly.

"Yes, sir."

"Were you in Jullundur when you heard of the disturbances in Amritsar?"

"Yes, sir."

"Did you ascertain that a military force had been sent from Jullundur to Amritsar?"

"Yes, sir."

His answers were like his facial expression, undeviatingly calm. Much to William's surprise he was soft-spoken, and as the preliminary interrogation proceeded he was amazed to note that the General seemed quite human, even civilized. He looked so typically British, the big-jawed ragged cliff of a face with its graying shrubbery under the nostril ledge, a brow as nobly broad as any peer's — it was almost a face to trust, to respect, a general's manly visage. That seemed somehow more terrible to him than all the nightmare visions evoked by the written testimony, which had prepared him for the scent of brimstone, horns, and a tail; for the frightfulness of a Prussian butcher of Belgian babes; or at least the blustering bombast of an Irish bully. How could he possibly be faced instead by an ordinary British brigadier?

"When did you arrive at Amritsar?"

The General shifted his weight and lowered his eyes. "I could not say exactly. I think it was about nine or nine-thirty — it was around nine anyway."

"At that time the headquarters of the Amritsar garrison was at the Amritsar railway station?"

"Yes, sir."

"Did you see Mr. Miles Irving, the Deputy Commissioner, and Mr. Plomer?"

"They were both at the railway station," he answered, sounding tired.

"Did you have a conference with them in the railway camp?"

"Yes."

"What information did you receive from Mr. Miles Irving?"

4

"He said he could not deal with the situation any longer," Rex began, but then he had to pause to try to remember it, that April night seven months ago. . . .

There was a stench of blood and carrion in the smoke-laden air of that grimy station. A black cloud hovered over the city. He had seen it driving in, the awful genie of death and terror whose home is India, rubbed from his lamp over Amritsar, grinning darkly at the damage done to White life and property. He sensed it in his blood, in his still fractured bowel, where the pain was like a jagged knife tearing open his intestines, he felt it the way his mother used to feel the monsoon in her rheumatoid shoulder, which he rubbed for her with unguent as a boy. He knew it well, that special brand of Terror, the anguish and fear burned indelibly into every bloodshot eye turned toward him, beseeching, begging his help. He'd known it all his life, from his first year at Murree, where ghosts of The Mutiny lurked behind every shadow, and his father, uncles, and brothers relived all the scenes of murder, arson, and rape from Meerut to Cawnpore, from Delhi to Lucknow. Those were lessons none of them could afford to forget.

The Gurkha guard snapped to as they reached the station gate, and Tommy drove onto the platform itself, where a covey of rumpled civilians in their sweat-stained jackets stood waiting beside the armor-plated coach they used for temporary headquarters. Tommy jumped out to open his door, saluting and bringing every Londoner rifle, Gurkha, and Baluchi within half a mile to attention with the blistering bark of his voice. He was all soldier, that boy, as smart, handsome, and tough as they came in the British regular army, and there were none better — the whole world had learned that during the past five blood-strewn

5

years. He was the best brigade major any general ever had.

Rex locked his jaw as he swung his legs around and stood up. The pain in his groin was worse standing than when he sat. No one had thought he would survive that fall at Akora two years ago, when his artillery horse reared up from the crumbling edge of a dirt trench and lurched over backwards, all but crushing him flat, the stiff rim of his saddle rammed into his gut. A weaker man would have died of the shock alone. Rex was on his feet again within two months, and back in command at Jullundur in time to celebrate the Armistice last November. He still felt it when he stood up, and had to move with deliberation.

"Good of you to come so quickly, General," said the thin civilian, who walked up briskly to greet him. "Irving, sir, Deputy Commissioner." He spoke in the nasal tone of the Surrey set, whose stately mansions had never been opened to Rex for weekends during his cold year at Sandhurst, more than three decades ago.

"What in hell's been happening around here, Irving?"

"It's been a blaze, I'm afraid, sir — rather more than we'd anticipated." He had that pallor civilians got from wasting so much of their lives reading useless files and writing stupid reports.

They all went inside the railway coach that had maps of Amritsar spread over an improvised table, and two sluggish fans rattling noisily at water-soaked muslin curtains hung from the ceiling, keeping the air just bearable. The red velvet drapes were drawn at each tightly shut window. There were bottles of gin and lime juice and trays of stale tea sandwiches. Rex settled back in a velvet seat, and Tommy lit his cigarette, then fixed him a drink.

Irving sat facing him, gnawing momentarily at his lip before starting to explain, "It all happened so swiftly,

I'm not quite certain any of us have sorted things out as yet, General. The mob gathered just south of here at Aitchison Park about noon yesterday. We'd deported two of the leading troublemakers at eleven, you see — I don't know if the names Kitchlew and Satyapal mean anything to you chaps at Jullundur?"

Rex had never heard of either of them, and wished Irving would stop being so damned long-winded in his briefing.

"I won't burden you with details, but they have been rather bothersome to us in Amritsar. They're Gandhi's leading spokesmen here, you see, and His Honour felt it would probably be best all round if —"

"What did the mob do?" Rex interrupted, flicking the ash from his cigarette onto the carpet.

"They tried crossing over into Civil Lines."

"How many?"

"About twenty or thirty thousand, I should think. Wouldn't you agree, Richard?"

He turned for confirmation to Mr. Plomer, the Deputy Superintendent of Police, a short barrel-chested man who muttered, "Twenty to thirty thousand, I should think. Yes, sir."

"How many bridges are there?" Rex asked.

"Three, and a level crossing."

"Couldn't you picket them?"

"Yes, that was the plan, of course, and actually we did hold them back, you see, but not without some fire," Miles explained. He had a nervous tic in one cheek, and it kept him silent for a moment. He poured himself some gin and swallowed it neat. "They broke into the goods yard around then and murdered Sergeant Rowlands. Another lot wrecked the telegraph office and bludgeoned our guard, Robinson, to death. Then we saw the fires from the city — the National Bank was sacked and burned, and

7

Stuart and Scott were both murdered, so was Thomson at Alliance Bank. They robbed the Chartered Bank, too, but its agents escaped to the Kotwali. We brought them out last night after your reinforcements arrived." He paused, his gaunt face white as the collar of his shirt, his eyes bloodshot.

"So they're not afraid to murder our men any more, are they?" Rex whispered. He snuffed the burning tip of the cigarette.

"They've gone for our women, too, I'm afraid," Miles continued. "Poor Mrs. Easdon over at the Zenana Hospital just barely escaped with her life when they broke in calling for her blood, and the buggers caught and beat Miss Sherwood, a blessed Mission lady who was cycling alone in the city and left for dead in the street, we've been told by those who found her. She's in hospital now."

The wire he'd received this morning had mentioned two Englishmen dead, but the shock of this report about natives attacking Englishwomen left him numb with rage at the monstrous gall of those savage beasts. He'd just kissed his niece, Alice, farewell, barely three hours east, at Jullundur. The most beautiful soul on God's earth, that girl, delicate, frail as a flower. Fragrant as a flower. He could still smell the sweetness of her perfumed breath, even here in this crucible of hell. He could see the fine dew of pearly moisture on her downy lip as it smiled at him, "Hurry back, Uncle Reggie! Do hurry, and God bless!" And his wife there alone with her niece, an invalid and a helpless girl. He shook himself like a great bear, rocking the very carriage on its tracks; he shuddered to his feet, and stood staring dumbly down at them, clenching both fists.

"I'm afraid we may have another Mutiny on our hands, General," Irving said. "There's been no sign of penitence today for yesterday's slaughter. I've only been in Amritsar

8

a few months, but I've served my twenty years in India in the Punjab, and this is the first time I've seen natives of this province kill sahibs without turning in the culprits overnight, and sending a delegation to humbly beg forgiveness of Government. Till yesterday I thought I knew these people. God help me, I thought I could trust some of them, the black cricket-playing lovers of Wordsworth! Terrorist scum. Not one of them's come to me all bloody day today — not one messenger! I don't know any of them, I'm afraid."

"I do," said Dr. Henry Smith, the white-haired broad-shouldered civil surgeon, whose face was as deeply lined as the riverine soil of the Punjab itself. "I've lived in this city for a decade, Gentlemen, longer than any of you, I daresay, and I know their black innards as well as their faces, Miles, and I know what they think. There's been a good deal of bluff hereabouts of late, General — the usual guff about responsible rule, political rights for natives, and all the rest of it, you know. Their stupid rags have been printing that drivel for half a decade or more, ever since the War began, and they sensed we needed them to help us fight — as we did, in fact. But that's part of it, you see, because your Punjabi veteran of the Marne is back living in Chouk Hall Bazaar now, and he's too lazy to find himself a job and too spoiled by the wages we paid him for fighting overseas and too puffed up with pride and his memories of power —" The Doctor paused, and bit into his pipe stem.

"Even this show may have started as bluff," he cautioned, "but it's got out of hand. They've tasted blood. They know it's too late to turn back, so they'll go for the lot now — for the White man root and branch. That's my diagnosis, General. The cure's up to you."

Rex did not reply immediately, but left the solemn weight of that warning to sink deep into the consciousness of everyone present at this momentous meeting. The Doctor's words moved him. Was it not said in Scripture: *Honor a physician with the honor due unto him . . . for the Lord hath created him.* Rex remembered the Lenten sermon he'd listened to last Sunday — "What means death? What is the mystery of pain? Why does Christ reign from the tree, instead of from the throne prepared for Him beyond the stars? Sin goes on, it baffles religion, civilization, progress, all prudential considerations. Why is it? What is the secret of its malignity and power? . . . It is not only that man is weak, frail, and rebellious, that he carries about with him a body prone and liable to fall, but that all this delicate and complicated machinery of will, desire, and motive, is acted upon from without — that there is a tempter who, as the devil, the accuser, is anxious to promote a crime or subject of accusation; as Satan, is desirous to stop the Christian in his path; as the serpent, lies in wait to deceive him; as the roaring lion, terrifies him by his boldness; as the father of lies, alienates him from God; as the murderer, seeks his death here and hereafter . . ."

"Gentlemen," he began, moistening his lips as he moved his eyes from one haggard, sweating face to the next, stopping to confront the pale gray eyes of Dr. Smith. "I have been sent here to restore law and order, and I assure you I will do that. You have lived ten years in this city, Doctor, and you have served for twenty in this province, Commissioner, but I was born in this pagan land — more than half a century ago. I have sucked the withered tit of this sordid soil, and I know the bitch whore as I knew my sainted mother, God rest and preserve her soul, and as I know this right fist." He held his clenched fist out for all of them to observe and admire. There were few bigger hands in his brigade, or any other. He'd used that fist to pacify the Mohmund Pathan, and the tribes of Sir-hand in many a blaze along the border from Pindi to Peshawar. "As God is my witness, Gentlemen, the White blood spilled in Amritsar will not go unavenged. I consider this city to be in open rebellion against His Majesty, our King Emperor, and as commanding officer here I hold it my sacred duty to defeat the enemy, to punish and chasten him, and then to restore this region to the peaceful order of our blessed British Raj."

"Amen," Tommy Briggs shouted, in his clear, resonant voice.

"Thank God you've come to us, General," Dr. Smith said.

"Yes, I must say," Miles Irving remarked, "it's rather comforting to know we've got such firm military support. I'm afraid our regular garrison here has never been very impressive, and though we'd thought our police force substantial enough to protect the city — it collapsed entirely, you see."

"Why in God's name was that, Plomer?"

"Don't know, General. I kept twenty-five men with me to guard the Civil Lines, sir. Ashraf Khan had the other seventy-five police under him at the Kotwali."

"A bloody native?"

"Yes, sir, but he's had thirty-one years in the Punjab police."

"A native can't be trusted alone," Rex replied, shaking his head slowly, confirmed in all the misgivings he'd felt instinctively about Irving. "Where the hell was your Superintendent of Police?"

"Mr. Rehill drove Kitchlew and Satyapal up to Dharmsala — that's where they've been deported for detention. He's the only one who knew the way and could drive his own car, you see," Irving explained, lamely. "He should be back tomorrow morning."

"He's not needed any longer," Rex replied. "I'll want

to speak to your native policeman though, Irving. Where is he?"

"At the Kotwali — in the city."

"Take us there."

"Now?" Miles looked more tired than terrified, though Rex suspected it was something of both he felt.

"Of course, now. Come along, Tommy — and bring a hundred rifles!"

He felt no pain leaving the railway coach. His stride was faster, firmer than before. He felt younger than he had — since his last war.

They drove between the troops, Tommy and Plomer up front, he and Irving in the rear seat of the Rolls. It was a fast march pace Briggs set for the men, though barely a crawl for the car, yet no one gathered to watch them drive by. And no dark heads emerged from the shuttered windows as they passed through Hall Gate into Amritsar proper. The resounding tread of a hundred heavy boots slapping cobblestone was the only sound they heard in this city of the Golden Temple, named for the nectar of immortality. Yet he sensed that they watched him, scurrying like rats, furtive and foul, sharp-nosed creatures born to crawl; his instinct told him that they peered from every crack in wooden shutter or stuccoed wall. He could smell them nearby. They'd spent their fury for the moment. Their orgy was over, and all of them lay limp and languid sated with the blood drawn from royal hearts. It was nothing less than regicide, the murder of Englishmen by Indians.

He told Tommy to halt the column as they came abreast of the scarred and still smoldering skeleton of what had been the National Bank of India. The steel ribs of the roof had buckled and reached down like hands lowered in prayer from the sky. He left the car, and walked into the rubble, ignoring the fatuous native police inspector, whose detail guarded the ruins and offered to take the general-sahib on a "tour." He stepped into the sacred shrine alone. The scars of war, powdered stone and mangled steel, were familiar to him, but this had been the pyre of two Englishmen, and that made it hallowed ground. He looked up, and through the gnarled knuckles of God's fingers he saw a glowing Cross in the heavens, a Cross of distant stars, whose fire, much like his own, burned cold, but with a brightness that endured, a power that prevailed. Then he remembered the words of the Apostle. *For every house is builded by some man; but He that built all things is God.* And bending his head, he removed the visor cap and bending one knee to the charred but sacred rubble, he prayed, touching his fingers to the ash.

"How far's the Kotwali?" he asked Irving, getting back inside the car.

"Just a few hundred yards along this road."

"Seventy-five armed policemen stayed there, while this bank was gutted?"

"I'm afraid so, sir."

"Double time, Briggs," he ordered.

"Double time it is, General!" Tommy replied, transmitting the order up and down the line, gunning the motor as they lurched ahead.

Inspector Ashraf Khan was a heavy-set swarthy man, a man of many lusts, Rex suspected, fine foods and voluptuous women, hashish, and perhaps young boys. He was a singularly greedy serpent, the foulest form of native low life, sleek and corpulent, lazy, lecherous, bred here as all of India's police were, on the yeast of crime, prostitution, dope addiction. They grew like fungus in every quarter of a native city's bazaars, such creatures. His eyes implored as his fat lips moved sensuously, repeating:

"We knew nothing, General. I swear it to you, inside

these walls we knew *nothing* what was happening out there, until it was too late . . ."

"Lies!"

"Please, General, do not call me a liar, sir."

"Blasphemous lies!"

"Mr. Irving, sir, Mr. Plomer, will you be so kind as to tell him of my record of faithful service —?" His face trembled, his hands gesticulated prayerfully as he turned to them for support.

"He has always been cooperative, General," Irving said.

"He's cooperated with them, all right! He's given every Pandy in Amritsar the chance to burn, murder, loot —"

"I did whatever I could, as soon as I found out! I took my men to the Chartered Bank, and saved it —"

"Twenty yards from here," Rex sneered. "Aren't you the hero? We should pin a medal on you for that! Why didn't you walk another hundred yards to save the National?"

"I did not know it — it — it was too late." His voice broke.

"You deserve to die, Khan, for letting sahibs burn," Rex whispered.

"Please, General, Excellency, sir —" He started moving away from Rex, back toward the door of his Kotwali office, but turning, he found Tommy standing firmly athwart his path, and turning again, faced Rex, who moved in closer.

"I should kill you for that, Khan, and you know it, dog that you are —"

"Please, Mr. Irving!"

"Pig that you are," Rex continued.

"Please ask him, sirs! Ask him to stop insulting me!"

"You greasy son of swine, I'm going to poke you with my stick," Rex whispered, moving the naked blade of a jewel-handled dagger a Maharaja friend had given him to within half an inch of the trembling Inspector's double chin.

"No, please! Don't kill me! Mr. Irving, help!"

Rex saw that Miles looked anxious for the swine, "I'm going to make you bleed, Khan, to see if your blood is as black as your heart," he whispered, poking him gently, merely enough to draw a rivulet from the soft underswelling of Ashraf's chins.

The Inspector shrieked as though he'd been shot, and tears mixed with the blood that ran onto his tunic. "I'm bleeding to death! Help!"

"General, I must say this is —" Miles started again.

Rex ignored him entirely, speaking, spitting the words into Inspector Khan's face, "You let them die, while you sat — Stuart, Scott —"

"I didn't know — please, help me!"

"Mrs. Easdon, Miss Sherwood," he continued, intoning the names of those martyrs, those innocents slaughtered here yesterday, who would, with the victims of Calcutta's Black Hole, and Cawnpore's bloody Well, be inscribed for Eternity in the hagiology of Empire. "You did nothing but cower here, guarding your filthy flesh —"

Rex smashed his fist into the tear-lined face, sending Khan falling back onto the stone floor.

"Get up," he shouted, kicking his boot into Ashraf's belly. "Get up on your feet, pig! I'm going to give you one chance, and *only* one chance, to save your life!"

"God will bless you for it, General," the Inspector muttered. The blows had prepared him for death — now everything seemed a gift of God.

"I want a list of names from you, Khan!"

"Yes, yes, names," he muttered, dabbing at his chin with his handkerchief, crying as he continued to find fresh blood flowing from the wound.

"Just press the cloth tightly over the cut," Mr. Plomer advised him. "It'll stop soon."

"I want the name of every rebel dog in Amritsar, Khan."

"I have lists, General, diaries, I keep records — ask Mr. Irving, I have shown him —"

"Every thief, every pimp —"

"Whatever I know, General, it will become your knowledge," he cried. "Trust me, I swear it upon Holy Koran!"

" —every badmash lout, every opium peddler. I want them all, Khan!"

"It will take me some time, General —"

"I want my list — and I want it before midnight, Khan!"

"Very well, you shall have it, General — Bugga, Ratto, they are the leaders. They are the ones."

"I want a list of no less than fifty names."

"Fifty? Oh, but my God, that is not possible. I would have to fill it with innocent people," he slobbered, tears rolling down his cheeks. "Mr. Irving —"

"General —" Miles began, and from his tone as well as the expression on his sickly face, Rex could see he was softened by Khan's wily plea.

"Keep out of this, Irving," he ordered. He saw how shocked the Deputy Commissioner was to find he no longer ran this show. He noticed Miles's face change from crimson to dead white as he realized the futility of trying to fight, and recognized his own impotence, the pointlessness of his rage against the very man who'd been sent down to save him. He looked like a bishop, who had caught himself disagreeing with God . . .

"He said he could not deal with the situation any longer, General," William repeated, leaning forward and asking, somewhat louder, "then what?"

". . . that it was beyond all civil control, and that I could take matters in hand," Rex replied.

"I would like you to explain to me what you understood your position to be in consequence of Mr. Miles Irving's request to you?"

"Roughly speaking, I understood the position to be that civil law was at an end and that military law would have to take its place — for the time being."

"Is there any provision for such a situation on the assumption that martial law was not to be proclaimed?"

The General looked perplexed. He turned from His Lordship to gaze at the other members of the Inquiry Committee. Two of those faces were dark — native faces staring with naked arrogance at him — half the number of English faces on that panel! What in God's name was India coming to? Were black natives going to sit there and ask questions of *him* about how he performed his duty? Black lawyers and politicians? Why there was only one general on the whole damnable board. One general officer and two natives. Why had he been ordered to return from the mouth of the Khyber to face these people, anyhow? He turned slowly in his seat and stared round at the crowd that packed the large room — every chair was filled, and many of them were natives too — reporters, clerks, God only knew what they were, he didn't.

"Did you not hear my question, General?" William repeated it.

"It was necessary for me to act without the actual declaration of war or martial law," he explained, staring at his thick calloused fingers, which for thirty-five years had held the sword that held India. "It was handed to me," he added, failing to understand why any Englishman had to ask such stupid questions. "The power was placed in my hands!"

The hearing room packed with officials, journalists, and generals was certainly warm enough, even for late November. Yet William felt a chill pass through his short, solid frame as he realized that the Brigadier really seemed to think there was nothing wrong with marching his troops into a city and usurping the power of the properly constituted civil authority.

"Was it your opinion that that relieved you of any necessity of consulting Mr. Miles Irving as the civil authority in the district?" he asked.

"I think it relieved me of that." He responded without a moment's hesitation, without a tremor of doubt. He said it, in fact, with such certainty, such confidence in his ultimate wisdom, such perfect assurance of the right of his action, that William himself was shaken. Surely Truth alone carried such conviction. William understood more easily then how a young man like Irving had capitulated, leaving the city's entire population at the mercy of this totally irresponsible military terror-monger.

No, I must not prejudge this man, he thought, scratching that opinion from his consciousness, cautioning himself to be doubly careful to reserve judgment till all the oral testimony had been heard, because of the revulsion he'd felt in reading the General's written statement. He pursued his questioning much more scrupulously now, filtering all emotion from his voice, trying to the finite limits of his capacity to find out what it was that actually did happen in Amritsar between that morning of tenth April last and the evening of the thirteenth . . .

Amritsar

April 10, 1919

2

SAIF-UD-DIN KITCHLEW slept late on the morning of April 10. It was past seven before he dressed and came down to the sitting room. His wife had been busy in the kitchen more than an hour by then, and the boys were hotly arguing as he descended the stairs. Akbar, who was a serious six, was trying with scant success to teach his "baby" brother of five something Hasan preferred not to learn.

"No, it is *not* a Muslim holiday," Akbar scolded, maneuvering to get into a position from which he could look directly into his brother's eyes, as Hasan kept turning away from him, coyly tucking his head against one upraised shoulder, pretending not to listen. "Why are you so stupid?"

"I'm right," Hasan shrugged.

"You're *not* right. I'm right. Ask Papa! Papa tell him! Don't I know more than he does?"

"First you must say good morning," he insisted.

"Papa, Papa, good morning, good, good, Papa," Hasan shouted, running over to him, jumping up and climbing onto his shoulders, patting his head and preempting his paternal attention, while Akbar, who was more restrained, stared at them silently with something of reproach in his luminously expressive dark eyes. He was a handsome boy, with his mother's slight frame, but a fine strength in his facial features, and a pensive quality, which Saif-ud-din suspected was his particular legacy to his first son.

"Enough, enough climbing," he told Hasan, hauling him off his head, depositing the sturdy tumbler with a double bounce on the hassock, and seating himself cross-legged between the boys on the rug. "Very well, Akbar, now you may present your case," he said, speaking in the formal tone he used with clients and when pleading at court.

"If it please Your Honor," Akbar began, "Hasan is all wrong, and so stupid he does not even know the difference between a Hindu and a Muslim holiday."

"Stupid, stupid you," mimicked Hasan, sticking out his tongue.

"He's out of order," Akbar cried, almost in tears.

"Silence in the court!"

"Goodness, I have never heard so much noise," his wife said, bringing in the tray with his breakfast, setting it down before him, and telling the boys, "Why don't you stop bothering your father with silly questions, and come help me make chappatis."

"In a moment, Madam, I will send them," he promised, "but first we must finish this trial."

"I don't mind — if you have time for such things," she said. Her reproof was never more explicit than that, but he knew she considered most of his public work wasted effort. Seven years ago when they married (their parents had arranged everything, including the lavish dowry), he had just returned from Cambridge and Münster, a British-trained barrister, armed with an M.A. and Ph.D. His father-in-law had urged him to come to Lahore, where the

22

High Court would give him scope for developing a princely practice. There were, in fact, several Muslim maharajas to whom his father-in-law sold jewelry, who would have been willing to take him on as one of their pleaders. Kitchlew preferred to remain in the city of his birth, contenting himself with a modest practice at the Municipal Court, devoting most of his energies and time to the unremunerative labors he loved.

"I thought you would be down earlier," she said. "Are the chappatis too cold?" She rarely asked him a question unrelated to food. He had tried in the first years of their marriage to teach her about some of the things his mind had been opened to during his years of study abroad, but she retreated more and more into the role of a traditional Muslim wife. She had never received any formal education.

"The chappatis are fine, Madam," he said. It was all she waited to hear, returning to the rear quarters of the house.

"Now tell me, Akbar, what is the point of contention?" he asked, winking at Hasan, who crept stealthily off the hassock and onto his lap.

"The point is about Sunday, which he thinks is a Muslim holiday, but I have told him, and Mama has told him that Grandpa always told her, it is only the Hindu's New Years Day, not ours! Am I right?"

"Yes, in one respect," he was forced to admit, much as it pained him to realize that she was poisoning their minds with the same disease of religious orthodoxy that had crippled her own. He had been kept so busy for the past few weeks organizing the protest movement throughout Amritsar that he had scarcely spent a moment talking to his own children. He was usually finished with breakfast and out with Satyapal by now. Ever since Mr. Irving's restraining order had prohibited them from addressing any crowds at public meetings, they had begun touring the bazaars, speaking individually with shopkeepers, mer-

chants and artisans, even to tongawallas. Kitchlew personally had convinced hundreds to join last Sunday's general
strike. The boys were usually sleeping by the time he
returned home. After the success of yesterday's celebration
and march he felt he had earned an extra hour's rest.

"See, I told you!" Akbar shouted triumphantly at Hasan.

"No, but in a more important, a much more important
sense, my dears, this next Sunday *is* our holiday too, and
we will celebrate it as joyfully as any Hindu family. Just
as we celebrated yesterday. Was that not beautiful, Akbar,
yesterday's parade? Didn't you boys eat the delicious sweets
made by Hindu ladies?"

"I ate four," said Hasan, holding up three fingers.

"Good, but that is why you weigh so much this morning," he said, patting his bottom as he eased Hasan off his
lap, calling Akbar to sit at his side. "Tell me, son, what
was yesterday's holiday called?"

"Ram Naumi, Papa — you know that," he answered,
shyly glancing up at his father's face as Kitchlew rested one
hand gently on his shoulder.

"Yes, but why should we celebrate the birthday of
Rama? Isn't he a Hindu God?"

"I know it is to do with the Hindu-Muslim unity," he
said quickly, repeating the slogan their National Congress
had coined for this year, "but Hindus are not Muslims,
are they?"

"They — and we — are *Indians*," he explained, his eyes
glowing. "And that is why we celebrated Ram Naumi yesterday, and why we will have such a fine time on Sunday,
the thirteenth! We are Muslims, too, of course, and Dr.
Satyapal is Hindu, but he and I are brothers, don't you see
that — just like you and Hasan. We are brothers of the
same Nation, born to the same Motherland, so how can we
help but celebrate our festivals and holidays together?"

"Then why does Grandpa say Hindus are all wicked people, who cheat and lie and steal?"

"He doesn't really mean it, my dear. It's just that sometimes — you know how you and Hasan will get angry and argue or fight sometimes, and you may say things about each other —"

"He calls me stupid," prompted Hasan, inching back onto his father's folded legs.

"That's right, and you said the same about him, but neither of you meant it, did you?"

"Meant what?" asked Maqbool, bursting into the room, grinning from one tip of his bushy moustache to the other as he bent his bulky torso to ruffle Akbar's hair and tickle Hasan's ribs. "How could two girls like these mean anything, eh?"

"We're not *girls*, Uncle Maqbool," Hasan yelled, giggling and squirming out of Kitchlew's arms and away from the fast fingers of his father's oldest friend and fellow barrister.

"What? Not girls any more? Since when? What's happened to them, Kitchlew?"

"You're joking, aren't you, Uncle Maqbool?" Akbar asked earnestly.

"Ah, what is the use of trying to trick these fellows," he sighed, leaning back against the hassock. "What are you eating there, Kitchlew — chappati?"

"Take one." He pushed the tray toward his friend, who protested that he was not hungry, but quickly dipped a piece in ghee and swallowed it.

"I have more for both of you," his wife said, bringing out a fresh batch. "Come, boys, you can help me cook."

"Can we make sweets for Sunday's holiday, Mama?" Akbar asked, following her, with Hasan dogging his steps, echoing, "Sweets, sweets!"

"You are a lucky man, Kitchlew." Maqbool sucked the

golden ghee from his fingertips. His wife had borne six children, but none survived the first year of life.

"Yes, I have been richly blessed, my dear, but see how spoiled I'm becoming — I stayed in bed past sunup today! What is the news? Oh, here is Hansraj now — he will tell us! Welcome, brother."

"Greetings, Maulanaji," saluted the gaunt young man, whose entire body was the color of their palms, his hair light as rust. It was rumored that nine months before Hansraj's birth, the Viceroy had come to Amritsar on tour. Kitchlew suspected his mother may have started that rumor. At any rate she seemed to enjoy the story, and though clearly past her prime by now, continued to attract a select clientele of male callers. "Everyone awaits your word today! I have never seen such spirit in this city. All the vendors are giving things away! Look at this pan Khusru gave me," he said, marveling as he displayed the beautifully packed betel leaf. "He has never given me anything but curses before! We must strike while the iron is hot! Government can be forced to its knees today!" He clenched his bony fist, and gnashed his betel-stained teeth.

"Force yourself to your knees," suggested Maqbool, "and have a chappati. You don't eat enough, that's your trouble, Hansraj."

"And you only eat! I am nourished by my dreams of Freedom! Hunger helps me understand how our starving millions feel, day in, day out, all their short years of life, plagued by starvation and suffering so that Englishmen can grow fat on our flesh and the fruits of our toil! You eat, Maqbool. I will starve till my Nation is free!"

"You may have to starve longer than you think, my young friend."

"If everyone was like you, Maqbool, I know it would take more than one lifetime! Why do you put up with him,

Maulanaji? He has sold his soul to the British — it's all there, you can see it coming out of his stomach!"

"Enough arguing," said Kitchlew. "Have we not learned by now that fighting among ourselves benefits no one but the foreign ruler? That was the beauty of yesterday, the wonder of it, eh, Maqbool?" He leaned forward and tapped his friend's knee, and with a warm smile reassured him of his unshaken confidence. "How unified we were — Muslims, Hindus, and also Sikhs were there. It was a great march, and how perfectly disciplined we remained! We have proved to our British friends that we can control ourselves, and work together peacefully. It may not be so far away any longer, the dawn of our Freedom. A year ago I dared not dream it could happen — what we witnessed yesterday — a parade of one hundred thousand Hindus and Muslims through this city, with no police in sight, only our own cadres to keep order, and yet no outbreak of violence — perfect discipline and self-control! We have become masters in our own home again, my dears. We have shown Government that we can rule ourselves."

"Yes, yes, but do not think Mr. Irving slept as well as you last night," Maqbool cautioned, morosely. "I watched him there on the balcony of the National Bank when the volunteers marched by, clapping hands and shouting, 'Victory to Gandhi — Victory to Kitchlew — Victory to Satyapal!' I will tell you something — his face looked blacker than mine."

"He has good reason to tremble today," whispered Hansraj, popping the pan into his mouth and chewing it with a vengeance, his pale eyes narrowed to secretive slits as he slowly nodded his head to the rhythm of his bite.

"But why?" Kitchlew asked. He did not want to dampen Hansraj's ardor any more than necessary, for he knew the value of youthful exuberance in a land where apathy reigned at every stage of life. "Why should he tremble? We bear him no malice, nor for that matter to any man —"

"I hate every Englishman, Maulanaji."

"How many have you known, my dear?"

"I have eyes. I see what they do to us. They have raped and enslaved our Nation! What more need I know of them?"

"No, we are as much to blame for what we have become as the English — more so! We were not defeated by a handful of merchants, our millions and hundreds of millions, we destroyed ourselves and each other. That much I have learned from my studies in Germany, where I read books about our History that I could not find even in Cambridge, none of which ever come here. We lost our vital spark of independent spirit, our human fire of integrity, and first we destroyed one another, Mughals murdered Marathas, and Afghans butchered both — the Nizam raided Bengal, Mysore attacked Madras, Peshawar plundered Malwa, Oudh hired British troops to crush Rohilla, and so it went, Indians killing Indians, till there was no India left, only regions eternally at war with their neighbors, and communities forever in arms against each other. We surrendered our priceless heritage of Freedom to foreigners who were wise enough to remain united in their ambition, and avaricious enough to exploit what weakness they found. Yes, I admit they were greedy and rapacious, but so were our ancestors, who were also more foolish. Yet surely you do not hate them? But tell me what is the use of hatred? It has all but destroyed the World in the last five years — War, War, War, for what? To what end? Germany and England — how many of the proud, bright, and strong young men I studied with have killed each other by now, I wonder?" He remembered the beer cellars in Münster where they sat huddled around varnished wooden tables, and other young men named Hans spoke with passion about their hatred of the English.

A servant interrupted his reverie to report that a messenger had arrived, and insisted upon delivering his letter personally to the doctor-sahib.

"Show him in then."

He was an elderly skeleton, who had not yet caught his breath, and stood with the glow of perspiration polishing the knotty mahogany of his naked legs. He wore a khaki jacket and shorts, and had a military pouch of leather bound firmly to his torso. "From Commissioner Bahadur for you, Doctor-sahib," he announced, saluting, and handing over the sealed envelope.

It was a short message written in the neat little hand of the Deputy Commissioner. "Please come to my bungalow at 10 A.M. I must speak with you about a most emergent matter. M. Irving, I.C.S."

"Well, what does he want?" asked Maqbool, nervously.

"He wants to speak with me about something," Kitchlew replied, going to his desk to write his answer, which he sealed and handed to the messenger.

"You're not going, are you?" Hansraj gasped.

"Of course I'm going."

"But — tell him to wait!" As the messenger departed, Hansraj stood ready to race after him. He sounded terrified. "Maulanaji, don't go to them!"

"Calm down, my dear. I have no reason to hide from anyone —"

"It may be a trap!"

"No, that's nonsense. We must stop fearing the English as well as hating them. I lived three years in Cambridge, and think I can claim some understanding of Englishmen. If there's one trait of character that may be called peculiarly English, it's fair play. Stop worrying, my dear."

"I rarely agree with him, as you know, but suppose Hansraj is right?" asked Maqbool, turning his hand back and forth as he spoke, shaking his shaggy head from side to side. "You could send him a letter saying you must humbly apologize and would like to come, but explaining it just so happens that today you are too busy —"

> *And thus the native hue of resolution*
> *Is sicklied o'er with the pale cast of thought,*
> *And enterprises of great pith and moment*
> *With this regard their currents turn awry,*
> *And lose the name of action,*

Kitchlew recited, smiling his saddest smile as he remembered the talks he and John often had at Trinity, the caustic rasp of his big-boned roommate's voice abrasively stripping the layers of self-deception from his soul, asking, "Why don't you chaps in India do more off your own bats, Kitch, and stop bloody-well complaining about us?"

"Recite all you like from Wordsworth," Maqbool told him, pausing to draw breath for further argument.

"Shakespeare! It's Hamlet's soliloquy."

"Yes, yes, I know it. We have all studied these things, but there is some knowledge you will not find in books, Kitchlew, and you must have learned in the years you have practiced law, that sometimes it is necessary to lie in order for truth to have its chance at justice."

"No, my good friend, but I have learned enough logic to realize that it is useless to complain about Government because it refuses to listen to our complaints, and on the next day, when we are called upon to speak, to refuse to appear. Shall I tell you why I think Mr. Irving has invited me to see him this morning?" His voice was richly resonant, and his face seemed to glow with some inner brightness. "It may be the dawn of a new era. Perhaps yesterday's peaceful parade has brought Government to its senses, and Mr. Irving sees now that we are not fools or knaves to be punished as naughty children or treated as inhuman slaves, but men, who must be respected as men, and who can be trusted with responsibility for our own affairs. It may be that the night of repression and terror has ended at last for our Nation, and the day of peace and brotherhood has begun."

"I cannot argue with a saint," Maqbool sighed, rolling another chappati, opening his mouth again only to pop it in.

"Do you really believe they will surrender to us without a fight?" asked Hansraj.

"We do not ask them to *surrender*, but rather to join our struggle for human dignity, for equal justice to all mankind, and as our brother Satyapal says, for truth, for love, and peace. Why is it so impossible to imagine that Mr. Irving might also want those things? Surely you and I and Maqbool want them — why not him?"

"Because he is a White sahib," Hansraj replied.

"Truth and love transcend color. They belong to no one race or clime. No, I refuse to accept your answer, Hansraj. I could not continue to hope if I believed that, and without hope there is no future for any of us. You must try not to love hatred so much. She is a treacherous mistress."

"Who is, Kitchlew?" Dr. Satyapal asked, coming through the dim archway and joining their circle on the rug. "I have never heard you gossip before." He was a tall, graceful man in his early thirties, whose raven-black hair had begun to go white at the temples. He wore a collarless cotton shirt and loose white slacks, and carried a small medicine kit in his smoothly veined surgeon's hand. He had fine aristocratic facial features, though he was only of the Khatri caste by birth.

31

He was just now talking of you, Dr. Satyapal," grinned Maqbool, waving his greeting.

"Good, then I have nothing to fear, since my only mistress is Truth." He had never found time to marry. After finishing high school first class first, he won the coveted Government scholarship to Punjab University, and continued to receive free education, thanks to his brilliant record, till he completed medical school. He was the only Indian doctor selected for a post in the I.M.S. that year, worked just before the War as Dr. Smith's surgical assistant, was shipped to Aden in 1917, and remained there till War's end, when he resigned Government service to open a private clinic. "Do you think her treacherous, Kitchlew?"

"No, only jealous, brother. What is your good news today?"

"I don't know if it's good or bad — I've been summoned to Mr. Irving's bungalow at ten. Perhaps he has dyspepsia."

"Probably not," Kitchlew laughed. "He wouldn't require both of us for that."

"Oh, have you been invited too?" He sounded at once more buoyant and apprehensive. "I wonder what he wants to see us about?"

"Perhaps he has decided to remove the restrictions on our public speaking. I don't know, but somehow I feel that our struggle is about to bear fruit —"

"You sound more and more like a Hindu each day, Kitchlew. Now you believe in karma, I see. What shall I do to make myself something of a Muslim, eh?"

"You could marry four wives," Maqbool suggested.

"Is there no easier path?" He rolled a chappati and joined them in laughter, all except Hansraj.

"I still think you should not go," he cautioned. "You tell him, Dr. Satyapal, he respects your opinion more than mine. Suppose it is a trap to arrest you both and — and,

and to transport you from Amritsar, or — who knows what they will do?"

"Yes," Satyapal said, sobering, "it may be. I have thought of that on my way here."

"No, but that would be madness, brother. Why should they arrest and transport us? We have obeyed the speaking ban. We have policed our own celebration for them, far more efficiently than that scoundrel Ashraf Khan could have done — and at no cost whatever to Government. It would be insane to deport us, and stir protest and resentment —"

"I myself will kill him, if he trys it, Maulanaji."

"No, no, no, please, Hansraj, please do not talk of violence any more — it solves nothing! It breeds nothing but more of the same, and then we have lost all this past month of patient unified nonviolent protest has gained for us, as Gandhiji promised it would. See how much we have achieved already in this one city, and don't forget, my dears, the same is happening all over this Nation of ours, in Calcutta, in Bombay, in Madras, in Delhi! No, they cannot stop us by deporting two insignificant people, and I am certain Mr. Irving would not lower his standard of ethics and treat us that way — it would be un-British of him. It would be beneath his dignity to invite men to his home and arrest them without warning. Whatever his faults, he is a gentleman."

The first time he had spoken to Irving, Kitchlew recalled, was when the Deputy Commissioner invited him to his bungalow to report that Kitchlew's defeated opponent on the Anjuman Council appeared to have "coached" his child with a "hoaxed up story" about having learned "seditious nonsense" from Dr. Kitchlew's conversations. A few minutes later the culprits were ushered in to confront him, and the boy was struck silent in shame, the father all but fainting from fright. Mr. Irving promised that day to inform Kitchlew of any malicious charges in future and give him the opportunity to refute them before Government would act against him. He was not obliged to do so, but he too was a Cambridge man, and old boys behaved as gentlemen, especially toward one another.

"But I wonder," Satyapal suggested, his long-fingered hands pressed tautly together, moving like bellows as he spoke, "I wonder if the very success we've had in controlling demonstrations — like yesterday's Ram Naumi — might not alarm Government more than any outburst of violence would? They're trained to cope with violence, after all, but what we've done is new, it's a different challenge, a different dimension of struggle. We fight by not fighting. We are ordered not to speak, so what do we do? You and I stand silent, but tens of thousands of voices shout our names, calling for Victory as they march by. Can Government silence an entire city? It may terrify them, Kitchlew. Don't you see, there is nothing more frightening than the unknown. Hansraj may be right. Twelve years ago they even deported Lalaji, after all."

"True, and in nine months they were obliged by the pressure of public protest to bring him home, and within a month of his return he was presiding over the National Congress. Till his deportation how many people outside Punjab knew the name Lala Lajpat Rai? Afterwards he became a national hero! Government officials may be terrified of what they do not understand, but they are not so stupid as to forget what they have learned by past error. Why should they crown us with the martyrdom of deportation, brother?"

"Why not?" countered Maqbool. "Who are you to escape the fate of every other saint?"

"It is his way of telling me I'm a fool," Kitchlew informed Satyapal, smiling as he removed his gold watch from the pocket of the open vest he wore. "Come, it is getting late."

"If I cannot dissuade you from going into the lion's den, at least let me accompany you," Maqbool muttered, his voice surprisingly gruff.

"I must come too," insisted Hansraj. "Please, Maula-naji."

"Very well," Kitchlew told them, putting one arm on the shoulder of each. "You will be our guardians, my dears, and that will caution the English from doing us harm." His laughter was infectiously warm. Before leaving the house, he called back to his wife that he would be home for the midday meal.

They stepped out into the bustling brightness and chaos of Hall Bazaar. It was a river of urban life, its endless flow of human traffic laced with the lazy meanderings of sacred cattle. There were turbaned and full-bearded Sikhs in gowns edged with gold, gaunt Pathans with the dust of the Khyber still clinging to their naked soles, purdah ladies in burkha tents that covered their very eyes, and some dazzling beauties in saris of diaphanous silk that scarcely hid the puckered nipples of their bosoms. The villagers had come in their finest costumes for the New Year's festivities, and many peasants brought their choice cattle for Sunday's Baisakhi fair, the annual cattle show, which drew crowds from villages twenty miles around Amritsar.

They were greeted by dozens of neighbors, who lounged in the shade of the overhanging balconies, and grinned and waved or touched their headgear jubilantly as they sighted this distinguished company, calling, "Hey, there is Dr. Kitchlew! And Dr. Satyapal! Victory to the both of you! Victory to the Hindu-Muslim Unity!" A crowd of onlookers gathered to cheer, especially children who tugged at their garments for attention. Kitchlew found himself surrounded by a shabby rabble of boys, and shouted down at them, "Let's see which of you can find us a tonga fastest? Whoever does will get his reward!" That sent them racing off in all directions, shouting like a covey of birds startled by a loud noise. In a few moments they were back with a large tonga, but all of them were hanging onto it, each insisting he had been the first to find it. "Then each of you must be rewarded, eh?" replied Kitchlew, frowning in mock anger. "That is quite an expensive service, I must say — however," and then he smiled, extracting a fistful of pice from his purse, handing one to each boy, while Maqbool climbed onto the tonga, muttering, "He spoils the beggars every day. What is the use of trying to teach him anything?"

Merchants along the road waved as they drove at a leisurely pace through the old city, their cheering escort of children following them, stirring every dog in the Hall Bazaar to bark its greeting. It was almost a repetition of yesterday's parade, especially as they passed beneath the festive arches of papier-mâché and tinsel strung across the road where the grandstand had been erected. Colorful ribbons were still hanging everywhere, and Hansraj stood, catching hold of one, dragging it down to the accompaniment of cheers, leaving it to stream behind their tonga as it started to pick up speed, where the road widened as traffic thinned out. Soon the boys stopped running and stood waving in the distance, and fewer merchants noticed them go by, so they could settle back in their seats.

"It has been a great week for our Nation, Satyapal," Kitchlew remarked, clasping his brother's strong arm. Through Hall Gate they drove, skirting the station and veering toward the new Carriage Bridge. The distant whistle of an approaching train wailed its warning from Lahore side, and the last-minute rush of travelers hefting bedrolls and bundles, moving hurriedly toward the track's

empty edge, imparted an air of excitement, a stir of antici-
pation and promise to the station region.

They rattled over the wooden planks of the railway
bridge onto the empty highways of the Civil Lines. The
boulevards were broad enough here to rush a brigade of
soldiers from one manicured official bungalow to another
a mile away in less time than it took to walk half a block
along Hall Bazaar Road. A brightly polished brougham
passed them, and as it raced ahead he noticed a pale bon-
neted head peering back at him, in what struck Kitchlew
as a tantalizing blend of curiosity and trepidation at the
sight of natives. He had known an Englishwoman once,
the daughter of his headmaster. She was a haunting creature, pale and pensive, eternally sad. They often "talked,"
saying nothing really, and several times they walked alone
in the churchyard. He had touched her trembling hand
there — only for a moment. After that she was never at
home to him. She answered none of his letters.

They reached the gatehouse at Mr. Irving's bungalow
at a quarter of ten. The carriage was stopped, and a
British subaltern in command of the guard ordered them
to walk the rest of the way to the front door.

"Do European visitors also walk?" Kitchlew asked,
speaking in his most polished Cambridge accent.

"I don't make regulations," the soldier snapped, turning his back to them and striding off.

They asked the tongawalla to wait, and started to walk.
The "bungalow" was set back some one hundred yards
from the gate. It was a grandiose neoclassic mansion,
above whose fluted white columns flew the Union Jack.
There were royal palms, eternally braced like plume-
topped horse guards, lining both sides of the gravel road.
The scent of honeysuckle and rose perfumed the air. Several gardeners hovered around the neatly pruned bushes
and hedges, whose leaves were trimmed as though they

37

were British hair. The only noise heard in this garden was the scratch of pebbles scuffed up by their sandals, and the mellifluous chirping of canaries. Two peacocks strutted like courtiers round the lush green lawn. The sky seemed much nearer here, more richly blue.

The front door opened before any of them could touch its brightly polished brass knocker. A young Englishman asked which of them were Doctors Kitchlew and Satyapal? They were to follow him. Hansraj and Maqbool were told to wait by the cloak closet. They looked apprehensive, and were about to protest, but Kitchlew calmed them with a reassuring smile. "We won't be long," he promised.

There was an empty sitting room beyond the foyer, and passing through that they entered a larger room, which appeared to be Mr. Irving's study. He was seated behind his desk, and did not rise to greet them, though he nodded as they entered. Kitchlew sensed it was meant for their escort, that nod, for just then the door closed behind them, and turning he saw the young Englishman standing braced against it. He felt like joking that it would not be very wise for them to try and run from this room, so the poor chap might as well relax, but looking back at Irving's face he could not quite bring himself to banter. Dr. Smith was standing behind the Deputy Commissioner, glancing out through the tall windows, puffing nervously at his pipe. Mr. Rehill, the Superintendent of Police, was also there. He stood in front of the desk at the side opposite Smith. He wore a loose hunting jacket, heavy knickers and woolen knee socks. He was much too warmly dressed for Amritsar, and his heavily freckled face bubbled with perspiration. His stiff topi was tucked under one arm, and he held a gazetteer in his thick-fingered hands, from which he started to read at once.

"Act IV of 1915 . . . to secure the public safety and the

defence of British India . . ." He read in the dry, dull, bored drone of a court bailiff, the Law, which had been passed during the War, ostensibly as an emergency measure for the "duration and six months," to help protect India from enemy agents and sabotage by putting due process in storage, and arming Government with the expedient powers it so urgently needed to defend the realm. Only no sooner had the War ended than the first Bill introduced in Delhi was a redrafted version of this Emergency Act (which would expire next month), this time to arm Government with expedient powers urgently needed to defend the realm during Peace. Gandhi called it the Black Act.

". . . rules under this section may be made . . . to empower any civil or military authority where, in the opinion of such authority, there are reasonable grounds for suspecting that any person has acted, is acting or is about to act in a manner prejudicial to the public safety, to direct that such person shall not enter, reside or remain in any area specified in writing by any such authority . . ." The drone continued to hammer against his brain, repeating words he knew by heart, as he knew most of the Code, entire volumes of which he could conjure up on the screen of his mind with the ease of a magician producing invisible rabbits. Why then was this dim-witted overdressed man reading these words to him, keeping him standing like a common criminal in this brightly decorated cell? He felt like shouting the questions in rage, but the next moment he wanted to laugh at the absurdity, the preposterous pretense of it all — this banal gesture to jurisprudential practice, reading the Law aloud! What Law? Whose Law? He was too stunned, too paralyzed, too dazed at the realization that Hansraj, a boy half his age, who had never studied in Cambridge, was right after all! He was right, and Saif-ud-din Kitchlew, LL.B., M.A. (Cam.),

Ph.D., Chairman of the Anjuman Board, and elected Member of the Municipal Governing Board of Amritsar, was naively, humiliatingly, disastrously wrong. He could utter no words as he watched and listened to these grown men, who seemed like amateur actors in a dismal comedy. When Mr. Rehill finished reading, Mr. Irving began.

"By the power vested in me under section 2 (f) of the Act, I hereby order that Dr. Kitchlew and Dr. Satyapal, both present in attendance, shall be transported immediately out of the District of Amritsar, to remain in protective detention outside said District, until such time as it may be deemed advisable, in the best interests of public safety, to permit either or both of the forenamed to return to residence in this District of the Punjab." He scribbled his name at the end of that document, and looked up. His eyes were cold.

"You must not do this, Mr. Irving," Kitchlew whispered, somewhat startled to hear that he found his voice.

"That's incorrect, Kitchlew. I must, in fact," he replied, pushing away from his desk and rising like a man who had been obliged to finish a tasteless meal.

"Why? What earthly reason can you have? Surely you don't believe that Satyapal and I endanger public safety? You have seen how scrupulously we obeyed your order restraining our public speech —"

"It's getting late, Miles," Dr. Smith remarked.

"So it is, yes. I'm sorry, Kitchlew, we've no time to discuss this now. Rehill —"

"But you can't," he shouted, stepping toward the desk, halting as he found himself blocked by Rehill's barrel-chested sweat-stained jacket. "You can't just sneak us off this way, like prostitutes chased out the rear door! What is wrong with you people, have you gone altogether mad? Do you not think Dr. Satyapal and I will be missed in

Amritsar? Do you imagine there is no one — no man, no woman, or child, who will ask within one hour, or two at most, 'But what has happened to them?' First you lack the courage, or was it rather the manners, to notify us of your intention in your letters —"

"This had to be done quietly to avoid fuss," Irving snapped, his cheeks blazing at hearing himself accused in the same breath of the two traits he most despised, cowardice and bad manners.

"I see, sir," continued Kitchlew, nodding, "and so that is why you would spirit us away without saying one parting word to our friends, who accompanied us and wait outside, without so much as leaving a hastily scrawled message for our families — 'To avoid fuss'? And is it in the 'interest of public safety' as well that you will allow our compatriots to assume that you have murdered us?"

"Miles, why are you listening to this seditious drivel?" asked Smith, who seemed the most bored.

"He may be right, you know," whispered Irving. "They do have a way of suspecting the worst of us —"

"The buggers will do that whatever we give them."

"How would you know?" asked Satyapal. "Have you ever tried dispensing anything but poison?"

"You are a wretched, contemptible, insolent —"

"I am a doctor," Satyapal answered softly. "What are you?"

"Miles, I'm going to murder that insolent monkey," Smith warned. "If you don't get him out of here —"

"You are a murderer, that's true! You could have saved the lives of hundreds of Indian soldiers in Mesopotamia by simply sending me the medicine I wrote and begged you for, but instead you kept your own empty clinic stuffed with unused morphine —"

"Shut up, damn you! Shut up, shut up, you black liar!"

41

He was ready to lunge at Satyapal, but Irving restrained him, ordering the young police officer to take Satyapal out back and keep him in the waiting motor car.

"All right, Kitchlew, you may write a note, but hurry it up, and be brief — and write in English!"

"It's the language I usually write in," he said stiffly, but then feeling so despondent a premonition of darkness that his voice broke and his hand trembled as he held the pen poised after writing, "My Dears," he cried out, "Don't do this, Mr. Irving! It's a terrible mistake, what you are doing. Please listen to me, sir. I know my people better than you. I am not begging for myself, though I cherish my Freedom as much as any Englishborn — yet I would gladly surrender it for all time if I thought that would save Amritsar. Please! I have never trembled so — my entire being shakes — "

He could not keep back the tears, so hot they ran like molten lava down his cheeks, burning brand marks of pain into his soul, yet even as he begged, pleading with eloquence, with passion, with reasoned restraint, and prophetic conviction, even as his voice echoed its thunder in his tingling ears, he knew it was to no avail, for the Law had been read aloud, and the deportation order had been signed by the Deputy Commissioner, and the motor cars that would transport them to the north were out back filled with petrol, waiting for him and Mr. Rehill to descend the dark stairs. And no words could change all that.

Dr. Kitchlew finished his brief farewell note, and was escorted hastily from the room.

3

MAQBOOL had quietly watched Hansraj pace the cloakroom hall, scratch his groin, hunt with pincer-poised fingers in the tangled underbrush of his hair, crack each of his knuckles — he watched the entire show, calmly remaining in the same seated position for almost an hour. Yet by now even he felt restless. Too many people had come and gone through the very same door which had swallowed Kitchlew and Satyapal — but still there was no sign of them.

"Excuse me, Sardarji," Maqbool said, clearing his throat and smiling at the tall Sikh, who guarded the front door. "My friend and I have been waiting some long time now for Doctors Kitchlew and Satyapal, who had, as you doubtless know, an appointment with the Deputy Commissioner at ten o'clock, and we would like to have some idea how much longer —?"

"I am not told such things." The reply was curt.

"That dummy," muttered Hansraj as he bit off another strip of fingernail and spit it aside, "I asked him a dozen times already! He couldn't tell you his own name!"

Maqbool, of course, had seen Hansraj interrogating

43

the big, silken-sashed and turbaned doorman, but he hoped that a civilized tone of voice from a man of his own substantial appearance might evoke a more enlightening response. "Well, it is not his job, you see," he explained to Hansraj, but he could not sit patiently any longer, and stood staring at the white door across the spacious foyer, tugging at his moustache.

"If Maulanaji doesn't come out of that door in another two minutes, Maqbool, I'm going into it!"

"Try not to be so impatient. I tell you what we'll do — let's make a wager to see who can guess closer to how high we would have to count before they come back? You can do the counting out loud for both of us and I will hold the bets —"

"Oh, go to hell, fat fool," he scowled, sitting and picking dirt from between his toes.

Then the door opened again, and this time it was Mr. Irving himself who came out, striding toward them with an envelope in his hand. He was followed by two other sahibs, both dressed in officer's uniforms, wearing side arms and carrying short clubs. The Sikh doorman snapped to attention and saluted.

"Are these the ones who came with Kitchlew?" the Deputy Commissioner asked the Sikh, as though he and Hansraj spoke no English.

"I am the Pleader Maqbool, sir, Dr. Kitchlew's friend." His voice was respectful, though he felt a flutter of tension in his chest and suspected he missed a heartbeat before Mr. Irving addressed him.

"I see. Well, this is for you then." He held out the envelope. "We've had Kitchlew and Satyapal transported —"

"What? Why?"

"In the interests of public safety. I'm not at liberty to say more than that."

44

"B-but where — *where* have they gone?" Maqbool felt himself choking as he clutched the letter, staring at this flimsy envelope, all that remained of his dearest friend.

"I'm not at liberty to disclose that."

"But for how long? Wh-when will you return them to us?"

"Impossible to estimate," he snapped. "I've nothing more to tell you. Captain Massey will see you to the gate. Good day," he said, abruptly doing an about-face and striding with perfect poise and composure back to his office.

Maqbool moved his lips. No sound emerged. His brain, his entire body, felt as though it were wax, left too long in the sun, he was softly sinking into the ground, and though he wanted desperately to explain that he was not a mere ball of wax, no jellied inanimate substance to be dismissed so and left with a thousand questions unanswered, unstated, he could not whisper so much as one word. He felt as he used to in his years at the University, whenever an English professor called upon him, though he had the answer clearly stored in his brain. He stood shaking like a dish of rice pudding, a deaf-mute imbecile, hopelessly lost, totally inarticulate. His father, who was one of the Punjab's first pleaders, a man of sterling intellect and steel will, had to spend weeks before every examination period, closeted alone with him, losing countless rupees from his practice, simply to tutor his inept son. Maqbool passed. He passed with honors, in fact, but when he was scheduled to go abroad with Kitchlew he broke down, and since then had never really overcome the jellyfish fear he felt in the face of White authority.

"Let's get on with it," Captain Massey ordered, touching the small of Maqbool's back with the tip of his stick. The other officer stood braced a few paces away. The door was opened wide by the Sikh.

He watched the pebbles disappear, crushed under the tread of his toes and thong sandals, like tiny heads caught beneath a juggernaut, some rolling free or kicked aside. Like cattle they were herded to the gate. Like natives. He felt so sick walking back to the tonga beyond the gate that he could not even cry.

Till he opened the letter and saw the handwriting of his friend, and heard his voice speaking through the words, "My Dears, Dr. Satyapal and I have been ordered to leave Amritsar, and though our hearts are filled with sorrow we have agreed to leave peacefully, believing as we do that nonviolence is the only way for us to achieve our precious goal of freedom . . ." then he could hold back no longer, but covered his face with his handkerchief as he collapsed onto the seat of the tonga.

"Tears will not help him," Hansraj said, taking the letter from his hand, perusing it coldly.

He was startled to hear Hansraj's voice. He turned to find his young friend eyeing him so contemptuously that Maqbool almost smiled. From the moment Mr. Irving had come within sight and sound of them till the moment after Captain Massey had left them alone at the gate-house, Hansraj remained so perfectly silent that Maqbool actually forgot he was there.

"We must get away quickly," Hansraj muttered, ordering the tongawalla to hurry back to Hall Bazaar.

"But where are the Doctor-sahibs?" the driver asked.

"I said *hurry*," shouted Hansraj, nervously watching the gatehouse.

"Don't worry, they won't waste any money deporting you," Maqbool assured him.

"Tears are for women! The insults of a woman do not bother me!"

Maqbool did not trouble himself to answer that. What did it matter, these verbal taunts from a child? *Kitchlew*

46

was gone! And to where? For how long? How had they taken him? Were there irons on his wrists or ankles? "We have agreed to leave peacefully," the letter said, but after he'd finished writing that, then what? Suppose they had pushed him the way Captain Massey pushed me? What if he did not wish to go quite so quickly? He is no Maqbool, Maqbool thought, gnawing at his lower lip, while he stared at the grand houses they raced past, his vision too blurred to see anything but the smiling strong glow of Saif-ud-din's face. As boys they had walked to and from their first class in school together — in those days his father's home was next door to Kitchlew's house — and sometimes other classmates would join them and someone was always there to tell a joke about Maqbool — was he not too fat? Was his name not funny? His nose too long? His ears too small? All of them used him as a target for invective, all but Kitchlew. There was no pettiness about him, nothing mean or small-minded, even when he was small. He was always memorizing poetry, reciting it as they walked, and suddenly he would stop, looking puzzled, to ask, "What do you think it means, Maqbool? What is the truth of it?" How many times he asked that question — *What is the truth of it?* And now he was gone. To Maqbool the drive back seemed but to take one moment, an endless moment of mourning. He knew many people in Amritsar, the number of his relatives, his clients, his colleagues at court, and his longstanding acquaintances in public life was legion. He had but one friend.

"Hey, where is Kitchlew? Where is Satyapal?" people called as they slowed down along Hall Bazaar Road.

"Ask the Commissioner," shouted Hansraj. "He has taken them! Who knows? They may be murdered by now!"

"What?"

"What did he say?"

"He said the Commissioner has them!"

"No, no, he said the English have murdered them!"

"What?"

Merchants left their shops unattended to start running after the tonga, and as they ran others stopped them momentarily to ask what had happened, and as they explained it, others heard and turned to inform still more people. And so it went — like a flame. Like hot sparks fanned over sawdust waiting to ignite in the sun. Like a brush fire blown by high winds it spread — *Kitchlew and Satyapal are dead!*

The crowd got so thick around them that the tonga was brought to a halt before it could reach Kitchlew's house, and everyone was shouting, and Hansraj was standing yelling the loudest, "They have murdered Maulanaji. They want to murder us all."

"No, no, do not exaggerate," protested Maqbool faintly. Few people could hear his words, though everyone saw how he looked, and men of substance who would not have paid credence to the words of Hansraj alone gravely nodded to one another as they mournfully tugged turbans from their bowed heads, their eyes clouding with tears saying, "See how the Pleader Maqbool mourns with bitter tears the great man he loved! It must be true — they have killed him!"

Then Mrs. Kitchlew came racing from her house. The rumor had reached her ears in its most brutal form, carried by a widowed hag, who heard it from a beggar boy, and rushed to Kitchlew's kitchen to scream, "They've murdered your husband!" She ran like a Fury, clutching her terrified sons, her face naked and exposed to all for the first time in her adult life: unveiled she ran out into the glaring sunlight of the street that buzzed with stories of how they had tortured him first, dismembering his

body. The crowd moved back upon itself, like a sea
miraculously opening to let her pass to the tonga, to
Maqbool, who stepped down to meet her, taking both
boys in his arms, lifting them, cradling them, one in each
arm.

"Where is he?" she cried.

"I don't know, Madam," he said, for it was only true,
but hearing that confirmed her worst fears, and she fell
to the cobblestone road, smashing the bangles from her
wrists, tearing the marriage necklace from her throat,
wailing her widow's plaintive cry of desolation, for death
would be better than the living death that remained to her.
Then neighbors, covered in their burkha tents of per-
petual mourning, came and lifted her gently, leading her
back to her empty house. Maqbool followed with the
boys. Hasan screamed when he saw what his mother
had done, but Akbar made no sound, though his eyes
were saucers of sorrow overflowing.

Hansraj did not descend from the tonga, but ordered
his driver to proceed on to Dr. Satyapal's house. It was
not easy at first to clear the road ahead. Then several
sturdy men took hold of the donkey's reins and walked
as an advance escort, brushing people aside, scolding, "We
must get through to tell Dr. Satyapal's father! Clear the
path!" Those who moved aside from the front followed
behind the tonga as it rolled along, and soon there was a
sizable procession of men and boys, all of them bareheaded. And with each turn of the tonga's wheels, as the
word spread, the crowd of outraged mourners grew larger.

Satyapal's father was a carpenter. His shop was on the
ground floor of the house, in which he and his only son
lived alone. The old man had two daughters, older than
Satyapal. Both girls were married, and their husbands
worked for Government in Delhi, but what with so much
agitation and trouble everywhere they had decided not to

travel home this year for the holidays. Satyapal's mother had died twenty years ago. The old carpenter never remarried. During the War, when Satyapal went overseas, he lived as a recluse, closing all the doors of his shop. Behind his wooden curtains he worked on, and from the street you could hear the dull scraping of his saw. Friends considered him lost. "His mind has snapped from being too long alone," they said. But no sooner did his boy return than the shop opened wide again, and there was the old man, seated smiling in full view of the world, braced like a human vise round the plank he sawed, gouged, or chiseled, like the knotty branch of an old oak, toughened, wrinkled, weathered by time, unbroken.

He did not stop working the instant he heard the noise of the approaching procession, for nowadays in Amritsar you got accustomed to noisy crowds. Then he noticed that everyone was bareheaded, and they walked barefoot, as well. It was how people looked when they went to a funeral.

He saw they were coming to him.

That was when he set aside his tools, and stood up. But no one rushed forward to speak, not even Hansraj, whom he had known as a boy. Suddenly hushed silence fell like a weight upon that boisterous crowd, a silence as heavy as the last breath of moisture-laden air before a monsoon's first thunderclap.

"What has happened to Dr. Satyapal?" he called out, for though he loved no one as he loved his only son, he referred to him always in this respectful manner ever since he had become a doctor — the old man touched his feet with his wrinkled brow that day, even as he touched temple idols in worship. Satyapal had lifted him then and kissed his brow crying, "Father, it is I who must bow before you!" but he never since forgot the title when speaking to him or about him. It was, he believed, a miracle to see his own boy, the son of a carpenter, whose Khatri ancestors had always been carpenters, to watch this child, this seed of his loins, transformed into a healer of men, a doctor honored by Brahmans and British alike — it was a miracle, at which he never ceased to marvel.

"What has become of Dr. Satyapal?" he cried louder. Scarcely three hours ago the message had been delivered here, and he had left, saying only, "I am needed at the Commissioner's bungalow."

Still no one answered him.

"You — Hansraj," he said, extending the finger which was permanently bent from its years of gripping the saw frame, "why do you sit in the tonga so? Where have you come from?"

"From Civil Lines, sir. I accompanied Dr. Satyapal to the Commissioner's bungalow."

"And where — where is Dr. Satyapal now?"

"He and Dr. Kitchlew went into the Commissioner's office, and no one of us has seen them since . . ."

The old man removed the sawdust-covered cloth turban from his bald head, leaving the cloth to drop, leaving it with his worn sandals on the road. Two men helped him climb into the tonga, for he was too weak to lift himself, yet once inside he sat erect, bracing his arms stiffly against the board, an aged banyan braced by its own branches. He did not cry, and his voice was remarkably firm when he spoke, shouting as loud as he could:

"Let us go back then, and ask the Commissioner what has become of Dr. Satyapal!"

A chorus of gruff voices roared in response, and the driver cracked his whip against the donkey who lurched forward, as they all did, shouting as they marched, "Victory to Satyapal! Victory to Kitchlew! Victory to the Hindu-Muslim Unity!" It came flooding, rushing, raining from their lungs, from angrily gaping mouths, a monsoon of frustration and fury. And from every house now people ran to join them. From every street and byroad, from every narrow dim lane, from the very crevices and cracks of the city's cobblestone streets, from the peeling plaster over sun-dried brick walls, from windows and cellars, from stalls and shops in a dozen neighboring bazaars, they emerged, running, shouting, pushing each other aside, asking, "What has happened? Where are we going?"

It moved like a mighty magnet, that tonga, drawing much of the city behind its slow rolling wheels.

4

ARRY HUDSON was drinking his morning bracer of gin in the flat over the
Crown Theatre, of which he was founding owner and
resident manager, when he heard the noise outside.

"What's that commotion?" he asked, turning instinctively toward his "housekeeper," but her dark head
remained half hidden under the pillow, and her answer
was a snore. The bitch was as useless as she was beautiful.
He went to the window himself, peering cautiously
through a slat of the still closed shutter. He saw young
men running wildly about waving their arms, shouting
something that sounded like "Civil Lines!" The great wave
of noise, however, came from beyond his line of vision,
and though no word of it was clear enough for him to
decipher, Harry had lived in India long enough to understand the sound's transcendental meaning — Trouble.

He dressed like the quick-change artist he was, stooping
in front of his mirror while he slithered into soiled pajama-
like trousers and collarless Punjabi shirt, smearing tan
greasepaint onto his face and the backs of his hands and
wrists. He was short, slight enough to pass for a Hindu or

Muslim merchant, and his Punjabi slang was good enough to give him free access to the mob, wherever it wandered. He loved a life of many roles, but could never quite make it in the London theatre. Washed out at twenty-five, he invested his life's savings in the P. & O. passage to Bombay — thirty years ago. He hadn't been "Home" since, though the War had started him thinking about it again.

Harry stepped back from the glass and swiftly surveyed himself, deciding to add one earring and his black vest to his costume. Yes, that was much better. Only his teeth needed some betel juice stain. He kept his pan box well supplied, and hastily rolled himself a leaf, which he popped into his mouth. Excellent. Now he was Krishna of Hoshiapur, come to Amritsar for the Ram Naumi!

"— what is happening here?" he asked the first wild-eyed youth he could stop.

"We must go to Civil Lines to protest the murders!"

"Whose murders?"

"Kitchlew — Satyapal — where have you been? Are you from this place?"

"No, from Hoshiapur."

"Oh, Civil Lines are that way!"

Harry started to run. His theatre on Church Gate Road was not far from the Hall Bazaar, which was where the mainstream of the mob was moving now. He glimpsed a tonga surrounded by bareheaded men. The dark fury of their faces made him hesitate, forgetting for an instant he was in mufti. He'd been caught once by the tide of a mob in Ahmed as the White Mr. Hudson, English pukka-sahib. He had never really thought about skin color till then, more intrigued by its texture, especially that of the out-caste girls he'd been visiting, young prostitute slaves kept in cages and rented by their owners for any length of time desired. Driving back toward the Camp area of town the mob had stopped his carriage and forced his driver down,

54

closing around him, jeering, and shouting words he couldn't comprehend. They'd been outraged by some accident or other at one of the mills, he later learned, where a few Indian hands were lost in machinery run by an Englishman. At the time he understood nothing but that his skin color was wrong — which was really all they knew about him, yet they almost killed him for it.

He joined the throng surging along Hall Bazaar, headed north toward the station, jostled into the noisy main current of humanity by a burly figure, whom he asked, "What are we going to do when we get there?"

"Where are we going?" the fool replied, looking so ignorant of what was happening that Harry wondered if he too might not be English.

"I wish we had weapons," a young man remarked, clenching his fist.

"What would you do with them?" he asked.

"I would kill the Commissioner!"

"What does he look like?"

"White! I would know him if I see him! He has murdered our leaders! And they have told us to love the English! This is their reward! I hate every Englishman," he snapped, baring his large teeth, glaring so fiercely at him that Harry feared he was detected. "Don't you hate them too?"

"Yes, yes," he muttered. "Oh, there is my friend." He elbowed his way to the other side of the road, stepping on someone's toes with his shoes.

"Take off your shoes," the man told him. "We are in mourning. What is the matter with you?"

"I — I am not from this place," he said, feeling his heart pound faster at the realization that if he removed his shoes he was lost. He had not thought of painting his feet!

"What does it matter which place you are from? Kitchlew and Satyapal are heroes for all India!"

"Shame! Take off your shoes," the irate man insisted, and others took up the cry, "Shame, shame!" It echoed louder inside his head as he inched away from them. Now the full force of midmorning sun burned its flame against his skull, drawing moisture from his neck, where the streams of perspiration flowed, and he feared that the paint was washing off with it, washing his skin white again. Any moment, he sensed, they would all recognize him. He felt as though every eye in that flood of dark faces was focussed intently on his skin, and the tumult raised with the clouds of dust and dirt rang as *"Shame, shame! Take off your shoes!"* He tripped, going backwards, and would have fallen, but for a big man who grabbed his arms, and then he thought he was dead, fearing they had him in their clutches, and would now strip him naked, exposing his livid flesh, which shrank from the saving touch of the black man's grip, as he heard the mild words, "Careful, brother, or you'll fall."

He broke free, and ran, fast as his legs could carry him, up Khansamawalla lane toward the Christian Female Hospital run by Mrs. Easdon. The hospital was freshly painted white, and the cross atop its modest cupola was newly gilded. This building was in fact so cleanly Christian a sight that Hudson almost thought it an apparition as he raced through the outer gate and dashed across the courtyard in which a horse drawn tonga stood. The driver was talking to the gate guard, who stopped to shout angrily at him.

"Hey! Where do you think you are going?"

"I must see Mrs. Easdon," he told the startled guard, saying it in English rather than Punjabi, which made the servant lead him inside the cool, high ceilinged building. A native girl, dressed in the starched white uniform of a nurse, asked him to wait while she called Dr. Easdon.

"Tell her to hurry, for God's sake!" he shouted.

"What *are* you shouting about now, Mr. Hudson?" Mrs. Easdon asked, shaking her gray head, testy as ever, as she walked from her office to greet him.

"Hurry! I've got to reach Mr. Irving's bungalow before the bloody mob does. I'll drop you at the Fort — you'll be safe there."

"Oh, goodness," she sighed, appraising him with a look more laden with disgust than incredulity. "Drinking too much again, Mr. Hudson? Or is that your costume for a new drama?"

"I know you don't approve of my way of life, but never mind that for the moment, Mrs. Easdon — I'm trying my best to help save yours! Can't you hear that mob? They're calling for White blood, those niggers! They say Irving's murdered Kitchlew and Satyapal, and —"

"Oh, so that's what all the fuss is about! Well, I won't miss either of those anarchists, I assure you," she replied.

The native nurse looked faint, touching her throat with trembling fingers, whispering, "Excuse me," running out the front door.

"Where in heaven's name is she going?" Mrs. Easdon asked. "I wanted her to make the rounds with me now, and — oh, dear! What a nuisance!"

"Don't you see, you've got to come with me?" he pleaded. She was a head taller than him, and for all her years still a lovely woman, a Lady. He'd known fifteen years ago, when first he set eyes on her here in Amritsar that she wouldn't have the lowly likes of Harry Hudson.

"What in heaven's name *are* you talking about, Mr. Hudson? I have no intention of going anywhere but on the rounds of my hospital, and I should think you'd want to go about your business as well. Good day to you, Mr. Hudson."

"Good luck, Mrs. Easdon," he said. Then he hurried

out and ordered the tonga driver to take him to the Commissioner's bungalow. "But stay away from Hall Bazaar — go Hathi Gate! *Jaldi, jaldi!*"

They went as fast as the mare could move.

Miles stared toward the distant hills through the window behind his desk. The heat haze of midday obscured all but the faintest silhouette of those verdant heights. It was almost one. Rehill surely had them out of the district by this time, past Gurdaspur in all probability. He was a fast driver, and that far north at least the road wasn't half bad. They would reach Dharmsala before sundown, God willing! It had all gone off smoothly — according to plan. Yet he felt no elation at the job well done, only a gnawing sense of anxiety as he turned to stare at the phone. He kept thinking it would ring, but the longer it didn't, of course, the more certain it seemed that His Honour was right, and he had been quite wrong.

Not that Miles presumed to believe his own judgment as to how Kitchlew and Satyapal should be handled was really superior to that of the Governor. For the order had come down last night from Lahore, brought back personally by Smith, signed by Sir Michael himself. No man was half as fit to rule the Punjab, or all of India, for that matter, as Sir Michael. He knew its lore and languages far better than the Viceroy, and should have been made Viceroy (many an old hand in the Service said that), and might yet be the next one, even though he was ready to retire (some people at the Club mentioned the possibility as very real), if he would have the job. Clearly, His Honour was right. Natives could not be treated like Englishmen. The standards of fair conduct that applied back Home lost all relevance in the Orient. Deportation, swift and silent, surgical excision removing the diseased part from the body politic, that was the only cure for sedition here. It had worked before. The quicker the better. Once they were gone people would forget about them, and more importantly, forget their anarchistic preachings. Out of sight, out of mind.

Yet Miles had hoped to reach Kitchlew — another way. It was naive he suspected now, but he'd really thought about trying a new sort of experiment ever since he'd come to Amritsar. It was his first assignment as D.C., and he wanted to do something, well, not exactly different, but it had occurred to him that since so many Punjabis fought in the War and proved to be so loyal to the Raj, even with guns in their hands and live ammunition and all, that perhaps there was more to the native character than most Englishmen thought. He'd tried talking to Kitchlew, more man to man than he'd ever spoken to a Muslim barrister before. They had talked of Cambridge and Keats once. Miles almost forgot till Kitchlew mentioned the poet that he'd dabbled a bit in romantic verse himself, and used to call Keats's "When I have fears that I may cease to be," the "Most meaningful poem ever written." He wasn't sure what he meant by that any more, but he did think about building a bridge of common cultural interests with Kitchlew, to help draw him away from anarchist ideas like Gandhi's. He hadn't had time to work it out. There was always something more urgent to worry about.

Miles touched the bright red leather cover of his "Emergency Plan," which rested squarely central on the otherwise clear top of his desk. The letters were embossed in gold under the seal of Great Britain. It was some source of comfort to him, simply seeing that Plan there so solid yet beautiful, so simple but complete. It had been worked out with care and precision by his predecessors in this office, after long and learned consideration of what procedures would be best designed to secure Amritsar's Civil Lines and the White population from danger in times of unusual "disturbance." The rough plan had then been sent to Lahore, and there it had been scrutinized, studied in every detail for flaws of logic or failure to consider all possible contingencies, after which it was initialed by each officer whose desk it lay upon for so many days or weeks. And finally it traveled in a locked dispatch box to the empyrean heights of Simla, that eagle's perch above the Punjab plains, where the Viceroy and his Secretariat sat watching over all the realm, perusing the Plan again with eyes that caught every fault, minds that never misplaced a comma nor misspelled a word. There the Plan was certified by a final set of initials, printed in its perfect form, and sewn into the leather cover that Miles's fingers caressed as he thought about the steps outlined inside. He knew the Plan by heart.

He'd activated Step One after dismissing the friends of the deportees. That meant the bridges leading to Civil Lines would have several soldiers close by, though not obtrusively so, in the event of any rabble trying to cross over from city side. The thin guard could cope with most disturbances by simply closing off access roads. But if the mob was substantial and bent on mischief then Step Two might be needed, and for that he had briefed Massey, Plomer, and Smith before sending them on their several ways — Captain Massey to the Fort, where he would stay with his troops on the ready, Superintendent Plomer to police headquarters in Civil Lines, where he would wait with his alerted force, and Dr. Smith to the Civil Hospital, where he would keep the motor ambulance ready to evacuate all Whites from the city if called. Miles was to remain in his office, at his phone, ready to call or be called by any or all of them if the need arose. It was really quite simple.

He'd expected a call before now, and almost picked up

the phone half a dozen times to ring someone himself, but couldn't risk tying up the line just for a chat.

His secretary knocked, opening the door without waiting for his response. Hudson rushed up to him, smeared greasepaint still on his neck and ears.

"They're coming, sir — thousands 'a them! They're hungry for English blood, them niggers! I got here fast as I could, Mr. Irving!"

"Where were they headed?" Miles asked, cranking the phone handle hard before he picked up the earpiece. Harry Hudson wasn't good for much, but his information had proved reliable before, and he knew he would only be paid for trustworthy service.

"Up the Hall Bazaar, round 'bout Aitchison Park too — I seen them milling there less'n five minutes ago! Gawd, it's a blood-hungry mob, it is, sir."

"Plomer. Irving here. We'd best get on with Step Two. Right." He clicked off, and promptly rung Massey, then Smith, each with the same message. Altogether it took no more than a minute's time. The Plan was efficiently designed.

He strapped his pistol belt round his waist, and put on his topi, taking his longer riding crop, which he whisked against his high boot.

"What about me, Mr. Irving? Where should I go, sir?" Hudson asked, as they left the office.

"The Fort. Our Plan calls for evacuation of all civilians to the Fort. You'll be safe enough there."

"What about Mrs. Easdon, sir?"

"Dr. Smith will be rounding everyone up," he snapped, hurrying outside to his waiting horse. He no longer felt conscience-stricken. There was no time for remorse or anxiety now. Step Two was activated. His part in the Plan was to see that it all worked smoothly. He turned his horse toward the carriage bridge and dug in deep with his spurs.

61

5

HARI thought it was another Ram Naumi parade. He kept racing along in front of the tonga, laughing and waving his arms wildly, shouting "Ram, Ram!" He was quite tall and much older than he behaved, though no one actually knew his age, or his lineage — even his surname was a mystery. He lived in the Vishnu temple, and had all his life, since the time he'd been abandoned there, another mouth no one wished to feed. Somehow he survived, more or less, for though he grew taller and larger, the Brahmans who watched over him soon recognized that something was different about the boy's mind, something missing perhaps, though they preferred to say he was "intoxicated by God," and that is why they named him Hari, which is the name of great Vishnu himself.

Hari loved to see so many people celebrating. He loved *tamashas* of every kind, especially those at the temple when everyone brought some delicacy to eat. He could eat sweets all day. Sometimes he ate nothing but cane sugar and coconut. At night, when everybody left the temple and the Brahmans were not looking, he took the puja offerings from the trays left before the gods. He ate flower petals too, and the chief Brahman, an old man they called Dada-sahib, once scolded him harshly, shouting, "You must not eat from God's tray, Hari!" He asked in reply, "Which tray is not God's?" and for some reason he never understood old Dada-sahib stopped shouting then and his eyes filled with tears, and he began to chant the sacred mantras reserved for special holidays. After that everyone in the temple treated Hari more kindly. People came to see him when they were very sick or lame, and Dada-sahib would ask him to touch them.

He loved to run. His leg muscles were well trained. Often he would run for no reason, all round the bazaars, and people would greet him and give him cane sugar, and once he was lost for several days, but he was not afraid. He could see the tall trees across the wide bridge. He liked to climb trees like those. He climbed as fast as some monkeys. He enjoyed playing with them, catching hold of their tails. He wondered if there were monkeys in those trees?

"Soldiers," someone shouted. "Look out! They have rifles!"

"What have you done with Dr. Satyapal?"

"Where is Kitchlew?"

"*Kitchlew-ki-jai! Satyapal-ki-jai! Gandhi-ki-jai!*"

Everyone was shouting at once. It was a real *tamasha*! The noise was terrific! Hari loved loud noise. He too kept shouting as he ran, dancing, gesturing with his long arms and legs, laughing, and singing, "Ram, Ram — Ram, Ram — Ram, Ram, Hari!" It was a *bhajan* he learned in the temple, and every day he sang it — sometimes for hours and hours.

"They won't let us pass!" yelled a man behind him, looking very angry as he shook his fist toward the bridge.

"Don't let them stop us!" called out Hansraj, his hands cupped to his lips as he stood in the tonga.

63

Hari was way ahead of the tonga by now. He was able to run faster than any of them. He kept looking back as he ran though, because he liked to see familiar faces. He knew most of those faces, but names were harder for him to remember. He could never be sure of names, except for Dada-sahib, and the little crippled boy who shared the shed in which he slept in the temple compound — his name was Manu, and Hari knew that very well, because Manu was his friend. Manu sang songs to him at night, when he could not fall asleep, and on days when there was nothing to do, Manu told him stories. Manu told him the story about the mongoose and the cobra, and about the fox who tried to pretend he was a tiger . . .

"Watch out! The horse is kicking!"

He jumped back just in time! The horse had reared up and stood over him, waving his front legs. Hari waved back, laughing, and someone nearby rushed ahead of him and touched the horse's sweat-shining flank with a piece of bamboo. Then he saw a small stone fly against the iron railing of the bridge and bounce near his feet, so he picked it up and tossed it as far as he could, toward the trees. He could not reach the trees though, but now other stones were flying about and bouncing near him, and he picked up as many as he could hold in both hands. He liked to play a game like that with Manu, only they used the smooth pebbles they would find in the temple garden, and then —

"Look out! Run! *Run, Hari!*"

He heard his name, and that made him look around, and then he saw them running back from the bridge and waving to him, and he did not understand why, but he couldn't wave back without letting all the stones fall from his hands, and he wanted to bring them to Manu, to show him how many he could hold — but then he felt something bite into his back, like the time a scorpion bit him and

64

Dada-sahib sat so long at his side reciting the mantras, and it was so strange —

He could not understand what had happened, but somehow it was all burning fire inside and he had fallen, dropping the stones, and the sun blazed against his open eyes, and he was so thirsty he wanted to cry out — but he could not speak. He could not so much as move his tongue, or lift his arm or leg, he who was the fastest runner of them all. Then he heard someone crying:

"They've murdered Hari too! They shot him in the back! The murderers! What harm did he ever do?"

But where was Dada-sahib? Where was Manu? Why did the *tamasha* have to end . . .?

Lieutenant Dickie watched them fall back, the wave that had all but inundated him receding as though miraculously in midtide. He had watched the terrorists rolling toward him, crying their battle shouts of hate, doing their war dance of death, intoxicated he sensed with whatever drugs they took to work themselves into their frenzies. There was only one way to stop a mob like that. He had held his fire till he could smell the stink of their armpits. He had forced his horse to face them, though the leather rein he clutched almost cut through the leathery flesh of his locked hand. The three Indians in his painfully thin picket of six soldiers had fallen back in panic just as the mob came into view, rolling like a wall of molten lava out of the city's erupting crater. Happily he had three Englishmen as well, all stout fellows of the ammunition column, Northumbrians. They'd stood fast with him, but their horses were harder to hold, and two of them dismounted, keeping their rifles at the ready. He waited, hoping the reserves would come up from the Fort, but not a fresh troop was in sight. He'd shouted "Fire" when he could almost touch the vanguard of that rabble with his whip.

His men aimed well. The ringleader of the terrorists, a very tall ebony-skinned one, who had been goading the others along, collecting stones with which to harass the guard, went down with the first volley. Seeing their leader fall, the others withdrew from the bridge.

"Hold fire," Dickie ordered, turning his head to find two columns of mounted British troops galloping to his relief.

Miles was diverted by Beckett, one of his three Assistant Commissioners, who shouted as he galloped closer,

"The footbridge, sir! We can't hold them!"

One grew accustomed to mobs in India, yet even Miles found the roar of this one unnerving. It was a special breed of monster, the Mob, and its roar was peculiar to the species. It sounded, he thought, much like a stampeding herd of elephants must sound to a grasshopper. He'd been hunting black leopard once when he was nearly caught by stampeding elephants. He would have been trampled to dust had he been foolish enough to come down from his blind, yet every nerve of his body told him to do just that, to jump and run, to do anything to get away from that approaching earthquake — only his disciplined mind kept him rooted where he was, several feet above the herd that raced by below, shaking but safe in his mahogany perch.

The Mob stretched beyond the tracks, moving first in one direction, then in the other, probing and withdrawing, testing every road and bridge, trying to drag itself onto the white sands of the Civil Lines and destroy the very roots of civilized order, peace, and tranquility. There could be no dealing with this mindless Creature, no negotiating, no dickering, Miles knew, which was why he never for a moment so much as considered allowing the Mob to reach his bungalow, to state its case to him there. The Plan in its wisdom left him no such option, of course, for the first step was to picket the roads into Civil Lines, and the second to reinforce the first with local troops, and the third to call for military reserves from the regional brigadier, but all were designed with one axiom of security in mind — to hold the island of British purity free of native contamination.

Miles braced himself more firmly, balancing his body with his thighs alone, as he brought his horse to a halt directly in the center of the picket line that swayed like a ragged flag in a high wind.

"Go back!" Miles shouted, cupping his hands to his mouth, though he could barely hear his own voice above the din. "Go back or we'll shoot!"

He kept trying to focus on the faces of individuals in the front line, but none that he saw meant anything to him. He was trying to pick out the leaders, but no clear pattern emerged. A stone hit his boot, bouncing off without leaving more than a pinpoint of dust, but he saw other missiles flying now, and ordered his men to fall back fifty yards. Beckett's boyish face looked terrified, and some of the soldiers seemed uncertain as they glanced at him, their eyes wide with wonder as to how long he would hold their fire.

He wondered why it was taking so long for the Step Two reinforcements to arrive, but as he backed off with his line he saw the dust raised by Plomer's horse coming at a reckless gallop.

"Where the devil are your men?" Miles called.

"They're trying to save the telegraph, sir! Mob's gone mad over at Hall Bridge! Dickie had to fire —"

Several soldiers heard the word "fire" and discharged muskets, but their horses reared up, and the shots went flying over the heads of the Mob, serving merely to incite it. Wild-eyed they surged forward, and Miles was about to order his men to shoot, when he noticed a familiar face frantically waving a white cloth, shouting:

"Pleader Maqbool . . . I will try to make them go back! Wait! Please!"

He nodded, waiting as he watched the pudgy man with the walrus moustache desperately trying to make himself heard above the Mob's angry roar.

"Please, let us be sensible," Maqbool yelled, berating those closest to him with every argument he could find. The Pleader Salaria quickly joined him in seeking thus to reverse the volcanic flood, and together they rushed from one side of the crowd to the other, shouting and pushing people back, desperately trying to make themselves heard, and for a few moments it seemed they might do the impossible. People who had till this point given no thought to their immediate or ultimate goals in coming this far were suddenly confronted with the familiar faces of men they respected, and told, "This is madness! Turn back! Our protest must be peaceful!" It made them stop, those in the front rows, all but the wild boys, who cared for nothing but excitement. Some even turned to ask those behind, "Hey, why are we doing this?" But then a young man, whose head was shaved bald shouted, "That's *him*! He's the one who murdered them! That's the Commissioner!" Others took up the cry, pointing and pushing forward, shoving Maqbool and Salaria aside.

Miles watched the Monster move closer. He felt almost hypnotized by the sight of that rabble-turned-Beast inching toward him, like a boa constrictor — only blacker than a boa, he thought. He had never seen a black-skinned human for the first twenty years of his life. His nanny used to say that if he didn't wash with soap his skin would turn black, and the color of a person's skin was the color of his Soul. Nanny said black Souls lived in the lowest pit of perdition

where poison snakes and spiders and crocodiles went. He
had known nothing of India at all before he'd boned up
for his exams, which were no simpler than those for the
Home Service, but the cream had been skimmed off the
top of the year's "mind-batch" for the choice openings at
Whitehall. Miles had had his heart set on the Foreign
Office, and when he was told he hadn't come quite up to
the mark for that — well, it didn't seem to matter really
where he went. As long as it was far away from Home! He
couldn't really stomach the idea of staying within sight
and sound of those friends who'd made the grade and were
called up to London. He saw Beckett staring wide-eyed,
panic-stricken at him, and sensed his assistant (he was a
good boy, actually, though not too bright) feared he had
lost his nerve. Perhaps all of them did by now, Miles realized, looking at the other White faces, most of which
appeared tinged with green. There was a point, of course,
beyond which patience in Authority was translated as fear
— especially by natives. After that, all was lost.

"*Fire,*" he ordered. His voice sounded faint amid the
thunder in his ears, and he feared it was lost upon his
men, till the report of their rifles rang loud and fast
enough to burn the Beast. Miles kept his horse's head
down, and had to slap his rump several stinging blows
before he stopped jolting at the sharp reports of rifles on
either side. Horses were like natives, they understood the
whip, and only behaved properly under a firm hand. Miles
marveled at how simple it was. The Beast was as cowardly
as it was brutal, thank God!

Maqbool heard the bullet scream as it winged past his
ear, and turning in total disbelief, saw the red-faced soldiers firing! The white cloth of his unfurled turban was
still clutched in his trembling fist, and he waved it wildly
for a moment, as though that might make them stop. He

could not grasp it. Had Mr. Irving's men gone mad? Did they not know that he and Salaria were trying to calm people down? How could they just open fire, and with his back to their muskets? His thoughts raced with the speed of a whining bullet that sang its terror to his scorched ear, and the answers came with the sound of other missiles winged to their targets at every side of him.

Maqbool started to run. There was no difficulty now about pushing people back. They seemed to be blown toward the footbridge by enormous invisible fans generating hurricane winds, all their limbs were flying as they cried in horror and trampled one another down in their haste to escape the punishment that flew indiscriminately toward them. He paused to help an elderly man, who had been knocked down, pushed over, Maqbool thought, by the racing throng. He was a merchant of the Hall Bazaar, a vendor of oil, whom Maqbool and Kitchlew knew as boys, and who himself had three grown sons, two in the army still, one in France —

"Teli," he said, bending and lifting his arm. Then he saw the blood pouring like oil from his chest, and shouted, "Help! Help! This man is dying! Help! Help us! Somebody!"

But in front of him they were all being blown away, frantically screaming and running, and behind they sat on their horses like statues, deaf to any words a native might utter.

6

RATTO watched from his tonga parked at the edge of Aitchison Park to the rear of the crowd as they started to fall back, shouting, "They're shooting! The sahibs are shooting! Run! Run or they will kill us!"

He clutched the empty sleeve on his left side with his one emaciated hand, grimacing at the itch he felt in his amputated arm. He had lost the arm fifteen years ago, when he joined a crowd like this, outside the Governor's House in Lahore, and found himself facing a horse guard charge. His arm was pulverized by the full weight of a horse's hoof. "It's not working," he muttered, spitting a bloodlike stream of betel juice out of the tonga.

"What do we do now, Ratto?" Bugga asked, rubbing the polished top of his shaved head, which glistened like an ebony icon of the Buddha laughing. His bulky torso was naked but for a scarlet thread that hung like the sash of a noble order, diagonally across his belly. It was the emblem of their Club.

"If they lock all the doors and windows," Ratto whispered, his rotting teeth and bloodshot eyes imparting a grotesquely demonic aspect to his face when he grinned, "then we must burn down the walls."

"Where do you see walls, Ratto?" Bugga asked, staring toward the Civil Lines.

"Not that way," Ratto snapped, finding himself less patient of late with Bugga's stupidity. Not that he had picked his "partner" for intelligence, but ten years ago Bugga was at least trimly muscular, and skilled in the arts of Yoga and martial drill. Ratto had searched every gym and temple court in Amritsar before hiring the man who helped him develop his various enterprises. The loss of his arm taught him to rely upon his wits, and soon he learned that some wealthy men were willing to pay remarkably high sums for small quantities of opium. He saved enough to buy a hostel-cum-restaurant, and with Bugga to train the young men who worked for him, Ratto gradually developed his little kingdom.

"They are shooting, Master," Abdul reported, panting as he raced up to the tonga, gesturing wildly toward the yellow-gray puffs of smoke that wafted so innocently above the footbridge. "They will kill anyone who crosses the bridge!" Like Bugga, his head was shaved bald, and he wore the scarlet thread over his naked torso, as did all the "boys" in their Club. Abdul was young and lithe, his muscles rippled, languid snakes under the glowing dark luster of his skin. Ratto felt a sudden impulse to touch his moist belly, but sensed Bugga's jealous eye watching him.

"Are there no English then left on this side of the bridge, Abdul?"

"Why do you ask it, Master?" His face was still hairless, smooth as a girl's face. His eyes reflected the naive simplicity of his peasant nature. He had joined their Club during the War, after seeing his father and brothers herded off in a bullock cart by the White officer, the British troops, who came like vultures to recruit peasant "volunteers" in the fields. Abdul escaped thanks to a fortuitous call of nature, which had lured him behind a clump of tall grass, where he watched them fall upon their prey. He remained hidden till dark, when he ran home to his village. His mother urged him to leave for Amritsar immediately, to hide in the crowded bazaars. Soon after he reached the city, Abdul heard about Ratto and Bugga, and the free board they provided for young men who needed help — and hated the British.

"If the English murder us when we try to enter their city, why should we let them remain alive in ours?" Ratto replied, his pulse beating more swiftly as he stared into Abdul's brightening eyes.

"Ah," the boy whispered, starting to smile as he began to understand.

Many of the others had reached the command tonga by now, and the tallest among them, Ram, who was always quick to grasp Ratto's meaning, shouted, "The banks! There are English in the National Bank! Let us get them! Come on — we will make them pay for this — for spilling our blood!"

In no time at all the word spread along the edge of Aitchison Park, and people turned away from the bridges, and started running back toward Hall Bazaar. Bugga grabbed the whip and drove Ratto with Abdul and Ram hanging onto the tonga sides, shouting, "The English banks! Let's burn them! Loot them! They have killed us, the White dogs! To their banks!"

Ratto remembered his last visit to the National Bank — it was before the War — when he had considered investing some of his savings in Government bonds, which paid such handsome interest, and — well, why not? He had become something of a pillar in the Amritsar community, and it seemed somehow only proper that he should have dealings with the largest banking establishment. He asked, of course, to see the manager, and then sat for more than twenty minutes outside Mr. Stuart's office. He had never known twenty minutes could seem so long. The door remained closed, and Ratto naturally assumed that the manager of the National Bank was a most busy man, no doubt conferring with half a dozen entrepreneurs, till an English lady appeared, escorted by her Sikh bearer, and Mr. Stuart himself opened the door for her —"My dear Mrs. Tucker," he drawled, his voice smoothly unctuous as his combed white hair, "how delightful of you to drop by. I've just been sitting here wishing someone would join me for tea. Haven't had a visitor all morning!" The door slammed before Ratto could speak, and staring at the Sikh, who took a seat facing him, he realized that Mr. Stuart never had any intention of speaking with him, but because he had tipped the clerk, he was left to sit unmolested, ignored, outside the manager's door.

Bugga's boys had brought their lathis, short iron-tipped sticks half an inch thick which they used in drill training. They held the sticks high, waving them like rods of righteous avengers as they shouted, "Destroy the banks! Kill the English!" The cry was infectious. Everyone claimed to have seen a comrade fall. There was that bond of mutual terror which welded them, fused their spirits, into a force recklessly bent on retaliation. It surged through their blood, the cry of vengeance, the hunger for English flesh, the craving to destroy in kind that which administered such punishment upon them.

Mr. Stuart heard the shouts growing again in volume and shook his head slowly as he finished checking the ledger which had been brought to him for initialing. It was no

74

mystery to him that India remained so devilishly poor and backward. Most of the population spent much of its time marching through the streets shouting stupid slogans! There was no hope for such people. Eighteen years ago when Stuart had come out as deputy assistant manager of the Bombay branch of the National he'd had all sorts of ideas about what could be done to stir up the economy, to get things moving a bit here. He'd learned by now, as all his betters had told him, that nothing changed in the Orient. The Orient, as he informed his new men time and again, was "too many damned people bogged down between Kismet and karma." He was considered something of an authority on Oriental religions. For years he'd lectured the Ladies Auxiliary on "Exotic Cults and Practices of the East." He used to find that sort of thing amusing, but even the occult bored him nowadays. He'd begun to count the weeks till retirement would release him from Indian servitude — there were just fifty more left.

"Excuse me, sir." Scott peered round the private door that connected their offices. He was a terribly timid little man, and though he was perfectly competent as Number Two, Stuart couldn't quite bring himself to recommend his assistant for the Number One position at this branch. After ten years of loyal service here, he suspected Scott considered himself the natural heir to Number One, and — it will be a letdown for him, Stuart thought, sighing as he glanced at the dandruff that covered Scott's jacket shoulder.

"Yes? What is it, Mr. Scott?"

"The mob, sir — they're returning."

"I'm not deaf, Mr. Scott."

"Oh," he said, looking rather sheepishly ashamed at his alarm, starting to withdraw into his office, like a turtle whose nose had been touched by a twig.

75

Then the pane glass shattered downstairs, and the roar rushed in.

"My God." Mr. Stuart jumped to his feet, rushing to the vault, where he kept his life's savings, the Series A Government bonds, the Western Railway stock, the Ahmedabad Mills Managing Agency shares, the Class AA National Bank securities — he chewed his lower lip as he twirled the combination lock so fast that it flew past the correct number. He was on his knees, sweat pouring in such profusion from his forehead that he could not read the numbers.

"Have we any guns, sir?" Scott asked.

"What? Yes, that's right! My pistol," he muttered, rushing back to his desk and opening the bottom drawer. He'd never been obliged to use that pistol. He wasn't sure it was clean. His hands trembled too much to load it.

"Shall I do that, sir?" Scott asked, sounding remarkably calm and self-assured, even looking taller, more sturdy than he'd seemed in the past. Perhaps he would do for Number One at that, Stuart thought, handing him the pistol and the box of ammunition, smiling gratefully at his assistant.

But all the while the sea kept rising. The holds flooded; the ship was going down, and nothing they tried was of any avail. Before Scott could fill the chamber of his revolver with a single bullet, his door was battered from its hinges and a black wave of bald naked bodies poured into the carpeted office, waving lathis whose metal tips glittered.

"Don't," Stuart shouted, but the ocean flowed on, washing his body away with Scott's, two bits of flotsam piled onto the pyre of gutted furnishings below, cremated with the ledgers, stocks and debentures to which they had devoted their days and years, the flame consuming flesh and numbers alike in the undiscriminating cauldron . . .

George Thomson loaded his revolver long before the mob reached his bank. The Alliance was closer to the heart of the old city, and George was always on the alert for looters. He had caught two young men less than six months ago breaking into the bank's godown out back, trying to make off with three bolts of top quality cloth. His office window faced the godown door and he'd put a bullet through each of those black hides, though one nicked the white cloth too, and unfortunately dyed it with blood. George was an ardent sportsman. He took pride in his marksmanship. He had won the gold cup last year at the Club's annual Target Tournament for Civilians.

George kept his revolver in a holster close to his heart, and ordinarily it sufficed to set his mind at ease. Only to-day's noise sounded rather fiercer than the usual native ruckus. He picked up his phone and jiggled the earpiece holder. Nothing happened. No buzz or static. He cranked the handle. The line was dead.

"Munshi!" he shouted, rising to his formidable height as the bearer rushed into his office. "What in hell's going on out there? This phone's dead! What's all that damn noise about?"

"Yes, sahib, it is that Kitchlew and Satyapal were taken —"

"What the hell has that got to do with my phone? And stop picking your bloody nose when I talk to you! Where the hell's Ravi? *Ravi!*" His long-legged stride brought him to the door of his assistant's office just as it was opened by the young Indian graduate of Bombay University, whose father owned most of the Alliance Bank's stock, and who was, George suspected, sent here to try to learn enough to replace him.

"Did you call to me, Mr. Thomson?" Ravi asked. He wore rimless glasses, and looked and sounded more like a woman than a man to George Thomson.

77

"The damn phone's dead! What the devil are your people making all that damn racket about now? Someone's going to pay for this party!"

"I have been sitting at my desk, sir, as you know since before you yourself arrived this morning —" Ravi began, his voice trembling. He sounded like a pleader preparing his defense. All Indians had begun to sound exactly the same to George — sickeningly stupid. Why was it none of them ever answered his questions directly? They were all as long-winded as cathedral organs. If it weren't for the big game available hereabouts he would have packed in this job ten years ago. The more Ravi rambled on, in fact, with that sick roar of Babel in the background growing louder, the more convinced George became that he'd had India to his nostrils. There was fox to be followed back Home, and grouse up in Scotland, and always a pig or two to be stuck somewhere closer to civilized human company!

"Balls!" he shouted at Ravi's fat face, turning to take his topi from the hat rack, ordering Munshi to bring his carriage round. He was going home early today.

Halfway down the stairs, George saw them rush in. He had never really known terror before. But now he bolted back, taking the stairs four at one stride, whirling round the landing and heading up the narrower flight to the attic roof. From it he could reach the godown, and on from there to the backyard and the gate to an alley no one ever used. He could almost see himself free and clear — but the attic door was locked.

He had the key in his pocket. It was on a ring of more than twenty keys and George used it so rarely that he did not know instinctively which one fit the attic door. There was really no time to test the lot. He turned to face a mob of young bucks with lathis poised over their heads headed up the stairs two at a time.

His revolver held four bullets. He emptied it into the eyes of Abdul and Ram. Their polished skulls cracked like eggs, and the black turned to scarlet as they fell back, momentarily halting the herd, till those behind used the dead bodies as shields and advanced with both corpses in the vanguard, up the stairs.

George clutched the trigger convulsively. He released and pulled it again. Nothing happened. The scarlet masks of death inched closer. He hurled the useless pistol at them. It fell ineffectually, covered with blood. He kicked out in utter desperation, but as the advancing wall dropped back he felt himself going down with it. Fingers clutched his feet, his ankles. He felt them tearing at his flesh, a burning stinging searing pain in his loins, his belly, his back. He waited for it to end, but instead the pain intensified as a hundred claws dug into his body like the talons of starving condors tearing open his flesh for the feast. He tried to scream, but then a lathi tip was stuffed into his open mouth, and George Thomson felt no more . . .

Mrs. Easdon had just finished her rounds and stretched out on the divan for a few minutes of rest when Rakhi, her servant girl, rushed into the office, shouting.

"Oh, Doctor — there are *many* wounded!"

"Wounded?" She jumped up and started after the girl, expecting to find several patients in the waiting room, but it was empty. Her native nurse had not returned. "Where are the wounded, Rakhi?"

"Outside," she said. "They are all men!"

"But if they're men, who on earth would bring them here? Everyone knows this is a woman's hospital. Where did you see wounded men, Rakhi?" Mrs. Easdon was harsh. The girl was a notorious liar. She was hopelessly inefficient as well, and Mrs. Easdon would have discharged her months ago, had she not learned from bitter experience that Rakhi was no worse than the average Amritsar working girl.

"You d-don't believe me," she cried, covering her face with both hands, sobbing hysterically.

"Stop it." Mrs. Easdon slapped the idiot girl sharply to bring her to some semblance of coherence. "That's monstrous self-indulgence, Rakhi, and I won't stand for it! Now take me to where you saw those wounded men, and do so quickly!"

To Mrs. Easdon's surprise, Rakhi started running upstairs. She was still moaning, but had regained sufficient control to know where she was going. The second floor ward had a sun patio with a steel ladder leading to the flat roof of the large building. Rakhi spent much of her "working" time, Mrs. Easdon suspected, dreamily wandering about on the roof, flirting with boys in the street below.

The heat-choked air throbbed with the beat of rowdy voices, and climbing the ladder, Mrs. Easdon saw black smoke rising from the bustling center of Hall Bazaar. Every dog in Amritsar seemed to be barking at once. She wondered if any of her patients would be able to sleep.

"There! See!" shouted Rakhi, pointing at the street to the north of the hospital wall, where several dark bodies were laid out in front of Dr. Kidar Nath's house. The bodies were surrounded by a crowd of young men, some of whom were bent over them attentively. They all looked like ruffians. Dr. Kidar Nath himself was apparently inside, since the door to his house remained open, and people kept running in and out of it. She'd never trusted Kidar Nath, and suspected now that he was in league with the anarchists.

"That is Dr. Easdon!" someone shouted from the street, pointing up at her. Other heads turned to stare, among them the pallid face of Hansraj, who had brought the bodies here in his tonga.

"What are you watching?" Hansraj shouted angrily. "Why don't you come down, and help care for these people if you are a doctor? Your countrymen shot them!"

"Then I'm certain they deserved it," she snapped, shaking her head in disgust at the arrogance of these young rowdies, who had become a serious problem in Amritsar since the War. Five years ago no native male would have had the gall to speak to an Englishwoman unless he was spoken to, not to dream of berating her. So many English troops and officials had been away throughout the War that people forgot their manners. High time they relearned a few!

"What did she say?" someone asked Hansraj.

"She says they deserve to be shot! She wants to see us all shot!"

"She *what?*"

"She wants to kill us because we are Indians!"

"Then let us kill her!"

"Yes, *she* deserves it," shouted Hansraj, starting to climb over the wall of the compound. He was accompanied by four of his youthful comrades, all of whom shouted ugly curses as they climbed, using the most vile of sexual epithets in describing her.

"Don't you *dare* come into this hospital," Mrs. Easdon yelled. "This is strictly a woman's hospital — you stay out of here! You better — oh, my God," she added faintly, seeing them rush across the yard, hearing their vulgar voices entering the building, which for eighteen years she had kept as a shelter for sick females, ladies of every color and faith, nine of whom were now in their beds. She screamed for help as loud as she could scream, but on the street below saw only vile faces leering at her, tongues sticking out, lascivious laughter taunting her

81

cries, and all the while she could hear them running upstairs, polluting her hospital ward with their presence, like invaders of a nunnery, rushing bare-legged through the rooms in which sick ladies lay terrified. Mrs. Easdon kept a pistol in her desk drawer, but it was too late for her to attempt to reach that. Desperately, she looked around, running to the other side of the roof, where a gap of less than one yard separated her hospital from the home of Mr. Benjamin, a Bene Israel merchant, whose wife had delivered her four children in Mrs. Easdon's maternity room. Mrs. Benjamin heard her screams, and opened the skylight door, looking terrified as she called across:

"What is it, Doctor? What has happened to you?" She was a slight dark woman. Her raven black hair was tied in a bun garlanded with gardenias. Her elegantly embroidered sari gave her much the appearance of the average upper-class Hindu matron, except for the pendant Star of David she wore on her necklace.

"Help me," Dr. Easdon cried, hearing Hansraj's voice from the patio below, shouting, *"Out here!"*

"Of course," Mrs. Benjamin said, rushing to give her neighbor a hand as she jumped the parapet. Hand in hand they raced back to the skylight, hurried down the stairs, and closed the hatch just as Hansraj's red hair peered over the top of the other roof.

"Follow me," Mrs. Benjamin whispered, asking no questions, as she led her deftly through the labyrinth of her enormous home.

"Where did she go?" Hansraj asked Rakhi.

She shrank back coyly, and lowered her eyes, starting to giggle at the thought of Dr. Easdon's life suddenly placed within her power, hurled by the gods into her own mouth. She looked at the young men who circled her now.

"That way," she said, pointing to Mrs. Benjamin's skylight. "Mrs. Benjamin has taken her inside — to hide her!"

"Good girl," Hansraj said, touching her cheek, which felt like fire. But then he ran away, to Dr. Easdon. Rakhi felt betrayed — by her own betrayal.

Hansraj jumped the roof. One of his four followers had brought a piece of brick, which he used to shatter the skylight. They released the latch and opened it, climbing down inside, shouting, *"Where is she?"*

"How dare you break into my house?" Mrs. Benjamin demanded, her four boys standing before her, like guardians, frail though each of them was.

"We will do you no harm, Madam," Hansraj assured her. "We have come for that White witch of an English whore, who dares speak of herself as a doctor! Where is she? We know she has come this way!"

Mrs. Benjamin controlled her rage. What did words matter, after all? God in His infinite wisdom would punish the wicked, and for the righteous eternal salvation would be more than sufficient reward. She knew that her dark color would save her today from these monstrous boys, and if only she held her tongue perhaps Dr. Easdon might also be saved. "Yes, she came this way — but she has gone."

"Gone? Gone where? Gopal, run outside, and see if you can find her — Brij, you search the first floor, the rest of us will start up here. Jewess, I warn you — if you are lying to me, if that bitch whore is hidden in this house, you die with her! Do you understand? Are you lying to me?"

"Why should I lie to save the English?" she asked, praying divine forgiveness as she spoke. "What have they ever done for me, except to remind me that I am too dark to join their ladies clubs, and my children are too dark to go to their schools, and my husband is too dark for us to be permitted to live in the Civil Lines! Why would you think I lie to you to save an Englishwoman? She has run away, but search the house if you don't believe me."

"Why did you let her escape then?"

"How should I know you were after her? I was resting, and she knocked upon the skylight door. No sooner did I open it, then she ran down and hurried outside. We hardly exchanged a word!"

"Oh," he said, clearly shaken by the logic of her argument, and the calm assurance with which she spoke. "I see — but we must search the house —"

"You may do so, if you like, but you will only waste time, while she escapes outside."

"Yes, yes — hurry," he shouted to the others, and rushed off to open the door to the next room, looking into closets, bending to stare under the beds.

"Mama," her youngest child began.

"Hush," she cautioned. "Not a word!" She embraced him gently, rocking him in her arms, feeling her heart race as she listened to them slamming doors and pushing furniture aside, praying to God that they would not open the cupboard in the pantry. . . .

Mary Easdon heard them moving closer to the upright coffin in which she hid. She heard their footsteps, their muffled voices, and the sharp report of doors closing, like rifles firing all around her. Unable to catch her breath, crouched in that dark cramped space, she felt the final humiliation, the utter futility and failure of all she had attempted to achieve in almost half a century of life. As a girl she had met Florence Nightingale and listened enraptured as she told of the wonderful work of healing that needed doing in India. Mary's father was a doctor, and he encouraged his only child in her altruistic ambition. The day she graduated from medical school, she married her classmate, Dr. Easdon, and together they sailed for India, two decades ago. In less than two years he died of bubonic plague. She almost gave up then. She almost went home. Now she wished she had gone. She heard those wretched voices cursing in the next room. They were knocking over brass pots, breaking dishes in their senseless wrath, their malicious fury. She was tempted to push open the doors that hid her, to step forth and tell them a piece of her mind — she all but strangled, swallowing the words of reprimand that welled up inside.

She felt her tears running cold down her tired cheeks. Thrown away! Everything. Everything she had been and done and stood for and dreamed about achieving and prayed. To no avail. All to no avail. Even the sanctity of her tiny hospital island had been ravaged now and she could never sleep there another night knowing it might again be invaded that way. She felt as though her life's work had been raped by those savages. She had given her all to help them and this was her reward.

"She's not in the house, Hansraj," someone reported.

"No, I see she's escaped, damn whore! Let's go after her outside —"

They were running away. She heard their footsteps receding, just as they had come within a yard — She shook her head in disbelief, even after the front door slammed. She remained hidden, trembling, crying silently, feeling as though a bayonet had torn out her insides, feeling utterly abandoned, cold, alone, without hope, without purpose. The future was dead to her.

"Thank God, you're safe," Mrs. Benjamin cried, flinging open the cupboard door.

Hansraj raced along the narrow alley, sensing he was on her trail, determined not to stop running till he found her. He would make her pay for what she said, for that smug contempt with which she spoke of Indian life, the way they all did. The way Irving kept him waiting for Kitchlew, the way those soldiers murdered Hari, the way they raped his mother — he had watched once through a crack in the door when an Englishman came to her bedroom during the light of midday, the sickly pale pallor of his leg laying so harshly over her small brown body. He had heard her gasp, as though dying under the weight and pain inflicted by that brute. He had been ready then to force open the door, but just as he started to push his meager weight against it, the servant came to drag him away, beating him.

His head throbbed as he ran. He dared not hesitate even for a moment. His comrades were behind him. He could hear them at his heels. They were all slaves of the Mother-Goddess who was India, prostrate and powerless, chained by the foreign plunderers, the white killers from afar, who seduced Her with sweet words and promises, then lulled Her to sleep, and bound Her limbs and lashed Her body till it bled.

Sweat clouded his vision and every street began to appear the same, till he feared perhaps he was running in circles. Then he saw her — trying to escape on a bicycle.

"There she is!" Hansraj shouted. "Get her!"

Miss Marcella Sherwood looked around when she heard that cry, and desperately started to pedal faster. Her missionary habit was not exactly the easiest costume to cycle in, yet she had become quite skilled at cycling during her years in Amritsar, since it was the simplest way to make her rounds among her far-flung female converts to the Church of England. Most of them were widowed women, whose lot as Hindus would have been lower than pariahs. A few were too old and sick to leave their homes, and Marcella often did errands for them. She was in fact bringing some medicated ointment to one of her oldest ladies, though Sister Grace had warned her not to leave the Mission today. ·

Marcella's heart fluttered as she peddled more swiftly. She prayed no child would race across her path, for she was moving at a reckless pace, yet glancing over one shoulder, saw the maniacal face of a young man loom closer. She felt sick with fear.

"Dear God!" she cried, and that seemed to give her legs fresh force. She lurched ahead, swerving into the Kucha Kaurianwalla, a narrow lane where several converts lived. She kept praying that someone would appear to scare off these wild boys, who seemed to have mistaken her for someone else. But this usually crowded lane was deserted, as though a scourge had come to blight its population. As if someone forewarned these people to close their shutters with their eyes, to hide from the shame of what would transpire here. Shadows darkened the ugly lane. The lower edge of her gray garment caught in the pedal chain. Screaming, she lost her balance. Then she felt rough hands grab her arms, ripping cloth from her body . . .

Hansraj tore at her. He had never touched an Englishwoman before. He was warned as a child that memsahibs were mightier than their consorts, that though but a handful of Englishmen managed by their miraculous power to conquer all of India, they had done so for a woman — their Queen, who was mightiest of them all. One Englishwoman, it was said, could take in a hundred White men in one day, and reduce them all to impotence. There were special fluids inside White women, he had heard, which burned an Indian's penis off if ever it touched them, and some people said leprosy was the punishment inflicted upon any black body, in India or Africa, which tried to touch a White woman's private parts. He no longer believed any of that, nor did he crave to enter White flesh,

87

as he once used to — when he worked at the station, taking tickets. That was when the War left so many service vacancies that rules were eased. He hated his job, except for the opportunity it afforded him of seeing memsahibs step down from their carriages and cross the platform to step up onto the trains. He would see their ankles then, the lower part of their trim pale legs, and the ruffled crinoline of their underskirts. Each time he saw that he felt himself harden, and sweat oozed from every pore of his skin. He would have to bite hard on the inner flesh of his cheeks to keep from running closer and ramming his arm up the open bottom of dress and woman alike, from lurching himself full against her legs and wrapping them like a garland of flowers round his neck, imbibing their fragrance, drinking it in —

He kept pounding his fist into her belly, cursing as he beat her, meting out the punishment she deserved, bitch whore that she was for wanting every Indian shot down in the full bloom of his manhood, butchered, emasculated, left like a spermless eunuch to simper around the harem of harlots into which this country was converted by British rule — making every Indian woman a helpless slave to their lust, taking his poor mother night and day, beating her tiny body, flattening her breasts till they hung limp, lifeless —

"But Hansraj, this isn't the Doctor," one of his comrades shouted.

It jolted him, made him stop. He stared more carefully at her, and realized then that the face was different than that which had laughed down at them from the hospital roof. This was a younger face, and under the hat that had been torn off, the hair was full and richly golden, not gray. The eyes were closed, the mouth open; the skin splotched purple, bruised and scraped. Blood trickled slowly from both nostrils.

"She's a missionary, Hansraj — look at the cross," his friend whispered, handing him her crucifix, which had been ripped from her waist. "Have we killed her?" His voice trembled.

"What?" Hansraj muttered, staring, getting off her hip, which he'd straddled as though riding a horse, leaving the stain of his body's hot fluid on the wrinkled cloth that covered her. He felt strangely weak, his legs were light, his head dizzy. The sun emerged again from behind the cloud, and its glare momentarily blinded him.

"We better get away from here," his friends said, tugging at his arm. "Before they see us!"

One of the doors along the lane opened, and a dark head peered out, but quickly receded, hiding again behind the sturdy plank of chained wood.

"Hurry! Come on!" they were shouting, running as they called back. "Why are you standing there, Hansraj?"

Only then did it dawn upon him, what he had done, how he had spent himself upon her prostrate body, and the obscenity, the abysmal horror of his crime, so filled him with shame and terror that he was paralyzed, robbed now of his manhood, wet and trembling he stood there, wondering what retribution the gods overlooking this wretched world would fashion for him? He was too terrified to look back to see if she was indeed dead, as he ran frantically after his fast fleeing friends.

Marcella stared at the surface of the cobblestone, pitted, deeply scarred, covered with scum, the slime of an Indian gutter, its stone eroded by the urine of centuries. Her body was numb. She dared not look at herself. She felt nothing, not even the pain, which had mercifully robbed her of consciousness soon after she was dragged to the gutter. She heard what sounded like a distant moan, a thin cry of anguish, and did not at once connect it with herself. Soon she saw a door open, and watched two elderly people hobbling toward her, wringing their wrinkled hands as they came, glancing about apprehensively. The woman squatted beside her, asking if she could walk by herself, only to the door, to come inside?

Marcella tried to stand up, but her legs refused to move. The best she could do was crawl slowly, like a wounded creature inching itself toward a cave. She began to whisper the Lord's Prayer, but could not quite bring herself to say, "as we forgive those who trespass against us." Not yet. She crawled inside the house, and fainted again.

Outside, Amritsar was burning.

7

COLONEL SMITH ordered his driver to leave the motor running, as he jumped out of the ambulance and raced up the steps of Saint Catherine's Mission Hospital. One of the Indian Sisters was seated at the receiving desk and rose respectfully to greet him.

"Where's your mother superior? I've got to see her immediately!"

"Please sit down, Doctor. I will try to find her—"

"I've no time to sit! Where is she? *Mother superior!*" He shouted through cupped hands. His voice reverberated down the long stone corridor, bouncing from one Gothic arch to the next. That did the trick, all right. Not only the mother superior, but her two English assistants as well, came fluttering towards him, fingering their beads as they rushed along.

"Oh, it's *you*, Dr. Smith," Sister Catherine said, sounding relieved as she came close enough to recognize him. Her eyes had grown quite dim of late, and though he'd told her last year that she needed both cataracts removed, she kept postponing the operation. "My goodness, you frightened us by shouting so."

"Sorry, Sister, but there's no time to waste. My ambulance is waiting outside. I've come to evacuate the three of you."

"You have?" She shook her head uncomprehendingly. "But why on earth would you want to do that?"

"*Why*? Haven't you heard the bloody mob? They're burning and killing everything White they can damn well find!"

"Oh, dear," she whispered, crossing herself, but he wasn't sure if it was for what he'd said or the way he'd said it.

"Come along now," he insisted. "I've half a dozen more stops to make!"

"You go on, Colonel. We'll be safe here. Don't worry —"

"Catherine, I am not *asking* you to come," he shouted, "I'm ordering you to evacuate this hospital! This is not friendly medical advice for you to ignore in your own inimitable *stubborn* —"

"Oh, I see." She crossed herself once more. "You mean you've been ordered to take *all* of us to the Civil Lines?"

"Yes, the three of you," he said, relieved at having finally gotten through to this most exasperating, frustratingly stubborn human being. She reminded him of his own sister, who despite her constitutional frailty and his advice against early marriage, allowed her husband to bully her into breeding five sons for him, dying as the last of them was born. Henry never forgave himself for not having been more firm in protecting his sister. Nor did he personally ever fall victim to marriage.

"Three?" the mother superior repeated in surprise. "But there are thirty-four of us here, Colonel."

"What in God's name are you talking about?" he asked, hastily removing the list from his inner jacket pocket. Every White name in Amritsar was on that list, with the most recent address of each adjacent to the name. One of

Irving's secretaries did practically nothing but check the accuracy of this list. Sure enough, precisely as he'd remembered it, there were three names noted at the Mission Hospital. Smiling triumphantly, he held out the list to her.

"Henry, you know perfectly well I can't see such fine print," she reminded him. "You tell me what it says, why don't you?" She had the gentlest voice, but there was just a trace of mischief about the way she spoke, an almost impish quality of teasing. She'd confessed to him once that as a girl she dreamed of becoming an actress — if she wasn't quite good enough to be a nun.

"It lists only three of you, Catherine. Now let's get on with it, Sisters!"

"Oh, *that* sort of list," she whispered, starting to count her beads again. "I must say, I wasn't thinking of that, Colonel. We're thirty-four *Christian* Sisters in the order now, you see, and I just never think of any smaller number."

"But good God," he began, glancing at the dark native Sister, who remained close enough to hear their every word, "the whole damned ambulance won't hold thirty-four!"

"Of course," she replied, no longer looking at him, facing the small brown beads as she ticked them off. "We understand, Colonel, and there's no need to be upset or anxious about us. We're perfectly safe here."

"You are *not* safe! Not the three of you with White skins at least! The others —"

"The *others*, Colonel Smith," she interrupted, looking at him with suddenly watering eyes, her voice sounding very close to its breaking point, "as you so politely put it — the others are all Christian Sisters, and there is no difference, no spiritual difference whatsoever, Doctor, between any one of them and myself."

He stared at her dumbstruck, shaking his head at the

futility of trying to talk sensibly with this woman. On the matter of racial difference, at any rate, she was totally blind.

"Are you trying to tell us, Sister Catherine," he whispered, putting his face to within six inches of hers, "that white is black, and black is white?"

"Oh, dear Colonel Smith, I am afraid you're upset with me. Do forgive me for troubling you so. I am sorry, believe me, to be such a nuisance, and here you're thinking only of my safety, but I simply couldn't abide myself, don't you see, if I'd abandoned my Sisters — any one of them. They're all so precious to me —" She had to stop. She closed her eyes and crossed herself.

"All right." He felt as though he'd been straining his every nerve at the operating table for hours, finding himself trembling with frustrated emotion. "I'll take all of you — every last blessed one! But hurry, before it's too late for any of us to get back across to Civil Lines!"

"Oh, Henry, you *are* splendid," she said, clapping her hands, telling the other Sisters to ring the bells. "Fortunately, we haven't any inpatients to worry about, so there *will* be only the thirty-four of us!"

"Thank God for that," he said.

Smoke billowed black from several sections of the city by the time they were ready to leave Mission Hospital. The noise of the mob had fragmented, and savage cries could be heard from every direction, which convinced Henry that he could not hope to complete his rounds and return safely with his cargo. Even if there were room in the overcrowded ambulance for more passengers, which there really wasn't. The Indian Sisters were so small-boned and compressible that they managed to squeeze in, stacked on each other's laps in what Colonel Smith hardly considered proper posture for the transport of ladies! Still and all he could not turn back without stopping at the

Mission Girls School, which was hardly more than half a mile from the hospital.

The fires intensified the heat of midafternoon, and as they started chugging lamely along the road, the air itself seemed a barrier to their progress. Laden with kerosene fumes and the soot of carnage, it felt thick enough to clutch. A raucous gang of hoodlums raced across the road barely ten yards ahead carrying their loot of cloth bolts and brassware, laughing like lunatics, intoxicated to find themselves holding the keys to their own ward. He was sorry he had not been able to talk Sister Catherine into sitting beside him in the cab, so that she might see for herself how they behaved — the sort of criminal bestiality that was natural to natives, as soon as they felt the restraining hand of authority go lax.

Only once in his life had Henry doubted the universality of that rule. For a while he'd been deceived by Satyapal into thinking perhaps that his view of natives was unduly simplistic. When the young doctor first came to work as his assistant at Jubilee Hospital, Henry was so impressed by his competence and apparent humility that he began to question many axioms of his understanding of India — for if even one of them was different, if one of them could prove himself worthy of total trust and confidence, could indeed behave, think, act, and react the way a white Englishman did, it would have profoundly shaken Colonel Smith's convictions concerning the native mind and heart. After six months he'd actually stopped thinking of Satyapal as a native. He'd become curiously fond of the young man, and began to look forward to their afternoon teas together, which they took on the shaded porch of his private bungalow — unless a medical emergency called them back to the operating room. It was one of those daily rituals, which provided continuity without boredom, and did so much to help make the passage of time more than simply bearable.

Henry had begun feeling his age when Satyapal came to him, and he'd started brooding about things, mostly about the falling away of old friends, the progressive isolation, which seemed an irreversible part of life. His oldest, dearest friend had died of a liver ailment less than a year earlier. Satyapal always had some new story to relate, something amusing, or clever, which happened to him or one of his many friends — he peopled Henry's world with new names, and often they laughed together. He started planning their teas the night before, thinking of special sweets to offer his friend — he'd planned a virtual feast one day, when Satyapal told him, just as they were washing to leave hospital, that he couldn't come for tea. The next day Henry read the C.I.D. report, which informed him that his assistant, Dr. Satyapal, was one of the most inflammatory speakers at a secret meeting of the Arya Samaj. The meeting had been held during teatime.

The ambulance stopped at the front gate of the Girls School. A native guard salaamed and hurried to push the gate open. One form was playing croquet under the large banyan tree, and the Sister in attendance started toward the path as she noticed them riding up.

"We're evacuating all English to Civil Lines," he announced. "How many of you are here? Call them please and tell them to hurry — we're going to have to dash for it!"

He did not leave the ambulance. He would have invited Sister Catherine to stretch her legs while they stopped, but feared that opening the rear door would only unleash a flood of black Christians, whose conversions were purely opportunistic, he believed, as was everything they did to ingratiate, insinuate themselves — till the day when they turned to devour their benefactors.

"Reptiles," he muttered, watching the little dark girls in their white school dresses playing at trying to become

English. It would never work — not in a thousand years.

"Colonel-sahib?" his Sikh driver asked, thinking he'd issued an order.

"Uh — yes, blow the damn horn, Singh! We can't wait all day for them!"

While the horn was blowing, four pale passengers rushed from the school door. Henry hustled them into the crowded rear of the ambulance.

"Back to Civil Lines," he ordered, jumping into the cab beside his driver. "Stop for nothing, Singh — And don't spare the petrol!"

By 2 P.M., when Amritsar usually slept, the frenzied pace of looting and burning reached its peak. The Town Hall itself, that ornate Edwardian mansion, whose lawn ended where the central police station began, was set to the torch, finally forcing the cowering native police to abandon their Kotwali stronghold, to picket the fire lines as water was pumped manually onto the conflagration. Still the dervish of death danced on, and as the ambulance raced back toward Mahna Singh Gate, the only access road to Civil Lines that remained open, brickbats and stones were thrown by unseen snipers at its hurtling hulk. Every road was strewn with rubble, and Henry feared that the tires would puncture, leaving them all trapped in the camp of the Enemy. He vowed then that if he lived through all this he would exercise his option to retire and return Home to Bath. . . .

Miles galloped to the station, and handed his horse to a guard as he jumped down, running into the master's office. There was the acrid smell of coal fumes in that airless room. Soot seeped through the cracks in door and window frames to cover every surface with gray powder, as though the dust of time had already begun to settle on this monumental artifact of industrial civilization.

"Where's the stationmaster?" he asked a young guard, who sat forlornly puffing a soiled cigarette.

"Sir?" the youth exclaimed, dropping his smoke as he jumped up. "Ee's took a bit'a clobberin', ee'as, sir!"

Miles followed the guard to the master's bedroom, where the big man was lying with his arm in a sling, his head swathed in bandages. He'd gone out to the goods warehouse, he explained, when he heard the mob attacking it, and found young Robinson, one of his station guards, being bludgeoned to death there by a gang of toughs, wielding lathis. He'd tried to chase them off.

"I booted some'a them niggers in the butt, Commissioner," he said, stirred by the stimulus of that memory to rise halfway out of his bed, his face flaming.

"Try to keep calm, Mr. Bennett," Miles suggested. "As soon as Colonel Smith returns with the ambulance, I'll send him to see you. You'd best lie quietly. I shouldn't be troubling you at all, but I need a light engine to take one of my men up the line toward Lahore. I'm afraid the wires are cut, you see."

"Take Commissioner Irving to track five, Jimmy! There's a fine engine that's just had her tender filled there, sir. Will you be callin' in the troops?"

"Right," Miles said, for there was really nothing else to be done now but activate Step Three of the Plan. Massey's force held the bridges for the moment, yet the mob had control of the city, and there was no way of knowing when they would mass again to storm Civil Lines. Both telegraph and telephone were dead. Miles felt precariously isolated. His only lifeline was the railway, yet for all he knew right now the tracks might be broken half a mile up the line — in which case the countryside was in revolt, and this Amritsar blaze would be just one episode of a much bigger rebellion! In which case — he preferred not to think about that.

"The message is to General Officer Commanding the Sixteenth Division," Miles told the subaltern he chose to send. "Activate Step Three Amritsar Plan — my last name alone will suffice for the signature. Now remember, wire it as soon as possible. The lines may just be down in this immediate area, so there may be no need for you to ride all the way to Lahore. Understand?"

"Yes, sir," the red-cheeked youth replied, saluting, and turning to step onto the light engine's cab.

"Repeat the message please," Miles ordered.

"To G.O.C. Sixteenth Division Activate Step Three Amritsar Plan Stop Irving." He said it without faltering. That helped restore Miles's faith in the permanence of Empire.

Though watching the light engine chug its lonely way up the track, Miles knew just how tenuously that thread could be drawn, which at times like this preserved all of them from being submerged under India's darkly swirling sea.

8

MAQBOOL helped carry the wounded from the footbridge area to the house of Dr. Bashir. Immediately after the shooting he'd asked Mr. Irving for an ambulance, but the D.C. curtly informed him that no ambulance was available. He and Salaria then requested permission to cross over to the nearby Jubilee Hospital to call for quick medical assistance. That too was denied. It came as a ruder jolt to Maqbool's faith in authority, this denial of medical aid, than the firing itself. Though the soldiers had fired too soon! If they could only have waited five minutes longer, he might have convinced the crowd to fall back of its own volition. But Indian life was valued more cheaply than the price of patience to British nerves, so, of course, they fired as a first resort, rather than in the last extreme. Even so, he could have forgiven that, for he was a man of the law, he lived by the code of civil order. But how could anyone justify denial of medical aid to the wounded? Even in War — on the battle-field — an ambulance was permitted safe passage across terrain on which no man was permitted to step. Was not the red cross honored as a universal symbol of mercy? Or did that apply only to European Christians?

Dr. Bashir emerged from his operating room, silently shook his white-haired head, and sank wearily onto the chair facing Maqbool.

"Too late," he said. "They had lost too much blood." He was well into his seventies, and had retired some years ago from active practice, but maintained his office for old friends and relatives, who refused to liberate him from their ailments. He was one of that select coterie of Indians who could afford to live within sight of the Civil Lines.

"If they had given us an ambulance one hour ago," Maqbool began.

"Yes, yes," Bashir interjected impatiently. "Then those boys would be alive right now! And if two hours ago they stayed home instead of coming here to demonstrate, then they would never have received bullet wounds in the first instance."

"That is true, of course," Maqbool conceded respectfully, but saying it he rose to leave before he had to say something less equable to this old gentleman, whose conversative views were almost as renowned as his medical skill.

"When will you people learn that those who play with fire get burned?"

"Dr. Bashir, you must try to understand — "

"No, young man, it is *you* who must try to understand! I knew your father, Maqbool, and I will tell you something he said to me once — he said, 'I thank God for the British rule in this land of ours, Bashir!' That is what he said, in those very words! And do you know why he said it? He was a wise man, your father. He understood this land and its people better than any of us. He knew how hot-tempered we are, how impulsive, how easily we allow our blood to boil over — "

"While the English stay cool," Maqbool said.

"Exactly!"

"And that is why they opened fire without giving Salaria and myself two minutes to try to move the crowd back across the footbridge!" He felt his temper rising.

"The crowd had no business trying to storm into Civil Lines!"

"People were upset over Kitchlew's arrest —"

"Of course! Just what I mean to say about our people! They have a grievance for which they crave redress — but instead of petitioning calmly, or initiating some form of legal action, they run into the streets and shout slogans!" He shook his head. "It is all that man Gandhi's fault, stirring up impossible hopes, making people crazy with his talk of self-rule for an Indian Nation! When have we ever been a Nation? Where is the unity of nationhood? Do we have it in race, in religion, in language? The man is infatuated with a vision that bears no resemblance to reality. And what does he advocate, tell me? First of all, he tells people to break the law by signing his lunatic pledge —"

"But the Rowlatt Acts are evil law."

"Oh, yes, I have heard all about that, Maqbool! But show me a law which has never been called evil by some segment of society — even if it is only the one man who breaks it."

"No, with all due respect to you, Dr. Bashir, I feel it is justified to appeal to our people to sign a pledge of nonviolent civil disobedience —"

"Do you call that nonviolent, what is happening out there? Listen to those lunatics! That is all I have heard today — that mad screaming and wild shouting! It is what comes of all this nonsensical talk about freedom! Our trouble is too much of freedom, not too little! That is what closing the shops has done — it gives everyone free time. And what is more burdensome, tell me? It is the curse of your modern society — freedom for women, freedom for children, freedom for the workers, and soon there will be those who demand freedom for draft animals as well! That is why those two boys are dead now, Maqbool, because they had no work to occupy their time!"

"I admit it is awful, how our people are running so insanely. It is just what Kitchlew always warned us that we must not do," nodded Maqbool, tugging at his moustache. "But the English are at least as much to blame —"

"Not another word of such seditious nonsense," the elderly doctor insisted, rising angrily. "I have heard more than my fill of it, sir! Government is there to maintain order, and if the English shoot it is because no recourse is left to them to restore sanity among your lunatic friends. How are respectable people supposed to walk the streets today, tell me? What will control those mad men other than British bullets? You claim we are ready for nationhood? Well, where is your national militia?" A gang of youngsters rushed by outside shouting, *"Burn the Town Hall!"* "There is your Nation, Maqbool, burning down my city. Who will stop them? Will you?"

It was so disarmingly direct a challenge that Maqbool had no answer, but was shocked to speechless reflection. On any other day he would have named Kitchlew. Or Satyapal. Now who was there left to take a lead? Men like Bashir were too old to patrol the streets.

Just then Salaria returned with more wounded bodies, and they dragged them inside. Several of the younger pleaders had come along to help, and after Bashir chased them out of his operating room they all stood staring at one another, and no one seemed to know where to go next or what to do.

"We must stop this mad rioting before it is too late to bring back some sanity to our city," said Maqbool. He was surprised at how strong his voice sounded. "Salaria, you take two of these men as your helpers and go by Aitchison Park, and I will take the others with me down Hall Bazaar!" He opened the door.

"But what should we say to people?" Salaria asked, hesitating.

"Say that fire and murder will not bring us Freedom. Violence only weakens us. We are destroying ourselves by forgetting the teachings of our leaders. Wherever the English may transport Kitchlew and Satyapal they cannot remove them from our minds and hearts, if only we take the trouble to remember what they have taught us all these days! Tell everyone you see to go home and wait calmly for further instructions. Later, we will meet at my house, Salaria, and then we will plan what must be done to keep Amritsar quiet. We have no right to demand our freedom if we cannot discipline ourselves. Now let us go! There is much to be done!"

Whether it was his own sense of conviction, or the heat of that hour, or simply that the Madness had by now passed its peak — Maqbool found his self-appointed task easier than he'd anticipated. People seemed eager to be told what to do, anxious to go home by now, sick of the sight of blood and the smell of burning.

"We must restore order," he told them, and though they appeared dazed at first, after a moment they would nod and agree that it was madness, all this rushing about, doing damage to property. "Our great leaders all advocate non-violence. We only dishonor them by such destructive behavior," he explained, and soon many men gathered round to listen, and most agreed. Though in every group some young person shouted, "He is a lackey of the English! Don't listen to the traitor!" others would respond for him with cries of "Shame, shame" or louder shouts of "Be quiet, idiot!" Then they began to fight among themselves, and he said, "What is the point of it, to fight one another this way? Are we not brothers, each one of us? Is this not what our beloved Kitchlew and Satyapal have tried to teach us? Let us go home now and pray for them — my dears," he added, and quietly people went their separate ways, like children chastened by the words of a respected adult, like mourners reminded of their bereavement.

Soon he found other responsible citizens, who had independently started doing much what he and Salaria did. Todar Mal, one of the wealthier merchants in Amritsar, was riding his horse along Hall Bazaar shouting, "We must clear the streets! There will be a meeting at five in Jallian-wala Bagh!"

"Who has called the meeting, Todarji?" Maqbool asked, saluting the handsomely attired man, who sat so straight and tall on his dappled mare.

"Lala Dholan Das, and Duni Chand, and myself, Maq-bool, but do join us! We must try to calm people down!"

"Yes, of course, I will come. Jallianwala Bagh, did you say at five o'clock?"

"That is correct — in two hours. Pass the word." He turned then to speak to someone on his other side.

Maqbool managed to find a tonga, and with his young friends of the bar, went up and down every side street, announcing the meeting. It made more sense, he felt on reflection, to hold a public meeting at once, rather than to advise people to go home. Too much had happened for anyone to sit calmly in his own house tonight, and though Maqbool's sitting room would hold fifty friends, Jalle's Garden was spacious enough to accommodate fifty thou-sand. The Bagh was not really a "garden," though back in the days when Jalle lived (no one actually knew when that was, other than long ago) perhaps it had served as such. As far back as Maqbool could remember, Jallianwala Bagh had been the site of public gatherings, particularly reli-gious festivals and fairs, and recently, of political meetings as well. The first mass meeting at which Kitchlew and Satyapal spoke out against the Black Acts had been held in Jallianwala Bagh. It was in the heart of the old city, not far from the Golden Temple, a rectangle of several acres of undeveloped land bordered by brick walls of the cramped neighboring bazaars, the lungs of Amritsar, an open breathing space for children to play in.

Swiftly the word was passed. By five o'clock many thousands had assembled in the Bagh. The dead were brought there on charpoys and wooden planks, decked with flowers, edged with burning incense. Women shrouded in white sat wailing beside the corpses, swaying ghostlike as they chanted mantras of lament. Men gathered around the small platform on which speakers stood, squatting patiently on the unsown earth, sharing a pipe with their neighbors, saying scarcely a word as they watched the air above the platform, waiting for someone to stand up and talk to them. Young boys raced about, chasing each other around the stone well, running like threads on a loom among the few scraggly trees that grew nearby.

The sun dropped to the top of a minaret, lingering like the flame on a candle lit to commemorate Amritsar's dead. Todar Mal stepped onto the platform and held up both arms, saying:

"This is a day of great sadness for all of us." His voice did not carry much beyond the first dozen rows of squatting figures, but those too distant to hear the speaker were content to look at him, for that in itself was believed to bestow merit upon the viewer, this doing of darshan, watching a great man. "Our noble leaders, Doctors Kitchlew and Satyapal, were taken from us this morning —"

He paused while cries of "Victory to Kitchlew" and "Victory to Satyapal" rolled across the Bagh, as young men rose with fists clenched, shouting their battle cry. Todar Mal fanned his arms to silence them.

"Have we not had enough wild shouting today?" he asked.

A gruff voice yelled, "No! Not till they are returned to us!"

"We must calm down!" Todarji insisted, though he sounded less than completely composed, and looked rather flustered, as he continued, "We have only done damage to our cause by burning the banks and murdering English —"

"What have they done to us? Look at our dead! Have you counted them? There are twenty" Ratto shouted, waving his one clenched fist toward Todar Mal. It signaled Bugga and at least a dozen of his boys to stand and cup their hands to their mouths, yelling, "Sit down! Let Ratto speak! We want to hear Ratto!"

Maqbool became so enraged as he watched and realized what Ratto and Bugga were trying to do to this meeting that he jumped onto the platform beside the now totally frustrated figure of his friend, and pointing back at Ratto and then at Bugga, began to call out, "Shame! Shame!" Salaria and the others who organized the meeting took up the cry at once, and they too berated the "Club" members. The cry of "shame" became contagious as hundreds of voices shouted down the ruffians. Bugga began to push and shove people standing close to him, and for a few moments it seemed as though the meeting would end in a fistfight, but Ratto chose to leave instead, signaling his attendants to follow his walkout. Several others joined the Clubmen as they strode away, stiff-necked and sneering, but the overwhelming majority remained, and soon focused its undivided attention upon the platform.

"Maqbool, you must speak to them now please," Todar Mal said, still shaken by the heckling he'd received, stepping down from the platform.

"This morning I sat with my dearest friend, Maulanaji Kitchlew, and I heard him say how proud he felt at the beautiful unity and peacefulness of yesterday's Ram Naumi parade," he began, moistening his lips, feeling a strange heaviness descend upon his soul, standing there alone on that platform, facing the sky-sickening smoke that continued to rise from the ruins to the north of the Bagh. "But this evening I know that if Dr. Kitchlew will hear of what happened today, he would feel no pride in this city of his birth. There is nothing of beauty in what we have done today. What have we gained by our violence? Did any of our shouting or shoving at the bridges bring back our leaders? It has only cost us more lives! Has burning the banks restored even one of those? Has the murder of English in Hall Bazaar? Where is the sanity in it? Such crimes do not bring us closer to freedom. How can we hope to rule a Nation if we have not the self-control to guide our own passions?"

They listened in silence, and the only sounds to interrupt his speech were muted responses of "Hear, hear" that came from those closest to the platform.

"Now the question remains with us — what are we to do? How should we act to make ourselves heard by the English but at the same time not to hurt or be hurt by the English? By now it should be clear to anyone with eyes and mind in his head that Government will not permit all of us to go to see the Deputy Commissioner. So what must we do? We must send a deputation of delegates we trust —"

"We trust you," several voices shouted. "Send Maqbool. Victory to Maqbool!" He felt flattered, embarrassed, gratified, burdened, by their spontaneous show of faith in his leadership. He was at once amazed and distressed at how simple it had been for him to become their spokesman. No one knew his weakness half so well as he did, yet here he suddenly stood, listening to his name hailed in the way Kitchlew's had been hardly an hour ago. It terrified him. He held out his hands in a gesture imploring silence.

"I am not worthy to represent you —"

"You are! Victory to Maqbool!" The more he protested his incapacity, the more convinced they became of his virtue. It perplexed him, this inverse ratio of publicly announced self-appraisal and popular evaluation, but by the time he realized that if he wanted to escape the responsibilities of leadership he should have bragged of his meritorious capacity to lead, it was too late to back down. As twilight deepened, a flutter of night air wafted its chill breeze across the Bagh.

"Very well, I will go tomorrow morning to plead with Mr. Irving to release our beloved leaders, and to permit us peacefully to bury our dead — but I must ask you to persuade my wise and trusted friends, Salaria and Todarji Mal to join with me, so that we can be a united delegation of Hindu and Mussulman and Sikh brothers —"

Again the response was overwhelmingly enthusiastic, and while the crowd chanted, "Victory to the Hindu-Muslim-Sikh unity," Maqbool reached down to help Salaria and Todarji and the Lala and Duni climb up onto the platform, and all of them joined hands there, raising their arms in the symbol of unity, and then someone started to sing "Bande Mataram," anthem of the Nationalist struggle, and that vast throng of seated people straggled to their feet, singing softly at first:

> *Mother, we bow to Thee!*
> *Rich with Thy rushing streams,*
> *Bright with Thy orchard gleams,*
> *Cool with Thy winds of delight . . .*

Now the words rang out louder, and Maqbool felt his eyes fill as he stared beyond the faces of those who sang to the sheet-shrouded bodies of the dead.

MASSACRE AT JALLIANWALA BAGH

. . . Dark fields waving,
Mother of might, Mother free,
We bow to Thee.

9

COMMISSIONER KITCHIN watched with astonished alarm as his motor car rolled closer to the motley procession of vehicles crossing the road ahead. There were touring cars and lorries, tongas and ekkas, four-in-hands and rifle-bearing soldiers marching beside them on foot. The drive from Lahore until now had been so surprisingly uneventful and calm that Arthur Kitchin began wondering whether Irving might not have been a bit premature in writing to activate Step Three. Yet now he saw what must have been the entire white population of Amritsar's Civil Lines moving in disquieting disarray and with obvious haste in the direction of the Fort.

"Shall I sound the horn, sir?" his driver asked, bringing the Rolls to a virtual stop barely ten yards from the crossing convoy. They could see the pale faces of anxious passengers in the crowded carriages blocking their progress. Several infants were crying.

"Let them pass," the Commissioner ordered. "We can wait." He was a heavy-set phlegmatic man, who gave the impression of being rather bored or distracted whenever he spoke. Bright young probationers in the Civil Service generally underestimated his intelligence in their first few months of contact with Kitchin, and after a year or more, if they survived to serve in his division of the Punjab, they invariably overestimated him. He was one of those consistently mediocre men, whose lack of imagination, humor, and small talk was so thoroughgoing as to invest his dullness with an almost Oriental air of mystical wisdom. Everybody, but those who knew him intimately (and since his wife's death practically no one did), felt there *had* to be more to Arthur Kitchin than he revealed of himself. He was usually compared to an iceberg.

"This doesn't look at all good, sir," said Mr. Donald, the Deputy Inspector General of Police, who sat smartly decked out in full uniform beside Kitchin. "They seem to be evacuating Civil Lines."

Kitchin never bothered to acknowledge the obvious, nor did he so much as deign to glance in Donald's direction. He considered the Deputy Inspector General just a bit pushy, and found his various abortive efforts at small talk during their two-hour drive rather tiresome.

The sun had begun to set. Miles was supervising the convoy's progress from horseback, urging the tonga drivers to close in on the vehicles in front of them, when he noticed Kitchin's waiting motor, and spurred his horse over, respectfully touching his riding crop to his topi, bending forward to shout:

"How nice of you to come, sir! Sorry to hold you up. It won't take but a minute to clear the cross."

"Where can we talk?" the Commissioner asked, distressed to see how disheveled his Deputy appeared. Kitchin always made a point of emphasizing neatness, which many an old Punjab-hand considered eccentric of him, extolling as they did the virtues of the rough-and-ready school of frontier life. But precisely because of the

Punjab's ruggedness and proximity to the wild border Kitchin insisted upon the most scrupulous adherence to standards totally foreign to this native environment. Irving was quite familiar with his views on this particular matter by now, yet this wasn't the first time Kitchin had found his D.C. looking as grimy, rumpled, and stubble-jawed as a native munshi. Actually, he suspected that Miles Irving considered himself rather more intelligent than Arthur Kitchin, and may even have become so infatuated as to imagine he was better qualified to be Commissioner.

"We've set up temporary headquarters in the station, sir," Miles told him.

"Very well. Lead on."

"My God," Mr. Donald remarked as they drove ahead. "Isn't that the center of the city, where all that smoke's coming from?"

"Yes. Things do seem to have got rather out of hand hereabouts," Kitchin replied, which was more than he'd spoken all trip. At the station he listened attentively to what Irving said, and jotted cryptic notes on his memo pad. He knew better than to trust his memory, and thanks to his scrupulous scribbling and periodic perusal of the notes he took, Kitchin often scored a point of fact off his much brighter subordinates.

"And what's happened to the city police?" Kitchin asked, when Irving finished his briefing.

"We assume they're dead, sir."

"Any Whites left in the city?" he asked, staring at the point of his pencil.

"I should think about ten, sir."

"*About?* You mean you don't know precisely?" His eyes were very wide, his cheeks almost flushed as he looked up at his Deputy, deciding that he really wouldn't be able to write a very favorable report on Miles Irving this year.

"Colonel Smith's been in charge of evacuating the

city, sir. I've rather had my hands full trying to secure this side, and get everyone moved to the Fort before sundown."

"I see. Well, well," he muttered, tapping the point of his pencil so nervously against his pad that it broke. "I assume then that you assume those 'about ten' are all dead?"

"We've had no information from the city for three hours now, sir," Miles snapped. "Are the troop reinforcements I requested coming?"

"Oh, yes. They should be along most any time now. I think I should like to see what sort of arrangements you've made at the Fort, Irving."

They drove with a mounted escort over Rego Bridge to the fortress named Govind, a hulking elephant of stone built more than a century ago by Ranjit, the one-eyed wily Lion of the Punjab, who carved out a kingdom for Sikhs in this land of the five rivers. Yellowish fingers of light flickered from the now silent city, but Civil Lines lay cold under a curtain of darkness. No fire burned in the abandoned bungalows of the sahibs tonight. The fetid moat was filled with brackish green water, home of fungus, mosquitoes, and flies. The oak beam gate studded with spearheads of rusting iron was half closed and had to be dragged wider to admit their motor car. The damp walls of the narrow tunnel to the inner courtyard were coated with moss. For decades the Fort had been used only to house munitions, military hardware, and a skeleton guard. Within the hour it had become home for one hundred and thirty Englishwomen and children, and for forty men, who were too old to bear arms. The inner quadrangle was littered with vehicles of every description. The scene that greeted Kitchin's eyes was one of such disorder and confusion it bordered on chaos. Several women walked about bouncing bawling babies in futile attempts to silence the screaming. Men were busy dragging bedclothes and bundles into the blockhouse tower at the center of the quad. The top floor of the blockhouse was being converted into a dormitory. Sandflies and mosquitoes buzzed about bold as the bats, which swooped out of a hostile sky to terrify women, children, and pets alike. There were really no sanitary provisions worth mentioning, and practically no milk, though several milch buffalo had been left to graze inside. A group of trusted native servants were busily lugging sacks of wheat and rice into the dry storage godown, and a line of jug-bearing suppliants had formed outside the canteen, which housed the one precious tank of potable water. Sister Catherine organized a hospital room, but there was hardly a bed to spare, nor had anyone thought of bringing sufficient linens. One of the babies was running so high a fever that the Sisters feared it was typhoid, but were careful not to let out word of that diagnosis. Several ladies fainted soon after arriving in this haven, and others asked if voluntary subjugation to this sort of prison was not in fact worse than the risk of death in the comfort of one's own home. But most of the women were staunchly British; they bore the strain without fuss.

Arthur Kitchin insisted upon climbing to the top of the stout wall, and stood on the stone rampart facing the old city, vaguely outlined by sparks of light that flickered in native homes. There were three cannon atop the wall, each aimed at one of the city gates that opened within sight of the Fort, though no sign of movement could be seen along any of the roads, nor on the parade grounds between the city's wall and the Fort, which were kept clear of habitation as an emergency military preserve. The Beast had withdrawn — for the moment.

"Diseased," Kitchin muttered, staring out at Amritsar.

Then he looked at Henry Smith, who had joined them on the ramparts. "And highly contagious at that, wouldn't you agree, Colonel?"

"Oh yes, quite right, Arthur."

"Yes, we shall have to find some proper medicine, Irving." He had been District Officer at Kasur when the plague hit in 1907. People naively thought they could lock their doors and bolt their shutters to escape that, but he knew there was only one proper way to fight Black Death. First he cleared the houses, dragging them out, if necessary, every last loitering one of those human rats, who lived in their airless dark rooms, sex-soaked purdah quarters of sin, those harems of black passion — he knew what they did back there, the rabbits. He brought them all into the special camps created in the open, and while his men whitewashed the insides of their filthy homes, covering walls and floors with lime, he had them inoculated, where it did some good, right in their black bellies.

"That's the train from Lahore, sir," Miles said. "Those must be the troops, thank God. Shall we start back to the station?"

"Yes, I've seen quite enough here," Kitchin said. At the station they found Major MacDonald waiting while the last of his troops disembarked from the steaming, hissing train. Like MacDonald himself, one hundred and twenty-five of his soldiers were Britishers of the Sussex regiment, and another hundred and seventy-five were Baluchi Pathans.

"The city's diseased, Major," Kitchin informed him. "Our people here aren't equipped to cope with this sort of thing. As ranking military officer, you'll have to do whatever you judge best."

"But sir," the Major protested, "I've only been six months in Lahore, sir. I'm afraid I don't know the ground

awfully well as yet. Naturally, I'll do whatever you think
I should," he added, lamely.

The War was to blame for it! Practically every officer
worth his command had been siphoned off to the Western
Front, most as volunteers who died in the first year of
battle. Indian garrisons were stripped of British brains,
and since the Armistice, young men like MacDonald had
flowed back in impressive numbers, but it was still too soon
to expect them to understand India. Kitchin left the Major
to Irving, who undertook the task of briefing him. It
was almost eleven, too late to drive back tonight, though
he was anxious to return to Lahore, to make his report.

At eleven-thirty word reached them from Ashraf Khan
in the Kotwali, reporting that four Englishmen were safe
there, and that the police were in fact very much alive.
They also had confirmation of the murders of Stuart,
Scott, and Thomson, as well as two other whites.

"You'll want to send in a column to bring those four
men out, Major," Kitchin ordered. "Best make it a strong
column."

"Yes, sir! Will you wish to accompany us, sir?"

"No, you don't want to be hampered by any civilians,"
he replied, resentful at having been asked so awkward a
question. He suspected Irving turned aside just then to
avoid being caught sneering at his caution. Kitchin knew
that some of the younger men considered him excessively
"cautious." He trusted none were vile enough to call him
a coward! Cheap heroics were for fools, who understood
nothing of Indian treachery. Arthur Kitchin had seen
more than one proud figure of unarmed British manhood
blown to bloody bits by a native bomb tossed in the course
of a parade — during a presumably peaceful celebration.
He had seen the Viceroy himself almost murdered when
entering Delhi atop his viceregal elephant in 1912. He

wasn't *afraid* of death! He simply considered himself too valuable an asset to Empire to risk his life foolishly.

He went to bed when MacDonald's column left for the Kotwali. The drive down had been more exhausting than he'd realized. Tomorrow he would have to face the drive back to Lahore, and he wanted to be fresh as possible for his meeting with the Governor. A first-class coach was provided by Irving for his bedroom. Kitchin double-locked both doors, and wrote for a bit in his diary before turning out the lights.

Next morning the Commissioner had finished breakfast and was ready to leave for Lahore, when a deputation of Indians appeared at the station, requesting an interview with Mr. Irving.

"I expect they've come to beg forgiveness," Miles said, shaking his head angrily. "Just like children! First they spill the milk, then they cry over it!"

"Are you quite certain they're chastened?" Kitchin asked. "Let's have a look at them, Irving. I'm sure His Honour will be interested in hearing how natives behave the morning after they've butchered white men."

Maqbool, Salaria, and Todar Mal were permitted to enter the stationmaster's office, escorted to their audience with Irving and Kitchin by three Royal Sussex subalterns. They were greeted by stony-faced silence from the seated Commissioner and his Deputy.

"I am the Pleader Maqbool, sirs, a Mussulman by birth and conviction, a barrister of our local bar, and lifelong a resident of Amritsar, and these respected gentlemen —"

"Natives are not gentlemen," Kitchin interrupted.

"I may beg to differ —"

"You may not!" Miles snapped. "We're in no mood for lectures this morning! English blood has been spilled! What have you to say for yourselves? Speak up, and talk quickly!"

"Many more Indian lives have been lost yesterday—"

"Is that your reply to me?" Miles jumped to his feet. His voice was strained, hoarse, from having shouted too many orders. His hands trembled, though he tried to subdue his rage. He had slept but a few hours last night, and those were so filled with nightmare dreams that they brought no rest. "What have you come here for this morning?" He glared at their passive brown faces, and knew then that he did not know them, not truly. Nor would he fathom those dark minds if he lived to be a hundred. He hated them for that—for sealing themselves off the way they did. It was really hopeless, trying to reach such people, trying to communicate honestly with them! It was futile. He saw there was nothing chastened or apologetic about their manner or tone.

"We have come, sir, to ask permission to bury our Mussulman dead outside city walls—"

"No processions," Miles insisted. "I won't tolerate any more of your mobs."

"There will be no violence, sir," Maqbool replied. "You have our solemn word—"

"What good is your word to me? What have any of you ever told me but lies? How can I trust you to keep order today, when Englishmen were burned in their banks under your noses yesterday? Where were all of you then?"

"None of us imagined, sir, that the crowd would become so enraged," Salaria interjected, "and the police, after all, were much closer to the National Bank when it burned. Why didn't they—?"

"*No!*" Miles shouted, smashing his fist against the table-top, rattling every cup, saucer, plate, and silver piece of their breakfast service. "I will *not* discuss this further with you people!"

"But you are the highest civil officer in Amritsar," Maqbool persisted softly. "If we cannot bring our peaceful deputation to plead with you to avert further catastrophe —"

"Is that a threat?" Miles asked.

"No, sir. It is a statement of fact. Punish me if you will for speaking what must be said on behalf of my brothers, who mourn their dead as bitterly this day as you do yours, but I have been sent by them as one they trust to speak! I will not plead with you now to release my dearest friend, Dr. Kitchlew, as I hoped to do, for I see your mood is not to listen today. But do you ask me to return to my devout Mussulman brothers, to say that Government refuses them permission to bury their dead? Will you ask them to abandon religious practice at such a time of sorrow? Is this the message you tell us to deliver, sir?"

Miles did not answer on impulse. He bit deeply into his tongue, knowing that political agitation or civil disobedience could be handled in one way, but religious doctrine had to be dealt with differently. It was the unwritten first law of the I.C.S., never to tamper with religious practice. He had learned to swallow that bitter pill early in his career, during his first year of service, when he brought in a middle-aged bull of a Jat, whose wife of twelve had just died from internal bleeding. He was ready to charge the man with murderous rape, but his Commissioner tore up the report, and sat him down to explain, "Miles, lad, there are three hundred million of them, and hardly fifteen hundred of us in the Civil Service. Didja ever ask yourself how we rule 'em all? It's no easy trick tryin' to explain what we do, but the first thing we don't do is fool with their religions, and for all practical purposes that means marriage and death! Never mess with neither, lad, and you may live to collect yer pension!"

"The dead shall be buried," Miles said, speaking very slowly to filter all sound of hatred from his voice, "outside Sultanwind Gate — this afternoon, between two and four P.M. No single body is to be accompanied by more than four mourners —"

"But in the heat of midafternoon, Honorable Sir," Maqbool persisted, "how can just four people carry a dead body in a coffin? Especially if those persons closest are women and children? Then what are they to do? How will they manage to perform the ritual required by Allah?"

Miles closed his eyes. His head had begun to feel light; the faces in front of him seemed to sway precariously. He inhaled several times before speaking.

"Eight," he said. "I will permit eight." ·

"May Allah bless you for it," Maqbool told him.

He made no reply, nor did he exchange salutations with them as they left. He felt quite drained of energy, sitting down again.

"I must be going, Irving," Kitchin said, rising.

"You don't think it was wrong of me, do you, sir?"

"Well, under the circumstances," Arthur responded, leaving his sentence to dangle unfinished, its meaning characteristically vague, exasperatingly Kitchinesque. He said nothing more of substance before he got into his car, but as it started to leave, Kitchin waved his arm at Miles, and shouted, ludicrously enough, "Cheerio!"

10

SIR MICHAEL won both sets of tennis that morning and returned to his office feeling more fit than he had in some time. The touch of tremors that impelled him to activate his option of retirement from the Service last winter was no more than a miserable memory now, and as the date of his scheduled departure from India drew closer, he wished he had been less precipitous about hastening its arrival. Actually, of course, he had expected more of a fight from the Viceroy to prolong his service. He certainly anticipated more than the form letter he received from the secretariat at Simla. He should have known better. His Excellency was notorious for his disregard of the niceties of social courtesy, especially his aversion to letter writing. Sir Michael's friends at Simla reported that of late the Viceroy hardly even corresponded with the King. Things weren't done in proper style any more, certainly not as they had been thirty years ago. Perhaps it was just as well to be leaving India next week.

Sir Michael glanced at the new stack of ribboned green files, arranged so neatly on his desk by his secretary during the brief interlude of his visit to the Club. The Machine never stopped grinding them up to him, those files. He used to wonder how long it would take if he ever decided to read them all instead of simply signing them. But today he did not even feel like opening the ribbons to add his talismanic symbol of authority to the foolish things. He had signed enough documents in his six years at this desk to fill the Taj Mahal. Most of them were irrelevant scraps of paper. Sir Michael never developed the fetish, so common among his civil subordinates and contemporaries in the Simla secretariat, of believing that files were a legitimate substitute for administrative action. His secretary tapped timidly at the door, announcing the arrival of Kitchin.

"Come in, Arthur! Sit down — you look fagged! Bring us some tiffin, like a good chap," he told his secretary. "I've just beat the General at two sets, Arthur! Now what do you think of that?" He towered fully a head over his Commissioner, a square-jawed Irish head, crowned with its mane of wavy black hair as dark as his Irish eyes. Many a maiden from Dublin to Delhi, so he liked to imagine, waited breathless for Sir Michael's dark eye to blink in her direction.

"Very good, sir. Very good indeed! Yes, that is very good. Your game's improved, has it, sir?" Kitchin resorted so rarely to small talk that he always made a mess of it when he felt obliged to try.

"Sit down, Arthur, and tell me about Amritsar," he said, taking a cigar from his humidor, lighting it carefully while Kitchin began his report.

"The disease is particularly virulent there, Sir Michael. Six Englishmen have been murdered, and . . ." He spoke without visible emotion, blandly relating the details of damage to British life and property. The Governor puffed more swiftly, but otherwise revealed virtually no sign of emotion either, except that all levity drained from his handsome face as he listened.

Tiffin arrived just as Arthur was finishing, and the secretary left the tray before them without saying a word. After Kitchin finished his report, they sat in total silence. Then Sir Michael rose from his seat, and went to his desk, but simply stood staring down at its polished top, appearing to have forgotten what impelled him to move there, unless it was simply the solace of seeing familiar objects, his jeweled dagger and the elephant tusk, and the great seal of Government, the raw diamond paperweight, the silver bullets Sindhia gave him. He fingered the bullets distractedly as he spoke.

"It's what comes of having that Jew in Whitehall, Arthur."

"True enough, sir. He's not been a strong Secretary of State," Kitchin responded, feeling less awkward than he did when His Honour spoke denigratingly about other members of His Majesty's Government, particularly the Prime Minister.

"He's Gandhi's *friend*," Sir Michael sneered. "Isn't that what he told the Commons when I barred the dirty little terrorist fakir from my province? Didn't that Levantine lecher stand up then and say, 'I am proud to consider Mr. Gandhi one of my friends?'" He pitched his cigar into the gleaming brass spitoon, and followed it with a stream of phlegm that resounded like gunfire.

"Oh, yes, I *do* recollect now, Sir Michael. You're quite correct, Your Honour! That is precisely what he said. Imagine one of His Majesty's Secretaries of State saying a thing like that?"

"The niggers and the Jews, Arthur — they're birds of a feather!"

With that, Sir Michael fell upon his tiffin, stripping bare the bones of two chicken breasts in the time it took

Kitchin to butter his hot bun. He ate voraciously, sucking his fingers clean when he finished, Indian-style. He
swilled down two cups of coffee before speaking again.

"We've got to teach them a lesson, Arthur. They'll be
waiting now to see how we react to this sort of provocation.
If we take this lying down — we're all dead tomorrow,
every blessed one of us!"

"I do believe you're quite right about that, Sir Michael,"
Kitchin muttered.

"This sort of anarchy is what comes of pampering them,
Arthur. They've been testing us, the scum. Seeing just
how much of their excrement we'll swallow without shoving it back in their black faces! It's why I stopped that
charlatan fakir from entering the Punjab! Any man with
British brains in his head can see what that naked blackguard is up to — he's a blasted Bolshevik if ever there
was one! He's been testing the will of Government, that's
what all of these pledges he's had his rabble swear to
mean, and his hateful hartals — getting decent people to
close down their shops — for what possible reason? There's
only one explanation of it all, Arthur — to test our capacity to resist his anarchistic preachings, to test our will
to rule! We've surrendered so much by now that they
think we're all as flabby and foolish as that Shylock in
Whitehall!"

Sir Michael went to his phone and rang up the Major
General, whom he had just beaten at tennis.

"Robbie, who's your G.O.C. at Jullundur?" he asked.
"Oh, yes. He's rather a firm sort, wouldn't you say? Good.
I want you to send him down to Amritsar, Robbie. Soon
as he's ready — that's right. Tell him to take charge personally. We've got to get things straightened out down
there! Right." He hung up the earpiece. He stood staring
at the crystal chandelier poised above his Persian rug. In
the past five years he personally had recruited more troops

and laborers, and raised more money, to bolster the Allied War effort than any other man in India — perhaps in all the Empire!

"It's really aimed at me, you know," he whispered.

"Beg pardon, Your Honour."

"This insurrection, Arthur — this revolt. It's that beggar's way of trying to embarrass me before I leave office. They're afraid I'll be offered the viceroyalty, or a peerage." He was often mentioned for one or the other, and only a fortnight ago the *Civil and Military Gazette* ran a leader suggesting he richly deserved both.

"He hoped we'd lose the War, you know, the little fakir did." Sir Michael toyed with the dagger Sir Pertap had presented to him on his last birthday. *Blow hot or blow cold*, the shrewd Sikh warrior advised, when they talked of how to handle political agitation, *only never forget you hold India by the sword!*

"You can stop a spring with a twig," he said, quoting Sadi, "but let it flow unchecked, and even an elephant cannot cross it. Let's hope it's not too late for us to apply the twig, Arthur."

"I devoutly hope it may not be, Sir Michael."

"Every Sikh and Jat villager from here to Delhi, every sepoy who owns a rifle, every black, brown, and tan mother's son of them will be watching and waiting to see how we react to this challenge, Arthur." He tested the edge of his dagger along the horny nail of his thumb. It was still sharp enough to bite. "They'll sleep with their breath drawn tonight, with their eyes open, waiting — and tomorrow they'll wait again. They'll remain coiled now for a bit, but none will close his eyes or stop watching to see how we take this sort of treatment, and if we take it lying down God help us!"

He tugged the cord behind his desk. His secretary appeared at the door. "Wire His Excellency at Simla — in code, if you please." He paused for a moment to compose the telegram in his mind before dictating: "Amritsar dangerously disturbed. Arson, looting, murder of six Englishmen yesterday necessitated evacuation of Civil Lines. Am keeping close watch over situation, and consider it imperative to remain at my post till order fully restored throughout Punjab. Request permission to cancel scheduled departure indefinitely." His successor-designate was a Simla man, one of those paper-pushing secretaries to Government, who rose so rapidly in the Service by remaining at the Viceroy's ear.

"No, strike 'indefinitely,' " he ordered. He knew how jealous the Simlawallas were of his position here, how much they coveted his power, thinking him too enamoured of it. "Substitute, 'for the duration of emergency.' " That would give them less to cavil about. His secretary rushed off to code the wire and send it.

"Oh, that is *most* heartening news, sir!" Kitchin jumped to his feet. "It's a personal sacrifice for you, I know, Sir Michael, but you are absolutely indispensable to us now. God keep you with us always, sir!"

"Never fear, Arthur, I won't be leaving for a while! We shouldn't want little black brother to think it was his dirty little anarchist terror that frightened me off, should we? We won't be bullied and we won't be burned out, Arthur. Not today, not in a thousand years!"

He hefted the uncut diamond in his left hand, tossing it up like a tennis ball. His service had really been strong today. He hadn't wasted a swat.

"Arthur, I want you to drive to Jullundur for me now. Are you up to it?"

"I'll do anything you say, Sir Michael."

"Thank you, Arthur." He walked closer and set his right hand firmly on the stout shoulder of his Commissioner. "I want you to speak with G.O.C. Jullundur before he leaves for Amritsar. He won't be ready to go, I'm sure, for a few hours, and if the roads are clear you should have ample time to catch him —"

"I'm sure I will, sir. No difficulty on the roads."

"Tell him to punish them for me, Arthur." His voice was sonorous, vibrant and deep. "Tell him — tell him to see to it they never dare do such deeds again! I want every Sikh and Jat, every Mussulman peasant and soldier in the Punjab to hear my answer to this provocation. My unequivocal answer, Arthur! Will you tell him that for me?"

"Gladly, Your Honour!" His eye and voice had caught something of the spark of Sir Michael's zeal.

11

THE funeral procession moved slowly toward Sultanwind Gate that afternoon. It was Friday, April 11, and noon prayers at Amritsar's Masjid had drawn a larger crowd than any prayer meeting in the memory of elders in the community, yet there had been no disturbance. Even when Dr. Bashir, who recited the Khutbah, mentioned the King-Emperor in the usual terms of respect, acknowledging British sovereignty over India, no strident voice was raised in opposition, only a murmur of discontent, a ripple that went swiftly across the otherwise calm sea of bowed backs. A prayer was then said by Maqbool for the release of Kitchlew and Satyapal and for the souls of those who died in yesterday's rioting. By one o'clock it was over, and the worshippers walked quietly toward Sultanwind Gate, following the dead bodies, which were carried in simple coffins, all but hidden by garlands of gardenias and marigolds.

Several thousands had joined the procession by the time its front ranks reached the stone wall and its southern passageway, the gate closest to Jallianwala Bagh and the Golden Temple. Outside were the burial grounds of the

Muslims and the cremation grounds of Hindus and Sikhs. Actually the city itself flowed beyond the old wall in this southerly direction, for hundreds of ramshackle homes, many no more than makeshift lean-tos against the south face of the wall, clustered there, accommodations for the families of those outcastes, whose labor in life was to care for the dead. Others also settled in this run-down region, recent migrants from impoverished villages, wanderers, landless and jobless, who found no friendly welcome among the more affluent communities inside the wall, mendicants and sadhus, the lowly and the holy, hovered here within constant sight and smell of death.

Maqbool feared that the entire procession would try to march out behind the bodies in defiance of Mr. Irving's order limiting each funeral to eight mourners. He had announced the limitation at the Masjid, and asked his colleagues of the bar to help him enforce it, yet now that the crowd was virtually at the gate, despite its peaceful demeanor, he became anxious. He expected, of course, that many soldiers and police would be there, ready to enforce violently any infraction of the Deputy Commissioner's order. He had never seen half so many soldiers at Amritsar as he found at the station this morning. But even the usual few police, who generally loitered at every city gate, seeing what bribes they could extort from villagers for the "privilege" of entering Amritsar, were nowhere visible. Was it a trap? he wondered. Had Irving ordered his guard to remain out of sight, to test them? He hurried ahead of the first coffin and signaled several younger barristers to join him in forming a loose line across the gateway. As the crowd approached he held up both hands, extending the four fingers of each, shouting:

"No more than eight mourners are permitted to accompany each coffin. Please do not go beyond this gate unless you are one of those eight!"

"Whose order it that?" someone grumbled.

"It is our pledge! We must learn to discipline ourselves," Maqbool responded, and at first it seemed to work, for the coffins moved past him with only those bearing their weight in attendance, each followed by one or two burkha-clad spectral figures. He counted nine mourners at one coffin, but seven at another. Five coffins passed thus, without complaint or shoving from the crowd. After that the pressure of numbers gathering in greater depth increased, and Maqbool had to retreat several paces. No sooner did he move, however, than the space left open was filled.

"Who are you to stop us here? What if we have different business outside this gate?" a young man asked irately.

"Go about it then! But why have you come in this procession?"

"It is none of your affair!" He brushed past Maqbool, and with him went others, saying nothing. Maqbool turned and saw them all racing to catch up to one of the coffins. While his head was turned many people hurried by, and soon the entire crowd was moving.

"Please stop," he called out, and some did, but most of the mourners moved on, determined to follow their comrades to the burial ground. All went bareheaded and shoeless. Finally Maqbool gave up shouting at their moist-eyed faces. His voice was gruff, his throat felt like parched earth. Once again he had failed. His heart sank at the prospect of British troops arriving now, at any moment, to find not eight mourners but eight hundred following one coffin. He stared at the furnace of the sky's shimmering face, waiting for the inevitable clap of thunder.

Only it did not come. He held his breath, anticipating the worst, yet he heard no guns fired. No troops appeared at the scene. He dared not believe their good fortune, for with his eyes he had glimpsed the station bristling with British arms, and Gurkhas and Baluchis, as well. They would as soon shoot down Punjabis as chew tobacco. There were, he knew, hundreds and hundreds of them, bivouacked on the station platforms, ready to move at a single word of command. Yet none came within earshot or sight of Sultanwind Gate — as though Allah, by His miraculous powers, had cast His invisible cloak over the burial grounds and His weaponless worshippers, who went in such prolific numbers to weep for their dead.

"We must not let things continue so," Todar Mal said, rousing him from the torpor of fatalism into which he had lapsed. "I have asked the Lala, Master Duni, and several others to meet this afternoon in my house to discuss what to do. Will you join us, Maqbool?"

"Of course. What hour?"

"Four-thirty. We must try to get everyone back from the burial grounds by four. Otherwise — who can tell what may happen? You must go to the burial grounds, Maqbool, and urge everyone to return peacefully to the city as soon as the service is finished. I will do the same at the cremation grounds." Several fires had begun to crackle from the sandalwood pyres of Hindu dead. A chant of Sanskrit mantras rose with the ribbons of smoke, even as the bodies of Muslims were being lowered into the earth nearby to the accompaniment of Koranic verse.

Maqbool moved wearily toward his friends, who had just painfully taught him the lesson every leader of masses must learn, sooner or later: that a mob may be led where it wishes to go, but can hardly be diverted by mere words from its desired destiny. The sanity and order that appeared so ordinary, while it prevailed in society, seemed virtually a miracle of achievement as soon as it broke down. The balance of human interdependence, which like the cosmic solar system, kept man and his neighbors moving in their proper orbits, doing the jobs that incrementally added up to a city's daily life had suddenly ruptured, fragmenting, dissolving. The aftermath was chaos. Maqbool felt so shaken as he moved toward the ground saturated with death that unconsciously, for no one person in particular, he began silently to cry. The people who noticed him approach made way respectfully, and some gathered about him, for sorrow seeks its solace in numbers.

So he stood for many moments, shedding tears in that field of remorse, where his father lay buried, and all of his uncles, and his brother, who died of the influenza last year, when that blight was upon them. How many times more, he wondered, would he return to this spot to grieve before he too was interred in this earth of the same reddish-brown hue as his own skin? Then he thought of Kitchlew, and the memory of that strong smiling face brought him back to the work that remained undone. He called to those standing about:

"We must return peacefully to the city now that our dead have been decently buried."

Slowly they did return, and by four, when the distant church bell tolled its somber count, practically all were safe within the shelter of the city's wall. Maqbool hurried across the Jallianwala Bagh, taking this shortcut to the old house of Todar Mal, whose back wall formed a portion of the Bagh's rear border. He arrived a few minutes before four-thirty.

His host welcomed him with a brotherly embrace, leading him to the sitting room, whose floor was decked with freshly laundered mats and stout bolsters, against one of which the Lala was reclining.

"Greetings, Pleader," the Lala said in that slightly acerbic tone, which gave his most innocent remark an edge of sarcasm. He was a short, frail man, with rimless spectacles imparting a quizzical quality to his boyishly round face. But for a patch of gray on the otherwise black forelock of his hair he hardly seemed old enough to be a teacher, much less the principal of the Hindu Arya Samaj High School. "Have you had any word from Kitchlew?"

"None since he left."

"It is intolerable," the Lala said, shaking his head. "They treat the best of us as criminals, and the rest of us as children."

"After what happened yesterday," said Todarji, "I am not so certain that most of us deserve to be treated any better than that!"

"The English will not love you more because you condemn your own people, Maharaj," replied the Lala, dipping into his mango puree, noisily sucking it off his fingers. "I am fed up with this wearing of sackcloth and ashes every time a precious hair on a priceless English head is touched, or one shred of English property is damaged! Indian blood is no less precious, and they have shed much more of it yesterday. No thank you, Maharaj, I will not say mea culpa this evening!"

"What is the use now of arguing over blame," asked Maqbool, knowing how much the Lala enjoyed forensics. He talked a consistently extreme nationalist line, but was notorious for his reluctance to take action of any kind. "I thought we were going to discuss some practical matters, Todarji."

"Yes, this was my intention in calling you here today, Gentlemen," responded their host, suavely oblivious to the Lala's attack, rising to welcome the enormously fat guest who was being ushered in by the servant. "Ah, here is the Master Duni! Now we will have his sage advice to guide our deliberations!"

At which point, Duni Chand, M.A., lowered himself cautiously onto a bolster, which he all but crushed, belching, "The first thing we must do is stop this damned hartal! Business is being ruined by this damn work stoppage! The whole damn economy is going to collapse if we don't get people to open their shops!" Duni had completed his Master of Arts at Calcutta University, and since achieving that pinnacle of his intellectual aspiration, settled securely into his father's brokerage business.

"Hear, hear," echoed Todar Mal, who was actually the only shop owner present. His elegant shawl and sari shops had remained closed during last week's hartal, and were secured again immediately after news of the arrest of Kitchlew and Satyapal spread throughout the bazaars.

"But hartal is our only effective weapon," insisted the Lala. "What better way have we of demonstrating to the English that we stand united?"

"United for what purpose?" shouted Duni. "To starve? To strangle off our economic lifelines? If that's the sort of drivel your students are learning in high school, it's no wonder they behave like such damned idiots and irresponsible fools!"

"Todarji, I have not come here to be insulted and maligned in your house!"

"Oh, now, now," Todar responded, clicking his tongue, "after what you have said to others, Lalaji, you should not become so indignant over the Master Duni's remarks. We are all of us somewhat on edge today."

"I would say it to him any day, my good friend Todarji. The man's a damned fool if he thinks that hartal is doing any Indian any damn good!"

"And you, sir, are twice the fool you accuse me of being! No man of intellect calls another a fool. I may not be a Calcutta M.A. —"

"No, and you never will be one! I'm sick of you armchair revolutionaries with your brainless ideas of how to get things done! All you can think of is stop work! Stop work, close up shops, stay home from school! Who can't get practically every Indian fool to do those things? The trick is to find people to work and contribute something to the damned economy! That's the only way to build your Nation — with productive manpower and capital."

"I venture to say, sir, it will take just a slight bit more than that," said the Lala, rising and controlling his rage, though with obvious difficulty. "It requires some spirit as well, you see — the spirit of freedom! And that is something you will not be able to buy or sell, so naturally to you and your kind, sir, it may have no value, but —"

"Lalaji — Duni — what is the point of this argument?" Maqbool asked. "To prove that even today we have not the wisdom to unite? That is why the English always say we are not fit to govern ourselves! Well, perhaps they are right, after all."

"What are you saying, Pleader?" The Lala shook his ineffectual fist toward Maqbool's face. "Is this how you talk the day after your great friend is spirited away from your side? Are you not ashamed —?"

"Yes, I am very much ashamed, Lalaji! But not for the reason you imagine! I am ashamed that even in this room, even among two men of such high level of education and public spirit as you yourself and the Master Duni, and at a time of such crisis for all of us as today, there can be no constructive discussion of what is to be done to restore sanity to Amritsar tomorrow, but instead only petty bickering and personal attacks upon each other's bona fides! Yes, I am ashamed of that." He rose to his feet. "Excuse me, Todarji, and forgive me if I have been rude to your guests, but my heart is too full tonight to permit me the luxury of polite conversation."

"Sit down, Maqbool," shouted Duni. "We need more such reminders of why we have assembled here. I will hold back my tongue, I promise, though as you may guess — for a man of my appetite, it is never easy to stop my mouth from moving!"

That was, Maqbool realized, as close as the Master Duni had ever come to apologizing to anyone since he'd received his M.A., and even the Lala appeared to be moved by so tortured an effort on his corpulent adversary's part to poke fun at himself, for he also muttered something about talk coming easier than action, and sat down, hanging his head in silence.

"Tell us what you think we should do, Maqbool," urged Todar Mal. "Should we try to end the hartal or not?"

"We should try now, Todarji, to do whatever we can to prevent any more violence. There has been too much of bloodshed, and perhaps it would be best now to open shops again so that people will have work to keep them occupied, and places to go — I think for those reasons, Lala, not because I have forgotten my dearest friend, who lives now in every thought of my mind — but because I remember that first of all he wanted to avoid violence of any kind, that is why I think we should urge our brothers to open their shops."

"But have we not surrendered then to English tyranny? Are we not capitulating in the face of pressures?"

"I do not urge it for those reasons, Lala, so how can I feel that what I suggest is surrender or capitulation? And let us think for one moment about what is achieved and what is lost if we continue hartal instead of ending it. Do we punish the English or ourselves by keeping closed the shops at which we purchase our food as well as our household necessities? The only major English business in our part of the city, after all, was banking. No, I cannot see the sense of continuing this form of protest."

"Protest is its own justification, Pleader! Was it not Oliver Cromwell who said —"

Duni began to cough as though he were choking, drowning out the Lala's words, and heaving his massive form so furiously about on his mat that it seemed he was wrestling with some invisible spirit. Todar rushed toward the kitchen clapping his hands and calling for water. The Lala forgot which quotation he had intended to use, and to compound the confusion Hansraj appeared in the room, flanked by two of his youthful cohorts.

"We heard you were meeting, brothers," said Hansraj, addressing them with exaggerated politeness, "to formulate plans for continuing our struggle. We hope we're not unwelcome in this house, Shri Mal." Then without waiting for any invitation to do so, he sat on one of the empty mats and dipped his hand into the groundnut and raisin dish. "Sit! Sit and join us," he urged his more reticent coterie, who shyly edged onto the mat at either side of Hansraj. They were thick-limbed boys, and their eyes appeared bright, but neither of them spoke a word.

"We have been discussing the merits of ending the hartal as quickly as possible," Maqbool informed the late arrivals.

"Ending it?" Hansraj exclaimed. "Has Maulanaji been released?"

"No."

"Then how can we speak of ending our struggle? We must intensify it! How can anyone go back to work at such a time as this?"

"Since when have you begun working, Hansraj?" asked Duni.

"I am a full-time worker for my Nation, sir! Some people work only for their bellies!"

"Do you not mean *on* their bellies?" Duni responded. "And how *is* your mother these days?"

"I could kill you for that!" Hansraj jumped to his feet, his two shadows rising with him.

Todar and Maqbool moved at once to the Master Duni's side, and seeing their determination to stand by their friend, Hansraj backed off, muttering curses, his bony fists clenched white at the knuckles.

"There is your revolutionary hero, Lala," Duni scoffed. "Yesterday he kills the English, today he would kill me, and tomorrow? Who knows, Mr. Principal, perhaps you will be next on his schedule!"

"Pig," Hansraj whispered, spitting the word toward Duni's bloated stomach.

"I must ask you to apologize to my guest, the Master Duni, or else you will leave my house at once," said Todar.

"He is the one who should apologize to me! I would sooner die than tell that pig I am sorry—"

"Please leave this house!"

"With pleasure! I can see there are no patriots here," shouted Hansraj. "I would sooner let English bullets enter my heart than sit with you and talk about how to sell out my country! All of you are too old to have any true passion left, and without passion there is no patriotism! I love my Nation. I love India. She is my Mother! My Mother is glorious and beautiful and will one day be free — despite all of you pigs, who can think no higher than your pockets and your bellies! India will never surrender! Never! Victory to the Hartal! Victory to India!" He clenched his right fist and held it high. His comrades joined him in the gesture, which had of late become popular among students.

Then Hansraj expectorated upon the mat on which he had been reclining, and rushed out of the room. The shadows followed in his wake.

"He is a menace, that young man," said Duni. "He should be locked away."

"I do not think I am in agreement, sir," responded the Lala. "He is sincere in his feeling, his seeking for freedom. Naturally, he is young, so he speaks too quickly, and impulsively perhaps, but it is sincere patriotism—"

"Lunacy, you mean!"

"I do not believe that love of motherland is to be equated with mental retardedness, sir, but if you will now excuse me, Gentlemen," said the Lala, *namaskaring* as he rose to leave, "I have promised my wife I would be at home before it is dark."

"Yes, I too must be on my way," said Maqbool softly.

"What do you think, Maqbool?" asked Todar Mal.

"I think it may not be very easy to convince people to open their shops tomorrow." Hansraj would be visiting many houses tonight, he knew, urging patriots, young and old, to stand firm in their protest. And even those who would not be swayed by his rhetoric would doubtless feel reluctant to expose their wares so soon to the possible ravaging of looters. Bugga's boys would be abroad once the shadows of evening fell, and there were always others waiting for some form of civic disruption to emerge from their lairs and seek to exploit public chaos. Maqbool felt weary. He felt as though in the last two days he had aged ten years.

"We damn well better do something," said Duni. "I'll tell Dholan Das to call a meeting of the Chamber tomorrow, and we can move to get things started again there."

"Excellent idea, Master Duni," Todar told him, asking to be notified of the time as soon as the meeting was arranged.

There would have to be many more meetings, Maqbool knew, and each person attending would want his opportunity to speak his mind, and there would be more arguments, heated, acerbic, possibly violent, and all of it would take — how much time?

"It's late," he said, walking out toward the darkness gathering in Jallianwala Bagh.

12

THE General woke early on Saturday. His drive down from Jullundur had been exhausting, he had not returned from the Kotwali to Amritsar station before one-thirty, and then first moved his troops to Ram Bagh, the military cantonment in Civil Lines. The station was too vulnerable for military head-quarters. He'd considered moving into the Fort, but that was too crowded. Ram Bagh had a decent C.O.'s bunga-low, and by three Rex was asleep inside it. Barely four hours later he woke feeling fit — more fit than he had since his last campaign on the Afghan border, three years ago. He won his brigade thanks to that skirmish, but even then he was the oldest brigadier left of his Camberley batch. It was the price he'd been obliged to pay for sitting out the big War in India. Perhaps if this show was big enough he'd finally get his division!

"Briggs!" Hardly had the name of his brigade major rasped from his throat than the door opened revealing Tommy's straight and polished figure.

"Good morning, General. Your bath is drawn, sir. Will you breakfast with the staff, or alone?"

"Just the two of us, Tommy. Any developments?" He tried to touch his naked toes with his fingertips, but wasn't quite that much better.

"Telegraph master reports the wires still cut between ourselves and Lahore, sir. He's organized a line party, sent off with an armored train at Zero-one-twenty, but no word from them as of Zero-six-hundred —" Tommy paused to remove two neatly folded telegrams from his jacket pocket, glancing again at one of them. "Yes, sir, he sent the last wire at six. I received it half hour ago, but didn't want to trouble you —"

"No, there was no need," Rex replied, doing a few arm and finger exercises, which were less of a strain to his groin. "But those cut wires are a sure sign that this is much bigger than a local show, Tommy. This is a well-planned revolt, my boy. They're trying to isolate me! Trying to cut my lines of communication. Close me off! That's what they'd like to do, the buggers. It's part of the big picture . . ."

His voice trailed off as he went into the other room, where his bath water was still steaming in the half-filled tub. Since his accident, Rex tried to spend at least half an hour each morning in a hot tub, but he was careful not to let anyone but Briggs see how badly bruised he was. He knew how quickly rumor spread in India, and how jealous some of his Simla "friends" were, jealous and suspicious of everything he did. If any of them started talking about how badly crippled that horse had left him, the adjutant general might just be tempted to recommend his retirement for "medical reasons" — before he ever got a division! It was just the sort of miserable thing that would appeal to his old friend the commander in chief, who never learned to use his fists till Rex gave him his first boxing lessons — thirty-five years ago. He expected no gratitude, of course, not from so small-minded a man. Others often remarked though that from the looks of the general officer promotion lists, since friend-Charlie took his regal perch, anyone would conclude he was purposely discriminating against Rex. Then too, there were some upstart young colonels, he knew, who coveted his brigade. He knew more than he let on.

The General stripped off his underwear and tested the water with his toes, shouting, "Too damn hot!" Tommy had rolled up his sleeves, and quickly added a jar of cold. The servants had left an assortment of clay jars filled with hot and cold water on the floor beside the bath.

"That's good, Tommy," he said, clenching Briggs's hand as he eased into the water, which nearly scalded him. "That's good!"

"You look very fit today, sir."

"I feel fit! Give us another hot!"

"Yes, sir."

"Not *too* fast!"

"Sorry, sir."

Tommy was adding the hot water slowly when a guard outside tapped at the General's bedroom door. A message had just arrived from Lahore by airplane. Its bearer was the plane's copilot, a young captain in British India's first air squadron. Briggs told him to wait, while he delivered the sealed envelope to the bathroom.

"My hands are wet. Read it to me, Tommy."

"Yes, sir. It's from Division Genstaff. 'Telegraph line reported cut this morning. Lahore quiet. Kasur reports at six-ten armored train visited Khem Karan during night and found station wrecked but no casualties. Rioters in small numbers apparently organized for destruction left in direction of Sutlej. Train patrolled two stations beyond and all quiet, so returned to Kasur. Tried to wire you last night to return Royal Sussex to Lahore today relieving them by your Queens. Most important to get Sussex back here to-day as trouble anticipated here tomorrow. Please report your situation by bearer who is to return at once.' "

"Blast!" He angrily smashed his fist into the water, splashing a puddle out of the shallow tub.

Tommy had moved aside discreetly, while reading the message, and when the General's reaction erupted, managed to remain dry.

"I need every man I have here — specially those Sussex rifles! Who in hell signed that blasted wire?"

"Div Genstaff, sir."

"Damned blasted nuisance!" He lost his patience for hydrotherapy, and his face flamed as he strained to lift his hulking form out of the water, the scar tissue of his belly's welts and dark bruises giving his body the strangely striped appearance of some crustaceous creature clawing its way up from the deep.

"Let me help you, sir," Tommy offered, rushing closer and placing a firm hand under the General's elbow, covering his shoulders with his robe. Rex wrapped the cloth firmly around his bulging midsection, and dripped a trail of water as he walked barefoot into the bedroom, where the pilot messenger stood waiting.

"Who the devil handed you this message for me, Captain?"

"General Officer Commanding Lahore Division, sir."

"Himself?"

"Himself, sir."

"Oh," Rex muttered, turning away from the young captain, cursing as he reread the last lines of the message. There was no ambiguity about that order to return the Royal Sussex rifles today! He had hoped to be able to hold them another twenty-four hours at least. Man for man they were as good as the Queens he'd sent down from Jullundur, and there were twenty more of them. Returning the Sussex to Lahore would mean the attrition of his British force by more than a quarter, leaving him with barely three hundred and fifty White soldiers to subdue one hundred and fifty thousand Black rebels. It was a ratio that gave him pause.

"How many native troops have we, Briggs?"

"Seven hundred ten, sir."

"How many can be trusted?"

"There are two hundred seventy-seven Gurkhas, General, and one hundred eighty-one Baluchi rifles. I should think those will remain loyal. The rest are Sikhs, and Mussulman Punjabis. I wouldn't care to lean too heavily on them at the moment. I expect most have kinfolk in the Punjab."

Close to five hundred Gurkhas and Baluchis was a reassuring number to Rex. He spoke the language of both martial races. They were loyal to the Raj — always had been, ever since they were soundly beaten by British arms. Like wild stallions, once broken in they made the best mounts.

"Very well," he muttered. "MacDonald can return his Sussex rifles to Lahore today. Briggs, write up a message for me to Genstaff. You know the sort of thing . . ."

"Yes, sir," Tommy replied, sitting at the desk and dipping the pen there into the ink bottle without pausing a second, just starting to write away in his perfect penmanship that made every letter look as though it were printed. Rex couldn't understand how he did that, put his thoughts down on paper as fast as it took him to think them. He would agonize for an hour over a brief letter to his son. He'd always been too busy to write, of course, out in the field. The thing about Tommy was that he could soldier too. He was no shirker. Best damned marksman in the regiment last year, and still he could scribble away! That boy, Rex thought, watching his brigade major work, he'll make brigadier someday!

"Is this the sort of message you'll want to send, General?" Tommy asked, rising from the desk to hand him the neatly spaced holograph, which read: "Royal Sussex will return today to Lahore. My situation at Ram Bagh here in Civil Lines now secure. British women and children safe under armed guard in Govind Fort, and railway station firmly held, lines open in all directions. Amritsar city, however, in rebel hands. Situation of city at present quiet, but precarious. Surrounding villages have not yet joined rebellion, though cut wires indicate extent of rebel conspiracy. Next forty-eight hours most critical. I am taking whatever steps necessary to restore Law and Order throughout Amritsar city and environs."

"Right," the General said, as he finished reading his wire, "that should do! I could tell them lots of other details, but we can't spend all day writing messages. I'd just as soon make this one brief!"

"Yes, sir."

"Right! Put my name at the bottom there — and seal that damn thing up!" He turned to confront the waiting officer. "Are you flying this back, Captain?"

"Immediately, General."

"Any sign of rebels in any of the villages you passed coming out this morning?"

"The roads seemed more heavily traveled than ordinarily at this hour."

"Which way was the traffic moving?"

"Toward the city, sir."

"Briggs, did you hear that?"

"Yes, General. We've had reports of villagers coming toward Sultanwind Gate, looking for loot perhaps, though it may be that since we've stopped all third-class bookings on the railway, what with the Baisakhi cattle fair the Hindus have scheduled in Amritsar tomorrow — they could just be coming for that. Did you see many bringing cattle?" he asked the pilot.

"Some livestock, yes. There were empty carts too though —"

"For the buggers to fill with loot!" Rex rasped. "And they might just be bringing their cattle to help them pack more loot home! Your Punjabi peasant is a slimy chameleon, Tommy. Long as he thinks the Raj is strong, he lies low and remains loyal, but let him sniff a straw of weakness in the wind and out he rushes ready to grab whatever he can with both slippery fists! He'd knife the master he bowed to if he thought he could get away free! Let's not waste more time gabbing — I want to see those buggers with my own eyes this morning!"

The sun had baked from bright orange to white before the General and his troop column were ready to leave their bivouac at Ram Bagh. Rex decided to take the Royal Sussex along for at least this one show. They were too fine a fighting force to send back without so much as parading them. He took half of his Gurkhas and Baluchis too, and the armored cars that had rolled down from Jullundur. There were two steel-plated vehicles in his command, both with four mounted rapid-fire machine guns, manned by his Londoners. He'd had no opportunity as yet to use his armored vehicles. They were the latest addition to his arsenal, battle-tested in France, and sent to his brigade less than six months ago from ordnance headquarters at Meerut.

Tommy lined up the column as he ordered it — the Royal Sussex in the lead, all one hundred and twenty-five of them, followed by his command car in which Police Superintendent Rehill sat up front with the driver, he and Briggs in the back seat. They were followed by armored vehicle one, behind which came the Gurkhas, trailed by vehicle two. The Baluchis brought up the rear. The Royal Sussex drummers set the pace, quick march at about six miles an hour. Spread out on the move, the column itself stretched almost a quarter of a mile. He had considered carefully the alternative routes to Sultanwind Gate, the shorter direct route through Hall Gate, across the old city, or the circuit road round about the city wall, which was longer but free of congestion and possible hazards of harassment from the tops of high buildings that lined the old bazaar streets. Rehill reported receiving information of rebel threats to hurl brickbats, bottles, and bombs at any soldiers who tried to penetrate the city today. Rex had encountered no such harassment last night, of course, but knew enough about native terrorist tactics never to be lulled into a sense of false security. More important than the security advantage of the circuit road, however, was the time factor. He could proceed round it at quick march, and reach Sultanwind Gate in fifteen minutes, less than half what it would have taken his column to wend its way through the narrow lanes of the city proper.

It was a fine morning, one of those cloudless April days for which he waited all year in India, not too hot, nor so windy as to stir up sand or dust, but warm and dry, just enough of a rustle in the air to carry the scent of jasmine to his nostrils. Leaning back in the slow-rolling car, he remembered mornings at Simla when he strolled on the mountain trails with his brothers and sister Beth. There had been nine of them once. Rex was the youngest boy, and Beth was always fretting over him, treating him like a baby, till the morning they walked together when he was six and a terrifyingly long snake came towards them hissing with forked tongue, sending Beth into a panic of screaming paralysis. Rex lifted the largest rock he could find and dropped it with deadly accuracy on the viper's black head. Beth never called him a baby again, and even his brothers praised his heroism. His father was so pleased, he let Rex drink from his own glass at dinner that night. It was the best malt his dad's brewery made, and though it tasted bitter, the memory of that sip, taken to raucous cheers — remained sweet and fresh.

"There's a gang of them, General," Briggs said, pointing toward the wall at a group of young natives, who stood not far from the Sultanwind Gate, huddled conspiratorially together.

"Slow march," he ordered, leaning forward to stare at those surly faces. None of them looked straight. They were shifty-eyed, guilt-ridden, obviously embarrassed, caught off guard by his unexpected arrival. A dirty, disheveled lot of rubbish. Diseased, all of them. He could see sores on their arms and necks, pustules on their grinning dark faces. He could almost see the lice and other vermin crawling in their unkempt hair, the heads of wildmen, savages more suited to the jungle than fit for civilized sight. He was tempted to say the word that would erase them all from his line of vision. There was something so unsavory, so ugly, so singularly noxious about those lecherous sneering lips . . .

"Rehill, who are those scum?"

"Don't know, sir. This neighborhood rather attracts suspect types."

"Did you see that one spit?" Briggs asked, pointing with outstretched arm, color flooding his cheeks. It was a sign of contempt, for any native to expectorate within the sight of a sahib.

"Arrest him," Rex ordered.

The column came almost instantly to a halt. Tommy jumped out of the car and called up a jamadar major of Gurkhas, who rushed on the double from behind them, saluting smartly. But he seemed too stupid to understand which of the young rabble was the one to be arrested.

"Arrest them all," Rex shouted, feeling foolish sitting there while they sniggered and scowled, insolently fingering themselves under the dirty rags that barely covered their loins. The buggers! He could see what they were thinking about him, what they thought of all Whites.

The jamadar major called several men from his squadron. The rebels' faces changed quickly as they saw the tough little Nepalese run toward them with rifles clutched across their barrel chests, surrounding the group of ten or twelve badmashes, bringing them back to the column.

"But what have we done? With what crime are we charged?"

"Handcuff them to vehicle two," Rex ordered. Tommy had seen to it that irons and chain were loaded with munition belts in the armored vehicles. He had some of the Londoners bring down the hardware, helping the Gurkhas do their job swiftly.

"What is it we have done?" the ringleader cried more frantically, trying to break away. One of the guards rammed the butt of his rifle into the prisoner's lower back, bringing him simpering to his knees. He sounded less insolent now.

"Think we're impotent, do they?" Rex muttered, as Tommy returned to his side.

"You won't let them think so much longer, will you, General?" Briggs had a fine pink-cheeked face, not a pimple, not a scar or blemish on that soldier's skin. The neatly trimmed sideburns under his perfectly square visor cap were golden, his eyes Mediterranean blue. His lips were roseate, and smiled just ever so slightly, only enough so that Rex could recognize it, for Tommy was no exhibitionist. "I shouldn't think they'll be insolent much longer, now that you're here, sir."

"Slow march, Tommy. I want to see more of these heroes, who've been waging war against our King-Emperor. Perhaps they think the old lion is tired of war, eh?"

A larger group of rabble had collected at Sultanwind itself, some of the idlers attracted no doubt by the sight of so many soldiers, others by the shouts and cries of the prisoners. By the time they reached the high stone archway he estimated there were several hundreds standing at either side of it, boys climbing onto the old wall, clinging like monkeys to cracks and jutting bricks, gaping at him, leering, even daring to shout:

"Victory to the Hindu-Muslim Unity! Victory to Gandhi! Victory to Kitchlew! Victory to Satyapal!"

Once again he brought the column to a halt.

It became quite clear to him now that the entire city was infected. Had there been any semblance of loyalty left among these natives, any vestige of respect for the Raj, seeing him today, so soon after the murder of British subjects and the pillage and plunder of British property, they would have gone down on their knees and salaamed in proper style, bowing and begging forgiveness for their sins, praying to him as they prayed to their false gods, their craven images and idols of devilish destruction. Shame, if not decency, should have prompted them to hide their faces from his sight, had they merited his mercy. Or if they dared greet him, the one cry that could have justified so arrogant a posture as standing erect would have been "God Save the King!"

Instead they continued to bleat rebel slogans, goading him with their eyes and gestures, their derisive smiles. The seditious brutes were obviously animals of the lowest breed. He would have ordered the Sussex to open fire there and then, but for the dangerous closeness of quarters. The mob was barely five yards from his troop column, and with the wall behind most of them some bullets would surely have ricocheted, doing almost as much damage to his own men as they did to the enemy. It was an absurdly awkward position, precisely the sort he'd hoped to avoid by coming round the circuit road. Now that he was actually at the Gate he found he couldn't take the firm action called for without risking more loss of White blood, which was the one risk he would not take. Exasperatingly enough, there was really nothing he could do from a military point of view, primarily because he was overarmed. He should have sent the Sussex home as ordered!

"Have the Gurkhas arrest those blackguards, Briggs — as many as you've irons for! We've got to move on toward the Kotwali!" Half the column had stretched inside the Gate, and the enemy kept running in closer, teasing the soldiers, taunting them with seditious slogans. He felt boxed in, especially inside the car, and the air was foul here, pungent with odors of excrement and dead bodies from the nearby burial grounds.

The bazaar temperature seemed at least ten degrees higher than that of the air beyond its constricting walls. Wending its way up the Lakar Mandi toward Queen Bazaar, the column moved at a sluggish pace, and every other moment he glimpsed a pair of eyes staring down at them from half-closed shutters. He almost expected a bomb to be hurled from one of those ugly walls, and mused at how ironic it would be if he of all people were caught by a native rodent, after half a century of never finding his match on battlefield or in a boxing ring or polo ground — he'd lost count of the golden cups that lined his breakfront at headquarters. What a joke that would be, if the pygmies picked him off, a sitting duck in their own bazaar — what a feather for some cowardly native's cap!

More worrisome to Rex than his personal vulnerability, however, was the tactical problem posed by having to cope with an enemy hidden like an army of mice in a mountain of Swiss cheese. Every battle he'd ever fought had been in open country, mostly along the Afghan-Baluchi border. Even in Burma, in the valleys of the Irrawaddy and Salween, where jungle grew so thick you couldn't see sunlight at noon, the foliage served only as a veil, not as a shield for the cowering enemy. He'd never been faced before with the job of subduing an enemy hidden inside a labyrinth of brick and mortar. The more he saw of this city's dark and narrow interstices, the more implausible his position appeared to the General, from the purely military vantage point. His primary concern this morning was that he had too few soldiers, but perversely enough he saw now that he had too many. The column he'd brought was as cumbersome and unwieldy as a dinosaur trying to wend its way through a network of slit trenches.

"How much farther is the Kotwali, Rehill?"

"Not more than half a kilometer, sir."

Some of the buildings were three or four stories high and all had balconies from which the rebels could throw whatever missiles they liked. He would not even venture to estimate how long it might take to restore a city this size to its senses, unless, perhaps, the most modern of weapons was used — the airplane. He had never witnessed an air strike, but heard that bombs worked wonders in France. He was not averse to trying new methods. In fact, he began to suspect that a day or two of bombing might do the job, which would otherwise take him months, and could risk the loss of dozens of his soldiers. Trouble with any punitive action that took a good deal of time to execute was that it might stir more rebellion than it subdued. The word would spread among villagers that the sahibs couldn't finish their job of meting out punishment. Rumors of dauntless native resistance would fan all the embers of discontent. If only there were some way of getting them out into the open?

"Did you see those two, sir?" Tommy shouted. "The scum — they laughed and ran down that alley! I'd wager half a crown they were in that murdering mob day before yesterday! These streets reek of sedition, General!"

"They do indeed."

"You should issue a proclamation clearing them, sir. Then if we find anyone outside we'll know he's a bloody rebel and won't have to hesitate about firing!"

"Right," he rep ied. Tommy was always scrupulous about proper procedure. "You draw up something later and give it to Rehill to post." Rex preferred not to clutter his mind with details, when faced with a military problem of the dimension and complexity of this one. He knew these buildings with their brick, stone, and cement walls more than a foot thick — ordinary houses built like fortresses, to keep out the sun primarily. Yet there they stood, solid shields against his fire power, as formidable as anything the Hun could have improvised! Shrewdly they kept their shops closed, block after block, here in the densest part of town, hardly a blackguard to be seen. He was faced with a formidable enemy, worse than he'd anticipated. He sensed what he was up against, but was not one to turn away from the reality of a military position, no matter how tricky it appeared. He had to strike fast and hard, if he was to save the Raj from this rebellion. It would spread like wildfire unless he did something soon. Yet how could he punish an enemy too shrewd to show himself?

"The Kotwali, General," Rehill announced.

Ashraf Khan was waiting to greet him with unctuous salaams.

"Have you arrested all those rebels you listed for me?" Rex snapped

"B-but, General Sahib, I do not have enough of men —"

"Let him take the Gurkhas and an armored vehicle, Tommy! Rehill, you go along. Briggs and I will head back to camp with the Sussex."

He had begun feeling the heat. He had no intention whatever of helping Khan drag a few termites from their cracks. He was impatient to get on with the job he'd been sent down to do. General officers were no more needed to make house arrests than sledgehammers for crushing ants. This was a much bigger show than that. It had to be. And they knew it too, the buggers, which was why they kept out of sight — most of them. Biding their time. Waiting to see what move he would make.

"They're watching me, Tommy, wondering what my next move will be."

"Yes, General, I expect they are, sir."

"Well, I'm just going to let them wait a bit longer." He had to think this one out carefully. He'd never been faced before with an Enemy he couldn't find.

13

RATTO heard the rhythmic tread of marching before Bugga or any of the others did. They were rolling dice in the rear of his hostelry, and though he had been enjoying excellent luck, Ratto stopped shaking the amber cubes to ask, "What is that sound?"

"I don't hear any sound, but your dice," Bugga snapped, his temper as short as his diminished supply of rupees.

"Be quiet!" Ratto rose, and touched the naked arm of the young man who was standing closest to his chair. "Go see what that is. Hurry!"

The young athlete ran off, but hardly had he dashed outside than he was back again, shouting, "Police! Soldiers! Coming this way!"

Bugga almost knocked over the table as he jumped up, his belly lifting the edge under which it rested. The last of his rupees rolled across the restaurant floor, but he did not even bother to look after them. "What should we do, Ratto?"

By now the noise was like a drum beating ever louder. Ratto started up the stairs to his private apartment.

"Lock the doors," he ordered, and several of Bugga's boys rushed to secure the hostelry.

"What will we do with our bolts of silk, Ratto?" Bugga asked, dogging his steps, reminding him of the cloth they had stolen from the bank godowns and stored in one of the hostel's bedrooms.

"I told you to hide them someplace far away from here, idiot," Ratto replied, feeling much the same about his incubus partner as Bugga did about the incriminating bolts.

"Why do you call me names? Whose idea was it to loot the banks?"

"Be quiet, fool! Or do you want them all to hear you? Why don't you go to the window and shout?" That seemed to chasten him, at least for the moment. Bugga tugged moronically at his distended earlobe and looked more ashamed than terrified. "Now come in here, and listen to me," Ratto ordered.

Ratto locked the door of his private quarters behind them and, while Bugga sat on the edge of a hassock, hands clasped between his legs like a schoolboy punished for misbehavior, he removed the icon of Shiva from the wall niche that covered his safe. Deftly he spun the combination lock with his one hand, jerking open the fireproof door and taking out a small silver box. He shut the safe himself, and told Bugga to replace the Nataraja. Carefully he carried the box to his desk and opened it, peering at the diamonds on their satin cushion inside. There were five stones in all, the smallest fifteen carats, the largest twenty-five. Each was flawless. They were his stocks and bonds, his savings account, his accumulated treasure. Till today he had never been obliged to bring them to his aid. Ordinarily, a few rupees sufficed to placate his friends in the police force. Ashraf Khan required a steady supply of opium as well, but what was that, after all, compared to these gems? He kept these as security for his life itself, and much as he hated to part with even one of them, Ratto feared that today might cost him two. If he wished also to barter for Bugga's life, at least, and how else could he assure his own safety, but by paying as well for the portly fool, who shared his enterprise?

"Ratto, why don't you tell me what to do? What should I say?"

"Nothing. I will speak. Play what you are, Bugga!"

"What do you mean?"

"Never mind. Remove the Nataraja again, I must put these back in the safe." He pocketed the two smallest diamonds. Each was worth more than the lifetime salary of an Indian inspector of police. A life for a life, he thought. He could hear heavy hammering at the downstairs door.

There was really no way of avoiding them, he decided, going to the top of the stairs, and signaling a Club member to let them in.

Ashraf Khan entered first, followed by a line of soldiers, who kept their rifles at the ready. Then Rehill stepped inside, bracing his riding crop under one armpit, looking cool in his neatly starched short-sleeved shirt.

"Arrest them all," he ordered, speaking only to Ashraf, who shouted the order in Nepali to the Gurkhas.

Ratto felt his·amputated arm sending needles of pain, shock warnings, to his brain, which was somehow·so numbed by the sight of this Englishman and these strange soldiers in his hostel that he had not been able to move or speak. He had expected the familiar faces of Ashraf's slothful squad of simpletons. But now Ashraf himself was on his way up the stairs, fuming and fussing from the exertion of moving his bulky body so energetically.

"You are under arrest, Ratto. You too, Bugga. Come along with me."

"What are you saying, Khan? I must talk with you in private!"

"Move along! Come, come, let us see if anyone is hiding inside that room!" Ashraf shouted, pointing to Ratto's quarters, which he knew almost as well as the inside of his own home. "Hurry up, both of you! Get inside there!" He shut the door himself, and leaned his full weight against it, sadly shaking his heavy-jowled head.

"I am sorry, Ratto," Ashraf sighed. "I must arrest you today."

"Do not speak like an idiot, Khan. I have something for you —"

"No, no, it is not a matter of gifts today!"

"Wait! You have not seen what this is," he said, removing one of the diamonds from his vest pocket, holding it delicately balanced between thumb and forefinger, moving it so that beams of blue and silver light shot into Ashraf's ever widening eyes.

"Do you know what this is, Khan?"

"Yes, I know it, Ratto." His face trembled with temptation, moisture oozing from the fatty pores of his neck. He licked his lips, staring at the many faceted luminous lure. But very old and wise fish that he was, he did not bite.

"There is no price today, Ratto. It is not possible this time. Sahibs have been killed, and the General will not bargain . . ." His voice trailed off in helpless muttering as he shrugged, shaking his head like a toy doll.

"I have two of these!" He brought out the second diamond.

"Ratto, there is no price!"

"I have a third one — in my safe!" His amputated stump began to quiver uncontrollably. He refused to believe that Ashraf Khan meant what he kept so blandly repeating. He could not accept the fact that this man, without whose aid and continuing collusion he could never have built his small empire of illicit business, this virtual partner to all his shady deals, whose capacity for dishonest manipulation of the law exceeded that of the most ingenious of barristers, actually meant that no price was high enough! He thought it was Ashraf Khan's shrewdness at bargaining.

"All right, Khan — how much do you want? Name the figure! What is it this time? How much? I see you are determined to rob me of all I possess!"

"No, Ratto," he replied, all but crying, not for the plight of his friend, but from the realization that the king's ransom being offered was beyond his reach. He could speak no more, but merely shook his heavy perspiring head, as he opened the door. "You must come with me now," he said. "Both of you. You are under arrest!"

The Gurkhas stood waiting outside, their faces as expressionless as oxen. The blades of their naked bayonets, fixed to the black barrels of their rifles, did not glow like Ratto's diamonds: theirs was the dull oily glint of sharpened steel, an ugly, imperative light.

Ratto and Bugga went quietly.

Ashraf Khan had showed no favoritism in compiling his list. He was a man with many friends, but today he lost most of them as he drove round about the old city, with his entourage of crack troops. He had not slept since the General's visit last night. His greatest strength as a police inspector was Ashraf's knowledge of Amritsar's population. He rarely forgot a name. He never forgot a scandalous bit of gossip. He kept diaries and ledgers. He had lists, which no one had ever seen. Last night he brought all of them out of hiding, and from these various sources he compiled his Doomsday roll. It was a veritable social register of Amritsar's underworld. Not everyone Ashraf Khan visited now was waiting at home

for him to call, but at only one house did he ask Mr. Rehill to permit him to enter alone.

"All right," Rehill said, after hesitating a moment.
"I'll wait down here with the men."

"Thank you, sir. I will not be longer than a few minutes."

It was one of the poorer houses along Bazaar Burj
Meva Singh on the eastern side of Jallianwala Bagh. The
corridor was mercifully dim, the air heavy with Sandalwood incense and pungent fumes of cheap perfume. He
passed quickly through the curtain of glass bead strings,
stirring the musty air of the shabby sitting room to the dis-
cordant tinkling of a fragile tune.

"Oh, who is it please?" the thin voice that seemed always to hover on the brink of hysteria called anxiously
from the bedroom. "Who is there? Please sit down! I'm
indisposed, but I won't be very long!"

"Come now!" he replied. "And get rid of him — whoever it is! *Now!*"

He could hear the familiar whispering, the hasty shuf-
fling of limbs donning cloth, the desperate effort on her
part to keep her client from protesting too loudly at being dismissed in this frustrating, embarrassing manner.
It no longer tortured him really, certainly not as it used
to. Thirty years ago, when it first happened, he nearly
killed the man. He would have killed her as well, but her
screaming attracted others, and since then — his blood
had become cooler. Ashraf lit a cigarette, deciding that
if after three puffs she did not appear, he would kick open
the bedroom door.

On the second puff's exhalation she emerged, draped
in a sheer silk chemise, her hair flowing loose to her ample
hips, her eyes glowing green as a cat's. The wrinkles of
time hardly peered through the thick layers of paint she
used. Only in her neck did the years show themselves un-

disguised, for she always wore a foreign garment that gave her bosoms the curve and firmness of eternal youth.

"I wasn't expecting you, darling," she whispered. "Forgive me."

"Go to hell, damn bitch," he shouted. "I did not come for you. Where is Hansraj?"

"Why? What do you want of my boy? What has he done?"

"Never mind your questions. I am the one who will ask the questions — damn whore!"

"Ashraf, why must you be so cruel to me with words? Come, my darling, let me feel your hatred in my body. Let me taste you —"

"Do not touch me! I warn you — I must leave in half a moment! A whole regiment is waiting outside for me, with Mr. Rehill!"

She seemed so genuinely saddened by that news, that he could not help but wonder if perhaps it was true what she had told him these many years, that there was no other man in Amritsar half so manly as himself, and if only he spent less time being jealous, and more making love to her . . .

"Stop that!" he shouted, holding her by both shoulders at arm's length. "Has he been here today, that son of yours?"

"No, I swear not! I did not see him yesterday all day or today either, but tell me what it is, Ashraf, I beg you — if anything terrible happens to that boy I will kill myself. You know I mean that, Ashraf."

He suspected that for once she was telling the truth. He had long admired her fidelity to the bastard, on whom she lavished more care and devotion than his own mother had ever expended upon him. Hansraj was her only offspring.

"Protect him, Ashraf, I beg it of you. I will be your

slave for life — for all eternity. I will wash your feet with milk, Ashraf, night and day. Save him for me."

"I should have killed you thirty years ago, damned bitch of a whore," he muttered, hating his weakness, despising the sickness inside himself, which left him so vulnerable to her. For did he not know, as surely as the sun would set this evening, that soon after he left, another man would appear in this room. For one rupee he would take her body in his arms and keep her captive one hour, perhaps longer. He knew that. No prison cell was secure enough to preserve this slight body even in partial purity, to keep it chastely waiting for him alone — no lock was devised that could insure that. He hated her with a passion that all but destroyed his life, and often robbed him of sanity.

"You will save him, Ashraf? For me?"

"Listen carefully, whore, but repeat one word of what I say to you now as coming from my mouth and not only do you die, but that bastard —"

"I swear it," she interrupted, still sensitive to the mere sound of that word.

"There is only one way for Hansraj to save his life," he explained, whispering as he pointed out that the evidence he received was extensive, all of it implicating her son in the worst of the rioting on Thursday. "This time I cannot protect him — sahibs have been murdered. Only he can save himself."

"How, Ashraf? Whatever it is — he will do it. I swear to you, I will make him do it!"

"He must go to Mr. Irving and confess his crimes and offer to give testimony about others involved — as a Government approver."

"A turncoat, you mean? An informer? Hansraj?" She backed off.

"Call it what names you like! I have no more time to

waste with you, bitch!" He turned abruptly and started to leave.

"No, wait — please do not be angry! Of course, he will do it, if there is no other way! I will see to that, Ashraf, please, look at me, and tell me just how he is to approach Mr. Irving?"

"I will send the Commissioner his name. In such cases as this, it is always necessary for Government to have one approver to satisfy the laws of evidence, and this time we did not have anyone prepared. I will say that Hansraj came to me and agreed to give evidence. His life will be spared if he cooperates fully — "

"He will!"

"Well then, that is all," he muttered, turning abruptly.

"Ashraf!" She ran to him, clinging with both arms to his neck, showering kisses upon his perspiring face, then falling to his feet, embracing his legs, coiled like a snake round his legs. "Ashraf, you are my salvation, my lord and master for all eternity, my love."

"Let go of me, whore." He kicked her aside, all but stepping on her prostrate body as he left the room and hurried down the dark stairs, wondering what madness it was in him that made him risk his life, his job, his pension, and his good name, all for this prostitute and her bastard son, when he would not so much as consider doing the same for a king's ransom?

You are a mad crazy fool, Ashraf Khan, he told himself, stepping out again into the full blast of the sun's oven.

14

ON the other side of the city, Hansraj had just risen to address a crowded meeting in the Dhab Katikan.

"Brothers," he shouted, waving his arms, "if we vote to end hartal without one concession from Government, if we surrender today, I say God will curse us forever — and we would deserve to be cursed!"

There were several shouts of "Shame" emanating from those weighty figures seated on the platform behind him, but down on the floor itself most of the cries were hoarse and angry *"Bande Mataram's,"* accompanied by the raising of clenched fists.

"Where is Maulanaji, tell me?" the speaker continued. "Where is Satyapalji? How can people talk to us about ending hartal today and returning to business as usual, while for all any of us knows, our leaders are bleeding to death in some miserable lockup! That is the advice of traitors to the Motherland, not of patriots! That is what I say!" He turned and shook a reproving finger toward the Master Duni, who rose in rage after removing one of his stiff-toed Maharashtrian slippers, which he wielded as a weapon, advancing with it raised to smash against Hansraj's skull.

"Wait, Duni! Control yourself," shouted Maqbool, hurtling between the adversaries before they could come within range of one another, embracing the massive body of the Master Duni with outstretched arms. The Lala did much the same to Hansraj, and several youths jumped onto the platform hurling words of invective at their moderate elders. Actually, those of Maqbool's generation and temperament, pleaders, accountants, schoolteachers and shop keepers, outnumbered the young extremists in the airless hall, but the latter made more noise.

For almost ten minutes the struggle and raucous yelling continued, threatening to end the meeting without further ado, but as swiftly as it flared up, the excitement subsided, with Duni sitting down and putting his slipper back onto his foot after Hansraj whispered that he did not mean anything he said personally about anyone in this room, especially not the "noteworthy Master Duni!" Then he continued to address the audience:

"What I am trying to point out is that if we give up today, tomorrow they will step over us, and then we have lost the initiative!"

"He is right! Victory to Hansraj!"

"How can we surrender when so many of our brothers have been butchered? Are we men or cowards? You have been told that Mr. Irving is angry with you for being 'bad boys' — well, it is time we informed Mr. Irving that we are not *boys*! We are grown-up men and we must behave like grown-ups!"

The younger people cheered. Some of them raised both fists high.

"While we have the initiative we must use it to make our voice heard by the English rulers, who have been ignoring our every wish and demand. Hartal is giving us the solidarity we need to fight such things as Black Acts, but is it only those Acts we feel crushing down our backs? I say No! It is every minute of our lives that they are trying to choke off the air we breathe! That is why we must meet together to speak out how we feel!"

His words were underscored by repeated echoes from the hall, and many eyes glowed with pride as young Indians listened to one of their brothers tell them that their dreams of equality and freedom, their yearnings for dignity and pride, were not only possible of attainment, but surely a human right, which they as men should demand and labor to secure.

"We must rally together tomorrow and resolve our demands so that we can speak to Government in one united voice. We must prove to them now, before it is too late, that when they arrest one of us, thousands and thousands will rise up and protest such cruel and arbitrary punishments! Otherwise, where is the end of it? Yesterday it is Maulanaji who goes! Today you and me are taken off. Tomorrow the Pleader Maqbool perhaps, and then someday soon, believe me, it is no exaggeration what I predict, even the Master Duni will be carried away!"

This time a roar, half of laughter, half cheering, rolled over the hall, and Hansraj continued in a newly acquired tone of self-confidence and authority.

"Let us meet tomorrow afternoon in the Jallianwala Bagh," he announced. "Lala Kanhya Lal himself will preside over our deliberations —"

"But is not the Lala Kanhya Lal too old for public meetings?" Maqbool asked, turning in astonishment to Todar Mal, who shrugged his uncertainty concerning the current condition of Amritsar's senior barrister, the aged doyen of the local bar.

"— and we will be able to vote then on whether or not

to end our hartal next week, and what next steps should be taken in our protest movement!"

"What hour will the meeting begin?" someone shouted.

"Four o'clock," Hansraj replied, deciding it would be best not to start any earlier, since Lala Kanhya Lal was much too old to risk coming out during the heat of midday. He had not spoken to the Lala as yet about tomorrow's meeting, the idea for which had sprung into his mind as he heard himself being cheered a few moments ago. But Hansraj had no doubt whatever that the Lala would agree to preside when he told him why the meeting was being called, and he firmly intended to go directly to old Kanhya Lal's house as soon as this meeting was over. Unfortunately, Hansraj often equated thought with action, and having convinced himself and so many others that Lal Kanhya Lal agreed to preside at the Jallianwala Bagh meeting tomorrow afternoon, he did not worry much over annoying details, such as actually going to the Lala and inviting him to preside. Partially, it was his Hindu faith in the primacy of philosophical idealism over a maya-world of phenomenological illusion, which lulled him into a state of calm confidence (it would be less than fair to label it indifference) about the Lala's reaction to his proposal. Equally important, however, in causing Hansraj to delay his mission of personally visiting Kanhya Lal was his desire to continue to enjoy riding the crest of what had now become a flood tide of popularity and adulation. For by merely linking himself to the name of Lala Kanhya Lal he had, ingeniously enough, united the hitherto faction-torn audience of young and middle-aged men, joining moderates with extremists in the warmest outburst of genuinely national enthusiasm that occurred in Amritsar since the news of Kitchlew's arrest spread two days before. Secretly, perhaps he suspected that Kanhya Lal, whom he had met only twice and

then in the company of Maulanaji, would be less than
elated by the invitation to chair tomorrow's meeting. In
order to protect himself from the blow of rejection, Hansraj at once insisted within his own mind that the Lala did
accept his offer and simply found ways of postponing his
visit to the old man's house.

"How have you done it, Hansraj?" one admirer asked,
patting his back warmly. "In the. last six months I have
tried a dozen times to win over Kanhya Lal to chair one of
my association's meetings, but he has never agreed!"

"Hansraj has more appeal than you, Misra!"

"With the Lala Kanhya Lal presiding we shall achieve
a great deal tomorrow," Dholan Das predicted, pedantically
tickling off the reasons on his frail fingers. "First of all, he
is a man thoroughly familiar with parliamentary procedure,
and so we may be quite confident that everything will be run
according to Roberts' rules. No disruptions or disorderliness,
you see, and secondly —"

Hansraj moved away from that group and was immediately drawn into another circle, where he again became
the center of attention and adulation. Men who two days
ago would have lifted their canes and threatened to thrash
him had he come so close, now smiled and bowed their
salutations. He ' almost laughed in their faces, feeling
nothing higher than contempt for any of them, but in
his newfound role of Leader he sensed that levity would
have been misdirected, so he maintained a solemn facade,
gravely nodding his head as though he were listening and
agreeing to vapid, banal expressions of opinion about
what should be done next to "bolster our position" or
"rectify the wrongs which have been foisted upon us,
not with malice but from inadvertence to our just griev-
ances." He felt as though he walked among them in a
dream, or as if he were surrounded by a glass bell that
kept all of them at a distance and made their voices echo

faintly in his ears, like the distant rumbling of a train when you put your ear to the glistening steel of the rail. He used to spend many hours hovering near the tracks, waiting for an appropriate opportunity to do that.

Suddenly he felt exhausted. He left the meeting hall, followed by his two shadows. Both young men had raced after Mrs. Easdon with him, and all three joined in the attack upon Miss Sherwood. It united them inseparably, the bond of complicity, of shared terror and guilt. Each was in the ultimate sense his brother's keeper, and all stayed together since their crime, never speaking about it, but like clandestine lovers always aware of one another.

"I must take some rest now," Hansraj told them. He had not slept in two days, and felt light-headed, though his limbs were heavy, aching, as if he ran a high fever. "I will go to my mother's house. You should try to rest also."

"We will come with you," the taller of the two replied.

"No, it is not — I cannot bring people there," he snapped. "What is wrong with you two — have you no family or friends to visit? I will see you tomorrow afternoon in the Jallianwala Bagh."

With that he left them standing like stray dogs on the street, rushing away by himself toward the only home he had ever known.

"Who is it please? Who is there? Just one moment," she called, coming through the bedroom door curtain as he was about to enter. "Oh, it's you at last! You bad boy, where have you been? Forgetting all about your poor old mother! You should be ashamed." She caressed the back of his head with her smooth fingers, sending chills down his spine.

"Stop that! I have told you I don't like it when you do that!" He jerked away from her, out of reach of those serpentine bangled arms.

"Why are you yelling at me? What trouble have you gotten yourself into now?"

"What makes you ask that?"

"Oh, it is a mother's intuition! Come, come, you bad boy, I will give you something to eat. I have *dosa* prepared —"

"Ah, *dosa* is a good idea."

"You see, a mother still knows something about her boy's appetite. Come, sit down over here, where you will be most comfortable." She busied herself rearranging the satin pillows and cushions, which were kept in the corner nearest the kitchen, for very special guests, who stayed overnight and enjoyed a warm *dosa* with some tea the next morning.

"I have made you halva too," she announced, reporting her every move from the kitchen, chirping to him while she gathered his nourishment, the way she always used to, when he was barely old enough to understand one tenth of the things she told him — her voice from the kitchen had always been the soothing prelude to something sweet and good. . . .

"Yes, and I have a very special treat for you today, just for you, freshly made gur, the sweetest nectar squeezed by your mother's own hands for her darling boy, and I also have. . . ."

But by the time she had finished preparing the elaborate tray of delicacies, Hansraj was fast asleep. She set the food down and carefully eased him back onto the softest pillows, removing his slippers and quickly locking the downstairs door so that no one would come to disturb them. Then she bent to kiss his brow and sat with his head on her lap, gently stroking his fair hair. "My fair-haired baby," she whispered. It was a miracle, a wondrous blessing, to which she had never grown jaded, that someone as dark and ignorant as herself could give birth to so fair and brilliant a child! It was some sign she had felt at his birth of her special powers, magic powers, and now, as he slept, she called upon all of them to help her save him, to persuade him to save himself.

"You must do it, my darling baby," she whispered, softly stroking his hair. "You must tell them whatever they ask for — it is the only way to save you, Hansraj, and you must be saved for your higher Destiny . . ."

15

THE General found several wires waiting for him at Ram Bagh that afternoon. None brought good news. The message from Kasur down the line sounded distressingly familiar.

"Rioters attacked station Kasur at 9.58 date," it read, "telegraph instruments as well as wires broken, station building smashed and burned with all furniture, consumable stores, cash, and ticket books of third-class booking office looted. Two European military passengers of train No. 60 UP badly injured, one of them died while firing on rioters, military force urgently required."

"Shall I dispatch a company of Londoners with the armored train, sir?" Briggs asked.

The General continued drinking cigarette smoke with his tea for fully two minutes before responding, "They're trying to whittle me down."

"We could spare a company of the Londoners, General."

"No, but it's part of the pattern — Kasur to my south, Tarn Taran to my north — don't you see?" There had also been a message noting disturbances at Tarn Taran, the heartland of Sikh recruiting for the military. "The whole bloody Punjab's rising, Tommy, and I'm smack in the middle of it! I've just had to send back those Sussex. I can't spare a company of Londoners for Kasur!"

"I see, sir."

"Well, can I, dammit? Why in hell did you say it that way, Tommy?"

"Sorry, sir, it's just — well, whenever a White Christian has died at the hands of a native mob, I do feel we should send Englishmen to the scene, to restore the balance, General."

"Right. Send a squad with the armored train. Tell them to use the machine guns if they see any rebel mobs there!"

"Yes, sir! Thank you, General!" His smile was bright as the brass of his tunic's buttons.

It bolstered Rex's spirits to see that boy smile, but he would not be lulled into any false sense of security. The Revolt was on, possibly the whole Punjab ablaze by now, perhaps all of India would rise tomorrow. He knew it as surely as he felt the stabbing ache of ruptured blood vessels in his groin. This was War. He would have to act, and act with promptitude. He wished that he had not allowed that pilot to fly back to Lahore without dropping a few bombs. There had to be some way in which he could punish the Enemy — today. Now!

Then he thought of it. The idea flashed into his mind like a cabled message from Above. So simple, yet effective, he wondered why he hadn't thought of it before.

"Briggs!" The orderly outside his door reported that the brigade major had not returned as yet to the staff room, but a messenger was sent to look for him. Rex lit a fresh cigarette from the butt of his last. He thought more clearly when he smoked, and it eased the pain somewhat. He tried pacing the room a bit, but that didn't help at all.

Finally, after what seemed like an hour, but was less than ten minutes, Tommy returned.

"The Londoners are dispatched, General. Did you call, sir?"

"Tommy, we've got to cut off their water and power supplies!"

"Whose water and power, sir?"

"The Enemy, Tommy! Amritsar!"

It did not take long for Briggs to see the tactical wisdom of such a move, for in hardly a second his face lit up, and sagely he shook his head.

"Yes, I see what you mean, sir."

The filtered reservoir water was fed by main to Civil Lines-first, and passed from here on into the city, but there was always a cutoff valve built into the sanitary system. The electric power was even simpler to control. "Yes, that's a brilliant idea, General. Let them feel the pinch!"

"Right! Pass the word to Irving, Tommy. Tell him I want it cut off immediately. He should have had the sense to do it himself — two days ago, the bloody ass."

Briggs was still chortling as he left the room, but hardly seemed gone long enough this time to have reached the Fort and returned, when back he came with Miles Irving dogging his bootsteps.

"I'd like a word with you, General," Miles said, looking as though he'd slept in his clothes, as haggard and disheveled as a native clerk.

"Has Briggs told you my order, Irving?"

"He has — and that's another thing I'd like to talk to you about."

"Oh?" Rex rubbed the stubble of his chin with the back of his right hand. He felt an almost irresistible impulse to smash Irving's smug, stupid face against the wall. There was something positively effeminate about the

175

man, his whole manner was grossly offensive, the way he slouched and his tone of voice, as though he were talking to an inferior rather than the other way round! It was absurdly annoying to Rex, but he resolved not to give Irving the satisfaction of showing that he'd scored so much as one point with his insulting manners. "Go ahead, talk."

"Perhaps you'd rather I spoke to you alone," Miles said, glancing at Tommy.

"I've no secrets from my brigade major."

"Very well. I don't think indiscriminately punitive measures such as cutting off the city's water and power supplies are wise, sir. I shouldn't want natives who remain perfectly loyal to the Raj to suffer equal retribution —"

"There are no loyal natives in that city, Irving! The place reeks of rebellion. The streets are infested with anarchists. We're at War with those people!"

"General, I think I can fully understand how strongly you feel," Miles replied. "Two days ago I felt much the same way in assessing the situation. Even yesterday morning I thought the deputation which came to us asking for permission to bury their dead was arrogant in the extreme —"

"What are you trying to say, Irving?"

"I am saying, sir, and forgive me if I'm prolix about it — what I am trying to do is to think some of these things through in my own mind, and I will admit that I am no longer positively certain about *anything* —"

"I shouldn't brag about that if I were you. I've never been more certain of my Duty, Irving, nor of my faith in God and England and our unconquerable Destiny to endure here in India, to save these wretched savages from their own kind."

"Hear, hear, General!" Briggs said.

"Thank you, Tommy."

"Shall I pour you another cup of tea, sir?"

"Thank you, Tommy."

"General, I've had a dozen reports in the last twenty-four hours, and most of these are from my own people, C.I.D. agents with access to the city, and I must say all of them indicate that the vast majority of the population is as deep in mourning over what happened there on the tenth as we are, and as anxious to restore law and order —"

"I don't believe a word of it!"

"But that's why I've come here, sir, to tell you —"

"My eyes have told me all I need to know, Irving," he shouted, jumping to his feet, smashing his fist into his open palm. "When in God's name have you been inside that city wall last, eh? I was there two hours ago. They won't trick me with those simpering lying reports — I don't trust any of them, Irving. I'm a soldier. When I need to survey the terrain I do it for myself. Ask Briggs here, if you want to know 'what in hell's happening in that filthy arsehole of a city. You tell him, Tommy."

"I agree with every word the General's said, Mr. Irving."

"Yes, of course you do." Miles sounded very tired, and sighing he closed his eyes for a moment, pinching the bridge of his nose, looking much like a weary traveler who'd lost his way. When he started speaking again his voice sounded more distant, as though it came from the far end of a long corridor. It sounded feeble, terribly feeble. "General, what charges do you wish to bring against those young men Captain Briggs deposited at the Fort this morning?"

"He means the rabble we collected at Sultanwind Gate, sir."

"Oh, that lot! They were bloody well sniggering at me!"

"Did they do anything violent —?"

"I just damn well told you what they did! They were insolent, the buggers! They should have been shot! I don't care what you charge them with, Irving, that's your business."

"Thank you, sir. I'm glad you agree that as Deputy Commissioner I still have the responsibility for this district —"

"Now, wait! I don't think I understand what you're driving at, Mr. Irving."

"General, to put it most succinctly, sir, we are *not* at War with Amritsar. No proclamation of martial law has been issued for this district, and though all of us here are most grateful to you for coming to our assistance as promptly as you did —"

"That is impertinent, Mister," Rex interrupted, feeling the blood throbbing against his eyeballs as he spoke. "I was ordered to come down here by G.O.C. Lahore. I command this district's military force and I will defend it against rebel attack, whether you want me to or not, and I don't give one hae'penny hoot in hell for your grudging gratitude."

Miles opened his mouth to respond, but his voice appeared to fail him, or perhaps he had second thoughts about continuing to widen what was fast becoming an unbridgeable gulf between them, for he closed his mouth firmly and stood trembling, face flushed, eyes lowered. Then he spoke again, swiftly, calmly.

"What I came here to say to you, General, was that we really have no room or provisions in the Fort for prisoners, and when you deposit some fifty of them with us as you did a short while ago, and when it appears after interrogation of those prisoners that none of them seem to know why they were taken into custody, and all of them avow their loyalty to the Raj and insist they were not conscious of violating any statute, I should like to request, sir, in future, before arresting anyone for simply being on the streets or outside the city gate, or what-have-you, that you take the elementary prerequisite measure of publicly proclaiming whatever new laws you wish and intend to enforce, so that the population may at least have some idea of what is expected of them, and so that His Majesty's Government may not at some future date be embarrassed with the charge of having disregarded legal procedure entirely in our misguided zeal to preserve law and order. I trust you understand, General, that I am reminding you of this in my official capacity as Deputy Commissioner, charged with the Civil Government of Amritsar District, which to the best of my knowledge remains my official position of responsibility."

"Get him out of here." Rex shook visibly, but held himself in check.

Briggs stepped into position for ejecting Mr. Irving from the room.

"And I do want to thank you, General, for the courtesy you have shown me today," Miles remarked. "It's always gratifying to converse with gentlemen."

With that he bowed slightly and left the room.

"Put a guard on his trail, Tommy. I want a report on everything he does, where he goes, who he sees. I think the Pandys have got to that one! He's a rotten apple, Tommy."

"Yes, sir, agreed sir. I'll have Bates follow him." Briggs rushed out to do as he was bid.

Left to himself, Rex simmered down swiftly. He had never been one to hold a grudge or nurse his temper at white heat. He said what he felt, when he felt it. He played no politics, like some of them did — the C-in-C for one. There was a politician, always saying what the right people wanted to hear, sucking up to the Frocks, telling them how great they were to cut the army's budget till there were barely troops enough left on the Khyber to hold India! Rex knew those maneuvers too well. He'd seen Sir Charles in "action" at the Viceroy's Ball, and at great house receptions back home — the teacup campaigns. He'd never shone on such occasions. He always felt ill-at-ease in the company of low-bodiced ladies, who stood around talking politics and public affairs as though they weren't in the least bit aware of the fact that they were practically naked. He couldn't keep his mind on serious talk when women were heaving their bare breasts at his face — the immorality of civilian society sickened him. He preferred the rough and ready atmosphere of camp life. He liked being with men who were honest and aboveboard about people and things. You knew where you stood with open men like that. None of those smiles to your face and knives for your backside. That wasn't his way. Never had been. Never would be.

He felt perfectly calm by the time Tommy returned. He'd almost fallen asleep, in fact, just sitting bolt upright in the wicker chair. All the unpleasantness of his meeting with Irving was forgotten.

"You certainly gave him a stroke or two, sir," Briggs said, heartily smiling, robustly smashing his fist into his own palm. "He was chastened all right, General. White as a livid sheet, he looked, when I came out after him. Don't expect he's had a lashing like that since his school days, sir. Shook some good sense into him, you did, General. He asked me to tell you that he was ordering the water and power cut off! Expect he's afraid of court-martial for obstructing your orders or whatever the Frocks get for malfeasance of duty. I told Bates to keep an eye on him, as you ordered, sir."

"Good. How's our supply of gin holding, Tommy?"

"Splendid, sir. I'll have a gimlet fixed for you in half a minute." He had set up a small bar in the corner of the room and had everything efficiently at hand. While he worked at opening the bottles, cutting lemon, pouring the mix, Tommy spoke, rather hesitantly. "There was just one thing that Irving said, General, which made a slight bit of sense, and I have been thinking that perhaps it would be wise for us to issue a formal proclamation or two —" He paused, stirring the drink.

"I don't mean to say that we've acted improperly at all, you realize, sir, but with Shylock in Whitehall it might just appear to some long-nosed snoopers as if we hadn't gone by the book —"

"Do it," Rex replied.

"Sir?" He sounded startled, looking incredulous, as though he'd anticipated a drawn out verbal struggle to win his point. He could not quite accept so swift and painless a victory. There was just a bit of the politician in Tommy.

Rex enjoyed watching Briggs go through his mental hoops as he handed over the drink, trying to figure out whether his ears had betrayed him or if, in fact, the General had agreed to issuing proclamations. He liked to keep Tommy guessing at times. It was a useful trick in controlling people that he'd learned from his father, long ago. "Never let the man under you know all you're thinkin', lad, or he'll think he's good enough to be top!"

"You mean you agree that we should issue certain proclamations, General?"

"Of course. Write them up, Tommy. We'll have them read out tomorrow morning. We'll do it up right — drummer and all!"

"Yes, sir! I think that's a very wise decision, General. I'll draft the proclamations at once, sir, for your approval."

"Right." He sipped the drink slowly. It was just dry enough to draw in his cheeks a bit, making him smack his lips. It was perfect. He felt content enough to nap, drowsily lowering his eyelids as he watched Tommy sit smartly at the desk, writing away, putting the words in proper order, making the proclamations sound the way all the books said these particular proclamations were supposed to sound, so that the people who read all the books would nod their heads happily when they read these proclamations, and then the Frocks could sleep soundly in their silk and satin beds, knowing all was well with the world that was ruled the way all their books said it should be ruled.

Only none of their proclamations was worth the paper it was scribbled on. They were useless, such documents. Rex knew that. He knew it in his blood. But he didn't tell Tommy to stop writing. No, he encouraged him to write on, and rewrite, so that everything would be done the way it was supposed to be done, because otherwise the Frocks would shout.

And tomorrow morning, Rex thought, nodding his heavy head somnolently — we'll read all the words out loud. To the beat of a drum.

16

THE drum called them. Its beat summoned them from house and hovel, from rooftop and alleyway. It beat slowly, but did not stop. It beat on, without changing its rhythmic pattern, a tocsin that echoed dull and muted from the hollowed chamber covered with buffalo hide, beat by a shriveled turban-topped skeleton, who sat cross-legged in the bamboo cart, wrapped round his drum, pounding the single note of its imperative message.

In front of the drummer rode Ashraf Khan, seated on his white horse and behind him was Malik Fateh, who held the bundle of printed proclamations, and sat upon a donkey. Malik was a heavy-set jovial man, whose voice was often used for public pronouncements, since it was rich and deep and carried some distance, and its owner had a flair for the dramatic, especially the comic. He was quite popular with children, and this morning many of them came as soon as they heard Malik Fateh's voice, calling back to others, "Come, it must be something funny!"

But the elders were more cautious, for behind the

drummer cart and Malik marched fifty soldiers, all British, and behind these Londoners came two cars, one in which Mr. Irving sat beside Mr. Rehill, the other with the General and his brigade major. Finally, there were fifty more British troops, all mounted.

At Hall Gate the column stopped, but the drum continued, even while Malik Fateh read aloud the words which were printed in Urdu:

"It is hereby proclaimed to all the inhabitants of Amritsar that no person residing in the city is permitted or allowed to leave the city in his own private or hired conveyance or on foot, without a pass . . ."

There were only eight officials, authorized to issue such passes, and solemnly, sonorously, he pronounced each of their names and official titles. The second proclamation announced a curfew after 8:00 P.M., warning prospective violators that "Any persons found in the streets after 8:00 P.M. are liable to be shot." A shudder passed through the assembled crowd, and many eyes turned furtively toward the soldiers, whose guns glistened in the sunlight.

"Proclamation the third," shouted Malik Fateh, licking his thick lips as he held up the ink-stained piece of wrinkled paper to read. "No procession of any kind is permitted to parade the streets in the city or any part of the city or outside of it at any time. Any such processions or any gathering of four men will be looked upon and treated as an unlawful assembly and dispersed by force of arms, if necessary."

This time many people appeared puzzled, and a buzz of questioning began among the listeners, each turning to his neighbor to ask what had been proclaimed, no two hearers repeating quite the same thing. But then Malik Fateh himself reread the three proclamations, and everyone listened in hushed silence, while the drum kept beating, and soon the column of troops marched south round

184

the circular road to the next stopping place, Hathi Gate, and there Malik Fateh read aloud again.

From the Elephant Gate they went on to Lohgarh, gateway of the iron fortress, and there many people gathered, for by now word had spread that the sahibs were marching round the city with proclamations to be read, and young couriers raced hawking the news down dark alleys, and some townsfolk who had not dared to peer at the light for two days, emerged timidly to look and listen to the golden voice of Malik Fateh. Several hundreds assembled, and most stood respectfully silent, trying to hear and understand what news it was that Government was taking this trouble and time to convey to them, for many rumors had seeped with the wind through cracked shutters and doors, but few people had any true idea of what was happening. Last night, those who had water piped to their homes from the Civil Lines, and who could afford electricity, suddenly found themselves without either, and wild rumors circulated of a new outbreak of the plague, which had poisoned reservoirs and threatened all with imminent death. There were also reports of an Uprising in Lahore, and of Government's abdication at Delhi, but no two people said the same things, so many were eager to hear this official word, and stood with heads bowed, intently listening. But several young men were more interested in talking than listening, and a few disliked Malik Fateh's pompous manner as he read the weighty words, and some disliked the words themselves, especially those like "shot" and "dispersed by force of arms, if necessary," which they considered a challenge to their manhood, so they protested:

"It is all sham! They are trying to intimidate us! Don't believe a word of it!"

Ashraf Khan was quick to silence them, moving closer with his horse, and shaking a warning finger at the culprits, but a few took his gestures as part of a game, and broke away, running behind the mostly inert crowd, to reappear elsewhere, shouting again:

"Don't believe it! It is all for show!"

The General remained unmoving in the rear seat of the second car. His forehead blistered with perspiration under the thick visor of his cap, but he did not stir to wipe a single drop away. He barely blinked his eyes, for he wanted to see their faces, all of them, especially those who did the shouting.

"They're laughing at us," Tommy remarked, his voice strained taut as a coiled spring.

Rex did not reply. His jaw was locked too firmly for him to open it, simply to utter some futile sound. Most words were futile, whether in written or spoken form. He listened to the useless words read by Malik Fateh's fine voice, the words Tommy had labored so long to produce last night. He knew these people. These people were cattle. You did not expect cattle to count or tell time. You did not read proclamations to cattle. He almost said that to Tommy, but he felt too tense to talk, and talk was wasted. Wasted effort, wasted words.

On to Dhab Khatikan the drum beat them, to an open space by the well, where people gathered full of curiosity, and the proclamations were proclaimed. To Chauk Bhai Sant Singh they went, where many heads peered down at them from tall buildings, and others listened from narrow passageways between blocks of houses. The heat of midmorning hung heavy. The drum beat on, like distant thunder.

Everywhere they stopped, crowds gathered. People seemed less and less afraid to appear, for unlike yesterday morning, no arrests were made today — because it was Sunday, some said. On Sunday Christians did not make arrests. Even the hecklers were ignored after a while, even by Ashraf Khan, who no longer bothered so much as to wave a fist at them. People said the proclamations meant that the trouble was over, the sahibs wanted to get things back to normal again, that was why they were going to all this bother in the heat of day, and it was a good omen for the future of Amritsar, and soon Dr. Kitchlew and Dr. Satyapal would be returned, and everything would be all right.

But why the curfew then? someone asked.

Well, it was a thing that must be· done after troubles. That was just for a little while.

But why the rule against processions?

No, that was not meant so strictly!

But why the threats?

That was what Government must say — but actually, they did not want trouble to start again, so there was no need to worry.

Everyone appeared more relaxed. The mood of the crowd became almost festive. There was more talking, more calling out from one cluster of listeners to another — for many it was their first glimpse of old friends or relatives in three days — since that fateful morning of April 10th. The familiar figure of Ashraf Khan at the head of the procession, the soothing voice of Malik Fateh, even the monotonous drone of the drum, seemed to mollify the harshness of the proclamations themselves and the unsmiling stiffness of the white soldiers. South to Chauk Chitta Katra they marched amid the tumult of moving masses, and on to Katra Karam Singh's quarter of the city, then north again toward the Golden Temple, stopping at Chauk Nimak Mandi, and the Quilla Bhangian, site of Amritsar's oldest fortress, whose crumbled walls dated back four thousand years it was said, to the very dawn of Indian civilization.

For Rex Sundays had always been special. This was God's day, his mother had taught him. The other six might go to the Devil, but on Sundays His work would be done — on Earth as it was in Heaven. He always went to church on Sundays, whenever possible. He trusted God would understand that if he did not attend religious service today it was only because he had been ordered to serve the Lord in other ways. For thirty-four years now, since he'd passed out of Sandhurst, a gazetted subaltern, Rex considered himself a soldier in double service, to God and Crown. *For whatsoever is born of God overcometh the world.*

"And who is he that overcometh the world, but he that believeth that Jesus is the Son of God?" he added aloud, barely moving his lips as he spoke.

"Amen, sir," said Briggs. "It's remarkable how much of the Bible you've committed to memory, General."

"That's from John," he said.

"I expect your good wife and niece must be in church right now, wouldn't you say, sir?"

"God willing." He too had been thinking of Alice. He tried to imagine how all of this vile scene might look to her innocent eyes, and it sent a shiver of despair through his rugged frame. Poor babe that she was, how terrifying these savage faces, these ugly black bodies, would have appeared to her. He had taken his niece to see Delhi and the Taj with Mary just a fortnight ago, and driving through the old city of the capital, they had been accosted by a mob of young men, one of whom jumped onto the rear bumper of his motor and peered grinning apelike through the window. Luckily, Alice hadn't turned to see that lecherous face with saliva drooling from its red wretched lips, and the bugger dropped out of sight before either lady realized someone had attempted to attack them. The mere memory of it made Rex's brain feel cold.

To Majith Mandi they went, and Chauk Phullanwalla,

paced by the beat of the drum, and everywhere he saw the same faces, the same lewd eyes, the same lips grinning red, the same black fists with their bony knuckles.

"They think we're joking, General," Briggs said. "They think it's all just a *tamasha!*" Poor Tommy, he sounded shocked at the realization that all his words were wasted effort.

"It's rather warm," Rex remarked. "I should think we've done enough of this." Briggs passed the order to return to Ram Bagh. Back through Lohgarh Gate they went, north along the circular road.

His throat felt parched. It was more than mere thirst. The desert dust had infested his soul, and it lingered there inside his body, under the leather of his sun-dried skin, the grains of sand had lined all the tubes of his throat and left their coating on his lung walls as well. There was a dryness deep inside his being that no canteen seemed large enough to quench. The west wind was blowing. It brought the taste of sand dunes from Baluchistan, the barren dry dust of Afghan air reached his nostrils, and pricked his eyeballs with its invisible darts. The weathered wall of the city seemed to undulate as they drove, and everywhere he looked there were grays that burned silver and browns baked to gold, but he couldn't touch any of it. He was too dry, and it was passing too fast behind him. Long past. Long forgotten. Like Baluchi land, and Afghanistan, Pindi and the Khyber. He'd conquered each of them, not once, but many times. He'd set his brand upon the desert. He'd climbed the highest dune, and planted his regimental staff on top of mountains blown to Seistan.

The drum had stopped beating.

Tommy stood outside, waiting at attention, holding the door open for him.

"Very well, Brigade Major," he said, climbing from the motor like a great bear emerging from his lair, stretching to full height in the sunlight. "Dismiss the column, and let's you and me have some tiffin!"

"*General*," Miles Irving shouted, running toward him as he was about to enter his headquarters bungalow. "Excuse me, General, but I've just been told by our intelligence people that a meeting's been called for four this afternoon in Jallianwala Bagh!"

He paused as though expecting some immediate response to his information, but Rex made no effort even to moisten his lips.

"*Today*, sir," Miles continued, looking toward Briggs, whose startled expression indicated at least that he understood the meaning and urgency of this matter. Miles turned to him the way one might turn toward an interpreter in trying to make sense to a foreign speaker. "Inspector Khan also told me just now that he distinctly heard two people announcing this meeting as we marched through the city."

"Let's have our tiffin, Tommy," Rex repeated.

"Shouldn't something be done, General, to warn them —" Miles began.

"They've been warned," he replied.

And with that, he went inside.

17

MAQBOOL heard of the proclamations shortly before noon. His neighbor's son had been visiting a friend in the Chauk Quilla Bhangian when the troops arrived. The boy raced home immediately after the column disappeared, and he and his father rushed in, breathless, to tell Maqbool.

For a while they all expected the column to appear in their own quarter of the city, so they sat anxiously waiting for the beat of the drum to announce its approach. But by one, when the Mission church bell tolled its lonely note, there had as yet been no sight or even distant sound of the proclamation procession, and Maqbool started to wonder about the authenticity of his informant's evidence. His years at the bar taught him to be skeptical of eyewitness reports.

"You say they were marching all round the city, Arjun?" Maqbool asked.

"Yes, yes, all over. They had come from Chitta Katra and — and — everyone saw them. It was a tremendous long column of soldiers, you see, and all sorts of vehicles and horses, and, and — drummers, and Malik Fateh was reading it out — don't you believe me, sir?"

"Why shouldn't I believe you, Arjun?"

"I can tell you why," shouted his father, who had from the first sensed it was a hoax. "Because he is always making up stories, that is one reason! And he is always daydreaming! Is this one of your ideas of a joke, Arjun? To come to your old father and the Pleader Maqbool with crazy stories? I warn you, I'm going to break your head —" The old man carried a cane, which he lifted with outraged swiftness, sending the terrified youth behind Maqbool's back.

"No, no, Maharaj," Maqbool soothed, "do not excite yourself for no reason. Arjun would not deceive us, I am certain of it. He has always been truthful with me. Please sit down now, both of you. Calm yourselves. Tell me exactly Arjun, what was it the proclamations said?"

"I think they said — I think — I —" Arjun kept glancing nervously at his father, and his voice became more and more high-pitched, and he touched his trembling fingers to his mouth. "I — I don't remember."

"I'll kill him!" The father was back on his feet.

"No. Wait, listen to me. Arjun, a little while ago when you came here with your father you said that you heard them proclaiming a curfew at eight P.M. —"

"Yes, that is it!" the boy shouted.

"Good. Now, you also said they proclaimed something about not leaving the city gates without a special pass, is it?"

"Yes, yes, that's right!"

"Good. And who could sign the pass?"

"Who? Yes, they told a list — but I don't remember."

"Idiot! And he wants to be a barrister! I should have given him away!" The father kept shouting, and Arjun

muttered ineffectually in self-defense. Maqbool managed
to calm the old man down.

"Was there anything else proclaimed?"

"I think so."

"There is no rush, Arjun. *Please* try to remember what
else was proclaimed."

"Something about processions — they are prohibited, I
think."

"I see. Well, you have an excellent memory," Maqbool
remarked, deciding to check into this matter himself. He
really wasn't sure of how accurate Arjun's account was, but
felt certain that something had been proclaimed.

The streets in his quarter of the city were all but
deserted as Maqbool left the house. He saw no tongas, and
though when he started walking he went toward the north
instinctively rather than with a fixed destination in mind,
he soon decided it might be best to visit his old mentor,
Lala Kanhya Lal, who lived just outside the Ghi Mandi
Gate. He had thought of his guru many times since Hansraj
announced that Kanhyaji would preside over today's meeting in the Bagh, and was at once amazed and delighted to
hear that the old man had finally come round to joining
the freedom struggle. Not that he truly doubted where the
sympathies of his legal mentor, his father's friend, would
ultimately reside, yet he could still remember how hard
poor Kitchlew had labored to convince him to sign one of
Gandhi's Satyagraha pledges less than a month ago — to
no avail.

He passed several householders, who sat inside the shade
of their doorways, sharing a midday pipe. He asked them
if they had heard news of the proclamations or of a British
column parading through the city. No one had heard a
thing! He began again to wonder about Arjun's report,
but was not kept long in doubt. As he approached the Ghi

Mandi Gate, Maqbool was challenged by two musket-pointing soldiers, each of whom shouted:

"Show your permit!"

"Is this a new regulation?" he asked.

"Have you not heard the proclamations? No one leaves the city without a special permit."

"And where may I apply for such a permit?"

"Do not ask us," the rude soldier replied. "Do you think we have nothing to do but answer your questions? Move away from here!"

There was a tongawalla near the Gate. Maqbool signaled to him, directing the driver to take him to the Kotwali, where he suspected the passes would be issued — for the proper price.

It was no simple matter, he soon found out, to procure the precious chit that would let him pass through the Gate he had freely used all his life. He had to speak to no less than six policemen in four separate rooms, and was kept waiting almost one hour, though he deposited one rupee, in four anna coins, into the greedy hands of those almighty munshis, who led him from desk to desk. The permit he finally procured was valid for one trip outside Ghi Mandi Gate, through which he would have to return before curfew.

Kanhyaji's bungalow was new, a somewhat smaller model of the Deputy Commissioner's mansion, more modest not from lack of resources on the part of its owner, who was reputed to be the wealthiest man in Amritsar as well as doyen of its bar, but in order to allay the envy of those in power. Most British, of course, resented any Indian intrusion into Civil Lines, but very wealthy natives were tolerated as long as they were not ostentatious in displaying their fortunes.

"Ah, Maqbool, so you have not entirely forgotten the address of an old man," the white-haired patriarch proclaimed, coming out of his study to welcome his guest with a wry smile, his Kashmiri shawl drawn tightly around his stooped shoulders. "Come, come, sit down, and tell me what has been happening? I have seen no one from the city in three days!"

"But — what? Have you not spoken with Hansraj?"

"With whom?"

The old man was so obviously unconscious of the very existence of Hansraj that Maqbool was too bewildered to respond.

"What has come over you, Maqbool? You look as though my innocent question was a sentence passed against you. Sit down here beside me, and tell me what is wrong?"

"I'm not sure I know, Kanhyaji," he muttered, suddenly feeling more anxious than he had since Kitchlew disappeared behind the door leading to Mr. Irving's office. He felt that singularly uneasy sense of anxiety, it was almost panic, generated by the realization that something totally irrational has occurred. For why would Hansraj publicly lie about something so easy to discover?

"You have not agreed to preside over a meeting in Jallianwala Bagh this afternoon?"

"What meeting? Maqbool, I must insist that you stop this line of interrogation, and tell me simply and directly what you are talking about. I have heard no news from the city in three days, I repeat. Now, please stop teasing me with meaningless questions!"

"I'm sorry. It's just — well, yesterday afternoon Hansraj announced that you would preside over today's meeting, and I think —"

"What? Was that said in a public place?"

"Yes, yes, in the Dhab Khatikan."

"The cheek! That mendacious scoundrel! He's the prostitute's bastard, isn't he? Yes, now I remember the one. Oh, he'll have to answer to *me* for this!" The old man became so outraged that he started coughing uncontrollably, and his housekeeper rushed in with two other servants, all standing helplessly about, till Maqbool ordered someone to bring water, which finally cleared Kanhyaji's throat.

"Forgive me, Kanhyaji. I've caused you nothing but trouble today."

"Never mind that. What is he up to, the scallywag? And why has that wretched drum been beating so long this morning?"

"So you heard it too? There were proclamations — a curfew, and passes — here is what I had to get before I could visit you —"

"What nonsense! Has the Raj grown so weak that it must lock city gates? Which officious fool ordered these things? Surely not Irving. I thought he had more sense than to resort to medieval methods for keeping the peace."

"The report I heard was that Mr. Irving was there, but as you must know, the General has taken control of things, it appears, and he has sent so many troops down . . ." Maqbool's voice trailed off as he hung his head, shaking in a gesture of despair.

"I don't know the General," Kanhyaji replied, and now he too sounded sad, which was hardly his normal mood, for despite the burden of some eighty years he was known for ebullient spirits, and could always be relied upon to address the annual Chamber of Commerce dinner in optimistic as well as humorous terms. "I've never mixed much with the military, Maqbool. They always talk about our caste system, but there's no Indian caste as ironclad as the British officer corps. I've never met a Brahman who wouldn't accept my hospitality, and I've yet to meet a British general who would."

It was the first time Kanhya Lal ever said a word to Maqbool about the social indignities he sustained. Sharing so intimate a confession of this proud patriarch's made him feel less upset. At last after two decades of distant adulation he was welcomed into the inner sanctum of Kanhyaji's mind. They continued talking not as guru and disciple, but as friends, as colleagues at the bar, as brother Indians. Maqbool reported everything, from the arrest of Kitchlew to yesterday's meeting. He told of the shooting and looting, of the violence and mourning, the madness followed by contrite suffering, the torment, the hatred. He told of the foolish acts he had witnessed, the cowardice and the courage of ordinary people, the passionate lust of young men, the patriotic ardor of others. He spoke softly, without declamatory gestures, yet with that intensity of feeling born of reliving the scenes emblazoned on his memory.

When he finished, the old man sat for several moments in troubled silence, then shook his head, whispering, "What is to come of it?"

"Perhaps now it will end. People are fed up with so much of trouble all these days, and if Government will only have the generous good sense of returning Kitchlew and Satyapal to us —"

"Oh, my dear Maqbool, my dear child," Kanhyaji remarked, shaking his head. "The Government of India is like the largest conceivable ocean liner, Maqbool, like a dreadnought, only more so. It does not turn instantly and reverse its course. No, that will not occur. Perhaps someday when things settle down and life is back to normal, we shall be able to institute, through proper channels, inquiries as to the whereabouts of our interned friends. Yes, that is quite proper to do, and I shall see to it myself when I have occasion next to speak with the Commissioner on matters of business. Yes, yes, that is quite proper."

"I'm sure you are right," Maqbool conceded. "I expect there is really nothing we can do but stop the hartal, and try in the days ahead to restore normal conditions, and then appeal to Government —"

"Exactly! This is the only course open to us now. And though I am not given to attempting to justify my past positions, you may recall, Maqbool, that some short time ago, in this very room, we sat together with Kitchlew and talked of the merits or otherwise connected with Gandhi's noncooperation movement and the pledge he wanted me to take —"

"Yes, I remember it."

"Do you remember then how I argued?"

"I think so. You — you took the position that refusing to obey the law would only lead to arrests and violence, and —"

"Exactly what has happened!"

He appeared to take too much satisfaction in having been able to say that, too much for Maqbool to tolerate seated comfortably in so finely furnished a room. It was not that he doubted the wisdom of Kanhyaji. He simply felt uneasy now in his company, uncomfortable, almost as though he were by his presence here somehow betraying Kitchlew. Politely he rose to take his leave.

"I know, I know more than you think, Maqbool. I understand your impatience, and Kitchlew's and Gandhi's."

"Kanhyaji, no one knows the law better than you, but tell me, is there no law higher than Government's penal code?"

"Laws are subject to change by legal means, Maqbool."

"And if the legal means prove unavailing?"

"Governments too are subject to change."

"But if the Government is foreign and autocratic?"

"Your head has been turned, I see, Maqbool. There is no rational way of explaining something to a person whose head has been turned by infatuating slogans."

The old man wrapped his shawl more tightly across his torso as he clenched both fists, keeping his white-haired head lowered, looking almost as though asleep. It was his posture of farewell, and though Maqbool stood for a while hoping that some magic formula of speech would occur to him, some golden phrase to convince Lala Kanhya Lal of the virtue, if not the wisdom, of the path he had chosen, nothing but a halting, silly-sounding, ineffectually weak, "I'm sorry," emerged from his lips.

It was almost 4:00 P.M. when Maqbool left that house, hearing from the not too distant cantonment of Ram Bagh a shrill cry of bugles, and the muffled clatter of rushing feet.

18

SUNDAR DAS and Mohan had left their village long before dawn. It was almost thirty kilometers to Amritsar, but the sturdy peasant and his young son were used to walking. They walked nearly as far each day, behind the plow or goading the bullock to raise water enough for irrigating their fields from the deep well. And today was so special a treat that they had covered the distance to Sultanwind Gate before stopping to eat their noonday meal. It was, after all, the Baisakhi Day, the Hindu New Year's Festival and cattle fair in Amritsar, and as though that were not wondrous enough, it also happened to be Mohan's birthday, his tenth. During the War years there had been no fair, and before that Mohan was too young to remember being brought to Amritsar. All year long he had been waiting for this day, and each morning he and his father had talked of it, planning it, their first long trip together, just the two of them, the two men in the family, for Sundar Das had three daughters, but Mohan was his only son.

"Dada, why is the wall so high?" Mohan asked as they came within sight of the city.

"That is to keep out strangers."

"But why do they make a gate, Dada?"

"To let us get inside," Sundar Das replied. "Now do not ask so many questions. Let us look around and observe what we see."

They entered with the continuous stream of villagers, some of whom came with their cattle to display at the fair; shortly before the proclamations had closed the gates to random traffic, they walked into the city, carrying their day's provision of rice and chappatis, which Mohan's mother had wrapped securely for them, armed with curds and ghee as well. Once inside they stopped at the nearest public square to squat in the shade of a pipal tree and take their food.

"Which is your village, friend?" a nearby peasant asked. He too had come with his boy.

"Ramgaon," Sundar Das replied. "And yours?"

"Haripur! Ah, my wife's family is from Ramgaon. What is your family name, tell me?"

"Das — and yours?"

Soon they established that they were not only of the same peasant caste, but that Sundar Das's cousin-brother was married to Raj's cousin-sister twice removed, and so they joined one another for lunch, sharing their food as well as exchanging the facts of peasant life, the size and price of last season's crop, the condition of this season's harvest, in their respective villages. The boys finished eating and ran off to explore the square and the neighboring alleyways of the bazaar, while Sundar and Raj shared a pipe. It was a happy start to their festive day in Amritsar.

"Where will the cattle be displayed?" Sundar asked.

"I have heard some young people talk of the fair being in Jallianwala Bagh," Raj replied.

"Oh, yes, I know where that is. Yes, it is a big enough place. Not too far from the Golden Temple, you see."

"Is it? So you will lead us there, friend. I am not very familiar with this place, but I see you know it from top to bottom."

"Not so complete as that, but, don't worry, we will find our way. There is time for us to smoke another pipe, I think, before we go — what do you say?"

"Why not? It is a holiday, after all. We should not rush ourselves."

Another hour they lingered, enjoying the shade, the smoke, the comfort of each other's company, waiting with bucolic wisdom and patience while the sun spent its fury on midday, before venturing to move on in search of the cattle fair they had come to see. Others paused to ask directions of them, and with the assurance of someone flattered by any inquiry, Sundar explained that the fair was in the Jallianwala Bagh, and pointed in that general direction. Then at last he called to Mohan, and the boys returned promptly from their play. Soon after they all headed off toward the Bagh.

It was past three before they found the lane at the end of Lakar Mandi Bazaar, where the passage narrowed through an iron gate and opened unexpectedly onto the acres of unused space in the center of the city. The Bagh had already attracted several thousand people, and Sundar was so excited to see the varied costumes displayed by the crowd that he did not even notice the paucity of cattle. Surely this was the fairground. Peasants and townies mixed almost in equal proportion strolled about, talking animatedly, listening to speakers, some of whom shouted and waved their arms. It was a first-class *tamasha*! Many young boys were there, racing round the stone well, hiding and seeking each other among the fig trees. Mohan and Raj's boy rushed off to join the play.

"When will the show start?" Sundar Das inquired of a young man, who appeared slick enough to be a towny.

"Four o'clock. Very soon now."

Sundar thanked him, and they strolled over to the large group that had gathered round the platform near the trees. He assumed that the best cattle in each category would be brought onto the stage for judging, and then prizes would be awarded, where most people could see what was happening.

Hansraj mounted the platform and stared out at the growing crowd. People kept pouring into the Bagh through its only real entranceway in a steady stream, like sand flowing to the bottom of an hourglass, dispersing in random symmetry after they entered the ample field. Many moved toward the platform, which had the largest cluster of turbaned heads poised about it. Others gathered round the samadh, an ancient graystone tomb at the distant side, and groups of picknickers squatted under the few isolated trees, taking refreshment. It gave Hansraj a peculiar feeling of power, seeing so many of them here, knowing they had come at his bidding, that they stood now like sheep waiting for him to speak, to initiate the program: that without him — but for him — none of this would be! He felt almost giddy at the realization of how mighty he'd become, how potent.

Then the dark memory of last night intruded to rob him of his sense of exaltation, and he felt as though his bones were spun of cotton thread. He felt puny, infantile, all because of her. How he hated her, her hair soaked in oil, that larvae of poisonous snakes, gleaming raven-like, lustrous coils of chain that bound him to her from birth. Her breasts, flat and shriveled as dry chappatis, how she rubbed them, how desperately she massaged them against his vital youth, turning his very organs of virility into sagging sacks of death, the way she sapped his independence of mind, seeking always to direct his thought, his action, his entire being. Seeking to "save" him!

203

All his life he had run from her Salvation, and today at last he would prove to her that he was a Man, not her infant, her darling boy, her toy to play with whenever the blood in her black heart moved her nature to the most vile, the most sickening passion that ever darkened the sun, as though like two maggots they lived in the black bowel of bubbling earth, maggots forced to feed upon one another.

Mother love!

"Comrades," Hansraj shouted, raising both arms, fists clenched, to help attract their attention. "Have we come here to surrender?"

His young friends, standing around the platform's edge, shouted in one voice, "Never!"

"Are we free men or slaves?"

"Free!"

"I cannot hear you, Comrades! Louder! Let me hear your voices!"

"Free, free!"

Sundar Das turned in bewilderment to his peasant friend. "What is that upstart shouting about?"

"Who knows? Perhaps his brain has gone soft. It happens to many people in a big city."

"Yes, that is true. Let us go look at the cattle, Raj."

He also wanted to be sure that he knew where Mohan was, for the crowd continued to grow, and so many people were milling about now that he could not see more than a few yards in any direction, and nowhere he looked was there any sign of the boy.

"Let us find our boys," Sundar suggested, as he and Raj moved away from the ranting figure on the platform.

Many of the peasant faces in this crowd looked familiar to Sundar Das, for though he had lived all forty of his years in Ramgaon, he made a special point of traveling to holy festivals and places of pilgrimage at least twice each year,

and he remembered faces. He was quite proud of his memory. He recognized a familiar face, smiled, and touched
his fingers to his white turban. "God be with you," he said
to a bearded peasant, who nodded, but looked at him
warily. "You don't remember me, but we met two years
ago at Hoshiarpur during Diwali."

"Ah, yes, yes, I do remember. So you have come to the
Baisakhi also?"

"Yes, I have brought my son. He is ten today."

"Ah, today, is it? That is most auspicious, to be born on
a holy day. Yes, that is good luck."

"Thank you."

"And who is that fellow up there?" the old man
inquired.

"Nobody knows. He is very noisy, and perhaps he has
had too much of sun today."

"Yes, yes, that happens."

"Well, I must find my boy. Happy New Year to you."

"And to you! Yes, yes, Happy New Year!"

He stopped to greet another man before getting much
further, and then someone stopped him to ask where the
cattle were. Sundar Das explained that he assumed the
cattle were at the far end of the Bagh, but this person
insisted that was not possible, because he had just come
from that side, and had been looking very carefully all
over, but no cattle were there.

"Do you mean to say there are no cattle at the other
end?"

"Not one head!"

"That is peculiar," he remarked, "to hold a cattle fair
without cattle?"

"Very peculiar, I must agree."

It was a puzzle neither of them could solve, so they
asked someone else, who simply shrugged and mutely
shook his head. He appeared to be either deaf or somewhat

slow-witted. Such people often gathered at fairs and places of pilgrimage. The lame and sick also came in unusual numbers, and Sundar Das had noticed many beggars about, especially those with limbs fractured early in life, who could never earn a living from hard labor in the fields.

"Unless," he said at last, for the puzzle persisted in troubling him, "unless this is not the proper place?"

"But see how many people have come here," his interrogator argued, and looking around Sundar Das saw there were indeed many many thousands, more people than he had seen at any fair or festival in years. "How could it be someplace else?"

"Yes, that is true," he whispered, glancing up at one of the fig trees. He saw a large crow there, which looked so sinister, he felt chill. The sun dipped lower. A breeze had come down from the north, bringing a sudden drop in the temperature.

He hurried off to seek Mohan, calling out the boy's name. But that made people turn and stare at him. Embarrassed, he muttered apologies, and continued walking in silence. Then he thought he saw Mohan racing off behind the old tomb.

"I think I see them, Raj," he reported, glancing back over his shoulder, for Raj was several paces behind.

His eye glimpsed the first soldiers running in through the entrance by which they had come here little more than an hour ago. For a moment the sight of those swift-moving troops, clad in battle gear and holding rifles across their chests as they ran, registered only on his eye, and he continued along the vector of his search for Mohan, but after two steps he stopped to look back again.

There was an earthen shelf of elevated ground just inside the entranceway, several yards wide, several feet high, a stage of soil that covered the water main, which ran through the Bagh. Like a chorus line the soldiers rushed onto that stage, fanning out to either side as they came through the entrance, moving with such seemingly effortless precision that the ninety of them appeared to be one man, or rather one strange claw of some mighty mechanism, thrust irrepressibly into the neck of this bottle-shaped garden. They spanned the full width of the earthen stage, and fifty of them in the front line kneeled and pointed rifles toward the crowd inside the Bagh, while forty of them, shouldering naked swords that gleamed silver in the setting sun, stood behind, and seeing them poised that way, Sundar Das wondered if this was not perhaps some special part of the fair? Because at many festivals there was a military band, and sometimes a martial parade.

Only then he heard the thunderous report of fifty rifles fired at once. Yet still he thought it was staged for the entertainment of the crowd. What was more exciting, after all, than the fireworks accompanying Diwali? The sight and sound of explosives was a great treat to Mohan also.

Surely they were firing blank cartridges, he thought, till the screaming reached his ears, a terrifyingly high-pitched cry of panic that rose above the repeated volleys of gunfire. Then a man quite close to him collapsed like a scarecrow that had lost its supporting stick. He knew now it was real bullets they fired. The throb inside his chest became a wild wail of fear —

"Mohan!" he yelled, running frantically toward the samadh, where he thought he had sighted his child. "Mohan!"

Everyone was running, except those who fell and lay still. Sundar Das was jolted by several fast-moving young men, who knocked his turban from his head, but he dared not pause or attempt to retrieve it. Once long ago he had nearly been caught by a herd of stampeding cattle, which the English army was driving across his father's field toward their camp to its north, and foolishly he had tried to save some cowrie shells he'd dropped while running out of the way, but his father lifted him bodily, and (though he kicked and writhed in the strong man's arms) carried him safely aside. For weeks he subsequently scraped over that patch of ground, but found no trace, not even a fragment, of his precious shells.

"Mohan!" He saw the boy running not too far away from him, and his heart was so buoyed by the sight of his son that he did not realize terror had completely confused the child, who rushed toward the soldiers, rather than away from them. He ran very swiftly, but Mohan too was a fine racer. He was a tall boy for his age, and his limbs were sturdy and straight, well-developed; not spindly, like the legs of a newborn calf, but firm. The legs of a Prince he had. It was Sundar Das's secret way of speaking about his son — "Mohan is a Prince," he often told his wife, when the children were asleep, and they talked in whispers of the future, of their hopes and dreams for their progeny. The girls he really did not think too much about, though he loved them, but girls were born to leave a father's home and rarely to return. A son was a different matter entirely. A son was always there. A son meant your name survived, not simply for one lifetime, but through the memorial ceremony of shraddha, forever. A son linked you to Eternity, specially if he was a son like Mohan, a good and cheerful boy, never one to shirk a day's labor in the fields, always ready to lend a hand, and so bright he had actually learned to read! No one in Sundar Das's family ever knew how to read before Mohan took it into his head, and in his first year of school he came home with the alphabet committed to memory, and on this trip whenever they passed a sign along the road, Mohan would read it. Was it any wonder he called the boy a Prince?

He had almost reached him, could almost touch his fast-moving arm, when Mohan fell.

He simply fell forward as though he tripped over a clod of earth, or twisted his ankle in a pothole. There were so many uneven spots on a field like this.

"Mohan," he shouted, though he could not hear his own voice above the din of fire and frenzy that filled the cauldron of this garden gone mad. He stooped to help his son rise, touching his shoulder, which felt very firm and strong. "Mohan," he called, bending his head close to the boy's ear.

But why did he not move?

Sundar Das turned his boy over, and stared at the chest, which had become a crimson scar, a gaping hole of mangled flesh and entrails. Mohan's eyes were open. His mouth was stuffed with dark soil. "Oh, God," Sundar called out, looking up.

Mercifully he had not long to wait before the impact of lead driven into his neck released Sundar Das from the agony of facing the sight of his murdered son. He covered his own gushing wound with both hands, and he prayed for death to bring its blessed end to this nightmare of incomprehensible brutality.

19

REX braced himself firmly as he watched the terrorists rush toward his fire in dark waves. They were trying to overwhelm him, to panic his thin line of Gurkhas and Baluchis with their countless numbers. Life meant nothing to Orientals, it was cheap, meaningless as the dirt of this disgusting "garden," a filthy field filled with rebellious natives.

He'd made up his mind, during the drive over here, to open fire without further warning. He'd given them all the notice any of them could ask for. Much more, in fact, than they deserved. He'd been patient as Job with these vermin. They were a pestilence, a blight defacing God's earth. They had to be crushed, ground under heel of boot into oblivion. Exterminated.

"Keep firing!" he roared. He kept his hand locked round his pistol, determined to put a bullet through the yellow brain of any Nepali or Baluchi brute who failed to obey his orders. But they were all true to their salt. He'd expected no less of this lot. They were soldiers.

"They're regrouping to try and flank us, General," Tommy shouted, pointing toward the nearest wall, where they were bunched like a fist drawn back and ready to punch against his right flank.

"Fire into that spearhead!" Rex rasped at the riflemen kneeling before him. "Aim for their balls! Don't waste a shot!"

He wished he'd been able to bring his armored vehicles through the narrow entranceway leading into the Bagh. He would have opened fire with his machine guns straightaway. He'd no idea the passage was so small. It obliged him to leave the vehicles outside the bazaar gateway, and stupidly enough there was no provision made for removing the rapid-fire guns from their vehicular mounts. He would have to write a memo on that to the adjutant general. It seemed a waste to have such fine guns, and then to be unable to use them. Especially here, where the targets were more ample than his men could take full advantage of. It was frustrating to see how many of them were running out of reach, scaling the walls, getting off scot-free.

"Don't let those men get away, damn you! Direct that fire at the wall over there! Look to it, you blackguards!"

Every fiber of his flesh tingled with excitement as Rex watched the buggers go down. All afternoon he'd prayed that they would hold this meeting as announced. He hadn't really believed they would be so idiotic as to give him so golden an opportunity. He'd feared it was too good to be true; too much to expect of the rodents. He thought them more cunning somehow. Yesterday's parade through deserted streets had made him less than sanguine about his chances of finding them gathered in any substantial numbers anywhere. Not to speak of anything as spacious and easily swept as this sort of field. It was almost as though God Himself intervened to give him this crack at the living lot of them.

After all he'd taken of their scowling, their sniggering,

and defiant laughter! Why don't you laugh now? he thought, watching them race with terror writ large on their lips, the scum, climbing over one another like rabbits on the run.

"Get those! Over there! Can't you aim that bloody piece? That's it! Now you've got a bead on them!"

He watched as one of the tallest beasts, a particularly vicious brute, whose tool was half an arm long and kept swinging as he raced naked across the field, and almost escaped to use that vile rod in subduing helpless women, virginal girls — watched him suddenly throw up both arms and come arching over backwards, caught by a bullet in his spine, to lay writhing, kicking out in all directions, to no avail, going limp at last, half arm and all, dead as the humping donkey deserved to be.

He would teach them a moral lesson they'd never forget. It was no pleasant duty. No, there wasn't anything lovely about death. He'd never been one to relish violence for its own sake. Yet to spare the rod was to spoil the child, and natives were children all their lives. It was an onerous duty, a difficult responsibility, but one he would never shirk. He could no more dream of turning away from this sight than he would think now of stopping his firing. That would have been too cruel a hoax to perpetrate on anyone, even these creatures, to give them just a whiff of grape and let the brutal mass of terrorists escape with blood boiling behind their eyeballs. It would have been like abandoning the hunt for a wounded tiger, knowing that every villager within reach would fall prey to his claws or fangs. Were he so weak-willed, so fainthearted as to call a halt to the shooting a mere minute or two after it had begun, then it would have been better never to have fired in the first place!

Of that he was certain. Half measures were worse than

none. He was not that sort of man. He'd never been one
to attend the fancy dress balls, to prance round a slippery
floor with a girdled waist in hand and bouncing bosoms
tickling his chest. He left that to the sweet talkers, all
words but no action, when the naked flesh was there. He
never started till he saw the field ahead clear for a successful charge, but then! He remembered the morning he
and Mary spent before they were married, in the central
hill country, the badlands of India. She'd come down
from Cawnpore with the regiment, the Colonel's daughter,
ripe as a mango in May, her hair flaming crimson. He'd
been picked as her "escort" by the Old Man, and was so
new to the game, a subaltern of twenty-one, that he actually thought it was protection the Colonel's daughter
wanted. Till she slipped going up a hill, and fell into
his arms, pressing her legs and hip to his muscle-stiffened
thigh, the two of them clenched so hard that they almost
rolled downhill together, but rushed instead to the plateau
above the barren plain. There he took her, while she cried
bitterly, and clawed blood from his back and arms.

"For God's sake, General, don't you think they've fired
enough?" Mr. Rehill asked, sounding as sickly as he
looked. He'd come along at Tommy's suggestion ("We
really should have a representative of the Civil Government accompany us, sir."), since Irving refused to join
them for this show. Rex was sorry now that he'd brought
Rehill. He'd thought a police officer might have had
sufficient training to control his emotions. "General, for
God's sake! Can't you hear me?"

"Keep firing, and don't waste any shots!" he ordered.
Rehill finally gave up, and turned away, leaving the
Bagh with his shadow, Plomer. Civilians hadn't the train-
ing of soldiers. They couldn't take the rough sledding.
It wasn't easy to rivet your eyes on death. It wasn't a pretty

213

sight — the spurting, gushing, spluttering fountains of blood. Yet there was no other cure for this disease. No alternative remained.

"General, sir," Tommy remarked, his eyes shifting nervously, "I don't think there's any — any other exit, sir. I — I thought for a while they were trying to charge us, General, but I do believe now that the reason they were coming this way, sir, is — is there's no other way out of this place.

"Did — did you hear what I said, General? Perhaps we should —?"

"Keep those men firing, Brigade Major! Get down the other end of this line!"

"Yes, sir," he responded, snapping to at once, but his eyes looked watery. Briggs would need a week's leave after this mess was over. Perhaps he'd let Alice go off with him — no, that wouldn't do. A girl like Alice was still too delicate, too sensitive, too young for wrestling with a man. He was surprised that Mary didn't see that herself — wanting to let her own niece risk getting skewered alive! Over his dead body! He'd never seen a girl as slight and frail as that child. Her hips were hardly broader than a boy's. Her legs were so delicately fine and thin — he could circle her calves with his hand.

He felt warm all over, the kind of warmth that came from good food and drink, from a good ride on a cool day, a good game of polo, or the end of a successful hunt. He'd savored life, the good moments of it. Why had they gone so swiftly by? He'd just begun, it seemed at times, and yet. He'd been cheated of all the fun. While others played and drank and danced, Rags did the work. Rags. He'd almost forgotten that nickname. His years were all torn, shredded rags, wasted, lost. It was their fault really. They were the ones who'd done it to him.

"Keep firing! Make those bullets count!"

He hated them. Yet he'd worked all his life to save and protect them, to defend their frontiers, to ward off the Enemy. He'd wasted his years, his talent, his vital forces on that. For them. For these blithering monkey terrorists, these ingrates. Did any of them appreciate his sacrifice?

The General locked his square assertive jaw, deciding that his Duty now was to do all these men unto death. Nothing less would really prove adequate by way of punishment for their crimes. Their presence here, in this Garden, attending this seditious treasonous meeting, was open rebellion against the King-Emperor. The penalty for treason was death, and death it would have to be. Not merely for some of them. That would be unjust. How to choose which should die? Only God could do that. He alone had that awesome power. There was no turning aside, no backing off. That would mean surrender. He would have felt obliged to turn himself in for court-martial, had he so much as faltered here and now, had he proved so cowardly as to stop. It was unthinkable.

He licked the briny sweat from his upper lip and felt a bit light-headed as the smell of their insides wafted with the smoke's sulfurous stench to his nostrils. *Multitudes, multitudes in the valley of decision: for the day of the Lord is near in the valley of decision.* The Prophet's words rang in his ears as he watched the sun darkened by the cloud of fire and dust that rose with their whining wail. *The Lord also shall roar . . . and the heavens and the earth shall shake.*

Maqbool tasted the dirt in his mouth. He dared not raise his head high enough to spit. He felt no pain in his leg any more. After the initial impact of the bullet, after he had dropped to his stomach, the leg unmoving felt numb. Or if pain was there, it had been deadened by the sight and sound of so much greater agony, which seemed

215

to cauterize his own consciousness of pain. He felt a dull throbbing, only that, like the calm steady flow of water from a pump, somewhere out of sight the pump was working, irrigating this soil. What harvest would be reaped here? He did not cry. Nor did he cry out. For each man he saw was himself afflicted or in flight, and many on death's dark doorway called plaintively to him for water, or a soothing touch of compassion. He could reach none of them. He tried to crawl several times, but had no strength for it. His arms felt numb, just as his legs did. He was too weak to stand. Even were it possible to stand without instant destruction.

Would it never stop?

He thought first they were firing blanks, for no one had shouted any warning. No one had ordered the crowd to disperse. Not a single word had been uttered by the General or his troops. Only their guns spoke. So surely he believed they were firing blanks, or firing overhead, by way of warning. He had come here to advise his friends to leave. When he learned that Kanhyaji would not appear to preside over the meeting, he decided it would be foolish to continue with the plan of holding such a meeting. What more would any of them be able to say just now, and what could be accomplished by so quickly defying the proclamations, except perhaps to test the will of the British, which had, after all, long since been tested elsewhere. Unfortunately, he reached the Bagh only a few minutes before the troops. There had been no time for him to converse at any length with anyone.

His throat felt dry. As though some dirt had seeped back there. He started to retch. Nothing came up. No drop of moisture, not even bile. He became angry now at his own helplessness. His very position angered him. Why should he be lying so, face ground to the soil? He was no creature that crawled the earth on his belly. He was no criminal to have to hide so. He was a man, a respected pleader of the bar. And this, this was his city — not theirs. By what right did they shoot at him this way, those Nepalese Gurkhas, who could not speak a word of Punjabi? Those Baluchi tribesmen, who had been recruited to join the British army from their nomadic existence in the desert. Who were they to open fire upon him, and here in his land, his homeland? It infuriated him so that he actually pushed his torso away from the ground, and sat up. He sat erect and stared at them, those killers, whose murders were absolved by the insignia they wore over cloth that was given to them by foreigners, who did not even pretend to claim India as their Home — only their colony.

"Who are you?" he shouted at them, yet though it strained his throat, the words were drowned by a responding crescendo of powder exploding.

He watched one young boy writhing and clutching his belly, curled up in the foetal position, his unlined face carved with newly hewn ridges of anguish, his eyes bulging like those of a wounded fawn, more eloquent in their silent plea than the shrillest shrieks of fleeing elders, thousands of whom continued to step upon one another, trying to escape over the stone walls. The mounds of dead and dying piled higher with each passing moment, each fusillade adding some fifty fresh casualties, for none of the bullets were wasted. Some indeed did double duty, passing through one limb or frail body, and lodging permanently in a second person's flesh. It was so frightful a sight, to see the unarmed and helpless caught this way, like chickens racing desperately about inside a closed pen, hopelessly seeking to elude the intrusive arm come to seize them, that now Maqbool did vomit. He trembled uncontrollably. It was rage that made him tremble, the futility of unavailing rage.

217

"Beasts!" he shouted, clenching his fist, desperately striving to rise. "Murderers! Killers! Who are you? Beasts!"

In all his life he had never held a gun. He never wished to before. He had always repudiated violence, partly because of his inherited respect for the Law, partly thanks to Kitchlew's adherence to Gandhian principles, but mostly for practical reasons, since it never seemed to him sensible or necessary really for Indians to resort to such means to attain greater independence and ultimately Freedom. On the one hand, the British were too powerful to be fought by Indian guns and clubs, and on the other hand, they were sufficiently wise in their restraint concerning the use of force and in their respect for legal procedures and constitutional measures so that in fact it was not necessary to attempt coercive or violent actions against them. So he had always thought. Thus he believed. Till now. Till five minutes, five irreversible minutes ago.

His hands itched for some weapon, a gun, a knife, a piece of blunt wood, a stone — something to use, to hurl against them, to throw back at them, these creatures of merciless brutality, these heartless things, who came in human form. He clawed at the earth, lifting a clod to toss, watching it lob to the ground several yards away. He was so outraged he started to cry, biting his lips, drawing blood to swallow for his burning mouth and throat.

The flow of blood had all but stopped from the wound on his leg, and though the soil around him was crimson, it seeped now merely in a trickle, oozing slowly from the half clotted puncture. He forced himself to his knees, and started to creep towards them, fixing his eyes upon their faces as he moved, each inch a tortuous struggle that seemed to drain the last dregs of his energy.

"When will you stop, murderers?" he called out.

Another bullet struck him, entering his shoulder, forcing him down, filling his chest with so fierce a burning pain that he could not bear the misery of it. He tried once more to lift his head, but he could no longer see them, the mechanical things that fired other mechanical things to destroy life. His eyes had grown too dim. The cloud, the veil was drawn over them. He felt the burning fire consuming his heart, and nowhere was there water to quench those flames. Not one drop of water.

So Maqbool the Pleader died in the Jallianwala Bagh, on Sunday, the thirteenth of April, as the sun was going down.

20

REX gnawed at the nail of his thumb, trying to count how many of them were still alive. It was difficult to reach any accurate estimate, since they kept running back and forth, and some fell dead just as he was counting them. It was infuriating. He felt strongly about the importance of precise numbers in his military reports, yet now he couldn't decide really whether there were closer to five, ten or twenty thousand of the buggers still running around inside this Bagh.

The thing that worried him most was that if the total was closer to twenty thousand, there wouldn't be enough time left to finish the job before dark. He estimated another fifty minutes of light, including twilight, but he would need at least half of that time to march his column back to Ram Bagh at a dignified pace. He couldn't risk remaining inside the native city after sundown, not with these troops. Which only gave him a scant thirty minutes more of firing time, and the trouble was that his men couldn't manage more than three rounds a minute. Rex had always been good at mathematics. That came to a kill total of under five thousand. There just wasn't enough time!

He wished he'd had the sense to bring twice his number of rifles. Those damnable useless machine guns tricked him into underestimating his rifle requirements. He'd made a fatal miscalculation. It wasn't as if he didn't have more rifles back at Ram Bagh. That was what bothered him most, the realization of this tactical error in calculation. It sent a shiver of anxiety down his back. What would G.O.C. Lahore say? How would the Adjutant General react when he learned there were forty Gurkhas standing around just holding their swords? It was unforgivably negligent of him. He felt like kicking himself soundly. He suddenly feared that he might not get his division for this show after all, and it enraged him.

The pain returned to his groin. His seed had turned black, dried up. For months he passed nothing but black urine from his body. Instead of taking up the division he had been training to handle, he wasted his days in wretched isolation on beds that turned black in the night. He'd lost all the locks to his body's doors. The doors swung free, loose and flaccid. It was their fault. For keeping him here, trapping him in this black hole of a country: luring his father to Simla with the money they lavished on his beer. As though there was anything worth buying in Simla! He remembered how bitterly his mother wept, how desperately she longed to go Home, how she fought to send him back for schooling, how she'd always wanted him to serve in Her Majesty's regulars, not out here, not here.

"General, sir, the men are running low on ammunition," Briggs reported, looking ghostlike, sounding frightened. "How much longer will you want to keep firing, sir?"

"Till we finish," he snapped. *Lord, how are they increased that trouble me? Many are they that rise up against me,* he thought, surveying the line of his kneeling soldiers. They weren't reloading quickly enough! They were hesitating, some of them were purposely slowing down, he could tell it. "You! What in hell are you waiting for? Load up! Fire, damn your hide!" That put some fear into their yellow skins. Yellows and blacks. He'd wasted his life trying to teach them some sense, trying to rouse them, these sick sleeping races, these subhuman species.

Wasted, drained, his years, his powers, the almost superhuman strength that animated his body. He'd given it all to them, to save this army of ingrates, this tumult of terrorists. Death by bullets was too good for them, too kind. They should have been flogged, stripped bare of skin, every last mother's son of them. Even flogging was too good. He'd never really minded the birch himself. And these were, after all, a lower form of life. The confusion came because they stood erect, like Man, but everyone who knew them, knew they were closer to creeping things. Crawling, he thought. There should be an order obliging them to crawl! Yes, that would make it easier to recognize the low life for what they were. Why hadn't anyone thought of that before? The trouble with civilian rule was its leniency. He'd never met a Frock who understood the native mind. Force was the only thing they honored, force and firmness. A month or two of crawling around Amritsar on their black bellies, and the buggers would bless every Britisher they met just for the privilege of standing on their two feet.

"General, I've counted the ammunition in the men's bags, sir," Tommy reported, returning to his side, speaking so close into his ear he could feel the touch of the boy's lips against his skin, the warmth of his breath. "There aren't more than thirty cartridges left in their bags, General. You've got to stop them soon, or we'll be obliged to return to camp without ammunition."

They were like rabbits, ants, too many. Like locusts. He remembered the first time he'd seen a cloud of locusts over Central India. He'd refused to believe it was anything but a storm cloud at first, though his older friends assured him it was the flying grasshopper, and then he heard their buzz, the strange high-pitched voice of their wings, and soon he saw them dropping from the sky to devour the stalks of sorghum and millet that grew scraggly on the grudging dry soil. It was a nightmare. There were too many of them to kill. Though he started stamping them out with his heavy boots, cursing and smashing, stamping in all directions, destroying hundreds, it wasn't possible to eliminate them all. There were too many of the cursed lot. They spent all of their time fornicating, reproducing more of their miserable kind. It was hopeless . . .

"Very well," Rex whispered, nodding slowly. "Cease firing."

"Cease firing!" Tommy repeated, roaring his command above the din.

The troops rushed out of the garden as swiftly as they had marched in — at double time. Rehill accosted him outside to ask if any provision would be made for the wounded, but Rex did not choose to reply to that sort of query. He was running an army, not a hospital corps. The cloak of darkness spread over the city's winding roads as they hurried back toward the cantonment in Civil Lines.

Inside the well it was darker still. Hansraj clung to the slimy stone, balanced precariously above the brackish water level, wondering if he'd gone deaf or if the firing had actually stopped. He'd jumped into the well after finding himself pinned flat to the ground for more than five minutes before the adjacent wall of the Bagh. The wall had become a tombstone for hundreds of fleeing bodies, caught by the deadly barrage of bullets that raked its top. Hansraj was the first to realize that the old circular well could afford excellent cover since its stone shaft was more than a foot thick, and the rough hewn stones inside were staggered sufficiently to allow a person to climb up or down. The water had long since ceased to be used for drinking, was covered with green moss, and smelled as vile as it looked. Others had followed his lead: one wounded man, who quickly succumbed and sank into the water; a corpse, which fell inside backwards, almost dragging him down with it as it dropped; and an old man, who jumped in unscathed, but failed to keep his balance on the wall, and was so unnerved to find himself in a pool with two dead men that he appeared to have lost his sanity, and kept trying to drag Hansraj down.

"Let go of me, you old fool," he shouted, kicking his legs angrily at the old man's shoulder, trying to extricate himself from the clinging fingers.

"Help me! I'm going to drown," he wailed, clawing at Hansraj's heel.

"I said *let go!*" He jerked his foot free and shot it back with such fury that he caught the old man's face with his sole and bashed his head against the stone. He had not intended to hurt the poor fool, and was stunned to watch him sinking into the water, joining the other corpses. He did not look back a second time. The firing had stopped. He climbed quickly out of the open grave.

Everywhere around the outside of the well bodies lay heaped like sacks of barley unloaded in haphazard disarray, left by some careless merchant for the kites that hovered overhead, poised with such effortless grace in the pale green sky, waiting to fall upon their prey. Several of the bodies moved, an arm, a head, many groaned. "Water," they cried. "Help. Give some water!"

He had to step on someone's belly to get away. He felt the soft flesh yielding to the pressure of his weight, his bare foot sinking into the jelly substance of human organs, like earth softened to clay by the rain. It made his stomach sick, that slippery feeling of flattened flesh and muscle. There were open eyes, staring up at him, staring accusations. Wherever he turned they were staring at him, attacking him, vilifying him! Why did they look at him that way?

"Water, please! Water!"

What did they expect him to do? How could he care for everyone? He had almost been killed himself! And who cared for Hansraj? They hated him, envied his fairness of skin, his hair. They wished they looked the way he did, light, almost White, like an Englishman. That was why they always reviled his ancestry, as though any of them — these stinking dark bodies — as if any one of them had better blood. He felt like laughing as he rushed past them, tens, hundreds of corpses, the dead and near-dead, the fallen, the lost, lost and unable to breathe again, unable to walk, to run, to taste one grain of rice, so many lives forsaken, destroyed! Yet amazingly, miraculously, he was unscathed, untouched by bullet, unscratched by so much as one flying fragment of shrapnel! He never felt healthier. He was giddy with a sense of euphoric power as he shoved dead limbs aside and squeezed through the narrow exit to Lakar Mandi Bazaar.

He felt free. Alive and free! It was the blissful release that came in the wake of seemingly certain death, the liberation that followed the most dread nightmare. He rushed away, adrenalin firing his limbs. He felt stronger than ever before. He knew now what it must have been like, to walk the earth as a pukka sahib, to fear nothing, no one, to command all you could see, rising colossus-like above the pygmies.

Dead bodies were piled outside the Bagh as well as within its walls, for many had scaled the walls to succumb a few paces beyond of wounds they carried away with them. Others lay dying, even now. Even as he hurried past them, he heard their groans, those hovering on the threshhold of death. One old woman lay before his path, clutching her net bag of onions and garlic that sprawled open, her precious possessions scattered unchased along the road.

"Help me, my child," she groaned.

For an instant he stood frozen, turned to ice by that hag's plaintive cry.

"Help an old woman. God will bless you for it," she cried.

He shook himself from the momentary paralysis that halted him, and ran away, avoiding her filthy body.

"Curse you!" she cried, gasping louder in what sounded like her last breath. "Bastard son of a whore, curse your polluted line for fifty generations!"

He felt his heart pounding as he ran. He continued to hear that curse, over and over again, it rang in his ears to the rhythmic pounding of his pulse. It served only to harden his determination to leave them, all of them, to leave them far behind him, to escape their black tongues, their vile curses and foul incest-ridden lives. to break free — now! Not in some mythical future year of National Freedom. Hansraj was also a Nation, to himself alone. He too deserved the Freedom he had labored so long to bring to others. More! He deserved it more than the rest of them, because he was better than any of them! Secretly he had always believed it. Except for Maulanaji perhaps, but Maulanaji was destroyed now, his magic powers had failed to save him from the English. The English were better, stronger, than him, than Satyapal too, than any of them — any but one, Hansraj!

He was panting uncontrollably when he reached the Kotwali. The native policeman who stood guard at the gate to the compound stared at him suspiciously, holding up his rifle.

"I must see Inspector Khan," he gasped.

"Why?"

"That is for his ears, not yours!"

"Who are you to speak so to me? Badmash, I should —" The dim-witted fellow lifted the butt of his rifle.

"Tell Inspector Khan Hansraj is here! And watch your step, or you will lose that rifle!" It brought the fool to his senses, for he seemed to detect by the mere tone of authority in Hansraj's voice that he dealt with a superior.

"Wait here," the policeman ordered, signaling to another guard, who came to take over the watch, as he went inside to deliver the message.

Hansraj did not have to wait long. He was soon escorted into the inner recesses of the Kotwali, to the office of Ashraf Khan, who told his assistant to wait outside.

"So you've come to be our approver?" Ashraf asked.

"You promise I am to go free — to any part of the country I choose?"

"Yes, yes, after you have testified," the portly inspector sighed. His voice sounded as disapproving as his face looked contemptuous. He hastily scribbled a note on a small piece of paper, handing it across his desk. "Show this chit to the guard at Hall Bazaar Gate. He'll take you to Mr. Irving."

"I thought you would take me yourself."

Ashraf ignored it, softly asking, "Have you just come from your mother?"

"No."

There was an imperative knock at the door.

"Yes, yes, now go on! Get along! I have no more time to waste on people like you! Yes, come in — who is there?"

It was one of his deputies, bringing in a wild-eyed young man whose hands were manacled.

"Hansraj!" the youth shouted, jubilant at first to see his comrade, then, realizing he was not also in irons, changing his tone to ask, "But what — why — what are you doing here?"

"Nothing," he snapped, feeling the blood like fire in his cheeks, hurrying out of that room, out of the Kotwali, through the compound and past the guard at the gate, who eyed him as though he were some form of poisonous snake, as though he were lower somehow, instead of taller, fairer, more exalted than he had ever been before.

He folded the chit into a small pad locked in his fist so that no one would see it as he hurried toward Hall Bazaar Gate, and instinctively he avoided the streets where his friends lived, slinking along strange alleys, down dark byways that took him off the direct path — as though he were lost and no longer knew his way, as though he were a stranger, an enemy in this place of his birth — but it was too late to turn back, for his comrade had seen him, and Ashraf Khan knew what he had done, and the bitch had cursed his line for fifty generations to come.

Hansraj gasped for air as he ran toward the guard at Hall Bazaar Gate, but the harder he tried to breathe freely, the more he felt himself strangling.

Lahore

November 19, 1919

21

"WHEN did you get information that a meeting would assemble at the Jallianwala Bagh?" William asked.

"I was in the city at the time," the General replied. "I cannot quite say what time it was. It may have been from one-thirty to two o'clock."

His Lordship placed his pince-nez over the ridge of his nose just above his nostrils, staring down at the written statement submitted to his committee by the General.

"I see in the report you say that at twelve-forty P.M. whilst yet in the city, on my way to the Ram Bagh, I was informed that in spite of my stern proclamation a big meeting would be held at the Jallianwala Bagh at four-thirty P.M. that afternoon!"

"Yes, that is correct."

"On the assumption that that is correct I want you to explain why you did not take measures for preventing the crowd from assembling at all at the Bagh?"

A murmur passed through the assembled crowd. The General shifted his eyes evasively before responding.

"I went there as soon as I could. I had to think the

matter out. I had to organize my forces and make up my mind as to where I might put my pickets. I thought I had done enough to make the crowd not meet if they were going to meet. I had to consider the military situation and make up my mind as to what to do, which took me a certain amount of time. I had warned them all day, that is, up to the time I went to Ram Bagh."

"When did you first receive definite information that a meeting was being held at Jallianwala Bagh?"

"About four o'clock."

"From Mr. Rehill?"

"Yes."

"When you received that information, what action did you take?"

"I marched off through the city."

"Had you with you picketing parties?"

"I had the picketing parties for marching off, and all marched off together."

"And your special party consisted of twenty-five rifles of the Gurkhas and twenty-five rifles of the Baluchis?"

"There were forty other Gurkhas."

"And you also had two armored cars?"

"Yes."

"As I understand, you proceeded to the Jallianwala Bagh at a usual pace?"

"At an ordinary walking pace."

"You did not consider any necessity for proceeding with any extra expedition?"

"No, sir."

"As you marched, the parties that were with you all dropped out?"

"They all dropped out, as they marched along. Some had to go in one direction and some in another. As we marched they took the most convenient road and they left us."

"As nearly as you can recollect, at what time did you reach the Jallianwala Bagh?"

"I should think about five or five-fifteen perhaps. I could not say." He looked around at the high walls of the large room, as though hoping to find a clock.

"When you arrived at the Jallianwala Bagh, what did you do?"

"I deployed my troops right and left of the entrance."

"You entered by the narrow entrance that leads in the Jallianwala Bagh. I think you left your motor cars behind?"

"I left the motor cars behind."

"Did you have the Gurkhas, who were armed, with you?"

"They all came in and went to the Bagh."

"You had forty Gurkhas and two columns of twenty-five men each, these fifty men being armed with rifles? That is on the high ground, on the north side of that rectangular space that goes by the name of Jallianwala Bagh?"

"Yes."

"That is a very wide piece of ground, and has very few exits?"

"I think three or four exits. There is one wide exit."

"When you got into the Jallianwala Bagh what did you do?"

"I opened fire."

"At once?"

"Immediately. I had thought about the matter, and it did not take me more than thirty seconds to make up my mind as to what my duty was."

"As regards the crowd, what was it doing at the time?"

"Holding a meeting. There was a man in the center of the place standing on something raised. You could see him above the crowd. His arms were moving about. He was evidently addressing a meeting."

"How far was the nearest man in the crowd from you?"

"When I entered first, about eight or nine yards off the wall. He ran away to the right, and there were a good many others who ran away and climbed over the wall there."

"Do I understand where you stationed armed soldiers there is a small ridge? Where was the man who was addressing the crowd standing?"

"He was absolutely in the center of the section, as far as one could judge; maybe within fifty or sixty yards from me. He seemed to be surrounded by them, but most of them were on the further side."

"So far as you know, was there any crying except this man's addressing the crowd?"

"No. I cannot say there was anything beyond that he was addressing the crowd."

"How many people were there in the crowd?"

"I then estimated it at five thousand. I heard there were many more."

"On the assumption that there was a crowd of something like five thousand and more, have you any doubt that many of these people must have been unaware of your proclamation?"

The General cleared his throat against his fist before answering: "It was being well issued and news spread very rapidly in places like that under prevailing conditions. At the same time, there may have been a good many who had not heard the proclamation."

"On the assumption that there was that risk of people being in the crowd who were not aware of the proclamation, did it not occur to you that it was a proper measure to ask the crowd to disperse before you took to actually firing upon them?"

"No, at the time it did not occur to me. I merely felt that my orders had not been obeyed, that martial law was flouted, and that it was my duty to immediately disperse it by rifle fire."

"Before you dispersed the crowd, had the crowd taken any action at all?"

"No, sir. They ran away, a few of them. When I began to fire in the center they began to run to the road."

"Martial law had not been proclaimed before you took that step, which was a serious step. Did you consider about the propriety of consulting the Deputy Commissioner who was the civil authority responsible for law and order?"

"There was no Deputy Commissioner there to consult at the time. I did not think it wise to ask anybody further. I had to make up my mind immediately as to what my action should be. I considered it from a military view that I should fire immediately, that if I did not do so, I should fail in my duty."

"When you left the Ram Bagh did it occur to you that you were going to fire if you found an assembly there?"

The General did not reply immediately. He sat in stony silence for fully a minute before saying, "I considered well the nature of my duty."

"Did not you think it proper to have a civil representative with you before you took that action?"

"I had a police officer with me."

"Who was that?"

"Mr. Rehill. Mr. Plomer."

"As I understand Mr. Rehill and Mr. Plomer came on the scene after you actually fired?"

"I think Mr. Rehill was there actually while the firing was going on."

"During the whole time?"

"I do not know whether he was there the whole time."

"Before firing, did you ask Mr. Rehill whether in his judgment it was necessary to fire?"

"No, sir. My mind was made up as I came along in my

motor car — if my orders were not obeyed, I would fire immediately."

"In firing was your object to disperse the crowd?"

"Yes."

"Any other object?"

"No, sir. I was going to fire until they dispersed."

"Did the crowd at once start to disperse as soon as you fired?"

"Immediately."

"Did you continue firing?"

"Yes."

There was an audible gasp, that echoed through this crowded room in response to that single word. His Lordship waited for silence to be restored, sitting with eyes lowered, hands clasped tightly on the long table that separated the committee from everyone else. The folds of his black robe pinched against the table's edge as he hunched forward, leaning heavily on his elbows, asking in a voice strained thin by incredulity:

"If the crowd was going to disperse, why did you not stop firing?"

"I thought it my duty to go on firing until it dispersed. If I fired a little, the effect would not be sufficient. If I had fired a little I should be wrong in firing at all."

"How long did the firing go on?"

"It may be ten minutes; it may be less, calculating from the number of rounds that we fired."

"Could you say whether there were any sticks with the people?"

"I cannot say that. I assume numbers had sticks. I knew they were going to be armed with sticks."

"Have you ever, in your military experience, used a similar method of dispersing an assembly?"

"Never, sir. It was an exceptional case."

"What reason had you to suppose that if you had

ordered the assembly to leave the Bagh they would not
have done so without the necessity of your firing, continued
firing for a length of time?"

"Yes. I think it quite possible that I could have dis-
spersed them perhaps even without firing."

"Why did you not adopt that course?" His Lordship
asked, shaking his head, more in wonder than horror, as
he asked the question.

"I could not disperse them for some time," the General
answered, speaking slowly, sounding distracted as he stared
over the heads of his judges, "then they would all come
back and laugh at me, and I considered I would be making
myself a fool."

A wave of startled comment greeted this remark, and
the clamor became so loud that His Lordship was obliged
to rap his gavel before continuing his interrogation.

"After the firing had taken place I think you returned
with your troops to the Ram Bagh?"

"Yes."

"And on examining the ammunition, you discovered
that one thousand six hundred and fifty rounds had been
fired?"

"Yes."

"Do you know the casualties imposed by the firing?"

"No. I formed a rough estimate from the number of
rounds. I calculated that number to be three hundred.
There would be more than that of casualties."

"You know that the casualties were something between
four hundred and five hundred?"

"Yes. I have seen it in the papers. I divided all my
rounds by five —" He paused and touched his fingertips to
his lips, staring vacantly at the ceiling, mumbling, "I am
in doubt whether by five or six — to arrive at the number."

"I understood that the shooting that took place was
individual shooting, and it was not volley shooting?"

"No, there was no volley shooting."

"The crowd was very dense?"

"It was very dense."

"It was unlikely that a man shooting into the crowd will miss?"

"No, according to the circumstances of the case," the General replied, shaking his head, sounding bewildered. "They were running, and I noticed only a certain number of men were hit. In the center of the section, the crowd was very dense and therefore if a man directed his fire well he should not miss."

"So that it is not impossible that the number of deaths may have been four hundred or five hundred from the number of rounds that were fired?"

"Quite possible," the General conceded.

William grimaced. One Indian member of the press jumped to his feet, shouting, "Frightfulness! Prussian butchery!" Two British guards moved swiftly to either side of the bespectacled young man, who waved his finger frantically toward the unmoving back of the General, and continued to hurl high-pitched expletives as he was jostled and dragged from the room.

"I must caution all of you," His Lordship remarked, after quiet had been restored, "that if there is any further outburst or disruption of that sort, I shall be obliged to clear this room of all visitors." He then continued questioning the witness.

"Martial law, I think, was actually proclaimed on the fifteenth at Amritsar?"

"I believe on the fifteenth. Maybe later perhaps," the General said. "I cannot remember."

"Under martial law a number of orders were issued?"

"Yes."

"I think martial law was continued for a considerable time?"

"It was."

"Was it continued until the sixth of June?"

"I believe it was up to sixth June."

"As regards flogging," His Lordship asked "that is a form of punishment that is recognized in the army?"

"Yes, after martial law specially."

"What do you think about public flogging as contrasted with flogging in private?"

"As a soldier, when we lash a man, he is lashed in public. The whole regiment parades there. The victim is lashed in public with a view to making an impression on other wrongdoers or would-be wrongdoers."

"Is it for the maintenance of discipline in the army?"

"Quite so."

"You had the same reason for flogging civilians under martial law?"

"Yes, I looked upon it as the same. It would make a good impression under martial law."

One old man, a white-haired Indian, who wore an elegant pinstripe suit and spats, rose silently from his seat and walked, somewhat unsteadily, to the door at the rear of the room, leaving without uttering a sound.

"Then people were whipped in the street where Miss Sherwood was attacked?"

"Both ends of the street were closed. I did not look upon it as a public thoroughfare."

"I suppose people could come from the ends of the street for seeing?"

"If they liked to come there, they would have seen," the General admitted.

"And the people who were living in the street could see?"

"Yes, sir."

"Would it not have been better if these whippings had taken place in private?"

"I cannot see it, sir."

"So far as the inhabitants of the street were concerned," Sir William explained, raising his voice just a bit, since the General looked so bewildered by his previous question that he suspected he might be hard of hearing. "Why should they in fact see the flogging? Why should the floggings have taken place in their neighborhood?"

"I think the population of Amritsar is about seventy thousand," the General replied, "so far as I know."

"It is a good deal more than that. I think about one hundred and sixty thousand."

"All the crowds who were present both at the firing and in other places," he continued, ignoring the correction, "it looked as if the majority of these were in it, I would not say the majority, but a very great number — were rebellious."

"Surely, General, you must admit that in a large population like one hundred and sixty thousand, there must have been many citizens who would not disperse, but who were quite willing to obey a lawful order?"

"They were not allowed to by some of the men," he answered truculently.

"Therefore there was an unruly minority that you had to get the mastery of?"

"Unfortunately for them, owing to the wicked acts of others," the General added, reverting to William's earlier question, "they came under martial law. And if they had to look at things like that, it may have been unfortunate, but under martial law, it could not be helped."

"In administering martial law, must you not as far as possible see that you do not permanently alienate the people or put them out of sympathy with the administration?"

"Quite so. I think we have to make examples. These men were doing wrong in spite of everything."

"In making examples, mustn't you, as far as possible, see

that you do not condemn the innocent at the same time that you are punishing the guilty?"

"I do not see that I was condemning the innocent."

"Take your order as regards crawling in that street. What was your object in passing that?"

"I felt a woman had been beaten. We look upon women as sacred or ought to. I was searching my brain for a suitable punishment to meet this awful case. I did not know how to meet it in a suitable manner. There was a little bit of accident in that. When I posted the pickets I went down and ordered a triangle to be erected. I felt the street ought to be looked upon as sacred. Therefore I posted a couple of pickets and I told them that no Indians were to pass along there. I then also said that if they had to pass, they must go on all fours. It never entered my brain that any sensible or sane man under those conditions would intentionally go through that street."

"You promulgated that order, I understand on the nineteenth or twentieth April, and the assault was committed on the tenth of April. Your object was to punish those who were guilty of this assault and so far as possible to avoid punishing those who might be innocent?"

"Yes."

"This street where you issued this proclamation was a street where there are many houses abutting. Is it not so?"

"A good many houses on both sides of it."

"As I understand, there are many houses that have no back entrances at all?"

"I was not aware of that at the time."

"If it be the case that many of the houses have no back entrances," His Lordship patiently persisted, "what justification is there for pronouncing an order that necessitated the inhabitants lawfully residing in these houses to crawl on all fours when they had to leave their homes?"

"They could leave at other times. My picket was only

241

there from six A.M. to eight P.M. I do not think it a very great inconvenience for them if they had to suffer a little for all that Amritsar had done. I thought it would do no harm under martial law. They could easily get the necessities of life by other means. It would not have taken much ingenuity to improvise other means of getting necessary things. They might have to suffer a little amount of inconvenience," he repeated, finally lapsing into sullen silence.

"How were they to get food if most of the houses had no back entrances?"

"Those who had not back entrances, if they had to get the necessities of life, might have gone on the roof and improvised means. If not, they could wait until eight o'clock in the night and then go out and get the things."

"All this thing might have a very different effect from the effect you wished," William suggested softly. "Instead of being a just punishment on those who were intended to be punished, it might cause a great deal of ill-feeling among those who resented treatment of this sort and who were not responsible for the acts that were done?".

"Amritsar had behaved very badly and I think most of the inhabitants of Amritsar either gave assistance or were waiting to see what was going to happen apparently. At any rate, they did not offer any help until after the firing, and if they suffered a little under martial law —"

"Do you admit that during a period of turmoil when the mob was having the upper hand," His Lordship interrupted, unable this time to restrain himself longer, "it is difficult for the peaceful citizen to give assistance in quelling the disturbances and it is just on that account that the extreme act of firing upon a mob is justified?"

"Yes, they were obstructing law-abiding citizens, I presume, but I think that on that occasion we only thought of punishing the wicked." His face had a strangely abstracted look as though he were just wakening to some long-forgotten memory. The words suddenly -tumbled from his mouth. "Men who had beaten Miss Sherwood who had to go through that street were punished. It was only with a view to make it what I call sacred. I was going to lash people there presently. That was the whole object. It might be that I could have done something else. But I was searching my brain for some suitable punishment at the time."

It was past noon. The interrogation had taken somewhat longer than William intended. He felt no further need to question the General. Other members of the committee would, however, doubtless want time to do so.

"I think we might recess for an hour at this point," he suggested. "Would the General please return here at one-fifteen?"

"Yes, sir."

"Very well then, we stand recessed." He rapped the gavel and rose quickly, speaking to no one as he left the hearing room.

22

WILLIAM disrobed with a deep sigh, and sank into the armchair in his chambers behind the hearing room.

"A sip of sherry will perk Your Lordship up a bit," Harold advised, limping off to hang the robe, which he'd carried about and kept clean of lint now for over twenty years. Poor Harold, his rheumatoid leg had been acting up since they embarked on their P & O voyage almost two months ago.

"Thank you, dear chap," William said, sipping the wine left for him on the end table beside his chair. He'd urged his servant to remain at home, to rest during this sojourn, but Harold merely replied, "Who would pour Your Lordship's sherry?"

There was a soft knock at the door. Harold opened it, admitting Justice Rankin, the only member of the committee who sat on Calcutta's High Court.

"Forgive me for intruding upon your privacy, Lord Hunter," the gentle-voiced white-haired judge remarked, "but I really must unburden myself to someone. I hope you won't mind talking about the testimony we've heard?"

"Of course not. Do sit down. Join me in some sherry."

"This is most kind of Your Lordship." The formality of his manner was, William sensed, a shield for his shyness. He glanced silently at Harold, and said no more till the servant had left the room to see about lunch for the judges. His face was ashen white as only the face of an Englishman who had spent most of his life in India could remain. In the past month alone, even William's face had turned tan.

"I don't know how you feel about it, Lord Hunter, but I was desperately distressed by the General's testimony," he began, speaking almost in a whisper, his eyes moving anxiously as though he feared someone might be lurking unnoticed in a corner of the room. "I must confess that the only appropriate word that comes to my mind for some of the things the General has admitted doing is — *frightful*. I don't know how you feel about that?"

William nodded his agreement, wondering as he observed Rankin's conspiratorial manner whether the gossips back Home weren't perhaps right in their denigration of Calcutta's High Court as the preserve of small-minded men! The Judicial Service of India was reputed at best to be second choice of those young Englishmen who couldn't quite qualify for the administrative plums of the I.C.S.

"I did suspect from your last few questions that we were in agreement about the frightfulness of the lashings and the crawling order, which is why I have taken the liberty of coming to trouble you this way."

"But you aren't troubling me at all, Rankin."

"That is most comforting to hear, Your Lordship. Most comforting indeed. I daresay, you know, I've not had much opportunity to make friends out here. One can't associate with the natives, and there seem to be fewer and fewer of our sort left who are worth cultivating. It's all worked out rather differently than one imagined . . ." His voice trailed off as he lapsed into nostalgic reverie. He finished his sherry and seemed to be waiting for William to respond in kind to his private confession of loneliness. When he realized that no such response would be forthcoming, he grinned self-consciously and said, "I don't know what led me off on that mofussil trail. Do you know the term mofussil?"

"Doesn't it mean provincial, or backwoods?"

"Exactly! Well I see you have been boning up on our Anglo vocabulary and lore! How *do* you find the time? With all the statements and testimony we've had to read, I must confess I've been hard put to keep up. But I shan't digress again! I am afraid I shall have to sound terribly blunt in putting this to you, yet since we do agree about the frightfulness of the General's testimony, I hope you will agree that for the remaining portion of it we should have the hearing room closed to all natives — and perhaps to all nonofficial British as well."

"I couldn't possibly agree to that," William replied, so startled to find a judge of the High Court making this request that he sounded more amazed than irate. "What on earth made you think I would do anything of that sort, Rankin?"

"But Lord Hunter, don't you understand, sir, that if the General's statements sound frightful to *our* ears, they must sound ten times as atrocious to the ears of natives?"

"I hadn't thought about it," William remarked. His closest friend on the bench had advised him to turn down the invitation from Whitehall, warning, "It's a thankless job, Willie! The scoundrels will curse you for doing them justice, and the just ones will curse you for doing the job they should have done, and the majority in between will curse you for being better than themselves. Only a fool like me will have sense enough to pity your sacrifice." William had shrugged off the warning with some banal reply about duty and his obligations to the law. Actually, he rather liked the idea of visiting India, and never had so flattering an invitation to do so before.

"Believe me, Your Lordship, I know the native mind. They tend to exaggerate everything. They are incapable of controlling emotions, you see, and this may simply inflame them all over again, and tomorrow we may be faced with a situation as volatile as last April's. I am not arguing for the suppression of truth. I am, as you know, appalled by what I've heard this morning, even shocked. I never thought I would hear one of my own race admit doing the sort of things the General says he's done. The Hun, yes. Or natives. Even some Mediterranean types, but never an Englishman! I must confess that I do persist in feeling that were he born in England and reared back Home, instead of out here in this corrupting clime, he *couldn't* have behaved so badly. But the point, don't you see, is that natives aren't ready for so strong a dose of truth. They're not capable of understanding it, of seeing how singular a case this particular one happens to be, how anomalous an Englishman he is, and all they will say and think is, 'Ah, there's your English justice! Haven't we always told you so?' They're like children, Lord Hunter."

"More sherry, Rankin?"

"Thank you, I shouldn't, but all right, just a touch," he said, holding out his glass. "You see what I'm trying to avert, don't you, Your Lordship?"

"Yes, of course."

"Good! I hoped I would make myself clear. Only sometimes, as I'm sure you know better than I, we are obliged to argue against just principle for overriding practical reasons, but there's really no use in poking our heads underground, pretending we don't live in the real world, is there?" He seemed genuinely concerned about that question. His brow was tightly wrinkled with lines of anxiety. He was a thoughtful man.

247

"No, I don't suppose any of us can ever fully escape the pressures of expediency," William conceded.

"I must say I've never liked that word. It's so — somehow invidious. I do believe there are times when higher wisdom dictates a particular action that might at other times seem rather reprehensible. Yes, I should prefer putting it *that* way, Your Lordship, and I must say I'm sure your decision to do this will be praised for precisely that reason, by everyone who really matters —"

"Oh, I am afraid you've misunderstood me, Rankin," he interrupted, shaking his head. "I couldn't possibly do what you've asked me to."

"But why? I thought you just said you appreciated the strength of my argument?"

"Oh, I do. Indeed I do. I'm sure we've risked a great deal by agreeing to hold this inquiry in the first instance, Rankin. A great deal," he repeated, distractedly tapping his knee. He had been warned by several people not to accept the Secretary of State's invitation, under any conditions. One particularly powerful peer, a former Indian Viceroy, cautioned him that an inquiry of this sort, at this particular juncture in history, might do nothing less than destroy the entire edifice of Britain's Empire over India. He had not lightly undertaken his task. "I hope that what we accomplish may be worth the risk, of course, but in any event, we have agreed to hold open hearings, and I shouldn't want to turn my back on that pledge."

"But the *danger* of incitement —"

"Yes, that's always a risk we run in our particular calling, wouldn't you agree, Justice Rankin?" He spoke very softly and smiled in his most engaging manner, for he did not want to hurt this gentle man's feelings, and he appreciated the ultimate altruism that motivated his request.

"B-but in dealing with natives —"

"I don't really see how that affects the merits of an

inquiry designed to investigate what you yourself describe as frightful acts of injustice. I don't for a moment deny your superior knowledge of India, Rankin, but natives *are* human, and by his own confession, our countryman appears to have treated them more atrociously than you or I should treat any beast, wild or domesticated, and I must confess I rather think it important that the native press be permitted to hear and report everything we do in the course of this inquiry, to make it perfectly clear to all natives, as well as to every Britisher serving our Government here, that Great Britain remains a Nation devoted to certain principles — I should have thought we just fought and won a War to help preserve some of those — rather important things, like freedom, and justice —"

"Back Home, yes, Your Lordship. But this is the Orient. Nothing is the same out here, not time, not principle itself. Believe me!"

He was almost shaken by the passionate outburst that animated Rankin's visage and voice, but before he was obliged to reply Harold returned with lunch, reminding them that they had less than half an hour in which to eat.

"I do so wish you would listen to me, Lord Hunter."

"But I have listened, Rankin. I've listened very carefully."

"Then will you close the hearing this afternoon?"

"Oh, no, I couldn't possibly," he repeated.

"You intend to permit the natives on our committee to interrogate him in public, just as you have done?" His voice trembled with disbelief.

"Yes, of course. Every member of our committee may ask whatever questions he likes of any witness who comes before us."

"But Setalvad and Narayan are much too clever for him, Your Lordship! They will destroy him, make a laughing stock of him, and in public, with natives present, it could prove a disastrous blow to our entire sense of racial superiority."

"Yes, I suppose it could," he conceded, pausing to taste a piece of his fried fish, pondering Rankin's apprehension as he chewed. "Pity the Brigadier didn't consider such matters some time ago," he added, sadly.

23

SIR CHIMANLAL H. SETALVAD was in some respects more English than any other member of the committee. His navy pinstripe suit was imported from Bond Street, as were his spats, cravat, and cuff links. He held a double First from Cambridge, and had been called to the bar of London's Inner Temple. His dark lustrous hair was combed perfectly flat against his high brow, and when he spoke it sounded as if all his words were generated inside the arched tunnels of his high-bridged nose.

"You heard about twelve-forty that the Jallianwala meeting was to be held?" Sir Chimanlal asked.

"Yes," Rex replied. He responded more gruffly than he had when answering Lord Hunter's questions, and did not look directly at the dusky face of his interrogator.

"When you heard that, you did not take any steps to warn the people against going to that place?"

"I had been warning them all the morning."

"You did not do so after you heard of it?"

"No. I began to organize my troops and think about it."

"You did not think it would be desirable, for instance, to put up posters at that place warning people?"

"I did not think there was any time to put up posters and write posters," the General snapped. "I had to organize my troops and look sharp, for if they were going to disobey my orders, the situation was really serious, and it was a much more serious situation than it appears now looking back at it. I had to get my troops ready."

"When you heard of the contemplated meeting at twelve-forty you made up your mind that if the meeting was going to be held you would go and fire?"

The General folded his arms across his thick, heavily ribboned chest before responding, "When I heard that they were coming and collecting I did not at first believe that they were coming, but if they were coming to defy my authority, and really to meet after all I had done that morning, I had made up my mind that I would fire immediately in order to save the military situation. The time had come now when we should delay no longer. If I had delayed any longer I was liable for court-martial."

"You took two armored cars with you?"

"Yes."

"Those cars had machine guns?"

"Yes."

"And when you took them you meant to use the machine guns against the crowd, did you?"

"If necessary."

"When you arrived there you were not able to take the armored cars in because the passage was too narrow?"

"Yes."

"Supposing the passage was sufficient to allow the armored cars to go in, would you have opened fire with the machine guns?"

"I think probably yes."

"In that case the casualties would have been very much higher?"

"Yes."

"And you did not open fire with the machine guns simply by the accident of the armored cars not being able to get in?"

"I have answered you," he shouted, turning his face sharply to glare for the first time directly into Setalvad's unblinking eyes. "I have said if they had been there the probability is that I would have opened fire with them!"

"With the machine guns straight?" he asked.

"With the machine guns."

Several gasps greeted this response, and Sir Chimanlal waited with head bowed and eyes closed before continuing his line of interrogation.

"I gather generally from what you put in your report," he began, looking up sharply, "that your idea in taking this action was really to strike terror? That is what you say. 'It was no longer a question of merely dispersing the crowd, but one of producing a sufficient moral effect!'"

"If they disobeyed my orders it showed that there was complete defiance of law, that there was something much more serious behind it than I imagined, that therefore these were rebels, and I must not treat them with gloves on. They had come out to fight if they defied me, and I was going to give them a lesson."

"I take it that your idea in taking that action was to strike terror?"

"Call it what you like," he replied, raising his chin. "I was going to punish them. My idea from the military point of view was to make a wide impression."

"To strike terror not only in the city of Amritsar, but throughout the Punjab?"

"Yes, throughout the Punjab. I wanted to reduce their

moral, the *moral* of the rebels," he repeated, clearly unconscious of his malapropism.

"You thought that by striking terror in that manner you would save the British *Raj*? You thought that the British *Raj* was in danger."

"No, the British *Raj* is a mighty thing," he replied, looking back and forth, like an animal bewildered by too many strange sounds at once, confused, troubled. "It would not be in great danger but it might bring about more bloodshed, more looting, more lives lost." He had lost the thread and became incoherent.

"You did not think your act was instituted in order to save the British *Raj*?" Setalvad asked calmly.

"No, never, I took action to save life and property and to prevent anybody who thought they could manage to mutiny from mutinying. It was a merciful act," he muttered, "but at the same time it was a horrible act and it took a lot of doing."

"Did it ever occur to you," Sir Chimanlal asked, driving the sword in clean with each perfectly articulated syllable, "that by adopting this method of 'frightfulness' — excuse the term — you were really doing a great disservice to the British *Raj* by driving discontent deep?"

"No," he insisted, half rising from his chair, reaching out his right arm, "it only struck me that at the time it was my duty to do this and that it was a horrible duty. I did not like the idea of doing it but I also realized that it was the only means of saving life and that any reasonable man with justice in his mind would realize that I had done the right thing." He stared hopefully at His Lordship's face, adding, "And it was a merciful act though a horrible act and they ought to be thankful to me for doing it."

"Did this aspect of the matter strike you," Setalvad repeated, driving his second blade in next to the first, "that

by doing an act of that character you were doing a great
disservice to the British *Raj*?"

"I thought it would be doing a jolly lot of good and
they would realize that they were not to be wicked," he
answered, sounding as distraught as he looked.

Major General Sir George Barrow, the only military
member of the committee, appreciated fully the damage
done by Sir Chimanlal's interrogation, and hastily
scribbled a note, which he passed to William, requesting
time for a few questions. William nodded.

"General, you received orders when you arrived at
Amritsar that you should take such measures that might
be found necessary to restore order?" General Barrow
began. He was a handsome man, whose features were as
sharp and clean as a classical bust, his brow as broad as a
Roman emperor's, his eyes widespread, fearless as a Greek
god's.

"Yes, sir," Rex responded.

"And although martial law had not been proclaimed
you considered that the situation was such that it was
necessary to carry out the instructions that you had received just in the same way as if martial law had been
proclaimed?"

"Yes, sir."

"In other words, you considered that war was being
waged against the Crown and that you had a right to antici-
pate the proclamation of martial law?"

"Yes, sir."

"Now coming on to the Jallianwala Bagh incident for
a minute, you perhaps know as well as I do, that an unlawful assembly may be dispersed even by force, if necessary, even though it has not actually resorted to acts of
violence?"

"Yes, sir."

Sir George nodded, taking a deep breath before he continued. The General was responding much too laconically. He sounded like a robot, repeating the same two word answer to every question. He had never been accused of having the quickest wit in his class, as George knew, but surely there was some way of getting this brigadier to speak intelligently in his own defense, in defense of the military posture he'd taken, which was, of course, perfectly proper. Exhaling slowly, George tried again, deciding to spell things out rather more carefully for his friend, who looked almost comatose at the moment.

"Now, with regard to the use of force against the crowd in the Jallianwala Bagh, do I take it from what you said this morning that you had taken a wider view of the whole situation, that you had looked at it not merely as an officer who was assisting the military, but you were acting in accordance with the directions given to you? In other words, I will read out to you the actual words to refresh your memory —" He spoke the last few words in a somewhat louder voice, trying to stir some life into Rex's glazed eyes, as he paused to open the martial law manual, reading, "Where a proclamation of martial law has been issued, any soldier who takes, in accordance with the official instructions laid down for the guidance of those administering martial law, such measures as honestly seem to be necessary for carrying such issue and the operation of restoring peace and preserving authority . . ." He stopped reading and looked up to see if he was getting through, and now he leaned forward, hammering out each word as though driving blunt metal into stone. "You, therefore, I understand, were acting under those words conveyed in the proclamation, that is, you honestly thought that it was necessary to use force for the successful issue of the operation of restoring peace and authority in the Punjab. Am I right?"

"Absolutely, sir."

George waited, nodding his encouragement, but the stone lips were sealed again, now that their quota of two words had emerged. At least one of the words was different! He braced himself and took another deep breath, prompting:

"And you were convinced honestly in your mind that when you fired on this crowd it was to prevent further trouble and bloodshed which might follow later on?"

"Absolutely, sir."

It was no use, he saw, asking a few more questions before surrendering the field with a faint sigh to the Honorable Pandit Jagat Narayan.

Narayan earned his title as an elected Member of the Legislative Council of the United Provinces. He was, however, called many names other than Honorable by the British administration of the Punjab, whose lieutenant governor had, in fact, developed so strong an aversion to the Pandit that he refused him permission to enter Amritsar during the months of April, May and June. Narayan was a small-boned frail-looking man, and in contrast to Setalvad and everyone else on the committee dressed simply, wearing only a white cotton shirt and pajama-like trousers, a peasant's turban of bleached cloth, and thong slippers. His face was thin, hollow-cheeked, his eyes glowed like coals, the ebony color of his skin.

"You arrived at Amritsar at about nine or ten P.M. on the eleventh?" Narayan began.

"Yes."

"Were you informed of any acts of lawlessness or violence that were committed by the mob on the eleventh?"

"No."

"Were you informed of any acts of lawlessness and violence that were committed by the mob on the twelfth?"

"I should think not, as far as I can remember."

257

"Therefore, may I take it that up to the thirteenth the only information which you had about the behavior of the mob inside the city was as to what they did on the tenth?"

"Outside the city a good deal happened."

"I am only asking you about Amritsar city," the Pandit replied sharply.

"So far as the Amritsar city was concerned, there was no further lawlessness."

"You have repeatedly been describing the citizens of Amritsar as rebels. Was your conclusion based on the facts that were supplied to you on the night of the eleventh as to what had happened on the tenth?"

"Not only in Amritsar city, but outside Amritsar. My mind was not made up on what had happened in Amritsar only."

"On the eleventh or on the morning of the twelfth at the railway station a number of names were given to you of the agitators by Ashraf Khan? May I know where that paper is? Can I get all these names that were taken down by you?"

"I am afraid you cannot have them. I have not got them now."

"Or the names that were taken down by Major Briggs that night?"

"It is a long time. We have been moving about a lot on the frontier," he muttered, shaking his head slowly. "He may have it. He is a very good brigade major. He may possibly have it." Why wasn't Tommy here? he wondered, glancing behind him at the rows of unfamiliar faces in the room, so many faces over uniforms, only none of them Tommy's.

"From the eleventh to fifteenth, had you ever been informed by anybody that any person inside the city of

Amritsar was seen with a firearm in his possession or used any firearm?"

"This is against the law."

"Or any of them used any firearm?"

"I do not know that any used any firearm."

"Therefore you had no information that even a single individual of the mob had a firearm!"

"No. They were going to do it with lathis!"

"Have not some of the orders promulgated by you a family likeness to similar orders promulgated in Belgium?"

"In my mind it had nothing to do with Belgium whatever."

"For instance, the order about salaaming and the curfew order?"

"I did what I thought right."

"Were not a large number of arrested persons kept in an open racket court throughout the day and the night for six or seven days inside the Fort?"

"In the night we had a little cover over the racket court. There were tarpaulins spread over. We did the best we could. There was no room."

"Therefore this allegation that they were kept in an open racket court during the day and the night the whole time is wrong?"

"A racket court is usually open."

"Without any shade for their heads? That is the allegation."

"My impression is that there was a shed over it."

"May I know what was the number of persons that were kept so in the racket court?"

"No, I cannot tell you."

"Can I get any record from which I may be able to get that information?"

"I think when you see Major Briggs, he will be able to

give you information on that point probably. I could not positively say, because we have been a long time away." They told him Tommy had been summoned to Lahore for today's hearing. Why hadn't he arrived as yet? He could have answered all these questions.

"You went on the night of the thirteenth inside the city to see that your curfew orders were obeyed?"

"That is so."

"And you found that your orders were obeyed?"

"That is quite true."

"And you intended that that order of yours should be obeyed on the night of the thirteenth? You intended that the curfew order should be obeyed?"

"If I gave an order, I intended it to be obeyed."

"You never gave a moment's thought," the Pandit began softly, though his voice got louder and more shrill as he spoke, "as to what would happen to the four hundred or five hundred persons that were killed inside the Jallianwala Bagh, as to how they would be attended to, as to how their relations would come and take them away, as to how any water would be administered to them, as to how any medicine would be administered to them? It never occurred to you as to how it would be possible after eight o'clock to remove the dead bodies?"

"I gave my permission that they might go and remove the dead bodies. Therefore I presume they could go."

"Did you in any way modify your curfew order? Did you make any proclamation that 'today I modify my curfew order and allow people to remain outside till twelve o'clock to remove dead bodies'?"

"I allowed them to go and remove the dead. Therefore they could go."

"Did you in any way modify your curfew order on the thirteenth?"

"It was probably modified," he said, anxiously removing a cigarette from his pocket, breaking it inadvertently between his fingers, leaving the tobacco to spill unnoticed onto his lap.

"Did you issue any proclamation?" Narayan persisted. "Is there any written order saying that the order that was passed by you on the morning of the twelfth was modified, and that people were allowed to remain outside their houses up to twelve o'clock or one o'clock?"

"I think they must have remained all the night. I saw all the dead bodies going by the next morning."

"You do not answer my point," he persisted angrily.

"I must answer it according to my light."

"Did you pass any written order and is there any written order in existence that the curfew order had been modified?"

"I allowed them to go ——"

"That is not the answer to my question!"

"I cannot tell you," he replied. "I gave them permission to remove and bury their dead. Therefore orders must have been given not to interfere with them."

"If your curfew order was modified, how was it that at nine P.M. you went inside the city to see whether your order was obeyed or not?"

"I do not know that I went at nine P.M."

"Supposing it was between nine and ten P.M."

"I think it was later," he whispered.

"It is clear that you came back to Ram Bagh at ten-thirty," Narayan reminded him. Rex had told William that this morning. He bit into his lip, staring mutely at the glossy black forehead of his interrogator, focusing on the spot where a single bullet would have put an end to the Honorable Pandit's questioning. "It was ten o'clock that I went round," he admitted at last.

"Supposing between four hundred and five hundred were killed, what would be the proportion of the wounded?"

"It was very close firing, you understand. I should say multiplied by three. It may be more I should think."

"Is it not a fact that it being close firing, one bullet could kill two or three at a time?"

"That is true. Quite possible."

A sepulchral hush had fallen over the crowded room. "Did you make any ambulance arrangements?"

"I had no time for that."

"You have told us that on the thirteenth the city was a model of law and order?"

"It was all quiet when I went round at ten. After the shooting it soon became a model of law and order."

There were no further questions.

24

G.O.C. LAHORE and the Adjutant General, down from Delhi for the show, took Rex to the Service Club immediately after the hearing ended. The A.G., who as a lieutenant general outranked G.O.C. Lahore, proposed the first toast:

"To the Savior of the Punjab, Gentlemen!" He rose smartly from his chair and held out his glass toward Rex.

"The Savior of the Punjab," G.O.C. Lahore repeated, and he too got up, though he'd gone heavy round the middle since getting his division, and everything he did seemed a bit slow and sloppy. Perhaps he resented the idea of finding his brigadier in the Punjab hailed as its savior. But none of the other staff officers in the senior officers' lounge appeared to Rex to harbor jealous reservations. They all added their lusty cheers, and every face turned with glowing admiration toward him. It was a moving tribute. He felt a rush of moisture to his eyes.

"Thank you, sir," he told the A.G.

"No, no, it's we who thank you, General," Sir Henry said.

"Yes, yes, well done," G.O.C. Lahore chimed in, grudgingly. "Of course, these things always look bad for us in the press. I rather wish Government hadn't started up the whole business again." He hung his heavy-jowled head over his glass.

"I don't know," Rex replied, inhaling the smoke of his cigarette as the gin's warmth spread its soothing fire through his blood. "I've never shied away from a battle yet. I'm not afraid of this one." He winked in the A.G.'s direction.

"Hear, hear," Sir Henry responded, winking back. "I'm inclined to agree with Reggie, Robbie. We certainly didn't ask for this inquiry, but it may turn out to be the best thing that's happened for us since the Armistice. People in Delhi have begun wondering how long we were going to sit round sucking our thumbs while seditious natives like Gandhi run wild preaching black rebellion. We've got to draw the line somewhere!"

"Of course, we've got to draw the line," Robbie agreed, retreating to safer ground now that he found himself flanked. "The only point I was trying to make is about this matter of publicity, which always mucks things up." He gestured vaguely with one hand.

"I can stand by every word I've spoken," Rex said. "I've answered them straight. Nothing to hide. Nothing I'm ashamed to say before God or man. I've done my duty. I'd do it again, by God. We can't let them rape our women, ruin our property. No, I won't abide that."

"Well said, Reggie! We've got to stand the shot, Gentlemen." Sir Henry refilled their glasses from the decanter that had been left at his elbow. "Confidentially, and perhaps I shouldn't be saying this, I've had my differences with C-in-C on this matter. He wanted to insist on closed hearings, especially for yourself, Reggie. Not that he doesn't support everything you've done, but precisely for the reasons Robbie mentioned. Well, quite frankly, I said, 'Sir, I disagree entirely!' And I told him why."

"Bully for you," Rex cheered. "I half expected to see him here today!"

"He wanted to stay close to the headquarters' wire with the Afghan pot still simmering."

"There's only one way to finish that job, Sir Henry," Rex said. "It would take me a division, but I'd move her right over the Khyber —"

"Snow's been falling all week up there," G.O.C. Lahore muttered wryly.

"Our men won't melt."

"It's freezing them that worries me," Robbie retorted.

"Yes, well it's the money that worries His Excellency," Henry explained, smiling tightly, refusing to get drawn any further into argument concerning the details of Afghan strategy or a lack of it. "But I must say, I can't help feeling rather proud of our record in handling the Amritsar revolt. Perhaps I should say *your* record, Reggie, but you know what I mean — I'm talking of the *military* record. I rather welcome the publicity, you know, because it will, after all, bolster confidence in us. The Frocks failed, let's face it. They couldn't hold the bloody mob in check for half a day. Some of our bleeding heart liberals in Delhi ask me why it was necessary to kill a few hundred of their black brothers to calm things down. Would you rather have waited till they killed a few thousand of your wives and sisters? I ask."

"Absolutely, sir."

"I say it's high time we stopped being afraid to say what we believe, and to do what we know is best for the well-being and security of our Empire," Sir Henry continued, warming to his subject as he spoke, displaying that eloquent command of speech for which he was renowned in senior officer clubs throughout India. "We stand on the ramparts, Gentlemen, and we stand there alone! The storm swirls beneath us, the darkness engulfs us at times, yet we follow our stars of light, and we emerge victorious and with our victory God and Country remain unscathed. I say let all the world know what we've done, what you've done, Reggie, and mothers, sisters, their sons and brothers at Home, and in every civilized corner of this earth, will bless you for the salvation you've brought them! *He* brought not Peace but the Sword, remember!"

"Thank you," Rex whispered.

"Hear, hear," Robbie called out. "I suppose you're right, Sir Henry. I expect it might be just as well to let everyone know that we won't tolerate anarchy or rebellion. My only point, you see, was to do whatever would best let us get on with our jobs of keeping things straight. Naturally, I agree we protect the civil arm, just as we do everything else, and I don't for one moment regret having ordered you personally down to Amritsar, Reggie, to take over there."

Rex stiffened and poured himself another jigger of gin. "Actually, I'd decided before your orders reached me, General, on the basis of reports I'd been receiving direct from Amritsar, that the situation was serious enough to demand my personal attention on the spot."

"Oh, did you?" G.O.C. Lahore sounded as though he'd swallowed his tongue.

"Well, you're both to be congratulated on handling this business firmly, and no nonsense about it," the Adjutant General remarked, adding with a faint smile, "The great strength of the military has always been our unity, Gentlemen. Ah, here's Georgie! *Georgie!*"

General Barrow had gone to a table at the other side of

the lounge, but was arrested by Henry's call, and walked over to take the empty chair opposite the A.G.

"Gentlemen," he said, nodding perfunctorily at Henry and Robbie as he sat, completing their circle. He carefully avoided looking at Rex, who did not, however, appear to notice the snub. Sir George was equally famous for his command of military law and his lack of civil manners.

"We've all been remarking about how well things went for us today, Georgie," the A.G. explained, filling his glass.

"Did they? I'm glad you told me, Henry. I never should have guessed it from where I was sitting. Cheers!"

"Oh? Didn't you think it went well for us, Georgie?"

"I think it was disastrous."

"Exactly how do you mean that?" Rex asked.

"Since you inquire, General, I mean that you said too much in answering questions you should have refused to answer entirely, and too little in answering others you should have used as springboards for your own defense."

"My *defense* for what? I don't consider myself on trial, sir! I've done nothing I'm ashamed of! I did my duty as I saw it, and there are many people who seem to feel I did it rather well!"

"Yes, I'm sure," Barrow replied, locking his lips.

Rex appeared ready to launch a still more truculent attack in response to so humiliatingly obvious a refusal on Barrow's part even to discuss the matter with him, when Henry set a restraining hand on his arm and softly inquired, "George, could you possibly be a bit more explicit about the sort of thing you feel Reggie did wrong today?"

"Oh, for God's sake, Henry, you must have noted it a hundred times — all of those absurd hypothetical traps he walked into — 'If you could have brought the machine guns into the Bagh, *would* you have used them?'"

"I answered them straight!"

"You shouldn't havȩ answered them at all!"

"Why not?"

"Be quiet a moment, Reggie," Henry remarked, tugging nervously at his trim moustache. "Yes, I do see your point there, Georgie. I rather prefer avoiding speculative inferences myself, but do you really think he sounded *badly*?"

"Setalvad made him sound a fool!"

"*Sir*?"

"No, no, no, don't be offended, Reggie," Henry told him, soothing him with strokes on his braided sleeve. "It's very *good* of Georgie to be so frank with us, letting us know how things appeared from the other side of the table, you see, and nothing he says now is meant personally! We're simply trying to see how this might affect us all tactically. We don't want to let the Frocks catch us unprepared, do we?" He smiled reassuringly, and refilled Rex's glass. "Tell us, Georgie, what do you think the committee's report will conclude?"

"I've no idea at the moment."

"But surely you've had opportunity to form some impression of the various members' predilections by now? How does His Lordship feel about things?"

"He's cold as a kipper and tight-lipped as a Scotch clam to me," George replied.

"Of course, that need not necessarily reflect his feelings about the military or Reggie's actions," Henry mused, clearly enjoying this opportunity of alluding to George's abrasive personality. Barrow did not bother taking him up, but continued speaking as though nothing had been said since his last remark.

"I can assure you, however, Gentlemen, that Lord Hunter is nobody's fool, and what really worries me is that he

268

may have been convinced by today's testimony that the doctrine of minimum force was abandoned without due process."

"Yes, that occurred to me also," G.O.C. Lahore said, nodding gravely.

"I'm afraid I don't follow," Rex confessed.

"It's quite simple really," Barrow began. "Ordinarily, when conditions of civil disorder call for military intervention we are, as you surely know, constrained by precedent to act with the minimum amount of force required to restore order in the immediately threatened area, in this particular case, the minimum force needed to disperse the crowd in Jallianwala Bagh on thirteen April —"

"But I was obliged to do much more than merely disperse the mob," Rex insisted. "It was my duty to produce a sufficient moral effect, not only on those present but throughout the Punjab!" He recited it almost as though it were the rote incantation of a sacred formula. It was what he'd written in his report.

"Yes, yes, I know all that," Barrow remarked. "The point I'm trying to make, and this is what I kept trying to get you to say for yourself at the hearing, is that the only legal justification for the sort of extreme action you took in the Bagh would be your conviction that you were faced with rebellion and acting under the aegis of martial law."

"I was!"

"Yes, I know you *think* you were, old chap, and personally I too *believe* you were, as we all do, you see," George told him, smiling ingenuously, gesturing with upraised palm to include their colorfully ribboned quartet of general officers. His smile faded and then he sounded quite glum, saying, "The trick is to convince the others."

"And you don't think we have done, Georgie?"

"I shall have a better idea tonight. His Lordship has asked us to dine with him this evening at the Polo Club. Now if you will excuse me, Gentlemen —"

"But wait half a moment, Georgie! You *will* explain how dreadfully important it is to each and every one of us in uniform for Reggie to be thoroughly supported, indeed I should hope he would be acclaimed by your committee for his heroism in acting to save the entire Punjab —"

"I'm sure I couldn't match your eloquence, Henry, but I will try to put our case properly — on its merits."

Sir George rose and bowed stiffly as his farewell salutation.

"Good luck, Georgie! We're counting on you."

"Good day, Gentlemen," he said. G.O.C. Lahore also rose from his chair, responding cordially, but Rex neither moved nor spoke.

"Georgie's a terribly clever chap," Henry remarked, after Barrow had left the lounge. "I'm sure he'll do the job."

"He talked as if *I* was on trial," Rex muttered. "I thought they called these damnable hearings to try the rebel natives. Isn't that what you told me?" he asked Robbie.

"Yes, yes, of course, but they're looking into the whole picture —"

"But the way *he* sounded, it was as if *I* was accused of something. I did my duty!"

"Of course you did, Reggie, and we honor you for doing it so superbly!"

"To hear him talk, you would have thought *I* was the one who'd rebelled against the Raj! I wish my brigade major was here today. He kept all the records. He has a better memory for dates and numbers than I do . . ." Rex hesitated, touching his forehead with trembling fingers. The throbbing head pain that had of late afflicted him returned with a vengeance, hammerblows aimed against the back side of his eyes.

"Feeling a bit fagged, Reggie?" Henry asked. "It has been rather a trying day for you, I imagine."

"No, I don't know what this is." He kept aspirin in his pocket, and took a few, washing them down with the gin. The brigade medics said it was probably a cold inside his head. He'd been up in the howling winds around the frontier passes last month. He heard a high-pitched buzzing sound like a fast drill whirling inside. "I'll be all right in a minute," he said.

"You need a good long rest, Reggie. I'm going to recommend a holiday back home for you," Henry offered.

"Very kind of you, sir."

"No, no, well-deserved. I'll speak to C-in-C about it soon as I return to Delhi. What's this?" An orderly had come up to their table with a cable in his gloved hand. Saluting, he handed the message to Rex.

It was from his brigade headquarters on the frontier. His fingers trembled as he tore open the envelope and unfolded the tear sheet of telegraph paper. Then he could not seem to focus properly on the neatly printed words.

"Would you read it to me, sir?" he asked Henry.

"Of course. It's from your adjutant — 'Regret to report Major Briggs just died on operating table —' "

"What did you say?" He had staggered to his feet, leaving his chair to tumble back onto the floor behind him, making a sound that brought all conversation to a halt in the lounge. "Did you say *Briggs*?"

"Reggie, *do* sit down," Sir Henry insisted, offering his own chair, gripping his arm firmly as he helped him to the seat. An orderly straightened the toppled chair, in which Henry now sat. "You must take hold of yourself, Reggie. Are you feeling better now?"

"Yes, sir." His face had gone ashen, his lips moved without making any sound.

"Have a bit more gin, Reggie!"

He only gagged on the drink, and started coughing uncontrollably. He seemed to have swallowed the gin in his windpipe.

The lounge remained otherwise silent, and each gasp, each choking cough, was magnified by a hush on all sides, every martial eye watching anxiously as the General fought to regain his breath. Several medical officers approached solicitously, but Sir Henry motioned them off, sensing that Rex was winning the battle on his own. A few moments later he had control of his respiration again, and everyone turned back to the conversations they'd suspended, like records from which all the Gramophone needles had momentarily been raised.

"Everything under control, Reggie?"

"Yes, sir."

"Good. Now shall I finish reading this cable, or would you rather wait a bit?"

"Please read it, sir. I've got a firm grip."

"Good . . .! 'Surgery for enteric unsuccessful. Fragments of glass perforated intestinal lining, indicating probable assassination. Investigation started.' The signature reads, 'Adjutant, Forty-fifth Brigade.' I'm afraid that's all, Reggie."

"Ground glass," G.O.C. Lahore muttered, shaking his head slowly. "We've lost three officers in the division to ground glass this year, Henry. It's getting to be more of a nuisance than the bomb."

"They're all cowards," Henry said. "If they want to fight, why in God's name don't they stand up and fight us like men, the buggers?"

"Tommy dead?" Rex asked, reaching out for the piece of yellowish paper.

"He was a good soldier, was he, Reggie?"

"Yes," he muttered, trying to read the words, but his eyes were too clouded.

25

WILLIAM'S dinner at the Club got off to an awkward start. The Honorable Pandit Narayan arrived at the posh main entrance clad in the same casual garb he had worn all day, and the doorman would have dislodged him forcibly from the grounds had not the Honorable Dr. Flower Rice, Additional Secretary to the Government of India's Home Department, seconded to the committee, arrived in his carriage directly behind Narayan's, jumping from it, shouting:

"Don't touch that man, you idiot! He's an invited guest!" Flower was the committee's youngest member, an Oxford don, who'd come to Simla before the War, served on the Viceroy's staff during it, and was by now generally reputed to be His Excellency's favorite, which made most of his seniors in the service dislike him.

The Club's manager listened phlegmatically to Dr. Rice's vigorous protest, but insisted that no one would gain admission to his dining room or lounge after sundown without the proper attire. The altercation had reached an impasse when William appeared, reporting that he'd decided to shift the venue of his party to his own bungalow at the Club, "Where we can have more privacy."

Harold labored valiantly at trying to rearrange the furniture inside His Lordship's bungalow so as to encourage conversation, but the dinner table, which was moved into the middle of the sitting room, was too large to allow anyone to do much beyond standing round it or sitting down at it. They stood round in virtual silence till Sir Chimanlal, General Barrow, and Justice Rankin arrived, and then, as much from fatigue as for the lack of anything better to do, they took their places at table.

No sooner were their wine glasses filled than Sir George snapped to his feet and toasted, "His Majesty, the King-Emperor." Pandit Narayan had just tucked his legs up onto his chair, and took time in unscrambling himself. Nor did he drink wine, but had to wait for water before they could complete the toast. William resented Barrow's usurpation of his role as toastmaster, especially since he mistimed the toasting, which should have come after they'd eaten. In India, of course, he knew many things were done backwards, and in military circles, he suspected, anyone who ate before toasting the King would be considered disloyal. So he refrained from reprimand, but could not help smiling when Sir Chimanlal asked, with his glass poised high, "Aren't we being slightly premature?"

William half suspected, from the expression on Barrow's face as he watched Setalvad and Narayan dutifully complete the ritual affirmation of loyalty, that the General may have hoped neither would be willing to do so, possibly thus bringing the dinner to a swift conclusion.

"We've had a long day," William began, as they settled down again, "and I apologize for imposing this further tax upon your time, Gentlemen, but I'm sure you all realize that the testimony we've heard today demands our earliest consideration —"

"Why so?" Sir George asked, softly.

"I beg your pardon, General. Did you say something?" Barrow had taken the chair opposite William at the end of the long table.

"I don't see why we should treat today's evidence any differently from anything else we've heard," Sir George explained. "We've scheduled another week of hearings here, and perhaps after that, if you like, before we move to Bombay, we might pause to consider all the Lahore testimony en masse."

"Oh," William said, breaking a hard little roll with his stubby fingers, but leaving both halves untasted on his bread plate. "You found nothing extraordinary about what we heard today, General?"

"All revolutions are extraordinary, Your Lordship. Inasmuch as today's testimony dealt with Amritsar in revolt against the Crown, I suppose it might be called extraordinary, but that's true of much of the evidence we've heard."

"No, no, Sir George, I'm speaking now of the *General's* behavior, of *his* action. Didn't you find *that* extraordinary?" He asked it as only a seasoned judge could ask the most obvious of questions, in so intensely open a manner as to disarm all but the most hardened of criminal liars.

"Well, I suppose — yes, inasmuch —"

"Oh, that's good," William injected, smiling and picking up half of his roll now to butter it. "Then you do agree we must consider this matter at once, and try, if possible, to reach some consensus amongst ourselves as to what recommendations we should make to Government concerning the General's rather frightful action —"

"Certainly not! I do not agree to that formulation at

all, sir! The General acted with firm restraint in the face of rebellion — "

"Do you call the murder of hundreds of unarmed villagers *restraint?*" interrupted Sir Chimanlal.

" — rebellion," Sir George continued, ignoring his interrogator, "induced by a total breakdown of civil government. Amritsar was in revolt against the Crown, under martial law."

"Is it showing restraint to flog innocent people and make them crawl on their bellies?" Narayan asked, visibly trembling with rage.

"Gentlemen, Gentlemen," William called, tapping his butter knife against his goblet to restore order. "I did hope we could discuss these matters calmly, as befits our weighty charge."

"Hear, hear," said Justice Rankin. "God help us if we here lack the good sense and restraint of — of others," he said, glancing fleetingly at General Barrow's icy visage. "Certainly the conduct of our deliberations should be orderly, and entirely free of those contentious remarks that generate heat without shedding greater light."

"Your Lordship, might we not best proceed by first of all reminding ourselves of how substantial an area of agreement concerning today's testimony all of us already share," Flower Rice suggested, exhibiting his gifts of synthesis and moderation, which helped win him such renown at Simla. "Surely, for example, we all deplore the murder of Europeans by the mob at' Amritsar on the tenth —" and he paused, focusing his innocently wide blue eyes first upon Sir Chimanlal's face, till he nodded his assent, then upon Narayan's, who also did the expected, " — and surely each of us finds most frightful the General's crawling order —" here he turned directly to confront Sir George " — which was, remember, rescinded by the General at the explicit order of the Government of this province."

"I am perfectly well aware of that, Dr. Rice," Barrow told him.

"Of course, you are, sir, and that's exactly what I mean, you see, that all of us *do* agree about most of the matters we've heard evidence on today."

"Then I say we must recommend immediate dismissal of the General from his post," Sir Chimanlal insisted.

"That's illegal," Sir George snapped, "as well as outrageous!"

"Anything less would be immoral," Setalvad replied.

"Soon, I expect, all the harlots in Lahore will start preaching to us about the immorality of our wives," Sir George remarked, addressing himself to Flower Rice, who was not married.

"Of whom are you speaking, sir?" Setalvad inquired, angrily tapping his finger against the white cloth. "Please state the precise name, sir, of whom you are calling a harlot, *if* you dare face the legal consequences?"

"If I *what*? Are you now ready to judge of my courage? And of the courage of other generals of His Majesty's forces as well?" He asked it with remarkable restraint and in so trenchant a tone that even Sir Chimanlal seemed taken aback at the realization that he may have lost the support of others at the table who till now were more favorably disposed to his position than to Barrow's. "I suppose you feel perfectly competent to pass judgment upon the Brigadier's qualifications for field command as well as the action he took in subduing rebellion, don't you?"

Setalvad pursed his lips, but before he could reply, Pandit Narayan spoke, in a voice that sounded very thin and mild, "I do not feel it is a question so much of recommending punishment for one man, though as you know, I myself feel that the General has committed many terrible, frightful crimes, but let us not dwell upon that in purely individual terms. What I mean to say, Your Lordship, is that we should find some way to strike out against the philosophy which breeds such men, such inhuman men, who do not care for life, who have no feelings of compassion, or, of sorrow, for what pain they inflict upon others. It is the phenomenon he represents, which we must attack, the whole fabric of violence in society, which encourages men to act so brutally."

"Excuse me, Pandit," Flower said, earnestly leaning toward his neighbor's chair, "are you saying, in effect, that our charge is to consider proposals for some general reorientation of society?"

"Yes, yes, and even beyond that, you see, to each and all of mankind, to effect something of a revolution in human spirit."

"That's most laudable, of course," Flower replied, "but I shouldn't think we could do very much along those lines within our committee's mandate, could we, Your Lordship?"

"Regrettably not," William agreed, rather insulted that Flower should feel the need to remind him, even so tactfully, of the limits of his power, as if he were so foolish as to forget, or so imprudent as to venture to overstep those bounds. "But there are, you know, many practical proposals we could make, which might move us a step or two in the direction of the goal so admirably described by the Honorable Pandit. For one thing I should like to see some strengthening of the statute obliging military commanders to refrain from usurping any of the prerogatives of civil authority —"

"There was no civil authority left in Amritsar!" Barrow boomed.

"I know that's what the Brigadier claims," William replied evenly.

"It's what the Commissioner himself reported, Your

Lordship. The situation had gone beyond the powers of civil control. G.O.C. was obliged to take over when he did, precisely at the insistence of civil authority! It was hardly a case of usurpation, but one rather of salvation. The mob was an army of disaffection against the Raj. There was no alternative to military administration, under de facto martial law. I find it rather shocking that Your Lordship should not grasp the obviously legal character of the temporary transfer of authority from civil to military control."

"Yet it was almost one week between the military coup," Sir Chimanlal argued, jumping eagerly to William's defense, "and the proclamation of martial law by His Honour! So how can you say it was not a usurpation of power?"

"It was not a usurpation of power," Barrow said, tucking his thumbs under the thick leather belt that tightly girded his waist, staring in unblinking defiance at Setalvad's outraged face.

"Isn't this rather a moot point, Your Lordship?" Flower asked. "Knowing something of the Simla labyrinth myself, I rather suspect that the difficulty we've had in judging the precise timing of the martial law proclamation is really attributable to the time elapsed between His Honour's request for permission from His Excellency and the official transmission back of H.E.'s sanction via the secretariat, you see, printing it up and all, to Lahore here, and then the further conveying of that document to Amritsar. What I do mean, Sir Chimanlal, is that the entire process might very easily have taken the week or so, but that the formal request was made immediately upon G.O.C.'s arrival, so that, in effect, both you and Sir George could be technically correct, though the point in dispute wouldn't actually exist."

He had such a facile delivery that for fully half a minute after he'd finished no one spoke, each of them seeming to require a bit of time to work it out for himself. William looked the most puzzled, and decided then that he would have to arrange a private interview with His Honour to clarify this matter. He had written the Governor some time ago, inviting him to appear before the committee in open hearing, but received only a terse negative reply, alluding to "pressures of prior responsibilities."

"Yes, I do see your point, Dr. Rice," Justice Rankin remarked, "and I must say, from what little experience I personally have had with official delays in requesting documents from Simla — oh, if we had the time, I could tell you some really lovely stories about bureaucratic bungling —"

"Gentlemen, I do think we should confine our conversation this evening to questions directly —"

"Agreed, Your Lordship, agreed. Please strike my digression from the record! But I prefaced my anecdotal introduction, you know, with the qualifying, '*if* we had the time,' expressly for that reason! There's no argument here, sir, none whatever."

Harold cleared their soup bowls and served the salad, then went round refilling the almost empty glasses of Sir George, Dr. Rice, and Justice Rankin. Since the initial toast, William hadn't touched his wine. He felt lightheaded enough by now.

"Leaving aside the question of usurpation of civil authority for the time being," William suggested, "I wonder if we couldn't agree on several points concerning the General's behavior at the Bagh on April thirteenth? I was most distressed by three aspects of that incident: first, his failure to give any warning to the crowd before opening fire —"

"He'd spent his entire morning warning them!"

"Yes, General, but I'm speaking now specifically of the crowd assembled inside the Bagh —"

"They knew they were breaking the law. That's why they went," Sir George insisted, "to test us!"

"Do you believe that was true of the villagers?" William asked.

"Yes, by and large."

"Of *all* the villagers there?"

"Not every one of them perhaps —"

"But if there was even *one*, one totally innocent man in that garden, surely all that each of us holds most sacred, the tenets of faith as well as law by which we order our lives must lead us to insist that that innocent man at least be given fair warning and the opportunity of leaving the Bagh before the firing should begin. Wouldn't each of us insist upon that? Wouldn't you, General?"

"Of course, I would try —"

"Naturally, you would," William answered. "We are agreed then on this matter of the Brigadier's failure to give prior warning —"

"I haven't finished my statement, Your Lordship! I would try under ordinary circumstances to give ample prior warning, but I do not agree that by not giving verbal warning the Brigadier erred. The situation was a military one, a most explosive revolutionary one, and could only be judged adequately by the military commander on the spot. There are circumstances in which verbal warning might be misconstrued as weakness, and with a crowd as large as the one assembled on the thirteenth any sign of weakness could easily have proved fatal to the troops."

"But how?" William asked. "They had their same weapons. They could always have opened fire, were they threatened —"

"Yes, you may say that quite smugly here in the Club, Your Lordship, but nothing seems so simple in the heat of battle, believe me, and few things work out exactly the way we plan them in headquarters. You must trust the man on the firing line. He's ready to lay down his life, if need be, for your security, for the comfort of all of us who drink fine wine and eat fine food. I should think that the least we could do in return is to support his judgment —"

"Even when it is in error?" Sir Chimanlal asked.

"You're in no position to judge of that!"

"Are we *never* able to pass such judgment?" William inquired. "Forgive me if I sound obtuse, General, but I must be sure I understand you properly, because I do think the position you've taken just now might in effect challenge the validity of our entire inquiry, might it not? Why create our committee in the first instance?"

"Yes, yes, it is what all their military people like us to think," Pandit Narayan remarked, "that no matter how much of our money they demand for their budgets, and no matter how many of our people they slaughter in our very streets, still whatever they do is beyond question or doubt!"

"Excuse me, Pandit," Flower injected swiftly, "could you explain why you speak of 'their military people' and 'our money'? Why the shift in pronoun?"

"You know what I mean," Narayan replied, gesturing vaguely with his dark hand.

"No, but I'm afraid I don't, you see. Would you mind explaining yourself please?"

William had not immediately realized why Flower Rice became so swiftly enraged, but noticed the obvious pleasure with which Sir George viewed this new exchange, and appreciated by now how foolish Narayan had been to speak impulsively in the idiom of revolutionary nationalism.

"I was talking of the military, the generals."

"No, but you spoke of *their* military, and *our* money,

and *our* people, and if memory serves, I do believe you even said *our* streets? Did I hear you incorrectly, sir?"

"It may be I said it." He sounded frightened.

"It *may* be?" Flower leaned toward him, and his voice rang with the timbre of arrogant assurance, unique to the voices of the powerful young.

"Well, and what if he did say it?" Sir Chimanlal asked, impatiently. "So what, dammit? If he did not say it, then I will! What are you trying to prove?"

"Obviously, I don't have to try any more, do I? And you're proud of it? You admit it?"

"Of what, sir? What the hell are you talking about? Why all this fuss over a pronoun?"

"I'm talking about your loyalty to the Raj, Gentlemen," Flower solemnly replied. "I happen to think of British India as *our* country, not of yours, nor of mine — of ours. I rather think that's an important distinction. Am I wrong, Justice Rankin?"

"Oh, no, no, I agree entirely. I must say I was rather shocked to hear the Honorable Pandit using such inflammatory language —"

"And is the imputation of disloyalty less inflammatory?" Sir Chimanlal shouted. "Is a lifetime of service to the Raj dismissed, canceled out, ignored, because of one pronoun uttered in the heat of debate concerning a matter involving the slaughter of hundreds, possibly a thousand, unarmed citizens? Is this how you now hope to exonerate the villainy, the Prussian frightfulness, of that brute who still wears the uniform of a brigadier —"

"I will not sit at the same table with this rebel," Sir George announced, rising, "and listen to him slander the good name of —"

"A murderer, sir! A man who dishonors the uniform he wears, and the nation which permits him —"

"Good night, Your Lordship," Barrow called out, tossing his napkin onto his plate, turning smartly on his heel, pausing only to pick up his hat and baton before leaving the bungalow.

"Oh dear, dear, dear, dear," muttered Rankin, sadly shaking his white-haired head.

"I rather think we owe the General a formal apology," Flower suggested. "Shall I try to catch him up before he leaves the Club grounds, Your Lordship?"

"I don't know that it would do any good," William said, turning anxiously to face Sir Chimanlal, the unspoken question in his weary eyes.

"I do apologize humbly to you, Your Lordship, for precipitating the disruption of your dinner party, but I will never apologize to him, nor will I alter my position concerning the Brigadier and the horrendous actions he took in Amritsar. You invited us here this evening to ask our opinions of the testimony we heard today. Mine, quite simply, is that the Brigadier, by his own admission, stands convicted of the crime of murder against an unarmed, defenseless, overwhelmingly innocent population, and that the least we can do is to recommend his immediate dishonorable dismissal from the service of His Majesty as partial punishment for what he has done, and in order to make it impossible for him to repeat such criminal actions in the future."

"I agree," said Narayan, turning to his friend as he spoke, "that this must be done, but after that, my point is, what measures can be taken to change the entire system whereby the military people have so much of power in their own hands that whenever they like, they can come onto our city streets, into our very homes, our temples, and treat us like animals . . .?" His voice trailed off as he realized that Sir Chimanlal had turned away from him, and was looking at Flower Rice, who silently rose from his seat.

"If I may be excused, Your Lordship," Flower said, bowing perfunctorily before turning to leave.

"Service officers are more concerned with old school ties than justice," Sir Chimanlal said, looking to Justice Rankin for some measure of support. "You've been on the High Court for more than ten years now, sir, you can understand how incensed we feel, I'm sure of it."

"Oh, my — Your Lordship, I've rather a nagging headache, I'm afraid," Rankin explained, sidling off his seat, and coming round to touch William's shoulder in a gesture, at once meant to reassure yet serving by its tremulous weakness only to deepen His Lordship's despair. "Well — tomorrow *is* another day," Rankin added, nodding with lowered lids in the general direction of Sir Chimanlal and the Pandit before departing.

"It seems they have all been too long in India," said Sir Chimanlal. "Thank God our Secretary of State had the wisdom to appoint Your Lordship to be president of this committee —"

"Yes, yes, it is a blessing," echoed the Pandit.

"Otherwise, you see for yourself how even men as upright and intelligent as Dr. Rice and Justice Rankin show their true feelings of prejudice —"

"I really don't think it proper, Sir Chimanlal, for us to discuss the merits of other members of this committee in their absence."

"I was only trying —"

"Yes, I know, you were being *kind* to me." He felt more repelled by Sir Chimanlal's flattery than he had been by his rudeness. Much as he'd tried to avoid all the stereotypes his friends used in discussing natives, William suddenly found himself thinking how typical it seemed for a native to pour flattery over one Englishman's head, while hurling a tarbrush full of insults at the back of another. But what disturbed him even more than this consciousness of Sir Chimanlal's inability to rise above the failings of his race was his own awareness that he was little more adept at that all but impossible act of mental acrobatics. For staring at the dark faces of his only remaining dinner companions William felt an almost irresistible compulsion to leave his place, to seek out the company of men of his own complexion with whom to dine. It was the first time he had ever sat alone with guests darker than himself, and the strangeness of it all but robbed him of any remaining appetite. He felt singularly awkward, strained, as though in a drunken stupor he had somehow blundered into the wrong room, and was too embarrassed to admit that he'd come here under false colors.

"If you would care to have my opinion," Pandit Narayan began, nodding his head to the singsong rhythm of his tone, "most of the troubles we have had here of late come from sahibs, who refuse absolutely to recognize that people are human beings, whatever the color of our skin happens to be —"

"Why do you say that to me?" William asked.

"No, no, I do not mean it is true of Your Lordship. Naturally, I would not mention it to you if I thought for one moment —"

"I see. Then you would say it behind my back?"

"No, no, I am afraid I have not expressed myself clearly."

"To return to the practical matter before us," Sir Chimanlal said, sounding more vigorous than he had at the start of the evening, "we trust you agree that our committee must recommend the immediate dismissal, or suspension, if that must come first, of the Brigadier, from all duties and responsibilities that would empower him to exercise command —"

"I don't think we can properly pursue this without the other members," William replied softly.

"But they're obviously opposed to any forthright recommendation of action —"

"Ah, but they do constitute half of our membership, and I'm sure you realize that as president of the committee, I should like to have us reach unanimity, if at all possible, on all the recommendations we propose to Government —"

"How in God's name is that possible, if they walk out as soon as we mention the only just punishment — and it is so mild, considering what crimes have been committed by that scoundrel?"

"We must try to be patient."

"Do you think we have not been patient? Is that all you can tell us seven months after the massacre? More than half a year has gone by, and the killer remains not only untouched, but still in position to do such killing today, or tomorrow — and do you think we have not been patient? Perhaps it is our trouble, Your Lordship, that we have been patient too long," Sir Chimanlal replied, rising. "I hoped this evening, when you first spoke as you did, that you at least fully understood how we felt, that you not only sympathized, for to express sympathy alone is not so difficult, but that you shared our sense of urgency and also of outrage."

"I do," he whispered.

"Then how can *you* wait any longer? What more evidence do we need than that which we have heard today — and from his own lips?"

"Our report will carry more weight if our recommendations are unanimous. I'm afraid that if only the three of us advise Government to take certain actions, His Excellency may choose to ignore our recommendations." He suspected that without Flower Rice's name on the document, the Viceroy might not even bother to read it.

"We have a saying in Sanskrit," the Pandit told him. *"Satyameva Jayate!* It means, the Truth alone conquers."

"But it doesn't say after how long," William replied, wishing that Rankin had remained. The four of them at least could have written a majority report, and though some of his friends would have called him a traitor to his own race, he was tough enough to withstand a bit more abuse.

"Why couldn't we write a majority report?" Chimanlal inquired, still standing, his napkin tucked into his vest.

"Because we aren't a majority, for one thing."

"And for another, because you would rather not have your name associated only with ours?"

"You said that, not I!" His cheeks flamed, as though he'd suddenly poked his face close to a blazing fire.

"But is it not what you were thinking, Your Lordship?"

"I don't want to discuss the matter further tonight, Sir Chimanlal."

"Very well. Then the Pandit and I will write our own report — a minority report! Government may ignore us entirely, but at least God and our conscience will know we have reached the right judgment."

With that he left. The Honorable Pandit followed him. William stared at the flickering flame of the candle closest to his place. The flame became brighter as the candle burned itself down.

"Will His Lordship want dessert now?" Harold asked softly, holding out his offering of rice pudding.

"They *are* right, you know," he whispered.

"Rice pudding, Your Lordship," Harold said, too discreet to indicate by so much as a murmur or facial expression that he'd heard his master's confession. "Do try some. It's quite soothing to the stomach."

But he'd lost his appetite entirely.

26

WILLIAM did not sleep well that night. Before dawn he abandoned his bed, leaving his bungalow while the grass was still jeweled with mist. He woke a cabby, who drove him to Government House, and astonished the guard at the outside gate, when he explained who he was, and whom he wished to see.

The sun hung blood red over the burnished minarets of Lahore's mosque, and the hills were purple as he entered the large room with its tall windows facing east.

"That's my Punjab," Sir Michael said, glancing round just long enough to catch William's attention, then turning back to his contemplation of the dawn, watching it reverentially, with the eye of a worshipper, of a lover. "Have you ever seen a more beautiful sunrise, Hunter?"

"I've come to speak with you about Amritsar, Your Honour."

"Of course you have," Sir Michael replied, still facing William with his back, hands clasped firmly behind it, "but that needn't spoil our appreciation of nature's wonders. Look at the color of those hills! What monarch wouldn't trade his regal robes for their splendor? That's the trouble with our modern civilization, it's taken us too far from nature, dulled our senses."

"Yes, I'm afraid many of us have become brutalized."

"I prefer to call it desensitized."

"But you're speaking of nature, I'm thinking about atrocities against our fellow men."

"Oh, I see," Sir Michael remarked, apparently losing interest in his window, coming round the polished desk. He seemed to grow taller as he moved closer to William, a formidably straight and sturdy figure. "Do come over here by the fire and sit, Hunter. Make yourself comfortable. It's awfully good of you to drop in and visit. I can well imagine how busy you are these days."

"This isn't really a social call, Your Honour, much as I would like it to be."

"The world is too much with us!"

"Yes, late and soon. Last night I convened my committee quite late to discuss the General's testimony, and soon I must write my report —"

"I'm glad you enjoy Wordsworth, Hunter. He was my favorite at Balliol." Sir Michael sat bolt upright on his high-backed chair facing the fireplace, reciting as he stared at the glowing coals, " 'When from our better selves we have too long been parted by the hurrying world, and droop, sick of its business, of its pleasures tired —' "

"Since you are much too busy to attend our hearings, Your Honour, I hope you won't mind if I put a few questions to you here?"

The Governor glanced at him, but continued bemused to finish the stanza, " '— How gracious, how benign, is Solitude.' "

"The timing of your proclamation of martial law for Amritsar, for one thing," William explained, feeling too fatigued and distraught to indulge Sir Michael's attempts at further taking his measure by prolonging this poetry

291

recital. "Could you recall the exact date on which you felt that the introduction of martial law had become a necessity?"

"I believe the proclamation has a date on it."

"Yes, it does, but would that be the day you decided it was necessary?"

"Of course it would. Why do you ask?"

"Forgive my obtuseness, Your Honour, but knowing as little as I do about Indian procedures, it occurred to me that perhaps several days might elapse between your wire to His Excellency recommending the proclamation and his responding wire of approval?"

"Nonsense! Not for emergent matters. I sent my wire 'clear-the-line,' and H.E. responded in kind. I had his approval in my pocket within three hours from the time I dictated my request! We may seem a provincial backwater to you, Hunter, but we can act with promptitude, if the situation warrants." His handsome face glowed with a smile of justifiable pride at the efficiency of his administration. Sir Michael enjoyed the reputation of being the most efficient of India's governors.

"Three hours *is* very impressive speed," William mused, rubbing the bristles under his chin. He hadn't shaved in his rush to come here this morning. "That would mean, of course, that you must have decided the proclamation was necessary on April fifteenth — the date it bears."

"Yes, I expect so." He sounded wary.

"Or possibly on the fourteenth? Perhaps you sent the wire late at night, do you recall?"

"No, but it may be. Yes, certainly either the fourteenth or fifteenth."

"But no earlier? I mean, considering the date on the proclamation itself being the fifteenth."

"Yes, yes, I've said that half a dozen times now! What the devil are you driving at?"

"Simply this, Your Honour. The firing at Jallianwala Bagh occurred on the thirteenth. The Brigadier opened fire on his own initiative, without consulting civil authority, yet since your proclamation of martial law throughout Amritsar district was not issued until the fifteenth, the Deputy Commissioner, Mr. Irving, was still legally responsible for the area — yet he wasn't even present at the time of the firing, nor did the General make any effort to reach him or obtain his prior approval."

"Oh, I see." Sir Michael left his seat by the fireplace, and returned stiff-legged to his desk.

William thought at first that the Governor sat at his desk in order to search for the original proclamation, to check the accuracy of its date, for without speaking further he began busily opening ribboned files, perusing the contents of one, setting another aside, glancing at papers in the folder beneath. In a few minutes he realized that Sir Michael had merely decided to go about his usual morning's work, as though he were entirely alone.

"That doesn't distress Your Honour?"

"I beg your pardon?"

"What I've just said," William explained, walking closer to the desk, "concerning the General's usurpation of civil authority."

"I've a very busy schedule this morning, Hunter — all day, in fact," he added, smiling a perfunctory grin, meant, it appeared, as his parting salutation.

"And I have hearings that are scheduled to begin in less than two hours, yet I have taken the trouble of rushing here before breakfast, and after a night, which I can see was far more troubled than yours, because I was foolish enough to imagine that as governor of this province you might possibly take some interest in its proper administration and, if I may be so indelicate as to mention *people* to a lover of nature, in the security and welfare of its populace!" He was trembling uncontrollably, and felt, as he watched Sir Michael's unabashed, imperious face, that he almost knew what it was like to be a native. "But I see I was mistaken! I won't disturb your *Solitude* any longer!"

He turned then to leave, yet found before he was much more than two paces toward the door that Sir Michael had hurried round his desk, and stood with face flaming, blocking his path.

"What in hell did you expect me to say, Hunter?"

"I really expect nothing at all of you any longer."

"Oh, yes you do! You're no different from all the rest of them, you know — every bleeding heart liberal member of the Commons who's come through Lahore during the past fifteen years — taking the two week circuit of India while their P and O loads its tanks and holds for the trip Home! Woe is the poor exploited native! How can brutes like myself behave so badly toward the begging black brother? The clergy also sing that sermon! We've heard your sort before, you see!"

"If you'll please permit me to leave," he whispered, stepping to one side in order to flank the Governor as he started again toward the door.

"No! No one talks that way to me and walks out! Sit down, Your Lordship! I've a few things to tell you about India!"

He half suspected that had he persisted in his intention of leaving just then he might have been knocked onto the seat he decided to take voluntarily. He was actually quite curious to hear what the Governor had to say for himself, and sensed that the posture of petty tyrant was much closer to the real Sir Michael than his earlier facade of poet.

"The first thing you've got to get into your head, Hunter, is that this is the Punjab! It's not Bombay, and it's not Madras, and it's not your bleeding bunghole of a Bengal — it's *the Punjab!* Does that mean *anything* at all to you? No, I can see your knowledge of India is as profound as my understanding of the law!" He shook his head wearily and sat down, leaning forward and speaking rather more slowly and a bit louder, the way adults often speak to small children in answering factual questions.

"There are really just two things about the Punjab that make it unique, you see — the first is its location, the second its population. We sit between Afghan tribes and India's heartland, that's what makes our location so important. We're the lock to the whole treasure box — crack us and you've got India! It's no secret. Every invading army that's ever marched into this continent has come through the Punjab! From Alexander to the Hun, they've all known that we're the path to power, we're the guardians of the palace, this is the moat and the high wall. Take the Punjab, break the Punjab, cross the Punjab, and you've won India!"

"This is all very instructive and interesting —"

"Yes, I know, but you're in a great rush! And so am I, Your Lordship, only I'm not the one who barged in on *you* this morning! And it wasn't I who had the gall to accuse you of knowing nothing about the law! Be patient now!"

William could not help smiling, hearing Sir Michael tell him the very thing he had said to Sir Chimanlal last night. The petty tyrant was a clever scoundrel.

"It's thanks to *where* we are that our population in the Punjab is what it is. I'm talking of your native now — the Punjabi. He's tough, a damned sight tougher than natives anywhere else in India, and that's why we use him so much in the army. Sikh, Jat, and Mussulman fighter, they're all Punjabis! They hold the Khyber for me, and the Bolan, and they've done a job for you people back Home of late, too, you might recollect — those were Punjabis we sent into the trenches by the end of '14, Hunter! I raised half a million more troops than we ordinarily recruit in this province during the War. Half a bloody million, Your Lordship!"

"I think most of us in Britain were not unaware of the Punjab's valiant contributions to the War effort, Sir Michael, and of your own personal role — "

"I'm not asking for your praise, Hunter! I don't need your flattery —"

"I assure you, I meant none!"

"Good. Now if you've followed what I said, you'll begin to appreciate how important the Punjab is to India — in fact, in many ways, the Punjab *is* India." His tone had softened and his eye wandered toward the windows, and for a moment William feared that Sir Michael was going to wax poetical again. But then his jaw muscles flicked and the Irish pendulum of his personality swung swiftly back to its opposite pole of toughness. "You can't govern the Punjab the way you'd govern Madras, Hunter — kindness is mistaken for cowardice by a Punjabi, hesitation for fear. He respects nothing but power, and he'll stay in line only so long as he knows that we have more of it than he does, but more important than having it — that we'll *use* it!" He smashed his fist against his open palm.

"Then you approved of the Brigadier's handling of Amritsar?"

"Of course I approved of it! I ordered it!"

"You — ordered it?" William could not help but repeat those words in a voice of utter incredulity, refusing to believe that he had correctly heard the Governor's statement, or imagining, if he did, that the Governor had misunderstood his earlier question. "You say you ordered the Brigadier to usurp civil authority, and to fire without warning upon an unarmed crowd, and then to continue firing into that crowd for almost fifteen minutes, while it was trying to escape from the Bagh? You *ordered* that?"

"It's the only thing that could have saved us, Hunter."

"You ordered that?"

"You still don't understand it, do you?"

"No." His voice was faint, like the whispered echo of one of those distant departed souls slaughtered in the midst of life, cut down by a vagrant bullet mercilessly aimed at the nearest body of fragile flesh.

"You don't realize that anything less firm and clear in response to the bludgeoning of Europeans and the burning of British property by Punjabis would have meant the uprising of every village Sikh, every farming Jat, every returned Mussulman peasant pensioned off from the Great War, and every native soldier in every cantonment throughout the Punjab would have joined the rebel army the day after, and by now this Empire would be a raging sea of British blood —"

"There were people in that garden who'd come to Amritsar that morning, for the fair —"

"Don't be a sentimental fool, Hunter! They were rebels. They went there for one reason only — to test our mettle!"

"I've heard that before," he whispered, starting to wonder if perhaps he wasn't the one who'd somehow gone insane, since all the rest of them seemed to agree about the wisdom and necessity of the Brigadier's act.

"They've been testing us all year, Hunter. This whole campaign by that charlatan fakir Gandhi is nothing but a test of Government's will. He's trying to break us, Hunter. He's using the Chinese water torture technique, and I'm afraid some of our people back Home have given up. I daresay, I expect you might even have come out here rather favorably predisposed toward Gandhi, mightn't you?"

"I hadn't thought much about him."

"There are some 'friends' of his in Whitehall, I know —"

"How extraordinary." He shook his head dumbly, feeling as though he were walking in his sleep, feeling suddenly very tired.

"Yes, I certainly think it is! I think any Englishman who would call that sedition-monger a 'friend'—"

"No, I mean — I was referring to something else, to why I'd come here this morning, actually," he whispered. He couldn't quite manage to speak much above a whisper, though he tried to talk louder. "You see, I'd decided last night that what the General had done was so frightful a crime that — well, I was hoping you would agree to help me see to it that he would be immediately relieved of his command."

"Are you mad, Hunter?"

He would have liked to have been able to laugh in response to that, but could only shake his head, staring bleary-eyed at the brightness of morning that glared painfully through the high windows.

"Have you any idea of how many of us hold India, Hunter? I'm talking of those of us who really count — not your British merchants in Bombay or your do-gooder missionaries in Calcutta — I mean men like myself and the Brigadier, those of us who do the day labor of Empire — we aren't more than two thousand strong. Yet we govern and control three hundred millions! Have you ever asked *how* we do it?"

"How do you do it?"

"By taking initiative, and doing what needs to be done *when* it needs doing, and never doubting, because we've no reason whatever to doubt, but that our superior in the service will back us up. To the hilt, Hunter! We stand behind each other, and we stand firm, and we don't cavil about details of what's been done by the man we send out to do a job, because we know that he'll do it right. He'll do it right, because he doesn't have to fear that after doing what he's done, his superior won't support him! Do you understand it now?"

"Yes, I think so."

"There's never been a service as efficient and remarkable as ours, never anywhere else in the world, never before in history — we're unique, and the Empire we hold is the greatest, the richest, the strongest thanks to our system, Hunter. And it's what's made Britain great as well, and rich, and powerful — powerful enough to win the War! We couldn't have done without India, you know!"

"It may be."

"Yet you seriously considered asking me to help you relieve the Brigadier of his command?"

It did sound strange to hear Sir Michael say it.

"Don't you see what sort of effect that could have on the morale of our people out here? Put aside the merits of the matter, which we needn't argue over — naturally I disagree with your judgment entirely, but that aside — I'm talking of the *effect* such an act would have *even if it were warranted*. The entire service would collapse overnight, Hunter! You wouldn't be able to find a staff officer worth his salt remaining in barracks! I'd have a hundred resignations on my desk by tomorrow morning, and by God, *I* wouldn't be here to answer the bloody things! I'd be on my way Home! And who's going to run India next day, Your Lordship? Are you ready to take on that job?"

He felt terrifyingly weakened by the mere thought of being called upon to take over the daily chore of administering this land of three hundred millions.

"No, I shouldn't think you would be, Hunter! It's not as simple as it appears, you know. We're sitting on the crater's rim, and at almost any moment the volcano could blow." He rose and moved swiftly to the windows behind his desk, those which opened as doors onto his balcony, throwing them ajar. "Listen to it — listen to the silence, Hunter, have you ever heard a more peacefully idyllic sound?"

There was a twittering of canaries, and the distant jangling sound of cowbells from the streets below.

"You should have heard the rumbling last April — it sounded like every kettledrum in hell, like the roar of ten thousand wounded lions, Hunter! From this very balcony! Nothing short of the action taken in Jallianwala Bagh could have squelched that. You can't put out forest fires with a garden hose, Your Lordship. India's not Belgravia."

"Yes, I've learned that much," he said, jumping up and hurrying closer to Sir Michael's formidable frame, angry and disgusted with himself for being so physically feeble, feeling so tired, so drained of strength. "I can see how different, how difficult your task is here — but how, in God's name, could you possibly justify what he did? Even if you argue that starting to fire without warning was required of the troops because of the sheer size of the crowd — though since it was unarmed, I don't agree that it presented any real threat to the Brigadier's force — how can anyone justify his *continued* firing for so long a time after the crowd started to disperse, attempting desperately to flee?"

"Short volleys only incense the blackguards."

"But they were running *away*!"

"Naturally! They're all cowards."

"Yet surely Your Honour is familiar with the legal doctrine of minimum force?"

"I don't claim any special knowledge of the law."

"There's nothing *special* about the idea that in dispersing an unarmed crowd, we are constrained, by all our ideals of Government as well as law, to use no more than the minimum amount of force required by a particular situation."

"If he let them escape on the thirteenth, they would

have sneaked round somewhere else to plot their bloody rebellion on the fourteenth!"

"But is a *military* man in the best position to decide such weighty matters of policy? Isn't the discontent you find among your native subjects really *political* in character? Can such issues be decided by bullets alone, Your Honour?"

"You sound as if you've been listening to some of our native Bolsheviks, Hunter!"

"Do I?" He pinched the bridge of his nose and closed his eyes. The lack of sleep left him feeling dizzy. He would have to return to the Club for a bit before attempting to go on with today's hearing. "What was that wonderful phrase Mr. Gladstone used when sponsoring 'lost causes'? Didn't he say he was appealing, not merely to parliament, but to the 'conscience of mankind'?"

"I never thought much of Gladstone," Sir Michael replied, closing his balcony doors, sitting down at his desk.

"Has it ever occurred to you, Your Honour, that some of the things the natives want most are the very things we've taught them to treasure — like freedom, and justice, and —"

"You're wrong, Hunter! They only want our Power!" And that's what they can't have, you see. And now, thanks to the General's handling of Jallianwala Bagh they know it!"

" 'Then was seen what we believe to be the most frightful of all spectacles,' " William recited, " 'the strength of civilization without its mercy.' "

"Another one of your Mr. Gladstone's pearls?"

"No. No, that's Macaulay. We British have had a rather long tradition of native Bolsheviks!"

"Lord Hunter's going now," Sir Michael informed his secretary, who had entered the office so silently that William was startled to find him hovering just a step behind. "Do show him out."

27

WILLIAM postponed the hearings for a day. He sent Harold round to the courthouse with a notice of cancellation, resting till he returned. They left the Club at nine, to catch the morning mail to Delhi.

He'd spoken only once before with the Viceroy, and then briefly, at a reception given in his honor more than a month ago. His Excellency had lived up to his reputation of being so true a Scot that he was thrifty even with his words. Yet his farewell offer echoed in William's mind during the train ride to India's capital — "Call on me if you need any help, Hunter. I'll never be too busy to see you."

There was an unexpected delay at Amritsar. The locomotive's boiler sprang a steam leak, and a new engine had to be brought for the remainder of the trip. The stationmaster personally informed his two first-class passengers of the delay, offering William the hospitality of his private sitting room for the hour or so before everything was fixed and ready to roll again.

"How long would it take me to drive to the Jallianwala Bagh?" he inquired.

"Oh, you wouldn't want to go there, sir."

"Why not?"

"Well, there's — nothing there, sir, but natives —"

"How long?"

"Oh, I suppose by carriage, ten or fifteen minutes."

"Shall we go, Harold?"

"Must we, Your Lordship?"

"Never mind. I'll go alone," he decided, at which point Harold, who always removed his shoes during train rides, relented, and started putting them on again, but William insisted that he preferred going alone. "I'll be back in half an hour," he promised.

"Don't be longer than forty-five minutes, sir," the stationmaster advised.

"Do be careful!" Harold called.

It was a swift ride over the bridge and down Hall Bazaar, but beyond the Kotwali the road narrowed, and then his tonga was brought to a halt while two native coolies argued about which of them had the right of way, blocking all traffic as they hurled invective at each other and left their sack-loaded carts jammed diagonally together barricading the road. His tonga was quickly surrounded by children, holding out dirty hands, begging for "baksheesh!" William searched his purse for coins, but found only silver rupees. He had no annas. There were fewer than twelve children. For one rupee he could have cheered the day for them all. He asked his driver for small change, but the heavy-set Sikh merely shook his turbaned head. He'd yet to find an Indian cabby who would admit to having change. The children were encouraged by his obvious sympathy and interest. They clamored louder, more persistently. Several children reached into the tonga to touch his shoes, kissing their fingers that had rubbed dirt from his soles.

"Don't do that," he shouted.

The Sikh flicked his whip at the boys. They scrambled out of reach.

"No need to whip them," he yelled at the driver. His voice had taken on an acerbic tone. The driver shrugged, put up his whip, and slumped on his perch. The children were encouraged to return, and seeing that the driver was determined to ignore them, they became bolder. Three or four of them climbed onto the tonga's running boards.

"Get down from there," William shouted. "I've no small change for you."

"Baksheesh, sahib!" they cried, grinning ingenuously, reaching out their bony arms, touching his legs, his feet, crying in chorus as they did so, like suppliants at prayer in a mosque. "Bak-sheesh!"

"No, stop that! Get down, I say! I've no coins for you!"

A group of shopkeepers had by now gathered around the arguing coolies, acting as intermediaries, helping them settle their dispute over which deserved the right of way, giving in to both by getting the owner of a third cart to move it from its parked position at the curb. Suddenly the road was clear up ahead. The Sikh slapped his horse's back with the reins.

Most of the boys jumped off as the tonga began to move, but one clung to the carriage frame, and continued to hold out his palm imploringly to William.

"Get down! Hurry, and jump down, you fool," he shouted, but the child hung on as the tonga gained speed.

"Wait," William called to the driver, yet even as he spoke, the boy either lost his grip or decided to leap away. But did not leap far enough. His leg was caught under the rear wheel of the tonga, the bone crushed beneath its iron rim.

The boy's scream echoed his anguish down the narrow street. Before William could convince his driver to bring the tonga to a halt, many people had rushed out of their shops and buildings, surrounding the pain-contorted body writhing on the cobbled road.

"Better to go on, sahib," the driver advised, sounding as nervous as he looked.

"Turn the carriage round," William ordered.

Driving back he noticed heads staring down at him from unshuttered windows. Dark sullen faces, bloodshot eyes that carried unspoken accusations. Many people on the street also turned to glare in his direction. None were White.

There were no familiar faces on this street. No one wore European dress. No police were within sight. No soldiers. No officials of any sort. He was totally isolated. Cut off. He felt suddenly vulnerable. Not frightened really — or was he?

His tonga had stopped. Yet he hesitated before putting his foot outside the relative security of its frame. He couldn't recall when last he'd felt frightened in a primitively physical sense. It was a most extraordinary experience to William. Fear had so long been foreign to his nature that he tended to think it was usually fabricated by others, for sympathy's sake perhaps. He wasn't sure he knew why. Yet now he felt it rushing over him, the dark tidal wave of mysterious terror. The clutching, chest-constricting, resolution-numbing grip of irrational insecurity. He didn't know what it was really. Why should he wonder now whether the faces staring down from a distant building might not want to toss a bomb at him? Or whether if he walked toward the young men crowded around the prostrate child, he might not be exposing himself to a violent assault? Such thoughts alone made him grimace as he stepped onto the road, ashamed of his cowardice.

He half expected them to stand fast, to block his way as he walked toward the knot of onlookers. He heard his own heart beating, and wondered then what he could do if they didn't move aside? Or how he should react if someone did strike a blow at his face? Or spat toward him? It all but paralyzed him — the terror he felt.

Yet a moment later the path before him was clear. Several people were bowing, salaaming respectfully to him. The beggar boy lay perfectly still on the cobbled road, moaning and staring mournfully up at the faces circling his body.

"Will some of you please lift him carefully and set him inside my tonga?" William urged.

No one moved.

He repeated what he'd said, staring at the sturdiest of the laborers in the crowd. There was a faint muttering reply from one or two of the young men, and he thought it presaged trouble, their sullen refusal to do as he asked, the dark hatred he saw for himself in several eyes, hatred, suspicion, mistrust, accusation. As though they said to him — you are to blame for this! You alone! Why did you come here to tempt this child to his fall? What business have you among us? Who are you to intrude this way into our workaday lives? Surely you cannot belong here? *You are not one of us!*

But then he realized that none of them understood what he said, for he heard a voice addressing him in Punjabi, and those words meant no more to his ears than his had to theirs. He called his driver over, and ordered the lazy man to translate what he'd said, but the Sikh shook his head sullenly, and whispered:

"Why ask for trouble, sahib? He did it purposely, the beggar! They all like to break a limb when they are young, and then they never have to work a day in their lives, you see, and people feel sorry for them because they must crawl

about. If you take him in the tonga, you will never escape
from the nuisance —"

"If you don't do as I ask at once, I'll see to it that your
license is revoked," William snapped.

"Very well! Hey," he shouted, ordering a young man to
set the boy inside the tonga.

As he was moved the child cried out again, and more
people ran over to inquire about what was happening now.
Several of the older men began to shake fists in his direction, and William could not understand what they were
shouting at him, so he asked the driver to translate.

"They say you are trying to steal the boy to keep him
for your servant," he reported, not without a smirk of
satisfaction. It left William feeling more helpless, bewildered, all but despairing by the time he managed to
squeeze back into the tonga, with the groaning child's
broken limb dangling purple and black before his eyes.

"Won't any of them come along to help comfort the boy
before his operation?" William asked the driver to inquire.

"He is an orphan, sahib! You have become his father-
and-mother now!"

He remembered the train then, and the time. He urged
the driver to hurry, to take them to the nearest hospital.
Luckily it was on the way back toward the station, Saint
Catherine's Mission Hospital. Several of the Sisters hurried
round to help transport the child safely inside. He
explained what had happened, how rushed he was. They
assured him the boy would be cared for properly, that the
fracture would be set, and the leg put into a cast. He
offered to pay for the operation, and medical care for the
boy, but they merely suggested he might donate something
someday to their Mission fund for orphaned children.

William returned to the station platform hardly more
than a minute before his train was ready to leave for Delhi.
Harold had taken their bag out of the carriage, and looked

very troubled as he paced the platform, muttering gruffly to himself, till he caught sight of his master.

"Your Lordship, thank God you're safe!" he shouted. It wasn't like Harold to be so emotional.

"What are you doing out here?" William asked, as he heard the shrill whistle of the conductor. "Shouldn't we be inside now?"

"We should, sir, yes. Are you all right, Your Lordship?"

"I'm fine, Harold," he replied, and no sooner did they step inside the plush carriage and settle down on their seats, than the train began to move with a steam-chugging lurch.

"Did you find that damnable garden, sir?"

"No. I never did get quite that far," he said, but then the rhythm of the wheels and the cumulative weight of exhaustion lulled him to sleep. He did not open his eyes again until they reached Delhi.

There were many people waiting in the Viceroy's outer office. Most were elegantly attired Indians, several with servants squatting beside them on the Persian carpeted floor. Harold whispered something to the secretary, who smiled at William and came round his desk at once to usher him into a larger antechamber, which was, but for its Louis Quatorze decor, empty.

"If Your Lordship would be so kind as to wait here," the young man, who looked and sounded like Flower Rice, suggested, "His Excellency will be free to see you in just a few moments. I'm sure it won't be longer than that."

Actually, it was less than ten minutes before the gold-knobbed door at the far end of the antechamber turned, and another young man, wearing the full dress tunic of a captain of the Viceroy's Guard, glittering saber, white breeches, polished jackboots, emerged, clicking his heels, and invited him into the inner sanctum of British Indian power.

The Viceroy finished signing his name to a magnificently designed document, which another aide removed from under his pen and carried out a side door, as William crossed the long expanse of carpet to the ornate desk.

"I was thinking of you this morning, Hunter, reading the accounts of yesterday's hearing," His Excellency said, coming round his desk, extending his hand to William. He was an unpretentious man, Calvinistically austere in appearance, bland in tone, his face unsmiling, almost looking as though it were so stiffly featured that any deviation from its sober norm would be physically impossible.

"I've postponed today's hearings to talk with you, Your Excellency. It's most generous of you to see me without notice."

"Not at all. You look as if you can use some tea." He nodded to his attaché, who promptly left the room to order their tea. They sat side by side on the sofa near the book-lined wall. The Viceroy folded his arms and stared at William, waiting.

"When I left Lahore this morning, I felt rather more confident about what I planned to tell you than I do now. We stopped inadvertently at Amritsar, and I went into the old city — " He paused. It was really too trivial a matter to relate to the Viceroy, and here in this insular, palatial atmosphere of total security it was virtually impossible for William to believe that the terror he'd felt so short a time ago had in fact been real. "I'm afraid I don't understand very much about India, Your Excellency."

"Nor do I, Hunter." He said it in so forthright a manner that there could be no mistaking the sincerity of his admission.

"Perhaps we've really no business being here then. I mean, of course, the national we — we British."

"Perhaps not. But we are."

"And so we must try to make the best of a bad lot?"

"I should think so. We are rather better than any possible alternative, you know."

"But are we really? That's what I thought, when I accepted the presidency of this committee —"

"Surely you must believe it still? Or would you replace me with Gandhi?"

It seemed so absurdly preposterous an idea that he smiled as he shook his head.

"The Amir of Afghanistan would·be even worse, of course, but I do think we've finally put him down," the Viceroy reported, saying it with something of a sigh. He bore his many burdens well.

"I would like to replace at least one of your brigadiers though, and one of your provincial governors," William said.

"I know the governor you mean, Hunter," the Viceroy replied, without a moment's hesitation. "I accepted his resignation more than six months ago, but we let him stay on for the 'emergency' period of martial law. Now that's over, and he'll be leaving within the fortnight."

"I'm relieved to hear that. We had a most unpleasant chat this morning."

"As to the Brigadier," His Excellency continued, "I've been awaiting your report."

"That's why I've come to trouble you, I'm afraid. My committee stands divided, but I tend to agree with our native members that what he did in Jallianwala Bagh was so frightful that he should be stripped at once of all command." He wouldn't have modified the strength of his agreement with the word "tend" before he'd reached Amritsar today.

"Perhaps we'd best ask the Commander in Chief to join us," the Viceroy said, ordering his attaché to call Sir Charles. Neither his voice nor his facial expression revealed the slightest indication of how he personally felt about William's recommendation. His eyes absorbed the harsh verdict without a flicker of emotion. He calmly sipped his tea, set down the cup, touched his linen napkin to his tight lips, and blandly asked, "How does Flower Rice feel about your idea?"

"Opposed."

"I see," he said, and that too without tipping one card in his hand. He sat perfectly still. He was a man at home with silences. A secretary entered the office and discreetly handed him a slip of note paper. He glanced at the brief message and nodded, returning the note. After another minute or so, the Commander in Chief arrived. He was surprisingly short, heavier round the hips than most military men, dressed in so casual a linen suit that at first glance William didn't recognize him.

"Charles, you've met Hunter, haven't you?"

"Yes, yes, of course! How nice to see you again, Your Lordship! I must say I never should have expected to find you in Delhi *today*!" He spoke in a bouncy way, as though words were a tennis ball jogging around inside his pudgy body.

"Do join us for tea, Charles," the Viceroy ordered. "Hunter's come up to recommend that you strip the Brigadier of his command because of his actions at Amritsar last April."

"Ah, that would explain why you're here, of course. I see! Well, well," he muttered, pouring himself a full cup, then trying unsuccessfully to lift it to his lips without spilling any.

"I expect you've read the reports of his testimony yesterday," William said.

"Yes, I have done. He's a terribly impulsive man, Rex is. Always has been," he explained, addressing the Viceroy.

"Hunter's committee is divided."

"Oh? Well, tell me, where does Barrow stand? I've enormous respect for Barrow."

"He's against my recommendation, I'm afraid."

"Oh, is he? My gracious."

"As is Flower Rice," the Viceroy reported.

"Flower too? Oh, dear. This does become terribly difficult! It's just you and Rankin, is it?"

"No, just myself and our — myself, and Sir Chimanlal and the Honorable Pandit Narayan," he said firmly.

"Only you and the *natives*?" Sir Charles asked. "Oh, my goodness gracious, how *dreadfully* awkward!"

"Perhaps it would be if we were wrong," William replied, "only we happen to be right!"

"One likes to believe that, of course," the Viceroy said.

"You've read the testimony yourself, Your Excellency. The reports were hardly exaggerated, I assure you. I think that a military commander who usurps civil prerogatives, opens fire upon an unarmed crowd without verbal warning, continues that fire long after the crowd has started to disperse, and admits he has done the latter for reasons of far-ranging policy rather than in response to an immediate and specific threat against the peace — I submit, Gentlemen, that such an officer has so clearly exceeded the limits of his responsibility as to pose a serious and continuing danger to the welfare of society, and should, therefore, be relieved of his martial powers as quickly as possible." He blurted it out with rather more passion than was his custom, yet this time the Viceroy's expression clearly indicated sympathy for William's position.

"Quite so," he agreed. "He showed very poor judgment!"

"Rex always has done, you see," Sir Charles chimed in, nodding earnestly. "He's a terribly good soldier, but he has poor judgment. It's why I won't trust him with a division!"

The Viceroy's secretary returned, this time handing him a longer note, which he excused himself to read.

"I am afraid I do have a luncheon engagement with the Nizam," he explained.

"Oh, my goodness, that reminds me of my luncheon with Bikaner!" said Sir Charles, jumping up. "Every time I keep him waiting I'm quite convinced he's ready either to run his saber through my heart or his own! These natives *are* dreadfully sensitive chaps, you know, Hunter! Awfully good seeing you again."

"But what will you do about —?"

"About Rex? Oh, yes." he muttered, gnawing at his nail and shifting his eyes toward the Viceroy, who was trying to remember whether he had agreed to call the Nizam Highness or Exalted Highness? "How does Your Excellency feel?"

"We shouldn't want to stir up a White Mutiny now that we've averted a Black one," the Viceroy said.

"Yes, that's the problem, you see. Were your committee unanimous, or even if you had Barrow say, *or* Rice, on your side of this thing — but with just the two natives, and yourself from back Home — Rex is awfully popular with our countrymen here, you see, and I'm afraid my soldiers wouldn't take kindly to any abrupt dismissal —"

"Yet his judgment *has* been faulty," the Viceroy interrupted. "Couldn't you possibly find some quiet way of relieving him of his duties, Charles?"

"Actually, he's applied for sick leave Home. He's been rather ill of late. I could grant the leave and then explain that he'll be reassigned by the war office after he's fully recovered —" He was thinking out loud. "Meanwhile, we could give his brigade to someone else —"

"And you could do that immediately, couldn't you, Charles?"

"Yes, I don't see why not." He was a most amiable man.

"But I must dash now. Your Lordship," he said, vigorously shaking William's hand, before bouncing himself out of the office.

"Well, Hunter, I trust you're pleased?" the Viceroy asked.

It all happened so quickly that William didn't quite realize till he heard the question that he'd just accomplished what he came up to Delhi to do.

"I am, yes. Thank you very much," he said, rising.

"Before you leave," the Viceroy began, walking back to his desk, scrawling a note to himself, then looking up, peering into William's eyes, "you do appreciate the delicacy of this matter — of your committee's report?"

"I'm not sure I understand what Your Excellency means."

"I'll speak to Flower, and Charles can tell Barrow — I'm certain they'll agree that the Brigadier showed an error of judgment in acting as harshly as he did, and I expect that Rankin will go along — wouldn't you say?"

"Go along?" William repeated in a questioning tone.

"With your majority report, Hunter. That is rather important for us out here — to present as solid a posture as possible to the natives — within the limits of conscience, of course."

"Ah, I see, that's my part of our bargain," he nodded. The verdict he handed down would be carried out as long as he agreed to modify it in its public form.

"I'm sorry you think of it as a bargain," His Excellency said, pronouncing that commercial word in a distasteful manner. He'd inherited his ten thousand acres of Scotland with his peerage. He accepted the viceroyalty of India, William knew, as a service to the Crown, not because he needed the job. "Some people back Home think we hold India by writ, Hunter, and others believe we hold her by the sword, but you know I've come to feel that it's neither right nor might which makes us masters here — it's something far more elusive yet in a way stronger than both word and deed — it's spirit, Hunter, our national spirit."

Scratch a dour Scot, William thought, and you find a mystic. "I'm sure you're right. That thought crossed my mind earlier today, in Amritsar, only —" He shifted his glance and noticed the Viceroy's secretary impatiently hovering at the edge of the desk, looking most distressed at the realization that His Exalted Highness, the Nizam of Hyderabad, was being kept waiting for lunch! "But I mustn't detain you any longer."

"When you've finished your hearings, Hunter, we must dine together — just the two of us, if —" He rose and looked questioningly at his secretary, while his attaché came round from the other side to gird his dress sword about his waist.

"Yes, I know, if either of us has the time," William said, laughing.

"But what were you going to say, Hunter, when you said 'only' —?"

"Nothing profound, Your Excellency. I was only wondering what would happen when the natives caught on to our secret, and developed a national spirit of their own?"

"Then we're finished, Hunter." He extended his hand. "Have a good journey back to Lahore."

"You shall have my majority report shortly, Your Excellency," he promised.

"Thank you, Hunter. Good day!" He followed his entourage out through the ceremonial door leading to the palatial dining room of the viceregal mansion.

William was surprised to find himself left alone in the Viceroy's office. He felt almost as if the awesome weight of responsibility for so many of the decisions that had to be reached in this room had descended upon his shoulders. He felt wearied by the mere thought of it, and walked hastily back across the long carpet to the door through which he'd entered this burdensome room.

Harold was snoring soundly in the antechamber. He looked so peaceful and happy that William was loath to disturb his sleep.

"Wake up, Harold," he said at last, touching the old man's stooped shoulder.

"Oh, excuse me, Your Lordship," he muttered, rousing himself with an anxious look. "Were you successful, sir?"

"I suppose I was," he responded, though he wondered about it as they started to leave.

"Oh, that is good, sir. Then shall we be going Home?"

"Soon," he promised. "Yes, I do think we'll be leaving for Home quite soon now."

Bibliography

PRIMARY SOURCES

The *Report* of Lord Hunter's *Committee on Disturbances in Bombay, Delhi, and the Punjab* was published by the Superintendent of Government Printing, Calcutta, India, in 1920, together with five volumes of "Minutes of Oral Evidence and Written Statements of Witnesses Presented before the Disorders Inquiry Committee." These volumes contain 1,371 pages of testimony by 229 witnesses to the "disturbances and disorders" in Northern India during the spring of 1919. Volume I contains all the evidence gathered in *Delhi*; Volume II, that heard in the *Bombay Presidency*; Volume III, *Amritsar*; Volume IV, *Lahore and Kasur*; Volume V, *Gujranwala, Gujrat, Lyallpur and Punjab Provincial.*

The Punjab Sub-Committee of the Indian National Congress appointed its own body of "Commissioners," led by Mohandas K. Gandhi, to conduct an all-Indian inquiry into the same disturbances and disorders. The 160-page *Report* of Mahatma Gandhi's Commission was published by its secretary, Mr. K. Santanam, in Bombay, in 1920, together with a 946-page *Volume of Evidence*, containing some 650 statements culled by the Commissioners from over 1700 accounts submitted by Indian witnesses.

The *Correspondence between the Government of India and the Secretary of State for India on the Report of Lord Hunter's Committee* was published by H.M.'s Stationery Office, London, in 1920, as a "Command" Paper (no. 705). The "Statement" of Brigadier General R. E. H. Dyer to the "Army Council" was "Presented to Parliament by Command of His Majesty" (Cmd. 771) in 1920.

SECONDARY SOURCES

Barrow, General Sir George, *Life of General Sir Charles Carmichael Monro*. London: Hutchinson, 1931.

Callwell, Major-General Sir C. E., *Life and Diaries of Field Marshal Sir Henry Wilson*. London: Cassell, 1927.

BIBLIOGRAPHY

Colvin, Ian, *The Life of General Dyer*. London: Blackwood, 1929.

Furneaux, Rupert, *Massacre at Amritsar*. London: Allen & Unwin, 1963.

Horniman, B. G., *Amritsar and Our Duty to India*. London: Unwin, 1920.

O'Dwyer, Sir Michael, *India as I Knew It*. London: Constable, 1925.

Swinson, Arthur, *Six Minutes to Sunset: The Story of General Dyer and the Amritsar Affair*. London: Davies, 1964.

MORE ABOUT PENGUINS

For further information about books available from Penguins in India write to Penguin Books (India) Ltd, B4/246, Safdarjung Enclave, New Delhi 110 029.

In the UK: For a complete list of books available from Penguins in the United Kingdom write to Dept. EP, Penguin Books Ltd, Harmondsworth, Middlesex UB7 0DA.

In the U.S.A.: For a complete list of books available from Penguins in the United States write to Dept. DG, Penguin Books, 299 Murray Hill Parkway, East Rutherford, New Jersey 07073.

In Canada: For a complete list of books available from Penguins in Canada write to Penguin Books Canada Ltd, 2801 John Street, Markham, Ontario L3R 1B4.

In Australia: For a complete list of books available from Penguins in Australia write to the Marketing Department, Penguin Books Australia Ltd, P.O. Box 257, Ringwood, Victoria 3134.

In New Zealand: For a complete list of books available from Penguins in New Zealand write to the Marketing Department, Penguin Books (N.Z.) Ltd, Private Bag, Takapuna, Auckland 9.

THE DEVIL'S WIND: NANA SAHEB'S STORY
Manohar Malgonkar

Nana Saheb was arguably India's greatest hero in the country's early battles against the British. This novel, by one of India's finest writers, brings alive the sequence of events that led the adopted son of the Maratha Peshwa Bajirao II to take on the British in the Great Revolt of 1857.

'A fascinating novel'—*The Sunday Times*

'A tragic and tremendous story'—*Pearl S. Buck*

'(Malgonkar writes) compellingly'—*Paul Scott*

ARJUN

Sunil Gangopadhyay

Arjun thinks he is in love with a beautiful college girl, but he falls prey to the fear that he is wooing someone far above his station. For Arjun is a poor, if brilliant and resourceful, refugee from East Bengal living in a squatter's settlement on the outskirts of Calcutta, whereas the girl he is keen on is the daughter of a wealthy doctor. But his love-life is the least of his problems, he soon discovers, as a crooked landlord and a disreputable factory owner join forces in an attempt to evict the people of Arjun's community from their hard-won land. Arjun now has to choose between fighting alongside the people he has grown up with, against the forces that threaten to engulf them all, or escaping to the safe haven his wealthy Bengali friends are willing to provide. He chooses to fight in a stunning climax to a powerful and sensitively written novel.

A DEATH IN DELHI :
Modern Hindi Short Stories
Translated & Edited by
Gordon C. Roadarmel

A collection of brilliant new stories from the writers who have revolutionized Hindi literature over the past forty years. The short stories in this volume take up from where Premchand (the greatest writer Hindi has ever produced) and his immediate successors left off and offer the reader an excellent and entertaining introduction to the diversity and richness that the modern short story at its best can offer. Among the writers represented are Nirmal Verma, Krishna Baldev Vaid, Shekhar Joshi Phanishwarnath 'Renu', Gyanranjan and Mohan Rakesh.

'By far the best collection of recent Hindi short stories to have appeared in English'.
—David Rubin